About the Author

Phil was born in Margate, Kent just after the war. His father was in the army so he was moved frequently from one country to the next as a child – Middle East, Far East, Germany, Malta and Cyprus.

He miraculously came away from school with six 'O' levels including English. He went straight into the RAF for many years and then into civilian street as a salesman for a short spell before joining   an engineering company, until retirement.

The author developed the reading bug when in some far-flung posting. Apart from 'Biggles', Phil's first real book was *Scaramouche* by Rafael Sabatini. Since then he enjoys a good read with unusual aspects to it.

The author has always enjoyed an active life, but these days it's more sedate activities like reading, music, golf – and hopefully, writing, which Phil now actually finds quite enjoyable.

Phil Webberley

THE ESSENCE OF GRACE

AUSTIN MACAULEY
PUBLISHERS LTD.

A CIP catalogue record for this title is available from the British Library.

ISBN 9781787100121 (Paperback)
ISBN 9781787100138 (Hardback)
ISBN 9781849634533 (E-Book)

www.austinmacauley.com

First Published (2017)
Austin Macauley Publishers Ltd.
25 Canada Square
Canary Wharf
London
E14 5LQ

Acknowledgments

Many thanks to the following who either by encouragement, advice or with information, helped me in their own way, to put this story together.

Caroline Hurrell

Stuart Wall

Carol Kershaw

Peter Fitton

Phil Astley-Jones

PROLOGUE

The Find – Germany 1944

It caught his attention immediately – a glint, a reflection from the sun on a piece of glass. The object was perched in amongst other tangled wiring and when Major Vetter tentatively shook the wreckage, it dropped out into the mud.

It looked unusual – and perhaps too small to be of real interest to the boffins. He called his assistant over.

'What do you think Schneider... what do you think it is?' asked Vetter. The wreckage was of a B-17 bomber that had been brought down earlier: the High Command was always on the lookout for new Allied equipment and Vetter's job was to look at wrecks for anything that might be 'new' that might give the Allies an advantage. Much could be learnt... even from wrecks, but rarely did they find items this small that provided any real interest in these large aircraft.

Schneider came over and looked at it, getting closer. 'Hmm... it is... different; quite small Herr Major.' He paused, pondering, 'I cannot think what it might be – it's probably a part of another component in the wreck,' he answered.

But both were remembering the earlier briefing:

"No matter how small it is, we want to know about it! We need to know exactly what the Allies are doing, what new technology they might be using – anything! So, we will do any investigations. Just bring what you find interesting or unusual to us. Do you understand?!"

These words from their Colonel were still ringing in Major Ralph Vetter's ears as he surveyed the wreckage. Before picking it up they took a photograph.

1

His first instincts told him it was just too small to be of importance… too slim. What he could see was neat, compact and out of place amongst all the big, dirty pieces of torn, smashed and burnt debris. He guessed they were close to the radio operator's position judging from the cables and plugs that were visible and he could see that the cockpit – a compact, crumpled mess – was two metres further forward.

However, it had taken his fancy; even though he could see it was obviously damaged, it looked superior – not unlike a classy cigarette case, which had been his first thought.

'So, what are you – *were* you – smoking, my American flyer?' he asked himself out loud.

He attempted to pick it up but it fell out of his grasp – it was slippery, smooth, probably covered in hydraulic oil or some other obnoxious substance. He picked it up again and turned it over in his hands – quite weighty for its size, compact; he looked for a clasp, couldn't find one so he tried to prize it open along one edge with his fingers. Gloves didn't help. No luck; wouldn't move, but now he could tell that it wasn't a cigarette case.

'Ach so, what have the Americans been up to – what could this be?' he muttered.

Like Schneider, he hadn't seen anything like this before. On closer examination, he could see that it was probably made of a plastic, nicely put together but not complete due to the crash and impact. No obvious markings were immediately visible however it could be cleaned up. He briefly considered leaving it behind – was it worth the effort? Perhaps not big enough to warrant further examination and all the paperwork, but he admired its difference.

In previous wrecks, he'd retrieved various pieces of personal kit that the USAAF supplied its crews like maps, small compasses or money. Some items were quite novel, some well-hidden in the flying clothing. The object he now held might also be personal kit, perhaps of a new design. With a closer look, he saw it also had what looked like tiny buttons or markings on it although too small to use wearing gloves. No, but he *had* heard about, and was on the lookout for, new miniaturised controls and switches the Allies were reputed to be developing for more advanced radar tuning and aiming systems.

'Shall I keep it…?' Then he also remembered the boss's words ringing out from their previous briefing, "So I repeat, be vigilant. Look out for everything and anything, big or *small*…" Blah blah blah, jahr jahr jahr.

'Perhaps we should take it back, Schneider,' Vetter said resignedly, 'And let them worry about it.'

...

.

PART 1

Chapter 1

UK today

'Take the day off,' my boss had said, – 'The deal's in the bag... worth a lot of money to the company and when word gets out, we could have a few more like these conversions,' he'd added.

In fact, he must have been in a real good mood because he told me to take the rest of the week off, which was right in front of my holidays anyway. Excellent.

'Go on that trip you keep promising your better half, that you keep telling me she wants.' True – with the sweet little bonus from this barn job, we could... quite easily.

Well, I might surprise her... pop in the travel place on the way back, pick up the tickets because we already know where we want to go – been nagged enough times – and then walk in the front door bearing gifts.

'Ta-dah!!'

Hang on... it's Thursday. She'll be under the sun-lamp at Kirsty's Parlour, something she always does today – on Thursday afternoons – so the surprise will have to wait 'til she gets back, looking brown with painted nails and a big grin on her pretty face.

These tickets will make her smile... even more.

Ah, she must be in. The front door is unlocked so I quickly look around downstairs – no sign so went upstairs – while disengaging myself from my iPod and ear plugs. She could be having a rest from the tanning – it's real hard work apparently; she's probably flat-out on the bed.

As I pulled my buds out I became aware of...

'Uh, uh, uh, uh, uh,' as I walked in through the bedroom door...

Yes... she *was* flat-out on the bed completely naked with some half-dressed Neanderthal on top. I froze – just stared at my girl in total shock:

they were oblivious for about two seconds then she screamed when she saw me.

I had had absolutely no idea...! Totally out of the blue. Not expecting *that*. Complete shock... and the things you see when you haven't got a gun...!

I was numb. I just collapsed to the floor in disbelief, sitting against the door-jamb vaguely aware of the mad scramble taking place on *our* bed... with her screaming and crying all at the same time. I avoided looking at him. I didn't want to see his face nor did I want any physical confrontation – I was no hero. I just stared at the tickets in my hand. So this is what she did on Thursday afternoons...

I simply said to her after he had legged it, 'And you can go too... never want to see you again.'

What a betrayal! I was crushed.

We were not married – but I thought we were headed that way; we'd been together for a while... had met a year or two after my wife had been killed in a road crash... had thought I was 'on my back from my tragedy and other spurious flings' – had thought this girl was going to be my salvation.

Wrong!

Women.

I just seemed to be hopeless with the other sex, always finding, or shacking up with the wrong kind of gal.

'I don't half pick them don't I Becks?' I said to Becky – a long-term friend of mine. My faith in them was now rock-bottom, but perhaps it was me, my fault, so I floundered, avoiding situations that might tempt me into more trouble.

And I hit the bottle – yes – I became that *Little Ol' Wine Drinker Me* that Dean Martin used to sing about only more, much more – the usual slide downhill, the slide that stops you shaving, cleaning your shoes, cleaning your teeth, combing your hair, which fortunately or unfortunately, I still possessed.

I asked myself again, was it my job as I knew I was away and 'out and about' a great deal? The money was good... but the pressure was high.

I spent several weeks like this, then...

Bugger it! It's no good – I have to change my life around somehow and the first thing I did was quit my job, to take the pressure off. Besides, I was an engineer at heart, and I liked music.

So now what do I do?

My two close friends Becky and Keith came to the rescue.

Becky did tell me when she first met 'whatshername'… that at first sight – instinctively – she disliked her. Pretty as my girl was, Becky became convinced very quickly that she was a foolish, empty, petulant creature and told me so. She was too obvious.

'She's trouble,' she simply said.

Becky was my confidante – but in this case, I had ignored her.

'Fancy a change of scenery? Fancy some music and dancing? You used to DJ in the past. Let's go and cheer you up this Friday… at the Golf Club do,' said Becky.

'Yep, great idea… you are *so* right… I need to change my life. As long as you promise that you won't let me get tangled up with another one like her… keep an eye out for me and all that – you will look after me won't you Becks…?'

'One day – one day… someone will turn up, you'll see,' she answered. 'Look, not all women are like the ones you seem to fall for… there are some good girls out there – trust me. Just don't try too hard… don't look desperate. Someone will fall for you.'

'Like some witch with a wart on the end of her nose you mean? Seriously Becks… I wish there were more like you,' I had answered.

Becky… someone who I considered both conciliatory and maternal.

The 'Golf Club Do' – the music – brought back memories from long ago, and one thing led to another…

Oh, and by the way, dear reader, my name is Bob Temple.

……….

Two years have passed since the bedroom incident, and yes, I'm still on my own… no partner.

But I now run a small dance group – or troupe – that performs in the local areas to the north of London.

9

Long story short, we play music while showing off various dances at gigs, usually once a fortnight, mostly evenings, occasionally afternoons. I say locally – we often venture into other counties further away.

There are five of us: me (boss), Keith and Becky (you've met them already), and Matt and Ruby. These two couples do most of the show-dancing while I generally organise the music to play at our events. I too can dance – at a push, usually helping out or to make up the numbers – although I'm nowhere near as good as the others.

We're on our way back from a gig in Peterborough – gone midnight, Range Rover purring along.

'So *when* is the next gig?' asked Ruby and Becky almost in unison.

'Either next Wednesday or the Wednesday after. I'll check.'

'And where is it again?' Keith asked.

'Kick-off at seven I think… and it's at Bury… Bury St Edmunds.'

'Bury St Edmunds? Where's that? I've heard of it. I take it it's in England?' asked Keith deadpan.

'No, it's not in England, it's in East Anglia.'

You have to go along with it.

'Actually, it's over towards Ipswich,' I said, continuing with the theme.

I'm used to this humour and exaggeration. good for morale. We bounce off each other, and yes, Keith and Becky were an item, just like Matt and Ruby, but Keith and Becky were closer to my age, which was on the wrong side of fifty – quite a bit on the wrong side.

As for Matt and Ruby, well, they looked like teenagers to me, but were in their thirties.

It never failed to surprise me the different shapes and sizes who wanted to dance and who were thoroughly enjoying themselves at the same time. That's what we were there for. I remember given half a chance years ago – and after a few pints, I'd get up and dance gleefully – and without shame.

…

How did I get into this dancing business? Well, to tell the truth I was on holiday at some Med hotel not too long ago and one evening I saw this real old couple – they had to be at least 120 years old, or even in their seventies – doing the Argentine tango! I thought 'wow' – not an easy dance to do even when you're fit and yet these old folk have to come all the way to some sunny place, for fun and to be able to dance! Why can't they dance at home?

So following the success of dancing on TV, and the fact there didn't seem to be much opportunity these days for *real* dancing apart from mind-numbing raves for twelve-year-olds, I'd come up with an idea. It was part of me wanting to change my life around. With some encouragement from Keith, I came up with the idea of forming a small dance combo to play music and dance in the local areas where we lived, or wherever we could find interested people or agents who had access to suitable premises. I would focus on arranging the gigs, setting up and playing the music while the others did most of the dancing. Not to be confused with tea-dancing, we operated, as I said before, mostly evenings.

Another reason for doing this is because I love music; it's in my DNA. My blood group – O Rhesus Music. To me most music is good, and good for the soul. I'm not fussed about playing new or old tunes come to that – as long as it's good in *my opinion,* and I'm the boss. It also has to be good to listen to, and also good for dancing. If it's a toss-up between the TV and the radio being on in a room, the TV always loses out, except perhaps if there's any dancing.

Plato declared in *The Republic* that, "Musical training is a more potent instrument than any other, because rhythm and harmony find their way into the inward places of the soul, on which they mightily fasten, imparting grace and making the soul of him who is rightly educated graceful". Yes. Amen to that – he hit the nail right on the head, thousands of years ago! The right music soothes the soul. To my mind, if there's no music in a society, no theatre, then it's shut off from humanity, but that's me. I do admit, however, that I sometimes like a little pain or quirkiness in my music.

Depends upon the mood.

Keith and I have been mates for decades. We have always liked a good gig, been to many in the past. We attended many concerts although that didn't stretch to Glastonbury; I'm a bit of a hothouse orchid when it comes to my creature comforts.

Keith was what you might call a 'real good egg', and a guy who made friends with people of all classes. He always had humour, was talkative, was true and was extremely generous – what was his was yours – and thought sarcasm, with sentiment, was the highest form of wit when used properly. He was tough and occasionally – just occasionally – could fly off the handle. When it came to authority, officialdom, bureaucracy and red tape, he was prejudiced against it: I was in harmony with him on that.

'And why is tape red?' he asked. 'Why can't it be some other colour – like purple? Jobsworths? Useless lot!'

He certainly attracted the dames. It wasn't so much his looks that attracted women to him, it was his honest curiosity and dry humour which was attractive in either gender, plus his patter, body language and keenness in spotting behaviour in people – he seemed to know instinctively what to say in most situations, usually with a small grin forming as he said it. Apart from a watch and ring, he wore no accoutrements at all – a bit like myself – no medallions, no bracelets and no earrings. As for body piercing –

'Well, I suppose it's a free world, but they look like bloody zits to me – I wonder if they realise that.' And sometimes he'd tell them.

Dancing was obviously popular. Everyone was watching it on the box. 'And it keeps you fit, so it's a win-win,' I thought. Can't be bad. Matt and Ruby were the younger, more energetic of the bunch with Matt, who was well built, often kitted out to show off his physique and six-pack. What a show-off. 'No comparison with my *one-pack,*' I kept telling myself.

The whole idea was to not only play music for punters to listen or dance to, but to play music and *show* the punters the technical aspects of the routines by instruction; this would really encourage the audience's participation once we'd kick off with a couple of exhibitions. Both Matt and Ruby liked to do these first dances, sometimes too much I thought.

Posers.

We realised that none of us would be an Artem, Anton or Flavia, but we all trained up – had proper lessons until we wouldn't be embarrassed, then we declared ourselves open for business, performing usually once a fortnight, to fit in with the day jobs.

For me…? It was almost like a busman's holiday – definitely not in it for the money. But we all loved the dancing and the music, especially as we could individually pick and choose the tracks and tailor the dances to suit us *and* the audience. And each time was different.

Yes, we all rubbed along together just fine, probably because we were not doing it every day. When we were together, it was just the quiet joy of friendship. It kept us fit too, as I mentioned.

And each time was different... especially Bury.

So – Bury next stop…

Chapter 2

USA – WWII
A Letter from Uncle Sam

'Barney – letter here for you!' shouted his Dad along the hall. 'Looks like our son will be working for Uncle Sam anytime soon,' muttered Dad, turning to Ma Muriel. Muriel knew it was inevitable.

'Coming!' Barney shouting back, bounding down the stairs.

As expected, the letter was his call-up. called up to report to a place a million miles away for training, Wendover Air Force Base.

He and his buddy Joe – they'd both written off over a month ago. They could see what was happening in Europe and knew it was just a matter of time they were eligible for call-up, so they made the first move, giving details of what they thought the recruiting people might want to know about. Pa still had friends in the right places to help things along. 'It's *who* you know son,' he would say.

Ever since he was knee-high, Barney was always tinkering with bits and pieces, pulling them apart to see what made them tick – especially electrical gear. He was mad on engineering and aircraft – he loved watching them doing displays and barnstorming. He had heard some wonderful stories about the Spitfire in the early air battles of the war in Europe. His school teacher complained about his mind being everywhere except on his school work, that he looked bored – 'He's constantly day-dreaming,' the teacher had told his Pa.

Truth be told, there was a part of Barney that craved excitement and adventure. He was always having scrapes on his bike or on his wheeled sledge he'd cobbled together from planks of wood and pram wheels.

'She's a real sumbitch to steer,' he'd say to Joe, sat behind him as they careered down the dusty track. They'd nearly always finish upside down on the side with scraped knees and scuffed knuckles – and a bunch of repairs to do on the trolley.

His other passion, his greatest passion, was music – listening, playing and dancing. Same with his close buddy Joe Tutucci. Barney could play the guitar, of sorts – his *gee-tar* as he liked to call it – and tinkled the ivories when he could get near a piano. Joe was a 'sax-man'; wow, he could blow and play that saxophone real good. At a push, he could also play with other brassy stuff as Barney called it. Now with his call-up Barney thought he might not get much chance with the music but was sure he'd get plenty of opportunity for engineering. They'd both written to the USAAF begging to do engineering if they were called – even to fly, if he could pass the tests. As for the army… no way! His Pa had done that in the last big fight.

'If you like digging, like mud, like crap food, then join the army. No, seriously, stay real clear of the army son. No fun at all!' Pa had said.

Every spare moment they had – when he wasn't pulling things apart – he and Joe would jam along with a couple of friends who made up the numbers. Ally (no one called him Aloysius) was the half black dude who could play the trumpet, the trombone and the bugle – just about anything made of brass, much better than Joe could. Satchmo was his hero. They just lacked Gene Krupa or Buddy Rich to hit drums, but they managed.

'Sounds like a load of damn noise if you ask me,' his Pa had said. 'What's the matter with Al Jolson, son? He sings real good.'

'You mean good for you – he's square!' laughed Barney, 'Dad! Can I use the phone?' He wanted to see if Joey'd also received his papers.

'Sure kid.'

He had. They were jubilant – school friends since year dot. Now they were just waiting for their travel orders.

'Where've you gotta go… Randolph?'

'No, Pa, Wendover.' 'Wendover bomber base here we come,' thought Barney. He didn't have a clue where it was though.

With his other interest however, Barney was frustrated with the music scene. He thought most of it boring, lacking excitement, even the likes of Glenn Miller sometimes. He *did* like Tommy Dorsey and Duke Ellington. He really was drawn more towards jazz and swing – a beat to get going with, to make your foot tap. He hadn't figured out yet how he could do all this just with a guitar. He wanted his to be louder, much louder – *somehow*. He needed something to compete with the noisy, ever-increasing brass players. His guitar didn't cut it, certainly not against Ally's trumpet. When he listened to the big orchestras, the guitars were nowhere to be heard – zilch. However, his interest in all things mechanical

14

and electrical had led him to do some experimenting with sound, perhaps with some kind of amplification. He dived into the books to find out, including Radio Shack. Joey was going to bring his catalogue with him.

Perfect.

Musical instruments had been around for thousands of years – guitars, or similar instruments included. Barney had read that a few keen musicians had tried in the past to make guitars louder just like he wanted his to be, even seen pictures of 'horns' attached to string instruments. Bizarre, definitely not cool, not looking right. It had to be cool. He didn't want some cockamamie rig-up.

But he also knew about the electric guitar.

'So, who made the first electric guitar?' he asked in the drug store with his bunch of friends.

'It was Leo Fender,' said Django.

'No. It was a guy called Rickenbacker,' said the store owner. Barney had heard of him too, a manufacturing and production guy. 'He did the messing around with acoustics and amplification.'

'No, no, no. It was none of these, it was a dude way back who started it all even before them – some guy called Beauchamp; he too, like Barney here, wanted more noise – a louder guitar. This was twenty years ago.'

'Rubbish!' chimed in Lizard, their local mechanic. 'It was some violin fella who played around with PA systems and microphones.'

'Come on guys, make up your minds.' Barney was getting confused – no one seemed to know, did they? All he knew was that several had already tried and failed, by adding those silly looking amplifying horns to their instruments, including Beauchamp. Somebody had also experimented by making a test guitar out of a board and a pickup from an electric phonograph. This experiment shaped thinking and put him on the right path. He even attended night-school classes in electronics.

'I'm telling you man, it was Rickenbacker,' repeated the owner.

'Nope – I just remembered, it was Les Paul,' said Lizzard.

'Les Paul? Who's he?' asked someone.

'Look. Listen, it was Rickenbacker and his Frying Pan,' said the store owner yet again.

'Frying Pan?'

'Yeah – his Frying Pan guitar!

15

Barney already knew that original electric guitars used tungsten pickups which basically converted the vibration of the strings into electrical current, which was then fed into the amplifier to produce the sound.

'I don't care who was first, I'm going to build my own... do it myself,' he announced.

...

This is what gave Barney his guidance and aspiration. He needed something to do and this was it.

The early experimenters had persevered. Further experiments followed with variations on the cone theme until eventually a working electric guitar was produced. Leo Fender, who also had a business in making and repairing amplifiers, produced his version of the electric guitar too.

The electric guitar's popularity began to increase during the Big Band era of the thirties and forties. Due to the loudness of the brass sections in jazz orchestras, just the problem Barney had even in his little group, he needed to have a guitar that could be heard above the other sections. An electric guitar, with the ability to be plugged into amplifiers, filled this void as far as Barney was concerned. He didn't really care who made it – he just wanted something like that! But it was beyond his means, so he reckoned that he might be able to do it himself, mess about and tinker... one day. He'd already pictured in his mind what he might do and looked forward to the challenge. And whenever he thought it was going to be too hard, he'd listen to Benny, Benny Goodman, one of his heroes. 'All your fault,' thought Barney. He was the first celebrated bandleader of the Swing Era, dubbed "The King of Swing," his emergence marking the beginning of the era. He was an accomplished clarinettist. His distinctive playing gave an identity both to his big band and to the smaller units he led simultaneously.

'All I gotta do one day,' he said to Joey, 'is to get some magnets into a coil so that it magnetizes the strings and these become themselves moving magnets that produce a current – a switchback current through the coil. Then I need an amplifier.' He reckoned that he understood the task.

Joe nodded along – he only had a rough idea what Barney was talking about. 'Where will all these gizmos go? Where will they fit?' asked Joe. 'I mean, it could be bigger and worse than the horns!'

'No, no, they are definitely not worse than them. They are smaller, much smaller. I'll have a bash at putting one together and even look at some kind of amplifier – a real small one. When it's finished, it has to be slim, Joe – and classy. Has to look the part, you know what I mean? I might need to have electrical adjustments on it for tuning, know what I mean Joe?'

'That's twice you said that. How big is it going to be – these amplifiers right now?' asked Joe.

'Big. Too big… and too many bucks too. I'll have to work on it Joey, maybe when we're *really* in the Air Force, get some parts.'

'Don't count your chickens just yet Barney. We gotta get through all them damn tests first.'

'It'll be a breeze, man.'

Good quality electric recordings were hard to come by – only some jazz compos, where nearly always the only thing you could hear was the singers and the brass. Barney had also heard that separate electrical amplification boxes were increasingly being experimented with to further increase and improve the sound. As he knew a thing or two about electrics, he thought that if he didn't get time on his tour, when he returned, this is what he would follow up on. Right now, the only thing he had to go on in his quest was to dabble with electrical gadgets and look longingly at a Radio Shack catalogue Joe had. Barney was going to make sure that when he reported to the USAAF, he'd take a copy along with him.

Chapter 3

USA WWII

Training – Wendover Field

Barney and Joe had been sent to Wendover Field, Utah. For much of the war the installation was the Army Air Force's only bombing and gunnery range. Although it was in the middle of nowhere, it was a big, busy airfield. Wendover's mission was to train heavy bomb groups. The bombing range was huge – over sixty miles long.

'If you miss here we'll send you home… in disgrace!' said one of the instructors.

'Boss tells me that there are more than ten thousand guys here,' said Joe. 'That's more than my home town!'

'Same here,' answered Barney. 'But let's hope there are some gals out here too – there's gotta be otherwise I'm done for!'

They found themselves teamed up with Walter Mitchell and Milton Baylis. Guys came in and guys went out if they couldn't keep up. Walt and Milt stuck with it and a bond formed amongst them. They were also quickly caught up with Barney and Joe's enthusiasm for music.

'Can't play a dang thing,' said Walt, but Milt could play a harmonica and trombone already.

'You could play the drums,' Barney suggested to Walt, 'Just keep a beat – keep us all in time.' So that's how Walter started on drums. Besides, he didn't want to miss out with his new buddies. He soon picked it up.

'Well, we've got six weeks to kill. If we can get Milt and Walt to get moving on their instruments we can get back to playing again,' Barney said to Joe. They needn't have worried – there were literally hundreds of buildings on the base including a hospital, gym, swimming pool and a library, not to mention a bowling alley and a proper movie house. They didn't have Ally with them – he'd joined the Navy, wanted to keep his feet on something a bit more solid than a thin piece of aluminium alloy.

The initial induction and training had determined that Barney was going to be a B-17 bombardier and Joe a wireless operator, huddled in his little 'shack' as he called it. That was fine by him. Barney also had to work the nose turret-gun as part of the bombardier's job. He couldn't just lie there in the nose for ten hours while everybody else was blasting away on the guns. Besides, there was only room for one right at the front. But the whole point of the B-17 was to get it over the target with the bombs for Barney to do his two-minute job, dropping them – on target.

When it came to the music, with Walt now on the drums, Milt – who could sing – had to be persuaded to carry on with the trombone; he could play but had left his at home thinking he wouldn't need it where he was going. It was only when they met up and started talking that they realized that for starters, there were four of them in the crew – a great bunch of buddies too – all who could play something, and therefore they had to play. It didn't take them long to find what they wanted on the base, or what they could borrow, to start jamming again.

'And when we get over to England, we'll just pick up where we left off,' said Joe.

But they had no illusions about how dangerous it was going to be. Many of the instructors had returned from Europe, hardened after many sorties. They pulled no punches on 'how things will be' during lessons. Casualty-wise, the waist gunners seemed to get it hardest followed by the man-in-the-nose… the bombardier, Barney's role. It did not surprise him. There was only a thin layer of plexiglass between him, shrapnel and a raging storm should it break… and it often did. But Barney had a plan for that, something an instructor had told him – an idea.

The instructor had said, 'On our outfit back in England we had one crew who took unauthorized steps to improve personal protection. A lot of crews did – it soon caught on and spread – until the boss heard about it. He initially said 'no' to it all until he realized, from mounting injuries, that it would be good for moral. So he turned a blind eye – as long as nothing interfered with the bomber's performance. The man in question who was, like Barney, a bombardier, made up himself a contraption he could mount in front of him in the nose to give some shrapnel protection – three Tommy tin hats mounted in a row on a half-inch bar of marine ply! The British helmets are flatter than ours – wider. He managed to get the limeys to 'find' what he needed. His ground engineers fixed it in place out of vision in such a manner that he could quickly swing it out of the way – then swing it back when his job was done. Naturally it couldn't completely protect him, he had to see where he was going and what he was shooting at. But he could also take it with him from plane to plane. Did it work? I can see by the quizzical look on your face. It sure did – two dented 'hats' with a nice big chunk of Krupp metal embedded in the ply. It was a draughty trip back home that's for sure!'

'Jeez, really! That sounds good, that's what I'll do – I'll get something rigged up when I get there,' said Barney.

'You do that son.'

'What about the others – what about them?' asked Joe. He didn't want to be left out. He took a little comfort in the fact that he was, in theory, better protected, hunkered down at his table.

'Sheets of steel or ply on the seat – have to protect your manhood – or fixed to the skin next to them; things like that,' said the instructor. 'But they couldn't be permanent – you never knew which kite you were going to fly until you got to it, so they had to be 'personal'… or you just hoped other crews and engineers did the same.'

Anyway, they felt a tad better after that little talk – the confidence of youth: 'It'll happen to someone else – but not to us.'

But the bomb-aiming was driving Barney nuts – the Norden bombsight was a sophisticated analogue computer that cost more than an average American home he was told. And while they were learning all this it was bitch cold up there. All his fingers felt like thumbs.

On a bombing run with the Norden, a target would be located visually; Barney would make calculations on wind direction, speed and altitude which he fed into the bombsight system – which would then take over the flying of the bomber, taking it on a course that would release the bombs at the right moment. 'Couldn't be easier,' said the teacher. Mind you, they had sixty miles to play in. Every time Barney dropped his dummy load he'd find out that the wind speed was different ten layers down, and he'd usually miss the circle.

'Shit!' he'd shout.

'We don't need to get the bomb into the bucket – we only need to hit the factory!' the instructor kept telling them. 'And Berlin and Munich are big places… real big.' But Barney – like all the other crews – had pride and wanted to be the best, wanted to win. The other crews used to laugh and rib, 'The Germans are going to be safe as houses when Barney's on a mission.'

Part of the buddy-banter.

Another problem was the long straight run required before dropping the bombs. This was needed so the pilot would have enough time to accurately account for the effects of wind, and get the proper angles set up with some level of accuracy. If anything changed during the bomb run, everything had to be set up again, but he did feel proud when they got a good result – and the skipper would often remind him that during the bombing run, Barney was in charge of flying the plane.

'Don't sneeze skipper!' Barney would call out.

But there was something else that kept both Barney and Joe busy between bombsights, lectures and flying. Before their arrival at Wendover, they had already been playing around on their own trying to get more noise out of a guitar with gadgets and gizmos. Joey, too, had picked up on the electrics and between them they had spent a whole lot of time down in the base's radio workshop trying to figure something out that would work on his guitar. Armed with the Radio Shack journal they dabbled and, with the help of the workshop guys, they came up with a small box of tricks, something they reckoned might do the job... rudimentary, but better than nothing. It wasn't exactly leading to the Frying Pan guitar just yet but it showed promise – a little black pick-up resin-made box with some leads, and small enough to fit into his big pockets.

'I'm not letting this out of my sight – it's staying with me no matter what until I can spend more time on it,' said Barney when they realised that they would be sent to England before the job could be finished. 'All we need now is a way of converting what comes out of this to a loud sound – some sort of electric booster. We'll get there one day Joe.'

'Amen to that,' Joe replied, '...but you might want to make it a bit flatter, maybe wider.'

They toiled together on perfecting their home-made guitar booster – Barney spending hours and hours on making his kit look good. 'It's has to look the piece Joey,' he would say trying to make it shine like a pin.

'Yeah – I get it, but if you keep polishing your gadgets all day long they'll disappear man... and it's still too big Barney.'

'Well, I'll get the grit-paper and keep rubbing it round and smooth over the edges – a few small clips to hold all together for now and some connectors for my wiring. Don't want it too big, man, just so it'll fit in my pockets. In fact Joe, I might put a little cut out round the outside for a small piece of Perspex to fit over the top surface so's I can see what's going on. What do you reckon eh? It'll be real cool man.'

'What? A guitar with a window in it. That's way too cool buddy.'

Eventually they were told where 'home' was going to be in England – a base called Knettishall in Suffolk, a county in Eastern England, part of the 388 Bomber Group. The crew quickly looked it up on the maps, and it began to dawn on them that the complete area was so small, the bases were almost on top of each other.

'Joe – this place, Suffolk, looks like we could walk from one end to the other in an afternoon! Hell man, 'teach' says that the whole of England is smaller than Texas. The Krauts can't miss!'

'Is it anywhere near London?' asked Joe. They'd heard of London.

'Well it looks a long way but really, no place is far from anywhere Joe. There's a town here called Norwich – seems to be the only place. Hey, they got to have chicks there… and look, there's Shipdham just north of us.' Some buddies they had met along the way were going there. They had no idea just how many bases there were that belonged to the USAAF. 'Those are ours – but look at all the RAF bases too Joe. Let's hope we can see where we are going – it must be murder flying at night! It'll be like Grand Central, how we gonna see each other?'

Chapter 4

USAAF in England

Spike Drops Out

Knettishall wasn't that bad – just strange, quiet, plenty of woods and a small town just down the road, Thetford, and an even smaller one in the opposite direction, Diss. The whole place had looked small on the maps back home but now that they were actually here, it was a long walk to anywhere.

After their arrival, there was some horse-trading with the crew members. Small cliques had formed during training school as was natural. These had continued until they reached England. The group and squadron assignments inevitably led to some splits from their training buddies but Barney, Joe and the others stayed together, just as they wanted it to be.

On only their fourth mission as a crew they were hit twice, the first time on the way in to the target, caught by a Fw190 that went screaming past from above and behind leaving a stitch of bullet holes down one side. Tail-end Charlie had hollered,

'One coming in from behind!!'

This gave Barney the warning as he readied for the 190 to go past – as it did – fast, too fast, going downwards while turning. Barney eventually let off a blast once he got his sights on it but couldn't catch it.

'Jeez. Dammit! Missed it!' he shouted, only to hear someone on the intercom say, 'Waist gunner's bought it. He's on the floor. I'll attend.' They'd all felt the strikes.

'Who is it – who's hurt?' asked the skipper.

'The new lad Spike,' answered Walt. 'He's in a bad way.' Not only had the shells hit the new waist gunner, one of them had hit the gun mount and knocked it clean across the fuselage. There were live ammo belts lying everywhere. The skipper called for a check. There didn't appear to be any lasting damage – engines were still humming, no rattles, no fires and they pressed on.

Meanwhile the gunners worked on Spike – beginning by removing his harness. Later, they had mused how come so much blood can come from someone and he still be alive. Spike had been hit through his side and had collapsed as deathly paleness spread across his face. Walt did his best, stemming the flow – reckoned that it was a ricochet that did the damage otherwise there would have been little left of Spike's belly.

There were two waist gunners on the B-17 but Spike wasn't an original crew member. He came courtesy of a motorbike accident – the original waist gunner having come off his machine bike two days before, returning to base late. He was now in hospital with a broken ankle. Spike was his replacement. Barney remembered his training back at Wendover when the instructor told him that of all crew members on a '17', waist gunners had the shortest life, with bombardiers not far behind. But Barney thought he was indestructible – if it was going to happen then it would not happen to him.

'Skip. He won't last the journey. He's bleeding inside somewhere. He'll just peg out before we get back. I've patched him up best I can,' said Walt.

He came back on a few moments later. 'He's getting paler Skip.' Walt knew that they could not be far from the target but nevertheless, it was still a long return slog home.

Skipper came on, 'If you're sure about that, Walt, then just give me a minute while we think. Try your best to keep him warm.' A couple of minutes passed before he was back on. 'You might not like what I'm going to say, but this is what we're gonna do… we are going to drop him out – with his 'chute already pulled. We'll do that as soon as we get clear of the target; we're only 15-20 minutes away.'

Spike – Frederic Nolec was his name – had crew-cut, straight up hair, so Spike became the easiest, quickest option. Now he was beginning to come around.

'He's opened his eyes Skipper.' They knew they had to keep him as warm as possible. Spike didn't say anything – just moaned a little but at least gave the impression of knowing where he was and what was going on. The gunners gave him an encouraging thumbs-up and a smile. It was good to see him respond with his own weak grin but it looked like he'd taken a knock on the head too.

Maybe he could make it all the way back, wondered Walt. But within five minutes Spike had lapsed into unconsciousness, his pallor returning to a blue/grey hue.

'Spike's gone again Skipper – don't look good,' he said. 'I thought he might pull through a bit. We got a smile out of him.'

'OK. You gunners keep him going – as the flak builds up towards the target they'll be less fighters around – they don't want to be hit by their own side. So stick with him and as soon as we're ten minutes on the way back we'll pop him out. We'll still be close enough to a town where he could get treatment. Got it? First make sure he's patched up and trussed up good. Joe – write a note with brief description of injury, as much as you know, and stick it in his top pocket; don't forget to put the time of his injury on his forehead.'

'Sure Skip.' Skip sounded real cool.

It took a few seconds for this to sink in… kick out Spike while still over Germany. They could see the sense in what the boss was saying – no point in dumping out in the sticks where he could hang in a forest for a day or two before being found.

'But boss, the Krauts will let him die even if they find him before it's too late,' said someone… couldn't tell who.

'Got a better idea? He'll probably be dead long before we cross the English coast. This way he has half a chance, guys.'

Walt looked down at Spike – still unconscious. 'Yeah Skipper – you're right, he's in a bad way.'

Skip went on, 'Two of you get around him, get his chute on, Walt – get him ready for my signal.'

It was a nerve-racking thirty minutes with flak making them jump around like a cork in a rough sea. Bombs were dropped OK, doors shut without problem. The plane moved about with the flak a lot more now the bombs had gone.

'Right, five minutes' time boys while we make sure we're clear. Top gun, tail man – are we clear behind? Joe Miller did two jobs – engineer and top turret. Lou Miagli was Tail-End Charlie, but he was just 'Lou'.

They weren't. About three hundred yards behind and just a little lower was another 17.

The skipper told them he'd slow down slightly so that they'd drift back over the lower machine for clear air and reduce height a little for when they dropped Spike. No doubt the other crew were just assuming they had a malfunction or something.

'Are we ready boys?' said Skipper.

'Yes boss, ready.'

Out went Spike – his 'chute opening almost immediately.

'Well done guys. He'll be in the cold air for a little on his way down which might work in his favour with his wounds. We can only hope they do the decent thing when they find him. So back to work, got to get this sonofabitch home.'

'She'll do it boss – got plenty chewing gum to plug these holes. She's a trusty ol' bird.'

'Did you say *rusty* old bird? Thanks!' said Skipper.

'No – *trusty* boss!' Barney thought a little humour might not go amiss while he pondered what they'd just done. The skipper was a clever man, Spike might have half a chance. It was cold enough down at ground level when they'd taken off so God knows how cold it was up there at 15,000 feet.

But it was just as well that they'd pushed Spike out; on the way back they received the attention of more fighters. One came head-on at the bomber in front which suffered some hits. Barney was ready behind his guns – ready to squeeze but suddenly became aware of debris hurtling towards him, debris that been blown off the kite in front. Instinctively he ducked. It missed but other pieces that came flying back didn't and clattered against their nose. Suddenly it was blowing a gale – a freezing cold gale. Noisy.

'My glass is busted Skipper... I gotta three-inch hole!' Barney did a quick check around him. 'Everything else looks OK. I'm sure that was an engine cowling skipper from the one in front that came past.' The bomber in front was still maintaining station then it started to slowly move back as the damage was felt. Missing a cowling or two was not going to make things easy.

'I reckon he's got some aero damage – can't see any smoke,' Skipper advised. 'He probably can't keep up.' He was hard to hear with all the noise.

Well that bomber had tried – it had kept up, but because it was using more fuel, and maybe because it had a punctured tank, it dropped out of formation to put down as soon as it had crossed the coast, looking for the nearest base they could find.

When they had landed, they had clambered out and done a quick external survey.

'Hey boss, you're bleeding,' said Lou. The skipper's face was encrusted with blood.

'Well just look up there fellas,' said the skipper, pointing up at the cockpit. They all looked up. It was only then that Barney realised he'd been lucky; some of that debris he'd seen flying past just above him had briefly wrapped itself around the windscreen before flying off – but not before it had punctured the glass which was a complete mess. 'I'm OK. I feel OK – didn't realise it looked this bad.'

The meat wagons were always on hand when the bombers returned – they called one over. The skipper was OK.

'You're gonna look ugly now boss... your gal won't want you looking like that. Can I take her out instead? I'm better looking than you now.'

Laughter... then it sank in. 'Don't forget about Spike,' Skipper reminded them. As for Barney – he didn't know why but when he'd first heard, during the mission, that a waist gunner was hit, he prayed instantly that it wasn't Walter. He was their drum man. He felt guilty and selfish for thinking that way but couldn't help it.

Their debrief took a little longer on account of Spike. They told their story.

They received notification through the grapevine a month later that Spike was alright; he was recovering. The Krauts had done the right thing. They had beers that night – many beers. 'Good call boss,' enjoined everyone.

Walt thought that in future, he'd take more gum.

Chapter 5

UK Today. – Our set-up

Hi reader – it's me again.... Bob Temple.

We've arrived at Bury and set ourselves up. It'd been a few minutes since we were 'all connected ready to go' but I stood up and looked around, taking in the whole scene....

Was it me...?

'Becky – don't you find this place........strange?'

'Yes... I know what you mean – strange atmosphere – and gloomy with it,' she replied.

For all of us, our journeys to Bury – Matt and Rubes on the bike, the rest of us in the Rover – had not been without incident. And there was confusion when we arrived just as it was getting dark...a mixed booking perhaps? The man we had supposed to be meeting – 'Andy' – was nowhere to be seen, instead we were met – or should I say, 'bumped into' a *Mr Rawlings* who was expecting somebody else completely different – 'The Fred Briggs Combo' – whoever they were.

I retrospect – when I look back – it should have been bloody obvious what had happened to us all, so let me back-track a little to pick up from just before we set off.......

...

The music we concentrated on was mostly pop of the older variety, mixed up with some new artists and with some good, solid oldies that are still popular today. We aimed and advertised ourselves for a more mature dancing audience – anyone over 21 these days was an oldie – going around local venues including town halls, pubs, converted barns and even private parties. You could say I was a child of the sixties… and no, never touched the stuff – ever.

We knew that anyone in their sixties, like myself, was familiar with all that went on back then, including the psychedelic flower power and beads. But Glenn Miller, Duke Ellington, Frank Sinatra, Bert Kaempfert, Nat King Cole and the like were not excluded, just in case some 'squares' did turn up. We took requests from our punters and just occasionally would have light-hearted competition for jiving – or some other dance. For my own consumption at home, I enjoyed a mix of both pop and classical – depending on my mood. I'm the first to admit that when it's all over, when the evening is past and the embers are low, I often need some chill-down with either some slow jazz for an hour before lights out… or some classical.

Must be getting old…

Keith, as a rule, partnered with Becky and Matt partnered with Ruby, however they were interchangeable – including me – at a push, so I was quite happy with this arrangement and mucked in when the others had a break which helped my own fitness.

As I watched my dancers I would often reflect on my own, single situation with just a little envy at times; they were comfortable together – made me feel real lonely these days.

'You need a woman,' Becky would say, '…and that's not an offer!'

'Shame. I'm getting on but trying my best,' I'd answer. '…and you know how good I am with females. Usually not good!'

To me old age wasn't just about numbers. I knew many who had given up when they reached 40 – and they looked it too, you could see it in their demeanour, their carriage, deportment, the way they walked…

'I'm beginning to check out!'

…was the message conveyed by many well before their time. And some just got too big. Grey didn't mean old either. It was all about attitude and approach to life, what you did – is there still a sparkle in your eyes and a smile on your lips? Is there humour in your mind? Of course, and yes, sometimes with a little help from your genes, it all counts.

If you've been dealt a bad hand from the word 'go', the struggle is bigger but is no reason to quit – character cannot be developed in ease and quiet. For many, as long as life pulsates in them, they move and approach life as if persuaded that it will never cease, therefore their infirmities and other 'issues' seldom set a term to their outlook and plans that concern their future. So when I saw that old couple doing the Argentine tango I thought, 'Wonderful.' The mind and spirit were there as were the flesh and bones, still wanting enjoyment in the late stages of their life.

Our format or routine was quite simple: we'd agree on a mix of tracks and dances then after getting set up I would play some safe, introductory pieces to gauge the mood of the audience – and adapt a playlist; I had all sorts. Matt & Ruby would be first up to 'boogie down' as they say – to break the ice and get the ball rolling. They were both good 'flappers' and often found the Charleston to be a good starting demo… 'But please not to *Happy Feet*,' I begged them, it drove me nuts. *Move It* and *Footloose* were ice-breakers we played – good, stomping jives. I was surprised just how energetic fifty-year-olds could be…

I was also amazed how the women still dressed up with stockings and suspender belts, even those older gals in their fifties and sixties. Obviously letting their hair down but keeping their skirts up, almost wanting to show their latest purchase from 'Naughty Knickers', displaying their *Intimissimi* or even posher *Myla* gear.

You don't ask, do you – 'Hey luv, are they *Hanro* specials or *Mimi Holidays*…?'

But we didn't complain… why would we? It was all great fun.

Our commitments were mostly local and neighbouring counties, travelling as far as practicable but occasionally we'd venture further, once as far as Sheffield up the A1. That's quite a way!

We'd all been surprised how popular dancing was right across the people's ages wherever we went so I played for all. Maybe one day we'll be surprised and see an eighty-year-old do a break-dance; I just hope that he doesn't lose his teeth when he's doing it – clackety-clack! Occasionally we'd have a bum audience, dull, unresponsive, fortunately not often. No feeling like pleasing an audience. We also realised that those in their sixties had more time on their hands, and didn't have to get up in the morning – mostly retired.

I sent an e-mail the next day to them confirming the arrangements.

…

'So Bob, how long to get to this place then – Bury St Edmunds?' asked Keith at lunch when they met up at their local.

'An hour plus maybe to get there but I'll give us a margin,' I replied. '…and Matt's got a late dental that day so we'll have to split the transport, us three in the Rover with the usual kit and maybe the small trailer. Matt will follow up with Ruby on his Trophy. I've sent the e-mails: direction? Well, straight across country more or less – get onto the A14 and stay on it; it takes us right there. I have been that way before but that was a long time ago. I think East Anglia was still attached to the mainland back then Keith.'

Becky was a 'fine lass' as Keith would say – slightly above average height, soft and curvy with the dancing keeping her trim and, like Ruby, a backside that could stop traffic. She exuded a delicious presence, had a ready laugh and, for many, a very seductive demeanour without it being obvious.

All down to chemistry, isn't it?

No wonder she was a favourite on the dance floor… and off! When I was younger I used to think women in their twenties were in the heyday of their looks – and those in their forties and fifties basically past it. But no longer – not these days and Becky was the proof, like an improving wine. To me, she represented what a real woman should look like – a proper shape, not like a figure 'one', straight up and down with no waist and no bum. Mind you, I'm not claiming to be an oil painting either – my features had long settled into a pleasant collaboration after all these years, even if they'd grown at different rates, giving me a curious but pleasant face (I'm told) that seemed to have been designed by a council committee…

And don't you dare say Picasso.

Unlike Matt, with his looks and physique, I wasn't too bothered if I walked into a room and the women didn't fasten their gaze upon me, but Matt, well… Rubes would say that's how she could tell if a woman was gay or not. I could see her point. I remember many moons ago when I was young and stupid, trying my best to impress the opposite sex with some silly chat-up line…

'Give them a false name that says, 'you're hard' – 'you're tough' – 'don't mess with me' kind of name,' my mates suggested, '…you know, the opposite of Rupert… or… Gideon.'

'You mean like… *Lance Savage*… or… *Brian Belter*…?

'Maybe not.'

Like I said... when I was young and stupid...

'Anyway – the bloke we're meeting at Bury is called Andy Baxter. Matt and Ruby can follow up later after Matt's had his teeth done. So we'll set off and they can catch up... perhaps meet up somewhere near Six Mile Bottom or thereabouts if you want – there's bound to be a pub or cafe there where we can have a coffee before getting to Bury, which will only be down the road. It won't take long for them to catch up, they can meet us wherever we stop.'

'Six Mile Bottom – is that a real place?' Keith again.

'It is for those that live there, and no, it's not a name for a fat-camp either,' said Becky. She was well acquainted with Keith's attempts at humour.

Before a gig, we always checked our kit because there was always a tendency to more or less throw it all in the wagon quickly at the end of the previous bash in order to get back on the road... and bed.

'Everything was working OK in Peterborough. Is it all there, Keith, and in the right places?' In preparation, we saddled up with sound-to-light, two flat screen TVs, our laptop, our iBattle pack – turntable of course and vinyl, plus the bigger stuff – mixer table. Oh – and a ghetto blaster... you never know. So all the usual paraphernalia.

I hadn't completely gone over to digital – not yet, but I was getting there. And as we were not providing a concert we just took our compact kit – smallish and easy enough to load, unload, get set up and get going. Today modern kit can pack a real punch while remaining small and compact. It was a tight fit in the Rover but we sometimes used a van and, in any case, we also had a low covered trailer. God knows what we would have done thirty years ago when kit was twice the size; no wonder they needed big vans or buses and although we would use the van it could not match the Rover for creature comforts.

On the gigs, I didn't do any real mixing – I just sorted and played the music saying few words; nor was I into talking over everything like some jocks do. I could quite easily just turn up with a pre-arranged track list on a stick, plug it into my laptop and just sit back and read the papers, like the 'raves'... but the punters were paying for something a little more exciting than that. Besides, I always listened out for a mood – and of course took requests. If I did say anything, it was only words associated with interesting facts of a track should there be any, such as did anybody know how the title came about for Buddy Holly's *That'll Be the Day*? Well folks, apparently he had the tune but couldn't think of a title for it and one day, when they were watching a John Wayne movie, *The*

Searchers, Wayne said during the film 'That'll Be the Day' five times. So I'm told. Little titbits like that. But because I occasionally had to dance, I usually let the music do the talking, if you know what I mean.

And another thing we had learnt on our travels – to *always* take an old round-pin plug or two with a lead and adaptors as part of the 'pack-up'; we were stymied once when they turned up at an old barn and the only power source was two old round-pin plugs… in this day and age! We had to do quick 'mods' to save the evening.

'How many costumes this time?' asked Bob.

'Two – I also have Matt and Ruby's spare outfits,' answered Keith. They usually took two each. They weren't going for any competition – not like *Strictly* but they all liked to dress up and look the part.

'You know, I could be sat behind my controls naked from the waist down and no one would notice,' I said.

'Good job too,' said Becky. I felt like saying that I could wear a fluffy red and white jock-strap for Christmas gigs.

'Let's hope the floor's been properly swept in this place,' added Keith. Nothing was worse than finding the premises had a floor like a Chinese tyre factory.

I suppose I had thousands upon thousands of tracks on my system backed up on nearly all my devices and usually if a selection went down well, we'd keep it with an annotation of where it was. But as it was, you never knew an audience 'til you arrived there and had a few bops. For Bury I thought I'd make some changes from the Peterborough selection. 'I've compiled some tracks in groups – different tracks from the last gig so we need to discuss what dances you want to exhibit. We'll do a twenty second sample on each and then you can tell me what suits you best.'

Chapter 6

UK – Setting Off to Bury

We packed the gear into the Rover and set off – me, Keith and Becky. Traffic was okay so we took it easy until Newmarket was not too far away. We turned off the main road and eventually spotted a pub and stopped.

'This place looks alright. Let's get in and I'll let Matt know where we are,' I said. Once inside and settled we found that Ruby had already responded – they were already on their way. The pub was unusual – it actually *was* like a pub as I remembered them from the past, with a welcoming atmosphere and no mindless sound blasting out nor any giant TV screens showing soccer. Here, they'd even had a fire going as it was April. 'Nice,' I thought. The joint wasn't too busy and while at the bar we struck up a chat with the barman after swapping the usual pleasantries. Keith told him what we were about – and where we were headed that evening. Over drinks Becky talked about the playlist and what dances went with the tracks. I made the changes on the laptop.

Historically, when music was composed and played going back two or three centuries, they were not short pieces. Just take some time out and listen to some classical movements and you'll see what I mean… if you can last that long, if you have a week. Not too exciting but at the time, cutting edge.

Looking back, it seemed that in the twenties and thirties everyone went mad with jazz and ragtime. Then it all became more organised with bigger bands with front-men singers and crooners before the war. How on earth they managed to pay the wages for these fifteen-piece bands amazed me – probably their downfall ultimately. Oh, and perhaps because of the emergence of the electric guitar. You cannot imagine Tommy Steele or Eddie Cochran fronting Glenn Miller now can you?

You don't have to answer that reader…

While Glenn Miller and his ilk had the youngsters jitterbugging in the aisles in the thirties and forties, after the war some artists started making music in smaller groups. The records got shorter, the outfits smaller – and cheaper. If you could play a guitar, strum a bass, hit some skin, blow a sax and sing just a little, you had a chance of making it. And of course in the US the jukebox played a significant part in the spread of what was becoming popular music. There were as many as a quarter of a million of them in the US come WWII. They soon caught on over here in the UK.

Welcome to pop.

And if you are wondering – most records became about three minutes long because of the time constraints on radio. and because of attention span… really. Yes I know, there have been modern records that go on and on… and on… zzzzzzzzzz.

Moving along now…

We don't dance to every track, of course, but the troupe liked to 'map out' what they were likely to be doing that evening. And for much of the time *we* became partners on account of being asked by audience members for a dance and a bit of tuition; some took it quite seriously which was good to see.

And just then Matt and Ruby walked in and joined the talk.

'Aha – just in time, we were about to talk music selection and dances. Get a drink, sit down and we'll go through it,' I said. '…and how's the face? Not mumbling like Marlon Brando then?'

'Okay ta, just a check-up,' answered Matt.

We set ourselves round one side of the table, eyes focussing on the laptop. We usually had a list of good 'starters' after doing several gigs, we knew what made the feet tap, heads bob and fingers snap. We also like to include a range of dances for Matt, Ruby, Keith and Becks to do at some stage of the evening, with Matt usually leading the way with the first dance. He knew from his own experience that the music could begin and play for quite a while before anybody took up the cudgel, brave enough to venture out onto the floor, so Matt and Ruby's first dance together usually did the trick and brought out the punters.

'I'll kick off with the usual *Take Five* – an intro, inoffensive but catchy, to get the punters settled and hopefully in the mood while we put the final touches together. Then for the first show dance it'll be… haven't decided yet, for your Charleston.' This was usually followed by a pick from a few rock 'n' roll tracks to showcase the jive by Matt and Ruby, such as *Candyman, Move It,* or maybe *Crazy Little Thing Called Love* to get the blood pumping. 'Which one?' I asked.

'Think we'll do *Move It* this time,' said Matt. They all nodded. If there was one record that never failed to get someone on the floor, it was *Move It* – a great combination of voice interspersed with flowing guitar. A fabulous example of a track where there are gaps in the lyrics beautifully filled by lead guitar. One of the first ever British rock 'n' roll records. Hats off to 'Sammy' Samwell who wrote it.

'OK. Hope you brushed up on your quickstep, rumba and tango. Have a few waltzes amongst this lot too.

'Waltz? Which one's that?' asked Ruby.

'A couple actually – *Interlude* and *Sweeter Than You* – so far.'

'What have we got for the rumba?' asked Becky.

'*Kokomo, Cry For Me* and maybe *Heart Attack and Vine*. But you don't have to do these dances, if you feel you have a better interpretation then go with your instincts. It's the same with the tango,' I went on, 'I've slotted in *Surrender.*'

'Ace. Not played that for a while,' said Ruby. 'But I'll tell you what, We're fed up of doing *Happy Feet* for the Charleston dance, aren't we Matt, so how about *Upside Down* instead?'

'Okay. Me too. When it comes to the Charleston, you're the boss, so fill your boots,' I said.

The barman called over to us.

'Where did you guys say you were going…?' He turned away. 'Hey Kevin, is that where they're having some sort of WWII re-enactment festival or fete or something – in Bury?' shouted the barman to someone round the back.

'Could be – not sure dad. Might be Thetford way maybe, but I could be wrong,' a disembodied voice responded from another room nearby. 'In fact, I think they're making a war film or something… something to do with the army,' the voice added.

'Did you get that…?' asked 'dad' barman, looking at us again.

'Seems a popular place for filming,' I said, remembering when *Memphis Belle* was done and the flying overhead at the time.

'Oh, Thetford… *Dad's Army* you mean?' chipped in Keith, raising his voice.

'No, I don't think it's that, something else. I thought I'd mention it because of traffic, but you should be alright if you're just going Bury way,' said the barman. 'Sometimes they start to close off the roads or make detours so be aware is all I'm saying.'

'Thanks anyway,' I answered. Must be *Dad's Army* out this way, I'd seen the TV. It was definitely out this way somewhere. But then Matt told us all that was all done years ago – must be something new, perhaps *Grandad's Army*! You could perhaps see why they came to this neck of the woods to film, it just seemed quieter, less spoilt, less built up – less crowded. Real quiet.

Keith and I well-remembered when we used to live up in Lancashire that in the summer, hardly a weekend went by without some kind of festival or vintage gathering taking place just down the road. We'd see old cars in convoys trundling past, or old motorbikes, lorries, old buses, Rolls Royce cars one after the other, and of course the usual rag-tag of mods on their polished-up scooters, in competition with each other to see who had the fanciest flag on the tallest aerials, festooned with about a million mirrors. But it was the 1940s festivals and WWII re-enactments that seemed to attract the biggest crowds, probably because of the links with the airbase nearby that had been American during the war. Army Jeeps and other transport could be seen headed towards the area a few days before the festival. It was usually a rehearsed event with German, British and US soldiers playing out some battle. All this took place on the large village green.

I was always amazed that in the high street, before and after these events, you would see WWII Brit, German and US uniforms sitting outside the cafes, apparently armed to the teeth – machine guns, rifles and pistols – sipping coffee alongside those with jeans, Glastonbury t-shirts, Nike trainers… and no one batting an eyelid, all part of the occasion, all good fun; it was a great atmosphere, not even spoilt when a 'Top Gun' jet from the nearby base made an appearance over the green.

But weird… men and women cyclists dressed up in lycra and all the headgear, mingling with storm-troopers wearing a different kind of headgear. Not Star Wars storm troopers, proper storm troopers.

And of cycling… it really has changed over the years; those mods with their scooters, huge aerials and exaggerated mirrors reminded me of when I cycled as a kid. I had things on my bike that would turn today's bikers green with envy. When I say 'things' – I'm talking gizmos.

For instance, I had indicators on my push-bike… yes, really! I was way ahead.

I'm not finished yet. On my bike I had *three* brakes – normal front and back wheel callipers, AND a back-pedal brake. So, while other cyclists struggled to stop when their wheels were all wet, I had – smugly – no problem.

Don't go reader…

I didn't just have a ting-a-ling bell – I had a wheel rim-mounted device activated by a lever on the handlebars. It sounded like an ambulance going past.

Mirrors? Of course – one each side but I have to admit they weren't heated. And oh yay! – I had a spirit level on the handlebars that told me if I was going up-hill or not. Yes. Seriously!

Stay with me…

Number of gears…? I remember that it was less than two hundred… probably about ten. Sufficient. I mean, who is so sad that that they need a calculator or indicator to tell them where they are with the gears? Come on!

Chunky tyres? Didn't need them – my bike was German, it already had wide tyres.

And no, one thing I did *not* have was forward-mounted machine guns or lasers – although today they could be useful these days. So, Hoy there, eat your heart out.

Happy thoughts, but I digress…

'If this re-enactment is in Bury, should make for a good gig then. Might even have to reschedule the kind of music we're going to play, loads of Glenn Miller and suchlike,' s. On the days they had these kinds of occasions back up north, the pubs and bars were always heaving.

'Yeah, but hold on,' said Matt. 'It's fine if it's something from the forties like *Dad's Army* because we can cater for that but what if it is a re-enactment from the Dark Ages – I mean this place is steeped in ancient history and death, Vikings and all that. Or there might be knights in armour too.'

'Loads of clanking – sounds noisy. I'll have a look tho' see if I've got an app for medieval music,' Keith added. 'Who knows, we could always play Black Sabbath.'

'Very funny – but you *could* play some Gregorian chants, although I'm not sure what kind of dance we'd do to that! Could be a 'first' coming up; Becky, what dance would you do to a Gregorian chant?'

'I'd do a jive wearing a monk's habit… or nun's habit if you prefer, even a sand dance.'

'Good luck with that, you'd be on your own,' Matt responded.

I cut in, 'OK, I think we're finished, so time to go. You can catch up – it's not far – just stay on the main road. If you fall into the North Sea, you've gone too far. And remember, no heroics on your bike – we know you can do 300 mph in first gear and all that. Take it easy. Difficult looking elegant with your leg in plaster trying to do the waltz.'

I liked to exaggerate occasionally.

'And while we are on our way, try and think about tunes and dances that would be setting the scene for any festival. You never know – it could be the First World War.'

'Or the War of the Roses – might simplify the music selection,' Ruby said. 'Guns and Roses…?'

Nice one. Pathetic.

'Finally – a reminder. No talking with any punters about war, politics or religion.'

When it came to the physics of dancing – the techniques, the moves and rules, I would leave it to Matt and Keith to ensure standards were maintained because, although it was almost like a busman's holiday and we were actually enjoying ourselves, we did want to convey the fact that we knew what we were doing. So occasional practice took place either at Matt's place or mine. The banter would flow…

'Remember, in the waltz we have body contact, lovely extensions, fluidity – and don't lift your feet. Just flow.' Often – and when we were split up by enthusiastic punters – we would be asked for tips and advice.

'Keep your chins up,' was always a joke as I had two – all mine.

'Keep the rise and fall… and open up your shoulders.'

Matt was particularly good with the Latin moves and could immerse and lose himself in the spirit of the dance. In a nanosecond, he was there. Me? I tended to flop about if I attempted anything too exacting.

'Come on Bob, in the cha-cha-cha you need more hip action; finish the moves in a clean way and no stomping – no flat feet! Yeah, and smile a bit.'

That's me told off. But I liked doing the samba. 'Your hip rolls could be disgustingly fabulous,' Ruby would say when we practised, so I had something going, even at my age.

Because of our mix of music the tango would be popular.

'Ok Ruby – must keep your head away, be more intense, upright and have good hold. Don't forget the staccato actions, and no rounded backs please.'

As for the jive – again, always popular – very few actually knew how to do it properly, technically. On many occasions when we partnered the audience, we'd find stompers, poor timing, missed holds and kicks that would do Johnnie Wilkinson proud. The jive was all about energy and enthusiasm, sharp flicks and kicks, timing, enjoyment, seen it even as far back as the Lindy hops in WWII which the Yanks had brought over. We didn't mind if they got it wrong – as long as the punters were enjoying themselves. But if advice was sought, we were there.

Chapter 7

En Route To Bury

'I wonder what sort of audience we'll get tonight?' I said out loud.

'You know what I mean; a good participating audience; snapping fingers, nodding heads, getting stuck in, asking requests and generally enjoying themselves, remember – it's all social dancing, we're there to give pleasure and entertainment and for everybody to *have* pleasure and entertainment.'

Before the war, it was all big orchestras and crooners, Fred and Ginger, smooth and polished – not raw, until I saw some very old pre-war clips. One that grabbed my attention was from the film *Sun Valley Serenade* with *Chattanooga Choo Choo* being played; great tune, but I was amazed just watching the drummer in Glenn Miller's band, bashing away – energetic, totally absorbed almost like Keith Moon or the Pretty Things except not so mad... and this in 1941! And he was wearing a bloody shirt and tie too; not quite sure who he was, possibly someone called Mo Purtil. It just goes to show that these guys had the passion and rhythm back then too – not just Elvis or Keith Moon.

When I told my gang all this, I mused, 'Hey, just imagine that lot getting together somehow. Have you seen this clip – or the film come to that?'

'Might have... pretty certain that I have seen a Glenn Miller film – I mean a proper Glenn Miller and not a Jimmie Stewart Glenn Miller film. Black and white, you know,' said Keith.

'Well I've downloaded the clip. I could always play it, put it on the projector/plasma when we come to it,' I said. 'It's always worth a play – get some good dancing. Might fit in well with any festival or theme they might be having.'

'Mmmm... I shall look forward to seeing the 1941 version of Keith Moon,' Becky added.

'Well, you might be disappointed. I don't think Mo went around smashing up his kit like Keith Moon did as far as I know.'

But I reckon one of the reasons Bill Haley, Eddie Cochran and Elvis became really popular was – apart from the music – because they didn't look like your mum or your dad. Let's face it, Russ Conway and Perry Como didn't dress 'cool', did they?

Hmmm… but what about Buddy Holly? Looked like a geek… could have done with a Specsavers down the road. I think he already did, looking at him.

Well alright then… the music helped.

....

We motored along. Keith was looking with dismay at the typical English roadside – it was spring and already with first buds, but the hedges and trash bins overflowed with litter. Crap everywhere: ditches with plastic bags and bottles cluttering up what should be a pretty English country picture. It looked more like downtown Cairo.

'Do you know it really pisses me off seeing all this shit lying around. Just look at it. Why *do* we act like slobs? Why can't people put their rubbish in the bins and why can't the councils pull their bloody fingers out and empty them?' he asked out loud to nobody in particular. 'You'd never see this kind of mess in places like Denmark or Switzerland, would you? Clean as a whistle.'

'I'm right on your side,' said Becky.

'Me too.' Here we go, I thought, he'll be on his soap-box in a minute. Keith had a thing about trash, litter and sloppiness, people generally not clearing up after themselves. The rubbish was always piled up and of course nature takes a hand – the wind blows it everywhere, scatters it all across the fields and up against those hedges.

'Did you complain?'

'Wrote a letter,' he said.

'Result?'

'Dunno – just felt better for making a stand on being ripped off. Anyway, I'm getting too old for those kinds of antics… but not quite 'pipe and slippers' yet.'

'You could always do the Egyptian sand dance wearing slippers,' added Becky. It went on like this for a little while – silly stuff.

We continued along with a pause in the conversation. Then Keith cut in. 'Listen… what's that…?' It was then that we heard an approaching, increasing roar that seemed to pass right over us like something flying extremely fast and low and then receding, except it receded in no particular direction. Nor was the noise focussed – it just felt like a blanket all around us, deep, like a storm, with a deep rumble that lasted longer than we expected.

'Christ!' exclaimed Becky. 'What the hell's that? Bloody noisy – scared the shit out of me.'

'I reckon a couple of low-flying planes – but they must have been damned low! Where are they… where have they gone? … can't see anything and I haven't a clue which way they were going,' answered Keith, looking up and around. No one could see anything, no winking lights even though it *was* approaching dusk.

It was strange; a silence fell upon us for a few seconds. The noise seemed to be all-encompassing with little sign of a source.

'Surely they're not allowed to fly that low,' Becky again.

'That's the point… I didn't see anything at all, just heard the bloody noise,' I said. They were all now glancing upwards to catch a glimpse of whatever it was that had blasted their eardrums, and I have to say, made my body shake. 'Well, we are in East Anglia now – always did have its fair share of air force bases, but not sure about that these days.' I knew what aeroplane noise sounded like. I wasn't convinced that what we heard was in fact that kind of noise but one thing I was sure of – it made my bloody hair stand on end, seemed to make the air crackle.

'They're supposed to have lights on them, aren't they? And keep your eyes on the bloody road,' admonished Becks. It was suddenly dead quiet now.

'Make a nice ring-tone though,' ventured Keith.

'Need a big battery for that noise.'

We carried on talking in this vein saying silly things until I remarked how quiet the road was traffic-wise – '…and where *was* this A14 road that we're supposed to be on?'

'Actually – this road used to be the A45 until they changed it a few years ago in the nineties as part of the M1/A1 link, so these old signs haven't been upgraded yet I reckon,' said Keith. 'Remember where we are; we are in East Anglia, so things might move a little more slowly here. But you could always put the sat nav on,' he added.

'Nah, I'll take your word for it. We can't be far off, but I seem to remember that it was a dual carriageway last time I was this way – but obviously I was wrong.'

'Wouldn't be the first time,' said Becky. 'And turn the heating up please, it suddenly feels cold. And I wonder how Matt and Rubes are getting on…?'

...

Meanwhile…….

After their pub break and a quick look at a map, the bikers Matt and Ruby had set off to follow a little later. They hadn't been on the road long, Ruby up front…

'Matt – not exactly sure where we are, I haven't seen any signs posts,' she said on the com. A couple of minutes passed and they began to drive slower.

'Well, pull off when you can,' answered Matt. They eventually came across a dusty lay-by that had seen better times and pulled into it. They climbed off, visors up. 'The sat nav's gone blue – typical! No probs – I'll give the others a ring.' Matt pulled out his phone, fiddled a bit and then said he couldn't get a signal.

'It doesn't surprise me when you see where we are. Must be in a dead spot; definitely on the wrong road, not usually this quiet, surely. I'll walk up the road a bit for a signal and try again ringing the others,' said Matt. A minute later Ruby saw Matt look up and shake his head. No luck, no signal.

'Let's get back on the road and retrace our steps for a mile or two,' said Ruby. She noticed that it had become quiet – and still. 'We wouldn't want to break down here, would we!'

'This baby won't break down – bikes aren't like they used to be back in the sixties and seventies Rubes, when you spent every weekend fixing your motor. My dad used to tear his hair out – there was always something going wrong, or going rusty,' Matt said, looking over his Triumph.

Just then they heard a car approaching, slowing down as it came around the long sweeping bend. It continued to slow down and joined them in the lay-by, tyres crunching on the gravel. It crept to a halt.

Of all the cars on the road, this was the last one Matt had expected to see – but his eyes lit up; he loved old cars and this was what looked like an old Wolseley, just like one of those old movie police cars, black of course, but perhaps even older than he first thought. 'Who's driving this?' he wondered as he walked towards it. He wanted to have a good look over it – get inside to smell the wood and leather. Even Ruby looked interested. Sure enough, the doors opened and out stepped two policemen – one a sergeant, the other the driver. 'Cool,' thought Matt; but no 'hello's or other acknowledgement – they seemed to have eyes only for their bike and, apparently, what they were wearing.

Matt knew a thing or two about old cars and had often attended many of the vintage and other old car rallies in the past.

'Fab car,' said Matt towards the two policemen. 'Am I right in saying it's a Wolseley... a Wolseley 14/56?' he asked, addressing the two uniforms, following up with, '...oh, and are we on the right road for Bury?'

'Yes, that's correct, this is the Bury road. I am Sergeant Pugh and this is PC Robinson,' answered the sergeant with an expression that hinted at both suspicion and a little aloofness.

'Good for you, mate,' responded Matt. '...good to see a plain blue police uniform these days instead of the usual 'Hi-Viz' crap they always seem to be wearing.' It dawned on Matt what the barman had said back in the pub earlier and these two must really be part of it all, having a few minutes out, and really into the spirit.

The sergeant looked at him a moment. 'Excuse me, sir, is this motorbike yours?' he asked – a little too abruptly thought Matt.

'Last time I looked it was. Help yourself if you want to have a closer look.' He turned to Ruby, continuing on the Wolseley theme while the plods walked round the bike. 'I think these motors were born way back with the beginnings of motoring – got into the usual financial troubles and, in the twenties, was taken over by none other than Sir William Morris. Nice motors and hey, look at this Rubes, it even has the police 'bell'!' He walked closer to the car, oblivious to the two uniforms who were doing exactly the same with their bike. 'Just look at the leather interior – looks original – and all that wood too... *and* that funny shaped speedo – not round – goes up to 90 mph. I think it's about 1800cc with six cylinders. Or was it a Wolseley 18.' He wasn't sure now. Last time he saw one of these the poor thing was in a car graveyard gathering rust. 'Must cost a bomb to…'

'Sir,' interrupted the serge. 'What bike is this – where did you get it from?'

Funny question.

'Like it says on the tin…it's a Trophy – a Triumph Trophy. It says it on the side – and we're from Milton Keynes. Not into the usual foreign rubbish; why, what's up – why do you ask?' Matt was still looking over the car but becoming slightly irritated with the mock, over-official tone of the silly questions. There was no sign of amiability, of friendliness in the policeman's words – no festival spirit; this guy looked strained, doesn't know how to connect does he thought Matt. But he considered he'd risk a friendly request. 'Do you mind if I get into your car for a second – feel the ambience and all that? I just love the inside smell of these old motors.' Matt opened the door for a closer look. The backward opening doors wouldn't have bothered him – open up and straight in. But it always amazed him about the seats in these older cars, the bench seats – when they went around corners, what stopped you sliding from side to side?! No seatbelts then. That's what the steering wheel was for – to hang onto. Funnily enough, no seatbelts in this one either. 'So, what's the story about the seatbelts – special permission for very old vehicles or something?'

'Old?' He looked upset at my enquiry.

Before he went on Ruby joined in with the chit-chat, 'Anything I can help you with?' she asked, watching the driver who was closely examining the bike's controls. She went over to him. 'It can do a hundred in third if you're that interested. These are the panniers for a couple of helmets,' she added, seeing him cast his eyes over them. '…and the tank holds about three gallons; most police seem to have BMWs these days, don't they?' she added, casting her eyes over the car.

He appeared startled when she spoke – as did the sergeant. A woman's voice…?

'Eh? What'll it do…? how fast does…?' before being cut off by his boss.

'Not now Robinson. Would you mind taking your helmets off please?' interrupted the sergeant.

Maybe he wants a *selfie* with us, thought Matt.

'Yeah, OK – whatever, they're just bog standard hats…the usual plastics – nothing special, some fiberglass with a bit of Kevlar thrown in –

and some expanded foam. Have a look; nice, don't you think – nice colour?' said Matt, offering his for a closer look. But it was when Ruby took hers off…

'Oh!' said the two uniforms almost in unison. 'A woman!'

On the ball, thought Matt sarcastically. 'Yeah – I know,' responded Matt seeing their faces, '…she always turns heads – a real cracker, aren't you sweetheart.' She flashed back a winning smile.

'Do you normally dress like this?' asked sergeant uniform.

Now *that* was an odd question. Matt had his hair cut quite modern he thought – the sides shaved leaving the rest of his mop up top.

'Eh? Doesn't everybody?' responded Matt with a grin. 'It's the *only* way to travel isn't it – cost a bomb though!'

'Half a moment sir,' said the sergeant, casting a knowing look at his deputy before he wandered over to their Wolseley.

'*Where* did you say you obtained this motorbike?' PC Plod asked again.

At this point, Matt started to wonder. Feeling his insides beginning to tighten, he was becoming irritated and felt uneasy…

'Like I said, Milton Keynes.'

He and Ruby seemed to be off the beaten track and began to resent the way these two dressed-up yokels were behaving. He had a gig to get to. 'Normal courtesy will be suspended – I can't be doing with twenty questions right now,' he said to himself. So-called Sergeant Robinson will probably be having a good laugh tonight over a pint of Adnams or Bods with his mates in Bury – either that or he and his sidekick were a couple of bozos.

Having got into his car, the sergeant now appeared to be on the radio or something.

'What's your sergeant doing? I'd love to have a look at your radio set up… can I?' asked Matt as a way of distracting plod's attention. Plod turned towards the Wolseley, uncertain.

'Rubes,' whispered Matt as he tilted his head towards her, '…I can't be doing with this. Put your lid on and get ready to do a very quick getaway… got it?' Ruby nodded at his urgent tone and casually put her helmet back on as she moved slowly towards the bike and quietly slipped onto it.

'Oi! Stop!' shouted Sergeant Plod, half out of his car, who had seen her move, while PC Plod turned back towards Matt and Ruby – but what he saw was Matt already on the back of the bike.

'GO!' shouted Matt. She needed no second urging. In one second the engine was running, in two more seconds it was away doing fifty… with a wheelie, just for fun.

The two locals stood stunned, mouths agape as the bike disappeared down the road in a cloud of dust. 'Did you see that guv…it had 180 on the dial!'

'Don't be bloody silly. Let's get after them – aren't you the slightest bit suspicious?'

'Suspicious? More like envious guv.'

Matt and Ruby, once they were out of sight, decided to do a detour just in case the locals decided to follow. In any case, a Wolseley versus their Trophy – 'no contest,' thought Ruby.

'I'd love to have seen their faces back then,' said Ruby.

They weren't exactly sure where they were going but decided to avoid the bigger roads and keep to the smaller, quaint back roads. Eventually, another lay-by beckoned – well hidden from the road. 'Could do with a fag and a swig of coffee after that little episode,' said Ruby, pulling into it. They sat on the verge keeping close to the bike.

'Still no signal Rubes,' said Matt after a while. 'Anyway, it can't be too far can it? Bloody quiet around here, don't you think?'

'Too bloody quiet if you ask me, almost creepy – those two included,' Ruby replied. After about ten minutes and another puff Matt said that they'd better be going.

Chapter 8

Mr Rawlings

Back in the Rover.

Apart from the noisy episode the rest of the journey was quiet, perhaps too quiet. And everything appeared dimmed down. We kept thinking that we were on the wrong road but Keith put it down to it being close to dusk, a rural area anyway, and past the evening rush hour so they made good time.

'Yeah – but where is everybody?' I asked out loud.

'Ooh look,' Becky exclaimed, 'A couple of army lorries over there… must be getting warm – like the man said in the pub.'

'I reckon they must have closed off some roads to keep the traffic in line, said Keith. 'Usually when *I'm* in a rural area like this I always seem to come up behind some ginormous tractor pulling a monster trailer full of sugar-beet or something, going fast enough not to able to overtake… you know what I mean… big motor, small road.'

'Yes… been there, got the t-shirt,' I concurred. Then… 'Look – a sign, and buildings. Hooray! Bury – I think, just got to find our way to the Guildhall or Town Hall or whatever it's called.' After a minute or two driving around I said, 'It looks a lot smaller than I remember it.'

In fact from what I *did* remember of BSE, dusk seemed to have given the place a quiet, eerie sadness – all colours muted. Dusk had been with us a little while now. '…and grey, isn't it,' I said rhetorically as we went into town. We motored towards the centre, keeping an eye out for a large important-looking building while ignoring everything else until we arrived at this big imposing structure, then we stopped by an entrance area just behind a courtyard wall. 'This'll do – I'll go inside and find Mr Baxter; won't be a moment. Stay put in case we have to move the car again.'

'Well, this *must* be it,' said Becky. I left the Rover in the small enclosure hoping that the entrance wouldn't be too far away and walked round to a door that was open, guessing it was the tradesman's entrance – I'm not proud – only to find I was being followed by the others. No sign of the Triumph. As I passed through I practically bumped into somebody coming out and who looked expectant – with fag in hand. 'Aha. Andy – Andy Baxter?' I asked hopefully.

'No, I'm Mr Rawlings. Who are you – who is Andy Baxter?'

'The entertainment guy I'm supposed to meet here --- I'm Bob Temple. We're here for the music; got the confirmation e-mail here on my phone.'

'Eh? Bob Temple? Ah – the entertainment; *you* are providing the music tonight, are you?' asked Mr Rawlings. 'Where's your transport, your bus; you *are* the band from Ipswich... the Fred Briggs Combo... I hope you are?' Mr Rawlings went on. There was a pause. We all stopped in the dim doorway.

'I'm afraid not Mr Rawlings, never heard of Fred Briggs,' I answered. 'And where's Andy Baxter? This is the Guildhall is it not... and this is Bury St Edmunds. I bloody well hope it is... it better be.'

'Yes, it is, but I do not know of any Mr Baxter. If you are not Fred Briggs then who are you?' He waved a piece of paper at us indicating we should look at it.

Keith peered at it, 'Paperwork? I'm too handsome to do paperwork,' and moved off looking at me with a big grin.

"Fred Briggs? Bus?' I responded. Me on a bus – I'm not that sad, not yet; could stretch to an SUV. And a lorry? No. I looked more closely at Mr Rawlings – he was rather over-dressed, a bit like how my dad used to be but nevertheless nicely turned out, wearing a sports jacket, tie and non-descript dark trousers but his shirt looked the worse for wear. He parted his hair on one side and with his pleasant, round face, I guessed he must have been in his late thirties with an air of social prestige, but tinged with a look of anxiety in his demeanour... no doubt worried about the events as they were unfolding, with no Fred Briggs.

'No. As I said, I'm Bob Temple and these are my partners in crime, well, two of them, Keith and Becky. We've got two more following up – at least I hope we have.' Becky and Matt both responded with a 'Hi,' Mr Rawlings with a 'Good evening. How do you do.'

'I was informed that it was Fred Briggs we were expecting tonight from Ipswich. So you must be a replacement. Where are your instruments Mr Temple? What...'

'Please call me Bob,' I interrupted. Mustn't stand on ceremony.

'I'm Chris,' said Mr Rawlings, 'and this is Albert who will help sort things out for you; we'll go inside and he'll show you a room you can use that we normally provide for these occasions, being used to six or seven players.'

Now Albert I immediately liked as soon as I set eyes on his smiling, lively countenance, an almost spitting image of Norman Wisdom as I remember him in the years when everything was in black and white. Not only did he have that look of permanent puzzlement and joy on his features, his face breaking into a huge smile as he said, 'Pleased to meet you,' he was actually wearing a cap too. The only aspect of his appearance missing as a clone of our old film star was the tight-fit jacket. And he was – or appeared to be – taller, but again, gave the impression in his movements and demeanour of an impatience – happy to help, constantly transferring his weight from one foot to the other, almost as a nervous characteristic.

'Hi. What do we call you?' I asked.

'Albert or just Bert,' he answered as his movements speeded up.

I grinned, 'Not Norm then?' I couldn't resist.

'Eh?' his movements pausing.

'Bert it is then.' I had the distinct impression that if I'd asked him to go away and build an exact copy of the large Egyptian pyramid, he'd have dashed off and then come back in two hours saying, 'It's done!'

Chris Rawlings then moved the conversation along. 'Albert will give you a hand with your instruments; just give the word. 'So *where are* your instruments – what do you play?' There was just a little suggestion of anxiety in his eyes as I could see that people were already arriving – standing outside another door. Inside, a couple of favourite seats and tables looked bagged already.

It was getting darker outside so we needed to hurry.

'In the Rover just round the back. We can manage OK – don't need a hand thanks, just let me know where the plugs are and we'll set ourselves up, and the bogs of course; actually, I need to go right now,' I said. 'As we asked last month, just need our own changing room – and a couple of tables and chairs here in the hall.' The inside of the hall looked dim. It's a good job I didn't have 'Carl Barriteau and his swing 15' with me. It would be rather crowded in my motor.

'What? I don't remember that,' responded Rawlings. 'And plugs? What plugs?'

'You know – plugs – juice. OK, tell you what Chris, leave it to us. Just show us the room and we'll quickly get our gear set up anyway; you're obviously expecting entertainment – and *that's* what we'll provide. Looks like you're stuck with us for now – the A-Team of course. If this 'Fred' turns up we can have another discussion, if you know what I mean, but we're here.' I continued, 'Ipswich is only just down the road and he should've been here by now. By the way – remind me, what *is* a combo?' But Bert was already headed towards the door before we stopped him. 'We'll let you know Bert as soon as…'

For your interest reader, a combo: a small jazz or dance band.

Didn't get an answer about the combo but Chris Rawlings looked a little more relieved after I told him we'd crack on. 'They were probably held up… sometimes it's very easy to get stuck, even now,' answered Rawlings.

'Know how you feel, police and army everywhere! Could be traffic – I remember back home during these occasions, you couldn't move on the roads. But they could at least have texted you, let you know. That reminds me, I must call my missing *two*.' Actually, the ride into Bury had been unnaturally quiet – thinking about it.

'There's a telephone in that room over there,' said Rawlings.

'It's a long time since I've heard anyone actually say the word 'telephone' – sounds strange doesn't it,' said Keith to me.

'Thanks Chris – no need,' I said as I whipped out my latest gadget. We might be all poor in the UK today but we all have our smartphones. 'I'll give them a quick ping on this.' Rawlings watched me intensely as I swiped away. 'Can't get a signal Chris – must be the building. I'll send a text – probably wasting my time though.'

'Signal? What is that?' asked Rawlings, eyeing my latest purchase.

'It's my super-duper, all-electric, mega-death-dealing, zillion-app comms machine – and it's not bloody working – can't get a signal! Typical!' I responded.

'Yeah, typical!' Keith added, 'You get the latest kit and it lets you down. It's a good job it hasn't got mag-alloy wheels on it as well – they'd probably have fallen off by now.'

'I'm just trying to picture that,' I muttered, 'and failing miserably. Well Chris, just show us what's what and we'll get the show on the road;

looks like it will be getting busy any time soon – don't want to disappoint the punters. We're just going to nip out to the Rover to bring our 'instruments' in and get set up – won't take a minute,' I said. I noticed that a few more were in, all dressed for the occasion I noticed. Must be a ticket 'do'.

When I asked Chris Rawlings why some were in and some were waiting outside he said he just wanted to make sure the musicians were going to be here first. 'I waited a while then let some in, expecting the music to arrive first earlier. When you didn't turn up I shut the doors. We've had bands not turn up as you can imagine,' he said.

'Well, give us a chance... won't be long, just a couple of hours. Joke,' Keith replied when he saw Mr Rawlings' face.

There was the typical raised platform area complete with a piano, an old Chappell. Makes a change. It was adjacent to us so we gravitated towards it and organised our stand, table and chairs there, with Keith and I looking around and scanning the premises. Albert showed us the room we could use, usefully situated in one corner at the back of the stage. We'd not been here before so while Keith and I organised where the kit was going, Becky pulled out her own phone and took a few pictures and a video for reference. Then Keith went down to the other end of the hall to get a feel of the acoustics, dodging the table and chairs – and a few stares – as he went. 'Must be the socks I'm wearing,' he said to himself, but he quickly checked his flies just to be sure... one sure way of getting attention. There were quite a number of tables and chairs dotted around the edge of the hall – civilised. Some places were just bare rooms – everyone standing, everybody a wallflower.

Mr Rawlings and Albert watched as we brought in a couple of small suitcase-sized black boxes and set them on the table in an interlocking fashion, snapping together a few connections and then putting the turntable to one side, alongside the laptop. It wasn't long before everything was ready to go, all connected up – speakers, the lot... *cooking on gas* as they say.

'See the glitter ball?' Becky pointed out. They set the lights to fire at it. Few places had glitter balls these days but they thought if it's there, let's use it. '...and look, just look at all those drapes they have here – place needs a make-over.' Her eyes scanned the audience that were in already and smiled – the hairdos on the girls. 'They're nearly all Rita Hayworth style,' Becky added. 'It must be a ticket do. Just look at all those curls – I've never seen so many. Nearly all of them. Fabulous.'

They were too. 'Well, won't have any problem sorting out the guys and girls then,' I said as I glanced around. 'They look a young lot as well, so far,' I said to no one in particular.

Keith called over, 'It's a bloody good job we have our adaptors, I've just had a quick butchers – this place is worse than that farm we went to last month. It's a shambles – the council should be ashamed of itself. The wiring looks ancient.'

I thought that odd – local councils were usually in the forefront on issues like this, Health and Safety and all that. Mr Rawlings looked puzzled at our exchange of words.

'What's the matter?' he enquired. 'Is there a problem?'

'Yeah... your electrics, they're shite, but no problem, we'll sort it – your hall needs a total rework on its electrics Chris,' answered Keith, 'Or is this place on the list for demolition sometime soon?'

'What do you mean – we do the best we can in difficult times.' responded Mr Rawlings. He was about to go on when I chimed in.

'Don't we all,' I answered. 'We *do* know how you feel. Still, we're OK for now, we'll manage. Keith has it covered. '

Then I became aware that a few from the audience had come forward to watch what we were doing while we'd been setting up.

'Don't you play instruments at all?' enquired Mr Rawlings, changing tack.

'No, not us – well not tonight anyway, not like your Fred Briggs and his boys. This baby does all the work,' I went on, pointing at our array. 'It packs a real punch, you'll see... or should I say, 'you'll hear'. But Becky does play the piano keyboard and we – Keith and I – can strum a guitar. I'm rubbish at it though.'

'Guitar? So, it's all recorded or something?' Rawlings again, frowning.

'Correct, vinyl, CDs, laptop etc. but don't worry Chris,' I said, looking at the expectant crowd close by. 'Won't be long folks; go and get another drink. Hey Chris – don't they do plastic glasses here?' I'd noticed it was all proper glass.

During setting up and after several minutes, Keith and Becky sidled up to me and muttered into my shell-like ear that the audience were *really* pushing out the boat for the occasion, almost surreal.

'I mean, just look at all those mid-calf floral dresses, Bob, all that material,' she said. '...and the blokes – well, jumpers and cardigans everywhere. Some guys even wearing ties! Even Mr Rawlings, he's just like my granddad used to dress. Looks strange to me. This gig should be fun,' she added in a strong whisper. She had a point – I had noticed the dress and styles but thought nothing of it, initially, but now I was beginning to wonder. Could this actually be a proper theme night or something else – some special, posh ticket event we'd stumbled into? I was, of course, dressed extremely casual, jeans and jersey – same with my dancers, until they changed of course.

'Mr Rawlings – this must be a strictly ticket admission because looking at our audience this evening, we seem to be the odd ones out with the dress code.'

He didn't respond, he just returned my inquiry with a quizzical expression, looking worried, probably mourning the loss of Mr Briggs and his *proper* musicians. There was no indication of this from my contact Andy Baxter, 'Just a normal gig,' he had said at the time, but it looked over the top and so far I hadn't spotted any of the more mature elements amongst the punters either... yet. Mr Rawlings seemed to be the oldest about. I was also conscious of the fact that Rawlings kept very close and seemed to be watching everything I was doing – following me everywhere; he seemed fascinated by it all. I wondered if he got out much.

'Oh well, we shan't disappoint them; I'll start with something in keeping with their dress mode – get those flowery dresses flying and those jumpers moving, but not just yet,' I said.

'What... like Val Doonican you mean?' replied Becky.

'Very funny. Mr Rawlings... Chris, looking at your crowd, what music do you suggest we play? What do they normally like to hear?' A few more had arrived.

'The men just want to let their hair down, have fun, I mean, look what they do all day, every day. They'll dance to anything, and probably with anybody,' he answered. I chuckled. Steady Bob...

'What about the girls? Can't they let their hair down too?' said Becks, making a point.

'Must admit, can't see much hair on the blokes – no Kevin Keegan hair dos, but the girls have really styled up.' Guys these days were into short hair – or no hair. Me... I was hanging on to every last follicle, but definitely no comb-overs. Not grey either. My hair would choose death rather than dishonour.

'And what *is it* that they do…?' asked Keith.

'I should imagine typing, or sitting at screens, fiddling with dials and controls – that sort of thing,' said Rawlings, before he was cut off by Becky.

'I know the feeling – chained to a screen, everybody has to do it these days it seems.'

Wow, I thought – and 'dials' too? What kind of desktops do this lot use I wondered – maybe new 'X' boxes or something or flight simulators? I carried on with putting the final touches, setting up the gear.

'Keith, did we get the big plasma out of the Rover? Where can we hang it?' We'd customised a couple of screens with two large, simple hooks so that they could view, play-back or simply play old clips that went with the tracks. We'd brought both along.

'I'm on it – soon sorted,' he answered.

. . . .

I looked around.

'Becky – don't you find this place… strange?'

'Yes, I know what you mean – strange atmosphere, and gloomy with it,' she replied.

Chapter 9

USAAF in England

The Dance Club

The crew was settled now and had flown several missions – formed a bond like a family, even after losing Spike. Richard (Ricky) Simms had filled the gap. And when they weren't flying, life was one long party with chicks and beer everywhere which they still hadn't quite mastered yet, but it was wet – and it was alcoholic. Also, they all had learnt a lesson, culturally – one not to be repeated: one pub they'd been to ('Walt – they're pubs, not bars,' Barney had to remind him) had run short of beer after a rowdy birthday party during the day.

'We've only got cider left,' said the barman. 'We've been drunk dry almost.'

'Cider! But that's a Goddamn woman's drink!' Barney remembers saying. '…but OK – it'll have to do, better than nothing!' No one had told them about scrumpy – or versions of it. How were they to know?!

They had to be poured back onto the transport to get home.

'Woman's drink my ass!' said Joe, nursing the worst head he'd ever had the next day. 'I thought I was gonna die. Give me the ack-ack and fighters over Nuremburg any day – strictly beer from now on!'

'Yeah, but you were adding rum to it! No wonder you looked dead! Still look dead!'

'He always looks dead,' Richard had retorted, '…actually, difficult to tell sometimes.'

'Say you guys, that stuff we could use in our fuel tanks!' added Milt. 'Potent!'

That was life. Desperate one day – fooling around the next.

It was a continuous party because if you dealt too long on the downside, the missing crews – other buddies who were with you last night at The Samson and Hercules dancing, were with you at breakfast this morning, now gone – it would drive you crazy. So they played real hard; they had to decompress. Yesterday had happened, tomorrow might never come so you lived for the day and the people who were there.

When they had first arrived at their base they soon found out that new crews got the old aircraft. No shiny new bird straight off the production line, just the older, clapped-out, hand-me-downs that usually flew in circles if you let them, or flew one wing higher than the other – or maybe the undercarriage played up occasionally and you had to crank it down by hand. Nor were the engines at their peak. 'Good job we got four of them,' someone remarked. Mind you, few aircraft lasted long in any case, such was the life expectancy, so *old* was a relative term. Then one day the topic of lucky charms and paint jobs came up.

'Hey Skip, what are we going to call her – what are we gonna paint on her nose?' Their B-17 was devoid of any frivolous markings.

'What, this old wreck? You wanna waste good paint on the old lady?' They chatted hard, with one after the other saying that all the other bombers had fancy nose art and catchy slogans.

'We have to have something sir. I'm beginning to get fond of the old girl,' said Lou. They were all nodding while mouthing possible slogans. The boss held up his hand.

'Actually guys, ever since they patched her up last time I've noticed that I always have to trim her for nose down because she's so damn tail heavy, no matter what. You're not stashing loads of Hershey bars down the back there are you Lou?' asked Skipper, chuckling. They all laughed together.

'No Skipper, it's his wallet – they pay him too much!' said Walt. A few more insults flew. The skipper turned to Lou, 'It's a good job you're not one of these big Kentucky farm boys sat at the back, otherwise we'd really be in trouble.'

'Tail heavy boss? Then let's call her Tail-heavy Betty,' said someone else.

It stuck.

Joe had good connections with the ground crew – he was the wireless operator and was always talking to the flight engineer and knew the ground crew boys so they left it with them. There were no such things as weekends but Joe told his skipper the art-work guys had been primed to pounce when a troublesome engine was due for some serious attention.

'Yeah, but what are they going to paint Joe – who has organised that?'

'It'll be a surprise Skipper.'

'Yeah – I can't wait.'

The engine problem turned into an engine change which, fortunately for the ground crew this time, meant the bomber was wheeled into the hangar; usually maintenance work took place outside – regardless of the weather.

When they all turned out to look at *Tail-heavy Betty* they gawked at the picture – and then laughed.

'Come on fellas – how else could you draw it!' There it was – a distorted picture of someone who looked like Betty Boop with a butt ten sizes too big – and a big grin, fluttering eyelashes, with teeth everywhere.

A voice came from near the hangar door, 'Hey you guys, make sure you look after her,' shouted one of the painters. The crew turned to look. No matter where you were in the world all painters and sprayers seemed to look the same -- old, scruffy, ill, and with boots the colour of a rainbow.

Skipper turned towards him, came to attention and gave a mock salute, 'Thanks Buddy. Nice work.' Everybody was happy. The skipper then looked at Lou, about to say something, but Richy Simms was first.

'I knew a girl like that back in high school – fat ass… well not quite as big as that but she was a real sweet girl.'

'Yeah, and comfortable too I reckon,' replied the skipper.

But although they were a crew of ten, they didn't always go out together. The skipper – who was real old, 26 years old – and that was *old* in Barney's books – would often do a day or two in London with some of the other officers from other crews. Both Barney and Joe had now been to London – the first big city they'd ever been to in their lives. 'Man – it's big!' they said to each other. They seemed to spend half an hour just getting into the place. There was rubble everywhere, with huge gaps where houses used to be. What a mess. They had heard third-hand about the Blitz and now they could see the results. But everyone seemed to be going about their own business – hurrying here, scuttling along there; it made them feel not too bad about their own missions over Germany. Now, when they had time off these days he preferred to stay local. Travelling was too erratic. You could get delayed quite easily, miss drinking time or be late back --- and be for the high jump.

'I have to get back to my guitar,' Barney mused with his crew. The crew had, musically, come together nicely. Barney had altogether Joe, Walt, Milt, Richard, and Ginge, all playing their part – Barney on guitar and occasionally on piano, Joe on saxophone or clarinet, Walt on drums and other noisy things, Milt on trombone and the harmonica – he could sing too. Ginge was real good on the ivories, real good. And Richard on… well, he just helped out – strung along, snapped his fingers. They needed a bass so they tried to set him up but like the drums they were not something you could drag around easily. And they'd not had much chance really to play together – drinking and dancing interfered too much except when the base was fog-bound, no flying and no transport, so they stayed put to entertain at the base.

'If our number comes up and we get captured, we'll have the best PoW camp entertainment,' someone said.

'What – you taking your sax with you?' They all laughed.

'We can bribe the guards – I always take a couple of pairs of nylons with me – you never know,' said Joe.

'What for yourself or for the ladies?' More laughs.

Barney still had his little guitar gizmo with him. They had popped into Norwich a few times to a music shop to see what was on offer. Not much, piss-poor actually.

'Well what do you expect?' said Joey. Norwich had not been bombed like London and Coventry but it still had had its visits from the Luftwaffe. Most of the gear was safely packed out of harm's way. Besides, what the shop had was only brassy kit. He did filch some thin cable from the base stores though and did just a little more work on his little box.

One day, Barney came over to Joe all excited.

'Joe, you know that crate that bounced off the runway a couple of days ago – Yankee Doo…'

'…Dandy…' Joe finished off Barney's words. 'Hell yes, who doesn't? They were lucky sons of bitches to get out of that before she went up!' One leg had collapsed putting the B-17 into a ground spin and onto the grass, almost flipping over. It was a complete wreck – but the fire was contained, and only one broken shoulder.

'Yep. Anyway Joe, the salvage guys have stripped it bare and when I asked them if I could have some bits off it they said help yourselves. I'm thinking of getting some aluminium, maybe some steel and some Perspex for my guitar.'

'Eh? What? You spent enough time on your little box already.'

'Well just look at this crap weather – no flying today and maybe even tomorrow. Plenty of time.'

'Don't forget the training session at two.' Inevitably, when you were grounded there were always quickly organised training lessons and other drills to attend. When they arrived at the salvage compound they spotted 'Yankee' lying forlorn – all crumpled. The crash teams were not fussy. All they were interested in was clearing the airfield as fast as possible, just bulldozing it off – after the explosives and other dangerous parts had been taken care of.

Barney went to work.

'What's your idea – remind me?' asked Joe.

'Gonna work the steel or aluminium to be like a fancy, shiny edging and then file some Perspex down, maybe lay it over the top. I haven't decided yet Joe. Then I'll polish up so that it won't look too much like some awful wooden cigar box. I'm telling you Joe, it'll shine like a pin.'

'You polish it too much it'll disappear... but is it going to work man?'

'It sure will buddy.'

'It's coming along. One day...' thought Barney.

It was a chance diversion on returning one evening from Stuttgart – their home base in Suffolk was fogged out so they'd been diverted to Horsham, right next to Norwich city. They had also heard that one of their own squadron bombers, short of fuel, had attempted to risk the mist at their base and had crash-landed on the runway, melting the surface. Fog, crash and more fog resulted in three days at the Horsham St. Faith base.

It was from here that the other aircrews, already familiar with the area, dragged Barney's crew to the Samson and Hercules dance hall in Norwich.

'Wow – I could get used to this,' said Joe, standing there with the crew surveying the ballroom and what seemed like hundreds of girls, the whole place moving, cigarette smoke hanging heavily. They all nodded in agreement. 'Right on their doorstep too. You could walk here.' It was the first time for them all to see a proper English town – big, but not too big –

with wonderful little side streets, chocolate factories and a huge cathedral, a cathedral Barney hadn't seen anything like before. The place was also heaving with pubs, 'Walt – they're pubs, not bars,' and few kept to the proper hours. Excellent... a blast.

So occasionally, when back at their home base, Norwich became part of the fun scene, if and when they could get transport as it was a bit of a way to go compared to their local towns and villages.

Barney was close to their squadron adjutant. He'd formed the relationship as soon as he found out that the adjutant was a 'Mr. Fixit' who knew when and where anything happened on the social scene. His girlfriend was English, local, a girl well supplied with nylons... and cigarettes.

'Next week, there's something going on in Ipswich, Thetford and Bury,' said Adj.

'Which Bury? There's *Burys* everywhere in England,' said Barney.

'Bury St Edmunds – the town hall I think. I'll let you know.'

'Oh yeah... good. We've been there before,' said Barney. Not too far away. Not Norwich, but always good.

'You guys remember,' said the skipper, '...I don't care who you shack up with on the outside – just make sure I don't have to come looking for you come briefing time otherwise it's the 'pen'...got it?!'

'Sure boss.'

Chapter 10

Yanks at Bury

As we were putting it all together…

Laughter…voices at the doorway. Sounded like American voices to me. It seems that a Yank element had arrived at the hall looking just like those guys on re-enactments I'd seen up near Blackpool. One of them came in sliding on his knees right into the middle of the floor, fag in mouth – big grin on his face, just like a footballer celebrating a goal, except wearing a big flying jacket… naturally.

Cocky bastard.

'Hi Mr Rawlings!' shouted the happy Yank when he got up, obviously a regular at the hall. Rawlings lifted an arm in acknowledgement.

Did I hear the words 'gobby shites' muttered from somewhere in the audience? Not quite sure.

'Ah, the smoking ban's been lifted then?' said Becky.

'Smoking ban…?' said Mr Rawlings.

'He'll do for me!' Becky answered, looking at Rawlings; she liked the occasional puff. They then realised that quite a few were smoking. She added, 'I can see a few fag burns happening on some of those skirts, and I'm not going anywhere near that lot over there… dancing and smoking at the same time! Definitely a no-no.'

'Don't blame you Becks,' said Keith. 'Just tell 'em, if they want to dance with you it's strictly no fags – a no fag girl. They'll get the message.'

As always, these so-called 'Yanks' had to play the noisy part, playing their exuberant selves, dressed in flying gear and showing off, but they weren't alone. Not to be outdone, there they were, a few 'Brylcreem Boys' for good measure with their own jackets – and some just wearing 'blues'; hooray for the RAF. They really were getting into the theme of things in this town... all set for a good gig. All we need now is for Captain Mannering to walk in...

I'd done some time in the 'blue mob' and hated the hairy uniforms we had to wear in training, especially the trousers, chafing your legs, horrible, unless you were as thin as a supermodel, but hey, after a few pints you wouldn't feel a thing.

The Yank who'd made the entrance, after he'd got to his feet, had looked around with a curious expression. He had paused, taking in the scene, then turned to his following friends and opened his arms with a quizzical look, as if asking, *'Where's the band – where's the music?'* Mr Rawlings, fanning out his hands in a helpless gesture, walked over to them and explained – no bus, no music, only me with hopefully, *four* dancers. The young Yank then paused a moment, eyeing us and my set up, which still wasn't powered up yet, and then wandered over to it, studying it for a while before saying to me in passing, 'Hi Pops,' and then going over to join his mates who had now sat down.

Cheeky sod.

Keith looked at me and laughed, 'Pops...? That's now your new name, Bob,' and he laughed again.

'Piss off! Anyway, need to get the show on the road, can't wait any longer for the other two; I wonder where the blood hell they are.'

'Reckon they've pulled into some lay-by,' said Becky, with a knowing smile.

'What – with all those leathers on... don't go there,' I responded.

'Anyway, give us five to change while you put some music on; might do the Charleston as a starter – but please, not to Kermit's *Happy Feet*, or *Chitty Chitty Bang Bang,'* said Keith.

'Will do. How about *Upside Down* for it as we said before? In fact while you're getting ready I'll start with some real cool jazz, *Take Five,* then into *A String of Pearls*, get into the mood... and then we'll shake it up a little with *Candyman,* seeing as they all look dressed for the occasion. Let me just have a quick look at the list and then I'll put the finishing touches to it all before I power up,' I said. I twiddled and fiddled, checked all the connections of the laptop, mixer and iPod and threw the switch: yep, the LED blockbuster came on – always a good sign. I never fail to be impressed by the sheer magic of the colours with LEDs every time I switch them on; hadn't had them long but LEDs have certainly changed the scene. And they were certainly grabbing the attention of this audience too.

'Need a quick sound check before *Take Five*,' I said to anyone who was listening and hit a key on the laptop. The first bars of a tune boomed out; I always do a check like this. I adjusted the level – perfect, that had the audience's attention. Then I set up the segue – you could have this 'on' or 'off' and I would select it according to my mood or what was playing.

What? You don't know what *segue* means…? It means following on swiftly without pausing – so it would be a seamless transition from one track to the next. Got it?

On went Dave Brubeck…

If it was a straight gig and no themes as we seemed to have tonight, we'd usually select tracks that would invite the various dancing styles to the floor to see if anybody was interested in foxtrots, quickstep, American smooth, and waltzes. And we would normally put on, amongst the first burst of activity, something like *Good Rockin' Tonight* (by Elvis – who else?) or *Crazy Little Thing Called Love*. The waltz or American smooth would follow this to entice other dancers onto the floor – see what the punters could do. Matt and Rubes usually showed the way and normally had things moving. It was 'taking the temperature'. I could soon shuffle tracks around to suit. To many, it didn't matter about the words, you hear the tune, you hear the music and just want to dance!

Now I don't know about you, reader, but there's some kind of music I do not like – chamber music being one. It's just me. I mean, who likes chamber music?! And yes, we all seemed to like jazz, or especially 'swing' jazz, however, although I liked *some* 'modern' jazz, I never did like the kind where each member of the band goes off in his own time doing his own thing, completely oblivious of the rest – like he'd suddenly woken up and was trying to catch up; makes you wonder what was the point of having a drummer, it was a mess, sounded like a band practice. We heard on the car radio one evening coming back from a gig this live jazz recording; everyone was doing their own thing – and it was almost tuneless. I felt like shouting, 'Oi! Shaddap!' The radio DJ cut in saying what a great performance that was. I was already reaching for my service revolver. What planet was he on?

'What crap!' I almost shouted. 'And some are even applauding – listen!?'

'That's because they're probably all stoned,' said Matt. 'Either that or they think it's a flower-power concert.'

'They must be stoned – and I'm not talking alcohol either!' I responded.

65

This music episode reminded me of a footballer I had in my team many years ago. When it came to dribbling he was a master – like having the ball attached to his foot with a piece of string. No one could get the ball away from him; he was brilliant, moving round the pitch with a gaggle of the opposition all around him desperately trying to get the ball – and doing this without any help from us, swerving left and right, stop start. The only trouble was he'd lose his bearings and start wandering towards his own goal amongst this gaggle until one of us shouted, 'Luke – over here, this way!' He'd look up for a nanosecond and work his way back in the right direction before passing the ball. Fantastic individuality – it's a good job he wasn't in a jazz band!

Keith and Becks came out dressed 'ready to party' – not quite like Moulin Rouge, but plenty of sheen and gloss, drawing both curious and envious glances from across the hall. They looked great. I always like this part because you never knew until the event what affect the first appearance and the first dance would have on the punters but it was nearly always good. The audience had come to dance, to get to grips with the opposite sex, but my little team came to dance *and show off!* I mouthed *Upside Down* and *Candyman* at them, both Keith and Becky giving a thumbs up in acknowledgement and moving to the floor area. Then I thought about that old couple doing the Argentine tango. Marvellous.

'The Swivels will be spot on this time,' said Keith, remembering what Matt had pointed out last time he watched them doing the Charleston.

Candyman, just like *Good Rocking Tonight, Move It* and *Footloose,* were always good for the early dances, both thumping great tracks that said, 'Get out of your chairs and get moving… or else.' And, with the accompanying show dancers to help it all along, they rarely failed to get the evening going. It was also a way to find out who could do the jive in the audience – there was nearly always a couple who were bloody good at it, usually those in their fifties or older! But in fact, it was Keith and Becky that everyone was now watching – at least at first – before a couple of the Yanks took up the cudgel, with a couple of girls, and started in true form, doing the jive. I knew that we all loved these more energetic dances, especially Matt and Ruby – dances that were derived from the old 'swing jazz' era such as the jitterbug the Lindy hop, now commonly called the jive. It was always useful to know the background when you performed and dancing was no exception, but the real origins of some of these moves and dances were difficult to pinpoint. I reflected on what we were now seeing on the floor… the jitterbug.

I'm told that the origins of the jitterbug and Lindy hop began way back in the twenties in black Harlem communities of New York. And some say that the 'hop' was originally called the Lindbergh hop – which didn't stick. It didn't take long before white people began copying the black dancers. I had seen old clips and was amazed to see acrobatic routines included, the kind of moves you normally saw Olympic gymnasts perform.

Brilliant. And how many times had I heard the word 'hop' in the lyrics of a fifties pop song such as *At the Hop* etc.?

Loads.

Then during WWII, American soldiers brought the moves to Europe in the early forties, where they soon were popular with the young. In the States the term 'swing' became the most common word used to describe the dance. In the UK, the words such as boogie-woogie and swing boogie became associated with jive until it became the generic name for the dance. A bit of background for you reader – I hope.

Meanwhile, back in the hall -

Keith and Becky were putting on a great show with the help of Glenn Miller and quite a few had stood up just to get a better view of the two. I reckoned that *what* she was wearing also had something to do with why they were all ogling. Even the 'airmen' who'd joined in now stood back and watched. When it had finished, they both flashed a smile at the crowd, took a bow, and gave me a wink. I knew just how much an energetic dance like that could take out of you in three minutes. The punters were clapping; it often happened after their first dances, but the blokes were whistling too – mostly our Yanks. I'd also noticed our lighting set up also had its admirers, with a couple of guys standing next to it mesmerised. I wouldn't get too close, I thought, unless you're wearing shades… but yes, a nice bit of kit.

The 'happy' Yank came over in a hurry with one of his side-kicks.

'WOWEE! They were darn good, man,' he exclaimed. 'Great moves – terrific! How did they get to be like that… where did they learn?'

Handed down by Tibetan monks I felt like saying.

On spotting our kit he asked., 'What's this?' His side-kick was also looking… keenly. 'But hey Pops, *who were they?*'

'That was Keith and Becky – and my name is Bob by the way, and you should just wait and see how good the other two are, when they get here,' I added.

'Gee sorry… no, no… the music – the singer; who is she? Is she one of the Andrews Sisters?'

'Pleased to meet you, Andrew Sisters?' I twigged. 'No, Christina Aguilera – with *Candyman*,' I answered.

'Eh? Christina *who?* Don't know her, do you know her Walt? Which band is she from?' the happy Yank persisted.

Walt shook his head, 'No idea. Maybe she fronts one of those new orchestras.'

New orchestra? Strange.

'Really, I thought the whole world knew her?' I responded, talking to them close up. I was aware that *Candyman* did in fact pay a kind of homage in style and presentation to an old Andrews Sisters song called *Boogie Woogie Bugle Boy* from 1941 – and said so, '…so you might be thinking of that instead, similar tunes aren't they.'

'Yeah, but that was only a couple of years ago – one of our favourites, real good swing. *This* song is definitely them, or someone doing a damn good imitation, and a great version too, especially in colour,' said 'happy'. His buddy Walt was nodding vigorously in agreement. I had put it on the plasma – which seemed to have a permanent little crowd around it.

'Three years…?' I paused, trying to get my head round this surprise. 'You mean more like seventy years ago.' These guys were now looking at me intently. Confusing – perhaps the local beer was stronger than I thought. 'Ah – yes. Actually it was quite recent,' I said, thinking about Christina.

'And your, your… what is all this anyway? Those lights… I'll bring the rest of the crew over…' said 'happy', casting his eyes over my mixer.

Still no sign of our tardy motorbike couple…

'So you fellas *really* are American,' I added, before they could move off. I'm thinking and wondering now about a string of events over the last hour, events not feeling right, but just then Matt and Ruby came in. And what an entrance they made, still with full motorbike kit on, plus helmets. Matt with black and gold leathers with helmet to match, visor up and Ruby in full blue and white with silver helmet, visor still down. The hall went silent for some reason. Rawlings was agape – and it takes a lot to shut up a Yank, but when they clapped eyes on these two, their jaws dropped. They just stared, not moving. Then Matt stopped, looked around and, spotting me, raised his arm, with thumbs up, smiling.

'What's up Chris, you look as if you've seen a ghost?' I said to Rawlings.

'Who are these people; do you know them?' he asked.

'Yeah – of course; it's my other two,' I replied. 'Told you we'd be okay.'

'Why are they dressed like that?' pressed Rawlings.

'They've come on their bike that's why; it's not exactly sunny California out there right now,' said Keith. Just then they both took off their gloves and Ruby popped her visor, lifted off her helmet and girlishly swished her hair.

'Gee…!' Whistles and voices erupted from a few – especially from 'happy' and his crowd.

'These guys don't get out much do they,' said Keith to Becky.

'The 'Yanks' actually sound like Yanks,' added Becky, hearing their voices.

'Either that or they really are taking this seriously; you know how the birds like a Yank,' muttered Keith to Becky, 'Real Yanks or not.'

'Actually, they really are American I think. I've just had an interesting chat with a couple of them,' I added. You could never tell these days. TV was full of US programmes where you thought the actors who were Yanks were in fact Brits – just look at 'House' – and many Yanks were doing the same over in the UK. Could be worse, could have been French… all silver plates and mercy buckets.

'Well – good luck to them,' Keith replied, '…but I wouldn't mind one of those jackets for myself though.'

The RAF blue was also evident, and a few army types. Don't ask me what outfits or which regiments they were supposed to be representing, they were, well, brown… hairy brown, poor buggers… the uniforms that is.

The presence of all these uniforms was amazing – just like 'up north' on the re-enactments, that if you were a 'flyer' it was almost mandatory you wore your flying jacket at these kind of gigs, poncing around like the big 'I am'. But there was no doubt about it – the women really did go for it. Had to chuckle. Must chat to them. I put three tracks online and made a quick bee-line to some boys in blue. to find out what the 'day job' was out of uniform. I was interested.

'How you guys doing?' I asked. 'If you want any kind of music played just ask. Looks like a good turnout, eh,' I added. I introduced myself – shook hands. 'What kind do you like?'

'Well I liked one of those songs you played earlier, the slow one, the woman – and the guy with the deep voice,' replied our man in blue, his name Gordon.

'Ah, I think you mean *Love and Affection* – yes, always popular. Good choice. I'll probably put it on again a bit later, just for you... when you've got a partner that is.' He went pink and looked a little hesitant.

Maybe shy.

'Some pretty girls here don't you think – you should get stuck in,' I said, looking around at the scene.

'Well last week we were down in London at our favourite club. Some wizard girls, much better than this boring place,' Gordon replied, encouraging agreement from the others who nodded vigorously.

'What – like the old Suivi Club or something?' I was surprised when they nodded!

'The Columbia Club too,' added Gordon.

It's been a long time since I've heard girls called 'wizard' – unless you were a Hooray Henry or a Rupert – must be friends of Mr. Cameron. And a 'club'...? Made it sound like my local.

Before I could ask what they did, one of them said, 'How are these tunes played – do you have recordings in that thing?' pointing at my mixer. He was 'Los' – short for Lawrence apparently.

This was another odd question, and I was just a teeny-weeny bit worried by it.

'Well yes... on my pod actually. Where are you lads from?' I asked, trying to draw them into a closer conversation.

'Lavenham,' they replied in unison.

Hmmm, I wondered where that is.

'And who are you?' I asked the third lad who had both fair hair and a fair complexion.

'Roland,' he replied, holding out his hand. 'Pleased to meet you,' he very politely said.

Roland. Of course you are. Maybe not a Rupert, but Roland would do – looked a bit light on the loafers. 'Do you know those other guys – those Yanks over there?' I asked, nodding towards their table.

70

'Not really. Some are okay – others are show-offs. There're usually more Yanks here at these shindigs but I guess some don't make it.'

Wizard. Mmmm – now *shindigs;* I like it. Must make a note…

'Could have been traffic; mind you it was dead quiet when we came through,' I replied.

'Traffic…?'

'Tell you what, when you're ready lads, come over to my play station over there and you can pick a tune or a band… anything. As long as it's not anything by *Jack Bean and the Runners.* Or you could ask your girlfriend what she likes – let her decide.' I had noticed a couple of girls hovering near these boys, one of them smiled when I made mention of a girlfriend.

'Yes please – thank you,' said Roland.

Very polite again.

'Then you can tell me what the day job is. Back in a minute.'

'See Becky? It's not just the Yanks that get the girls. Anyone with a flying jacket it seems. Or maybe even Matt's motorbike leathers might do it!'

'Don't tell him!' Becks replied, then added looking around, 'My God. They look young tonight.'

I was side-tracked. The Americans came over again, one of them asking, 'Mr Rawlings, where're they from… Mars?!' while still looking at Ruby.

I answered for Mr Rawlings, 'Milton Keynes, I'm afraid… they are part of my crowd – and just wait 'til you see her after she gets changed,' I added.

Spotting the look of query on my face Matt said, 'We got held up… a couple of local idiots dressed up as coppers in an old police car pulled up in a lay-by we'd stopped at, were all over us – kept asking questions about the bike. I got the distinct impression they didn't want us to leave, almost acting as if they *were* the police. They had nice wheels though, a real old Wolseley – black of course. It was quite surreal actually.'

'An old police car you say?' I asked. My interest was pricked just a little more than it should have been. 'The coppers… how were they dressed?'

'Not in hi-viz that's for sure; actually, I was too absorbed in the car to look too close, but they did look the business to me. What do you reckon Rubes?' asked Matt, turning to her.

'I thought it was OK at first but after about a minute, I actually thought it was quite creepy. You should have seen their faces when I took off my hat, especially as I was driving,' added Ruby.

'I can imagine – just like a minute ago; still getting used to it myself,' said Keith. 'I wouldn't let my *missus* anywhere near my wheels.'

'So where did you get to – how long were you stuck there?' I pressed.

'We skedaddled out of there as soon as we could when they started to get too personal, but we did go around a few back roads just to make sure we lost them – in case they *were* nutters. They weren't very forthcoming, were they Ruby, apart from telling us their names – 'Sergeant Pugh and a PC Robinson'. I remember that.'

'Well, better get yourselves sorted,' I said. Then I gave them a quick rundown on layout etc., introduced them to Rawlings – who still appeared to be in awe of Ruby – and told them the next run of tracks. 'Could be putting on Bert Kaempfert or James Last in a minute – and Adele. *Candyman* went down well with the jiving,' I added.

'What – you've played that already? That's one or our favourites. You owe us!'

'OK – get changed while I feed in the next lot of tracks and you can step on the floor whenever you're ready.' I checked back to my laptop and decided to re-arrange the music – I just had an idea and feeling that this lot of punters were not the same as our usual gigs. I called over Keith and Becky. 'I'm going to change over and move some of the tracks around tonight – I get the impression that this crowd might like something different, just a feeling I have.'

'You mean like the Midwitch Cuckoos,' chimed in Keith. 'I know what you mean.' He and Becks quickly checked out the next track they could see coming up while I got back to work.

It was a nice smooch – *Wonderland by Night* – to be getting on with, followed by *Rumour*. That'll separate the men from the boys, I thought.

We would always strive to mix the music for those that just liked to turn up and listen, or just chat over the music with pleasant talk, so I was careful not to do what many establishments did, which I hated – just blasting out music way too loud so that nobody could hear anything else. Okay if you were a zombie but not for me or my audiences. I'd also seen and learnt while travelling around Europe how the clever and successful establishments playing music would arrange the sound output so that no matter where you sat, you didn't miss out, while at the same time, just because you happened to be near a speaker, you didn't go home with your brains scrambled. Mind you, it was difficult to tell these days if some people had brains in the first place. Another lesson – the more drink consumed, the louder they liked the music.

Wonderland quickly had the floor packed. I found that Bert Kaempfert – and James Last I might add – went down well wherever we went so we always kept a few of their best on my track listings. But *Footloose* seemed to do almost the opposite for some reason, even while both Becks and Keith – with Matt & Ruby now in tow – were doing their best. 'I wonder why, what's going on?' I asked myself. Fickle lot.

How about *Money Honey;* try that. After playing *Ladybird* I was confronted by a young bloke who asked who was singing – it is an old record and perhaps not up there with the Beatles and the Stones but we always found it popular.

Then I became aware that a few lads had wandered over, including two of the 'Yanks' dead keen at what I was doing, especially with my toys, quizzical looks on their faces – none more so than on our 'breezy' Yank's face. Everybody knows that DJs have turntables and other kit for the shows these days and yet they always seem fascinated with the 'goings-on'. Now Elvis was on, singing *Trouble.*

'What's up folks?' I asked. 'How can I help? I take requests if you want – just name it. Or tuition maybe?'

'Do you have Glenn Miller sir?' one of them asked. I immediately recognised the local twang… talk about The Singing Postman. What a strong accent he had. And 'sir' as well, another polite one.

'Not only *do* we have Glenn Miller as you probably heard earlier – maybe you weren't in then – but I actually have a clip of him and can put him on the screen just over there with *Chattanooga Choo Choo,*' I indicated pointing to the wall and flicking it back on with the remote. 'Will that be OK for you… sir?' I said, tongue in cheek – and with just a little smile on my face. He looked surprised, '…and don't look *too* surprised,' I added. 'It's all part of the service.' They ambled off.

The plasma burst into life. I signalled to Matt while pointing at the screen, doing a little track shuffle at the same time. Matt gave thumbs up, maybe ready for a tap routine. Ruby looked good – a dress with a slight flare, bare back and x-over straps in a shimmering Ferrari Red, Matt with his one-piece, mustard-coloured.

Shit hot, right now they were all blaze and sparkle. What a couple. They soon had more on the floor – and many gathered round watching.

As I watched my couples dancing to the smoother dances, gliding across the floor in each other's arms, I felt envious. They love the dancing, love music and look… so happy.

Yes, Becky was right. I need a woman.

Chapter 11

Suspicions – and three girls

The young lad moved off looking pleased, still looking at the plasma, but the American and one of his buddies remained, hovering. 'Can I help you guys – remember me? I'm Bob Temple... or 'Pops' as you called me.'

They looked sheepish and laughed. *Chattanooga* was on the plasma just then. The clip from the film *Sun Valley Serenade* was, of course, in black and white, but that didn't stop a few suddenly getting up and crowding around it. The speaker set-ups for TV had moved on since the emergence of the thin, flat-screen screens with their thin, tinny sounds – Keith and I just pumped it out through the amps.

'You must know this one yeah?' I said. They nodded while watching the TV. 'So, you guys *are* Yanks; I thought for a moment it was just part of the gig theme.' I went on, 'Tell you what – if you go and sit down with your *buddies* I'll come over to your table and say 'hello' when I've finished juggling; I saw you looking at my kit. I'll bring Keith over too.' Keith was involved with his phone, fiddling, but he nodded.

'Sure... OK, sounds great,' they said, whilst looking at what Keith was doing.

Everybody seemed to be nosy, fussing about what we were doing and watching us all the time. I checked my feet, just making sure I hadn't come out wearing one shoe and one slipper – or different coloured socks. I'm told it happens.

But I *am* just a little bit out of sorts, concerned about the feel of this gig; there was a mix of events today – everyone responding the wrong way, almost like a peculiar dream, Mr Rawlings looking at me as if I had a wart on the end of my nose, and the punters not knowing their music. 'I'll clear this up when I go over and chat,' I muttered to myself. I had heard that in some parts of the States there were still areas that were quite, well, backward, yes, even today in the land of Apple iPhones; maybe these young lads came from the wrong side of the tracks. That could account for their gaucheness.

Then I took a swig from my flask and waited for our two young dancers. I watched briefly as Matt and Ruby started on a cha cha to *Train in Vain* – great hip action, straight legs with snappy moves. I needed to get up there too, with Becks, and do a couple of dances, once I'd chatted with the boys from across the pond, and maybe do a Foxtrot to *Millennium* or something – or *Walk Like a Man*. I'm never far from being rusty on dancing but it only takes a moment or two to get into the swing; I just can't be bothered to train too much though. Leave that to the experts.

'Right ladies and gentlemen – and all those still thinking about it, I'm going to play three hot tracks to get those arms and legs flying, and then afterwards some softer music, music where you can just melt into each other's arms and hang on. So, let's start with a drop of opera!'

That made the audience pay attention, and look a bit worried as the first notes played in the intro. It was, of course, *Rockaria* by ELO. There was obvious relief when it got going, and the Yank element took to it right way. This was to be followed by *Stood Up* and *Reet Petite.* Make them sweat – they'll drink more and therefore dance more… or fall over.

For the first soft, relaxing track I had *I'm Not in Love* ready. I remember years ago I had literally clung onto my dance partner for dear life with this track at the end of a hard night's drinking and dancing, more drinking than dancing, but don't tell anyone – a real saviour, preventing me collapsing onto the floor. *To Know Him is to Love Him* and *At Last* followed.

Then to interrupt my thoughts I noticed three girls headed in my direction, approaching nervously. One of them was older than the other two and dressed a little more soberly, more conservatively, a little more war-paint perhaps, maybe mum with two daughters? Yes – definitely 'mum'. It was their clothes – all similar, same styles, long skirts, almost same hairdos with the younger girls sporting brighter colours.

I was already expecting a question. 'Excuse me sir,' said the older one. 'Did you say that you would take requests earlier?' she asked in a rather pleasant but quiet voice with only a slight accent. Obviously not the Singing Postman's daughter…

And there it is again – 'sir'! Maybe I should wear a uniform or something – put stripes on my pyjamas.

'Yes, I certainly did – anything you like. And you girls?' I asked looking at the younger ones. They blushed.

'Oh sorry,' said the older woman. 'These are my daughters, Susan and Cecily. They wanted me to ask a request for them,' she added, just a little bit anxious. A crimson flush stole now into her cheeks, the girls turning even more pink.

'Really? Sounds like you have a couple of well-behaved girls there. Things must be different in this neck of the woods – my daughters would *tell* me, and that would be that – if I had daughters that is! But what's your name – apart from 'mum'? I'm Bob. Please *do* call me Bob – not sir. I've not been knighted, not yet; in the post I've been told. Tom Jones beat me to it.'

I could have got a bit creepy or obvious and say that she didn't look old enough to have these two girls as daughters, but I resisted temptation. I was surprised again when I saw how red they all turned – a real blush, like they'd just been caught on air saying, 'knickers to the queen' or suchlike. I also noticed that mum was still wearing her coat and guessed that she was in her forties maybe – and pretty? Yes, but understated, hidden away perhaps, although there seemed to me a promise that awaited in her clear blue eyes.

Mum, indeed, looked good! I remembered what Becky said – I shall keep my eye on this lady.

Daughters one and two were pretty in different ways, but both had frilly-bottomed skirts, blouses and cardigans, and dark hair, Susan lighter and looked more like her mum. I looked around, just wondering if they were blushing because some lads might be staring at them or had made some comment as they went past the tables.

'Oh… pleased to meet you. My name is Grace,' replied mum.

Really – 'Grace': not many of those around these days are there – unusual name.

'So, what'll it be ladies? Robbie? Boy Band? Adele? We've got the lot all the way from Glenn Miller, Elvis, Beatles, Take That, Bieber (please not!) to Madonna? Or Dean Martin? Sarah Vaughan… even Frank Sinatra? You name it. And if you want a nice waltz I even have Andre Rieu somewhere.'

No immediate answer… bafflement.

An awkward silence.

There was a ten second pause while they looked at each other… me with my headphones around my neck. 'Would you play that Andrews Sisters record again?' asked Cecily (or was it Susan). 'We liked that didn't we,' she said, getting bolder. Mum and the other sister nodded. 'And we were wondering if you would play a tune by Lionel Hampton or Maurice Winnik please?'

That stopped me.

'Do you mean Maurice Williams – of the Zodiacs?' Not heard of Maurice Winnik. Who's he I wondered?

There was a moment of silence so I continued, 'But of course, that's a 'yes' for the first one. Great choice – I'm not sure about Lionel (Lionel Hampton?). I'll have a shufti,' I replied with a chuckle on my lips. Lionel Hampton, Maurice Winnik? That'll teach me to leave my Victor Sylvester handbook behind. 'In fact, I'll put your first request on the screen just like Glenn Miller. And ladies, it's not the Andrews Sisters – as you will see – it is Christina Aguilera singing *Candyman,* as I had to tell those chappies over there,' I added, nodding towards the Americans.

What is it with these Andrews Sisters I asked myself? I suppose I could always play them *Strip Poker* by the Andrews Sisters – but probably not appropriate. I flipped out my iPod from the mixer, fiddled a bit and then put it back on the console. Mum and girls watched fascinated. 'Right, consider it done but I'll still need to look a little more for Lionel 'whatshisname' and Maurice 'thingamajig'; in fact I'm just going to do a playback for the Yanks – they thought the same as you. Keep your eyes on the screen over there if you want to watch *Christina*. See – how's that then?' I said. 'But 'Lionel' might take a bit longer.'

But Maurice Winnick? Lionel Hampton? I'm just not *that* old.

As I watched my dancers I would often reflect on my own, single situation with just a little envy at times; they were comfortable together – made me feel real lonely these days.,

And now I have Grace standing in front of me – just to rub it in.

These girls were into swing – old swing or quickstep by the sound of things, unusual. Very rarely were we asked to play pre-war music apart from Glenn Miller. Still – I will do what I can do.

'Was that Duke Ellington you played earlier?' chimed in the other young sister hopefully, and with a giggle.

'The Duke? No – not yet. I can if you want me to, but that was probably Bert, Bert Kaempfert and possibly with *The Bass Walks*; it always goes down well, always popular – anywhere. You don't know him do you,' I said rhetorically, judging by the look on their faces. 'But he *is* good, isn't he?' They nodded – still blushing and now sniggering between them. I had the impression that 'mum' Grace wanted to linger but was pulled away with a 'Come on mum' from Cecily. 'Hang on a mo,' I said. 'You'll need to take your coat off, Grace, if you're going to dance to *Christina*,' I said, smiling. There was more blushing, this time just from Grace. Yes, a pretty woman – I like her. Pretty girls too. 'Where's *Mr* Grace? Is he not here tonight?' I ventured.

'Oh – he's in Italy,' she replied almost solemnly.

'Lucky him; see you later,' I finished off.

'Oh, I won't be staying. I've only come to see them in safely,' she replied, looking at her two girls who now just wanted shot of her.

Yes, I remember that feeling from when I was young.

Parents.

'What a shame,' I answered, just a little dejectedly. She was still burning. Fleetingly, I had improper thoughts about her, but two seconds later I'm feeling at odds – a tad puzzled. The two sisters, although probably in their teens, looked both older and innocent at the same time. They were young, no doubt – I think it was the hair – lots of it down to the shoulders – large curls, with mum less so. But this isn't the eighties. They turned to go.

I suddenly had a thought cross my mind – an idea.

'Grace,' I called after her. They stopped and looked back. 'Just for you, I'll put on a song that I think you'll like, with the singer on the screen over there – when I can find it. I think you young girls will like it too, especially if you want to slow it down a little – later perhaps – when you've got your man so to speak... I'll make an announcement when I'm ready to play it and, if you don't mind, I'll dance with *you*... with you Grace – if you come back,' I said, fluttering my eyelids. The girls collapsed into sniggers as they moved off again, and I thought Grace looked stricken with embarrassment... me chatting up mum in front of her daughters. And what I had in mind music-wise was perhaps *Love Me Tender* by the one-and-only.

'Are they always giggling like this?' I asked, looking at Grace before she could move off. They reminded me of somebody. I looked at her daughters, 'Hey girls – have you seen *The Odd Couple*? You remind me of the girls – the English twins in that film.' I said with me motioning them to come back closer.

They looked at each other then back at me, '*The Odd Couple*? No, I don't think so,' said one of them – think it was Susan. They all shook their heads.

'Well, keep an eye out for it and remember the giggly English girls – at the end,' I added. They nodded, looked at each other saying, 'Odd Couple?' with more laughing. Very infectious. They certainly put a smile on my face.

Just then Ruby and Matt came by and stopped to look at the next listing, leaning over as they did so. I couldn't help noticing that one of the girls could not take her eyes off Ruby's gown – and the way it accentuated her bust which she was trying to adjust. Quite shapely was Ruby.

By way of an explanation she looked up and said matter-of-factly, 'This keeps slipping down, don't want my boobs popping out do we.' She struggled for a moment longer, Matt helping her before realising she had an audience. 'Oh I am sorry,' she said to the girls, who looked on fascinated. 'It happens – wardrobe malfunction again.' Her boobs weren't large – they were just a nice shape. Matt and Rubes then moved off.

'She does have nice ones doesn't she – and the costume helps,' I said to the young girls as they watched Ruby move away, then one of the girls mouthed the word *boobs* with a puzzled expression. They looked at me for a moment then looked at each other. 'Actually ladies, they shouldn't be called boobs, should they? Let's face it… boobs are 'mistakes'… they're called tits.'

Sharp intakes of breath. Did I say something wrong? Grace put her hand to her mouth while the girls creased up in muffled chuckles, not knowing where to look.

'Sorry ladies – didn't mean to embarrass you.' I think I had literally 'boobed' there… maybe they had a strict upbringing but I often call things by the name that belongs to them. 'Back to the twins and that film,' I ventured, trying to divert the topic away from ladies' chests.

They eventually recovered. '*They're* not twins; there's two years between them,' Grace said, looking after them proudly as they moved off.

'But I think you've been naughty haven't you Grace… I think the younger one, well, put it this way, you probably know the doorman to get her in, am I right?' I asked, touching my nose with a knowing smile.

Yep – her embarrassed look told me I was right, so I was thinking the younger one could be only sixteen? Difficult to tell. Perhaps I should play *Only Sixteen*…

Ruby was back. 'Do you know what, Bob? I think she's taken a shine to you,' she said as she watched the girls move away.

'Which one?' I asked with a grin.

'As if you didn't know,' she said with a sly look.

That would be a turn up, I thought to myself. But there was no doubt in my mind, I very much liked the look of Grace... I shall keep my eyes on her. You never know, it could lead to something... and her eyes – something about her eyes, the outsides slightly arched.

'Your boobs just caused me a spot of bother Rubes... I'll tell you about it later. It was quite funny actually.'

'Keith, Becky, over here,' I called to them. 'I'm going to put a couple of different tracks to the ones we decided upon originally and then go to have a chat with those guys over there about *Candyman* and the music. They, like those girls I was just talking to, think it's by the Andrews Sisters for some reason and they want to hear it again. Made me feel strange. Then it'll be *Woman,* then *Perfect* – a waltz perhaps – and then *Melina* with Elvis following, doing *New Orleans* or *Love Me Tender*. Haven't really decided yet. I'll leave the pod in the mixer. Then we'll bash on; must admit though, I'm getting vibes about this place...there's something odd. Have you had the chance to speak with any of the punters yet?'

They nodded. 'No, not yet but I know what you mean... they seem an awkward lot, quite restrained,' said Becky. 'But let's go dance!' It didn't really matter to my dancers what was put on because all they needed to hear was about two bars for them to instantly decide which dance to do... but Elvis was always easy to suss.

Elvis...

How do you describe the essence of someone like Elvis? Whenever I hear *Love Me Tender* I realise that he had a voice like no other – not necessarily like the crooners such as Tony Bennett or Andy Williams but as a pop and rock 'n' roll star, with a unique melancholy to his voice, a richness. He combined Hillbilly and Rockabilly with an appealing naughtiness... I mean – just watch his old black and white performances from the fifties; he was enjoying himself! And the youngsters loved him.

He could soar too – reach the notes actually singing, not shouting. Not easy to do. The kind of singing he did cannot be taught, it can't be studied in books, it can't be written down. Few pop stars could do it, although Freddie was maybe another...

Just like the girls before, a young lad, possibly mid-twenties, approached my station, somebody who looked untidy, with little gimlet eyes and rough round the edges, not smooth and sleek like those electro-pop boys of the eighties. He was sporting a real fancy stud on one ear and a ring on the other, and I think he had one arm or wrist in plaster, his hands grubby. When he opened his mouth, I guessed car mechanic or farm-hand, and pretty much a local. He was asking where I was from.

'Where do I live do you mean, or where I actually came from?' I responded.

'You're not like the other band people we have here. You dress funny,' he went on. 'Is it all part of the weird music you play? Can't you play proper music?'

Weird music? Nothing like being direct.

'Proper music being...?' I asked. 'What do you have in mind? Would you prefer some Northern Soul or perhaps Led Zep... or even a little sprinkling of rave with Danzel? Could I tempt you with James Last?' Silly suggestion – no way was he going to be a James Last person. Probably into Folk...

No immediate response. Then...

'Are you from the cinema people?' he continued, fingering his earring while looking at the plasma.

Now why would he ask a question like that?

'Cinema? No mate. It's just me and my troupe, going here and there making complete fools of ourselves – as you can see and hopefully having some fun... and trying to ensure you lot do too.' I quickly looked down to see if my chinos had sprung a leak or something but all was intact although I have to admit I'm a bit of a slob when it comes to clothes. I'm so uncool: been uncool for so long, I'm cool again! Then I added, looking at his ear ring, 'You do know that *Wham!* have split up, don't you?'

I did say it in English but I was under the impression, from his expression, that I'd spoken in Chinese. He hesitated, perhaps thinking of something else to say, then turned around and sloped off.

Weird music...? Weird bloke... one of the pint-sized Romeos and other 'wingless wonders' I had spotted tonight.

I reflected upon that encounter... another strange moment.

Chapter 12

Around the table with Barney

'Anybody with kids?' I asked over the mike. A couple of hands went up.

Is that all, I wondered… hardly any.

'Well for those who have, if you've left your kids at home tonight, just wonder what they might be doing while the cats away and take some comfort in my next track… *Baby Sittin' Boogie!'*

More jiving – going down well. 'You never know; kids start young these days,' I added.

I wandered over to Barney's table with a laptop. They looked up expectantly as I approached, plonking my phone on the table and opening up the computer.

'Remember me… Pops?' I reminded them. 'Bob's my name.'

'Yeah, sorry boss. I'm Barney – Barney Collins,' he said with an obvious US twang. We shook hands. 'But we wanted to know what kind of music you've been playing. I've never heard any of it before, especially that fast one just now.'

'Where you guys from?' I asked, looking at Barney's bunch sat around the table.

They looked around at each other first. There was a hesitancy to speak, almost glances of an anxious inquiry amongst themselves. Eventually, '388 Group,' Barney responded. 'This is Joe, that's Walt, Milt, Ricky and Ginge,' he said as he went around the table. A universal 'Hi' came back.

Nice to see a carrot-top.

One of them perked up, 'Say Mr Temple – back home guys your age are either in the cemetery or in a rocking chair on the porch.'

'Well, thanks for the compliment. If I'd known I was going to live this long I'd have looked after myself better. I'll be sure to bring the defibrillator along next time.'

'A de… what…?' one of them asked.

'Never mind. Besides, I'm really only twenty-one… from the waist down, otherwise I sometimes I feel about ninety.' It took just a little time while it sank in before more laughter followed. Did I really look that old? They were all laughing now.

Yes, maybe I was getting on but I thought that you could tell when someone *was* old by the way they moved – the way they walked and talked, indicators like that. It's true that the way *some* people moved, they were giving a sign that they were 'checking out' – headed for the exit. I thought I did OK in that respect – passed muster.

Barney continued, 'I mean – look at your gear man. We ain't seen nothing like that nor heard most of your music. Who ARE you guys?'

Well – not American, that's for sure. I supposed things might just be a bit different over here music-wise… and 388? 'New to me,' I responded. 'I've heard of M83 – have one of their tracks but it's good that we still have new ones coming along otherwise where *would* we be, eh,' I added. 'What's your poison when it comes to music? Let me guess… country…Dolly Parton? Jive, rock 'n' roll? As for my kit… well… I like to keep up, don't you?'

'Jazz… swing jazz,' two of them said almost in unison. 'Jitterbugging too, like them two did.'

'Oh, you mean the Lindy hop… or jive,' I continued. 'Well we could be in for an energetic night folks. I'll tell Matt and Ruby – they just love that stuff. It can be arranged.'

'Rock and roll?' asked one of the group sat next to Barney. 'Let's have some of that!'

'You guys obviously like dancing…'

'Yeah – but we also like to play as well, get together like a band,' interrupted Barney. 'We all play our own instruments; well we *try* and play: me on guitar and a bit of piano, Joe on saxophone and clarinet, Walt can play drums and Milt does trombone, harmonica and sings. Ginge is *real* good on the piano. Lou does bass – when he can find one; I told him it would be better if he played something smaller, like a violin! But he also sings. Richard here does nothing – ain't musical, leastwise not yet but we'll find something. We've not had much chance though. To be honest

Mr Temple – Bob, none of us is *really* any good apart from Ginge, so we just play mish-mash. We are quite hopeless, but one day...'

'Barney's crazy on guitars,' said Joe, '...even fixed himself up with a little box of tricks to make it louder – make it electric man.' Joe seemed the cooler, more sober guy than Barney. 'He takes it everywhere, no matter what.'

'An amp?' I chucked in. I knew a thing or two about guitars, '...or do you mean the pick-up? There's lots of little things that go into a guitar – the bridge, potentiometers. And amps of course... to boost the input signal from the guitar to drive the speakers. Well good luck and all credit on your DIY attempt. Is it a vacuum tube or solid state amp? And the wah-wah pedal...' I stopped. It was going over their heads. 'I can see that I'm boring you...' They were all looking at me, Barney just gaping.

'What the... gee. Wah-wah? What do you mean?'

'Sorry. Just me getting carried away.' Perhaps I was going too deep, '...but basically you wanna be heard, is that it... the 'twang's the thang' and all that.'

Which went straight over their heads... again. I'd have to practice more.

Barney cut in, 'Aw shucks fellas. Well I had to, otherwise you'd never hear me,' he retorted, looking around challenging for support. 'You're just as bad with your sax!' he said looking at Joe. They all laughed.

Now a real live *Aw shucks*! Good entertainment so far. I'd been to the States a few times but it's not often that you get off the beaten track to meet real country hicks – you usually stick to the well-worn tourist attractions.

I continued, 'Hey guys, I thought guitars were loud enough already. Are you into heavy metal or something? Deep Purple and Led Zep not loud *enough*? And where do you play?'

'What did he say?' asked Barney, turning to the others.

'No goddamn idea... something purple,' answered Joe who was keen to let Barney tell me more about the band.

'Well, we actually got together and started in Wendover but now we just jam together whenever we get the time, usually in the clubhouse back at Knettishall. Crap actually, but we have fun.'

'Speak for yourself,' they chimed together loudly. 'Yeah – but we have good times that's for sure.'

'How about a gorilla playing the drums?' I threw in. Must show that clip...

'Eh?'

Wendover? Memories... used to hang out near there years ago.

As I said, I knew a little about guitars so just a little background; I promise I won't bore you too much reader...

When I was young I did what many other kids did – try and play a guitar like Hank Marvin or Eddie Cochran, just as Barney's doing. Fortunately for music and the music industry, I mostly failed but did learn a little history about the instrument and who played which guitar, as part of my efforts.

Similar instruments to the guitar have been around for thousands of years. Who invented the electric guitar? I don't know *exactly* who but it was probably between Leo Fender or Rickenbacker just before WWII, perhaps even in the twenties. That's good enough for me. The first was manufactured in the 1930s by Rickenbacker... I'm informed.

Original electric guitars used tungsten pickups. Pickups basically convert the vibration of the strings into electrical current, which is then fed into the amplifier to produce the sound (via the speakers as I said above). The very earliest electric guitars featured smaller sound-holes in the body. These guitars are known as semi-hollow body electric guitars and still are somewhat popular today, mainly due to the fact that they are flexible guitars, but with the use of pickups, it was possible to create guitars *without* sound-holes that still had the ability to be heard, if plugged into amplifiers. These guitars are called solid body electric guitars.

Still with me? Keep up please.

Other names in the guitar world...? Gibson and Les Paul, who pioneered the solid body with Ted McCarty, introduced the invention to the world – the Gibson Les Paul – and it's still going strong today. Leo Fender came up with a solid body electric guitar of his own with iconic names such as the Fender Broadcaster, then the Stratocaster. Fender guitars were generally lighter compared to the Les Paul. Now there are many guitar makers.

As for the music – and I'm biased towards pop – there are many memorable guitar intros such as *It's All Over Now* by the Stones and Joe Moretti with *Shakin' All Over.*

So who played what? James Burton who played for both Elvis and Ricky Nelson used the Telecaster – as did Eric Clapton, and Danny

Gatton too. Mustn't forget Muddy Walters, Otis Reading and Clarence White who was big in country music apparently. 'Country' was not really my scene, although I gather he played with The Byrds. And who is this… yes, George Harrison no less, used a Telecaster during the recording sessions for the Beatles on some albums.

With rock music came Keith Richards, Status Quo and Jimmy Page of Led Zeppelin. Let's not forget possibly the greatest guitarist of them all – rock guitarist that is – Jimi Hendrix. But some of the above also used Les Paul guitars and I'm informed that Brian May (Queen) made up his own guitar called The Red Special presumably because it's red, although he had also used the other two makes. Others who used Les Paul instruments… there's Pete Townshend, Slash and Pete Green of Fleetwood Mac. I hadn't found out what guitar Joe Moretti played yet. I could tell Barney that even the famous Django Reinhardt – who really does deserve a mention – often used a *Selmer* guitar fitted with an electric pickup, but Selmers were only made in small numbers.

That should do it… but you could, folks, do a special chapter on Jimi Hendrix. But not here, suffice to say he was responsible for bringing in the *Fuzz Box* as a result of one of his engineers – Roger Meyer – designing for him the 'Octavia pedal', to provide some distortion.

Anyway… so well done Leo Fender.

See…that wasn't very painful was it?

I move on, back to Barney's crowd.

'Don't you also go to dances in Thetford?' I asked.

'No man, not much action there like there is here,' said Barney.

'Action…?'

'You know – chicks, broads, dames,' responded Walt.

'Ah – you mean skirt. Got you.' A typical American expression – *broads* – but not in the way we mean these days.

'The best place we been to so far for action is The Samson and Hercules,' somebody said.

'Eh? Say again… Samson and Hercules?' My ears had pricked up. I knew it from old, been there myself.

'In Nor-wich,' they all chimed.

They'll pronounce it right one day…

87

'Yes, I know where it is – still going strong is it?' I thought it'd closed a long time ago – I knew the place well from way back. 'When was this?'

'Last month when we were stranded at Horsham,' said Milt. Now they all started to talk and tell me about this girl, that girl and other juicy, illicit pleasures, each speaking in turn, cutting in the moment another paused for breath and sometimes they all spoke together. Their noisy, happy banter and the way they came across – surely American small-town boys, looking young enough to be straight out of high school, probably church-going too – made me think back, made me feel really old.

'Yeah OK – I get the message,' I said, holding my hands up to stop them all babbling on. 'So, you all had a good time, and you all live in Knettishall.'

I'm not sure how I felt just then – strange perhaps, warm under the collar with my mind trying to digest this information and other unnatural reactions over the last hour from some of the audience. No… it couldn't have been The Samson and Hercules. They must have got the wrong place – probably all pissed. I thought the place had been closed for years now, so they were probably getting mixed up with some other joint – easy to do when you are not local lads, in a strange town. No point in arguing about it.

But nice guys. Must ask them what they are doing across here.

Chapter 13

Gadgets, Bikes and Questions

They had mentioned the Andrews Sisters earlier on, as Grace had done. Well I had heard of them along with our own Beverley Sisters so I said to them…

'OK, but first let me just show you this clip again – just to show you that it really is Christina Aguilera and *not* the Andrews Sisters. I'll keep the volume down – don't want to disrupt the main gig do we now.' I opened up the laptop – I already had the clip primed – and stabbed the key, while at the same time clicking my phone on. 'Just feast your eyes on this,' I said to the table. Christina came on and I watched too. Always loved this track; she and her backers captured the essence and style of the song perfectly. Then I became aware that not only were these guys watching, they were totally and utterly absorbed. '…yes, I know – great picture, good colours, great dancing too; we usually only hear it on the radio, so you don't get to see it, do you?' I added. My gaze switched from the screen to the lads. It suddenly dawned on me that they might be seeing something they weren't used to down in the boondocks – especially when one of them picked up my phone, touching it – feeling it. They make smartphones so attractive these days you feel like wanting to lick it. I was also conscious of the fact that others nearby were also looking at *Candyman* playing on my computer.

'How come we've not heard of her if she's that good?' asked Walt, probably appreciating the beat. Walt was into drums remember.

'Man… she looks real sassy,' said Barney. The others were nodding. 'Like to get to know her better… yes sir!' he added. Now he was looking at my laptop closely, seeing what I was doing. 'Is this some kind of hi-fallutin' movie thing, a typewriter with a movie picture?' he was asking, looking closely at Christina.

Where have these guys been…? 'Movie thing'?!

Just then Matt and Ruby came over from speaking to Chris Rawlings, to see what was going on.

I made the introductions.

'Matt, Ruby, meet the American element – just showing them Christina with *Candyman*; guys – these are the two from Mars,' I added with a smile. And to our surprise, they all stood up with 'How d'ya dos' and shaking hands… couldn't take their eyes off these two, especially Ruby. I did a quick rerun of their previous conversation. 'These are the two who love the jive and do all those kind of dances, have even won competitions… and you're welcome to ask them to partner, ask them when they're not all sweat and hottie.'

'Gee… great, thanks. Hey, I like that – all *sweat and hottie.*' Barney repeating it as he laughed.

'It's called a spoonerism I believe,' said Matt.

'Tell you what,' I said, looking at Matt and Rubes, 'Do your showcase jive with *Good Vibrations* – I'll put it on next, show them how it's done. Take it away.'

'You got it,' they said as they moved to the floor.

'Just watch these two…' I motioned to Barney and co. Then I paused.

Me… I was still wondering about the typewriter… it made me feel uncomfortable. Did they live in some kind of protected home I wondered?

They were sure impressed with Matt and Rubes' rendition of the Beach Boys, in fact quite open-mouthed when they returned to the table.

'You see – all sweat and hottie!' I said. They were too.

'But who was singing?' asked Barney.

Oh, oh, another strange moment. Don't know who did *Good Vibrations…* really? The surfing thing must have passed these guys by, that's all I can say.

We continued chatting about various things, general chit-chat on music and women. Matt had told them that we'd been doing these gigs for a little while now.

'Just like Bob here, Rubes and I love music and dancing, keeps the body in trim too – along with a round of golf now and then. Used to like going bowling but the place closed down,' Matt added.

'Did you come here on your motorbike – dressed like we saw you?' asked Walt.

'On our Triumph – yes, we both own it and Rubes does her share of the driving. You definitely need the leathers,' said Matt. 'I don't want my baby getting scratched,' he added with a grin.

'Love to have a look at your bike. Can we have a look see?' asked Milt. 'With gear like that I'm dying to see the bike.'

'Sure, absolutely – when we have a longer break, I'll show you. Have you got a motorbike?' Matt asked.

'Well, my Pa has an Indian which he lets me ride. She's a real bitch – fallen off a few times,' said Milt laughing.

'That's why you look the way you do Milt – all bent and twisted!' said Barney. Now we all laughed. He added, 'Milt always wants to be one better than everybody else – go faster, play harder, dance better. You'll see.'

'Know what you mean,' I chimed in. 'I knew a colleague from a few years ago like that. We called him 'Two-shits Dave'. If you said you'd had a shit, he would say he'd had two... always one better.'

More laughter.

'An Indian you say? Fancy that – haven't seen one of those bikes for ages – at least not over here. Anyway, we'll give you a shout later and you can have a look at mine,' said Matt. More banter followed – more talk about music and dancing.

Walt spotted my phone.

'What's that on your gadget Mr Temple... Bob sir?'

'Just having a quick look at the calendar – got some appointments to check.'

'Is that the time on it?' Walt looked closer at it. 'Still early. Is that right... twelve minutes past eight?'

'Why? Got a hot date or something? You guys can't miss tonight – look around, loads of them,' I pointed out. They all looked around.

Although he grinned he was still looking at my phone. 'Crap!' he said, looking at his own watch. 'Mine is way out – going too fast!' It was well after nine on his. It looked noddy. Now they were all looking at their watches.

'Come on fellas, there's plenty of time – and yes it's well past nine. Get on the floor. I'm not going anywhere just yet.' I nudged them with a nod as I pocketed my phone.

The next thirty minutes flew by. I jiggled the tracks, cued a few to follow and eventually set the scene for our first robotic dance – a slow robotic jig, always a spectacle, always popular with songs like *Addicted to Love* and *Every One's a Winner*.

When my four do this, even I stop and watch. They're brilliant. Just watch out C3PO! The crowd was mesmerised too, with some of them coming up and asking, 'What was that?' and 'Where can you learn it?' etc.

I blame Kraftwerk.

'Ask them. They'll show you,' I answered. 'That's what we do; as well as showing the dance, we're also very happy to show you how the steps go – any dance you want.'

In the bigger towns, with the younger, more agile element of our dance audiences, we were quite used to someone getting up and doing the occasional acrobatic event or break-dance. Not tonight. Not yet, but my four 'robots' had the audience's interest, so I thought I'd push them in the right direction after a couple of real smoochies, *Move Over Darling* and *Sealed With a Kiss*... get the batteries recharged. My energetic enticer was *Pump it Up!* with my dancers showing the way. This usually does it; I thought there were enough youngsters in the hall for someone to get up and blow us all away with flick-flaks, somersaults and bum spins, but no... no one.

Disappointed.

What's the matter with them? Why is this audience so – apart from the Americans – bloody quiet? Did they all have six pork pies before they came out or is it just Bury? (Sorry folks if you're from Bury).

What else will get them to the floor?

How about a bigger question. What is it that grabs you with music I often asked myself? We would often mull this over amongst ourselves during our travelling when a particular song came on. What makes you *like* a tune?

For many it's not the lyrics – it's just the notes, the melody, or it could be the chord arrangements, an unexpected change in octave or just a plain good melody flow. I know from my youth that for me, *Wonderful Land* was one of the finest instrumental guitar records ever – a good flow of melody and terrific guitar play by Hank Marvin. Not clever, not really rock and roll, just good... great to listen to. There were many like that. Then, for others, perhaps as a minimum, there was the need for a solid beat. Who can resist your body parts – and I'm talking snapping fingers, bobbing knees, nodding heads, feet and hands all moving to something that makes your chemical make-up want to get up and take part in the twitching and tapping. Just listen to the intro to *Stupid Girl* and you'll know, just the first five seconds will do it. Or *Jailhouse Rock*.

If you sit still during these then go and see a doctor... or ask your nurse to take you home.

Mood counts too. I could not listen to my favourites 24/7. It would eventually drive me round the twist. It's probably why most shop staff are irritable or rude – or both – having to listen all day long to the same piped crap that you can't quite hear, but it's there nonetheless. Background, irritating noise. Feel sorry for them actually – must be mind-numbing.

I do recall quite clearly many moons ago, when I was at some far-flung outpost in the east, far east, we had a small radio station – very small. On one particular programme, the music was kicked off by the DJ who would then repeat the same record over and over until someone phoned in with a pledge for a different song, which would also be repeated ad infinitum. You get the picture. You could soon go off a tune after a thousand plays. It was an almost surreal place with facilities provided for only thirty people that you wouldn't get on much larger outfits – our own cinema, the latest papers, a library, a medical centre and a bar, of course. But it was the radio station where I spent much of my spare time because you had access to all those records, thousands of them. So I'd be sat there in the listening booth with my dog H&B sat beside me.

Dog? What dog, you ask?

Let me tell you about my dog called H&B who is probably the only dog in the world who has listened to all of Elvis and the Beatles ...oh, and maybe the Beach Boys. Without complaint... I think.

When I had first arrived at this outpost I was asked if I wanted to look after a dog. 'We have thirty of them – all strays now from previous owners who have gone back. Take your pick,' said the bloke showing me around. 'They'll starve otherwise.'

'Well OK, I like dogs – but I'm only here for three weeks. I'll have that one,' I said, pointing to a mutt that looked half-way decent. 'What's its name?'

'H&B,' he said.

'H&B? Why's it called that?' I asked, intrigued.

'Well just look at him... he's all head and bollocks,' he replied.

I cracked up, but yes, sure enough, it was… a big head and huge bollocks. Don't ask me what kind of dog it was because I didn't have a clue. He didn't starve but he became an expert on the Beatles and possibly the Beach Boys too.

Often, I would talk to my dog as there wasn't much to do. He would perk up and listen. When you talk to them – look at them directly, they have this habit of first cocking their heads one way, then another way, looking at you intently, as if you're stupid… which is probably true.

'So, who's your favourite artist then H&B… Howling Wolf maybe? And your top record? What… *Hound Dog*? Oh, come on… too easy man! What about *Ol' Shep*?'

Many people think the Beatles were only about jangly guitars (sorry Ringo) but actually they had many other strings to their bow – if you please excuse the pun – when it came to musical arrangements. For instance, they reintroduced older instruments into many of their arrangements.

Classical: *A Day in the Life.*

Brass band: *Sgt. Pepper.*

String quartet: *Yesterday.*

Harpsichord: *Fixing a Hole.*

Melodeon and fairground organ: *Benefit of Mr Kite.*

Mellotron: *Strawberry Fields*

There's more… recorder, drone, piccolo trumpet… too many… zzzzzz.

I digress… where was I?

There are of course others who do not like jangly, harsh, edgy stuff, where the balance is wrong, the noise too much and the instruments don't compliment the song. Or the voices are hard, there are too many gaps and stop-starts. Not smooth. And some records were… just too frantic. Perhaps, like a relative of mine, they may hate guitars, preferring instead something more soothing – maybe strings like the Mantovani brigade or the smooth orchestral Glenn Miller band, nothing wrong with that. Perhaps we can blame Charlie Christian and Benny Goodman back in 1939 for bringing on the first proper guitar records for the modern noisy pop.

And Bert Kaempfert was a modern bandleader who was successful in combining many of the more modern acceptable elements that went to make up successful tunes – steady, flowing music without being too bland, even turning out a top ten hit in the swinging sixties with *Bye-Bye Blues,* when usually it was either the Beatles or the Stones fighting for top spot, and occasionally the Beach Boys – mustn't forget Brian Wilson must we.

Some just don't like pop full stop. Let's face it, in all genres of music and back through the decades, an awful lot of crap was produced, much of it boring, unmemorable – auto-tuned pop rubbish, made side-by-side with the good stuff. Always has been. And we don't necessarily like, or go for, the good singing voices like they used to have in the past; what they go for these days is the beat, the hype, the tune – perhaps the celeb name', and the video of course.

But pop music happens. It happens without anybody's permission, unless you're in North Korea or other oppressive places. You cannot keep romance and music off the scene. There's no love without a song!

If you're into the singers, the writers, all you need is to hear – well, put it this way, if I said Bing, I wouldn't need to say *Crosby* as well would I? Same with Elvis – everybody knows who you're talking about. It's the same with Nat, Ella, Doris and Freddie. Adele is… well, Adele.

But for many it *is* the singer, not the song… maybe a generation thing, popular in the thirties, forties and fifties when famous singers fronted the big bands. I've known many who have simply said, as an example, 'As long as it's Frank Sinatra singing I don't care about the rest,' or Tony Bennett and Andy Williams, all those crooners with instantly recognisable, wonderful voices and great musical arrangements. But two of my great favourites, one with the fabulous, smoky voice, are the instantly recognisable Nat King Cole and Brook Benton. Come on Brook – fancy being named after a stream! But a great voice. We always played these guys at our gigs mixed in with Elvis and Freddie and, just occasionally, El Divo. Yes – El Divo – you heard right. What a combo! But along with the good stuff, there was a great deal of dross in every part of the music world as I said earlier. How many tracks were recorded just to make up the numbers, fulfil contracts etc. Too many.

However, people forget that it wasn't just Americans and Italians who could sing. The Brits too had some fine singers and our own crooners, who tended to be eclipsed by the big American names. Even Frank Sinatra paid tribute to a British singer often overlooked – Matt Monroe. 'Great limey singer,' or words to that affect. There was also another very good Brit singer called Michael Holliday. Michael who? Exactly. Just listen and wonder why he wasn't up there with the best.

Yes, even as a child of the sixties, I liked these guys and some of their records. Same with the dames – the moment Eartha Kitt opened her mouth you knew who it was – her voice was so distinctive. Some singers had special voices. You only had to hear them sing two words and you knew…like Doris Day. Now Doris could sing – and in a way few other females could emulate. Her voice had a ringing, lingering pulse to it, never harsh.

But you only have to look at what makes for a good song by the number of covers – the tunes that made it big, tunes all other artists record. If memory serves me right there are three that are outstanding. *Yesterday*, *My Way* and *Summertime*. If there's more – sorry I left them out. Simple tunes, great lyrics – none too fancy or elaborate.

This thinking gave me an idea. I called over, 'Matt, Rubes – when you're ready,' beckoning with my head. When they came over I said I'd change the emphasis a little towards some swingy, catchy tunes, easy on the ears but also good for the dance floor, starting with *I'm Coming Home Baby* by Mel Torme. When I put it on I was surprised – very popular, had them bopping, bobbing and clutching. Mel Torme – all our troupe liked him. He came down from immigrants – Jewish. Aren't most of the good composers Jewish? Seem to be. Talented lot. Torme made musical arrangements, could also play the drums and wrote loads of songs. He was also a very fast gun drawer (as in the Wild West). Yes, we didn't know that either. But apparently, he was not impressed with rock and roll. Well, I suppose no one's perfect; maybe he was ill at the time but no doubt he was one accomplished dude, was Mel. And the punters liked him too. I got a thumbs-up from one of Barney's lot as I glanced across.

So I then thought of trying Sukiyaki singing *I Look Up When I Walk* ('ue o muite aruko'), a surprise hit from the sixties. A really pleasant song even if I can't understand a word of it, and yes, it's looking good. They're dancing. The singer, poor man, came to a sticky end… he was on the JAL Jumbo that lost its fin over Japan. Can't remember if there were any survivors but they all knew they were going to die as the plane flew on for quite a while before crashing. Many wrote last farewell notes on scraps of paper, which were found. How tragic.

'Who was that?' asked Chris Rawlings. 'I rather liked that. What language was it – French?'

'I know what you mean – catchy tune – forget who it was,' I said, lying through my teeth. French would do for now because for some reason, I didn't want to say the word 'Japanese' to him. I was already harbouring a certain suspicion, then I thought again…

'No, Chinese maybe… I think.'

Safer answer.

Chapter 14

The scrap

We'd noticed a couple of blokes who were well-oiled, drifting and staggering a little around the dance floor, rather like my dancing... even when I'm sober. Some of the punters seemed to know them as they bumped their way through the crowds, talking out loud and making a general nuisance of themselves. I sensed trouble looming. It happens — music, women, strong local beer, not gnat's piss — all the ingredients necessary. We'd seen it many times before but usually there were 'big geezers' about who nipped it in the bud — but I couldn't see any big boy candidates tonight. I wondered if Chris Rawlings was watching and keeping tabs on the possibilities; I couldn't see him anywhere. Inevitably one of the drunks wandered into the close proximity of Matt and Ruby. He stood there watching them for just a little while in the middle of their moves, swaying slightly. No, not them — he was the one swaying. Then he opened his mouth.

'Big queer!' he said deliberately at Matt, loud enough so that both Matt and some of the audience could hear, while leering at Ruby. Matt, with his great dancing, was obviously getting up the bloke's nose — a green mist. I also heard those words and looked up; I'd briefly lost track of the development and could only see one of the local drunks sounding off. Of course Matt *had* heard — he was meant to. He fleetingly glanced at me after one of his *rondes*. I shook my head ever so slightly at Matt as if to say, 'he's not worth it'. Matt and Ruby carried on without a pause in their routine, but then drunk number two — the idiot, sozzled mate of drunk number one — chimed in, obviously emboldened by the first salvo.

'Yeah — big ponce!' he said even louder and went up to Matt and pushed him out the way. 'Have a dance with a man, a real man,' he said slobbering and ogling, spittle on his lips. He probably imagined that three pints of the local sauce made him look like George Clooney, able to fight like Bruce Lee — and probably sing like Caruso. I thought for a moment that Rubes was going to deck him — and she was quite capable of doing so

– having that look in her face right then. Whoever this bloke was, he had certainly picked the short straw in the looks department, probably born in a tree – an ugly tree, hitting every branch on the way down. He and his 'other' must have held hands during their frontal lobotomy judging from their command of the English language. Either that or their English teacher 'did time'.

Meanwhile Matt – seemingly amused with this turn of events – came back up to him and said, 'Excuse me *hammerhead*, that's my partner and I don't think she's really impressed or interested.'

It was the *hammerhead* that did it…

Looking at Matt, number two said, 'Who asked you?' almost with a vacant expression of idiocy that alcohol often brings – and then he made a big mistake. He took a swing at Matt who smartly ducked sideways while bringing his leg around to sweep the drunk's front foot away. The drunk wasn't expecting that… went down in a heap. But number one wanted some action too – and came in from the side.

If there was one thing my dancers were good at, it was being able to move, nimble-like. Matt turned into him and saw the primed fists. He wasted no time – hopped in, doing a front snap kick to the crown jewels. Just for a fleeting moment the drunk knew what was being unleashed so moved his head and arms down to belatedly protect his manly goods, only to see a fist come crashing into his face. But Matt was an expert; the kick was almost a feint – almost. A loose foot connected and hurt enough… just enough. Same with the punch – Matt relaxed his fist so that it became almost a slap. Still hurt a bit though. The guy was already going down, groaning about his meat-and-two-veg…and was out of it.

Me, I'm quickly on the mic. 'Ladies and gents, just a little altercation here. It'll soon be over. Carry on dancing… Matt will sort it.'

The fight was not quite finished yet though. Number two was up on his feet again cursing, after taking up the length of a cricket pitch to get to his feet, staggered around with the veins in his brow swelling visibly like ropes and immediately headed back towards Matt, coming in full frontal, fists and arms flailing like a tank minesweeper, hurling himself into the food-mixer. I knew what I'd do. And Matt did exactly that, again hopping in with a strong side kick to the paunch followed by a nice turning kick to the side of his head. Same leg, real quick. Smack! The side kick stopped the lumbering idiot and brought forth a 'oof' of exhaled breath; the turning kick knocked him over. But again, Matt slackened his foot, he didn't want to kill the bloke. Amazing how everything stops in the vicinity of a scrap – gasps from the other dancers, a couple of shrieks then it's all over. Both crawled away, number two rising carefully to his feet. He was in that condition in which to move with care is of the first importance, with the assistance now of Chris Rawlings, 'Norman' and a couple of other locals. He was now seriously mouthing off as he was dragged away, cursing left and right.

Such profanities! Sorry reader, but I refrain from penning them.

Rawlings and co. made sure they actually left the building. It was pitiful really. The fight was over – done cleanly, only a little blood and no broken glasses, almost as if everything was contrived in the most artful manner by Matt.

Show-off.

I began clapping. 'See, I told you so,' I said on the speakers.

Eventually Chris came rushing over – as did a few others – now looking at Matt differently, with respect and curiosity. I mouthed, 'Awesome,' to him with a thumbs-up. Keith and Becks clapped too. A few others joined in.

'How did he do that? He certainly dealt with them very well like some spiv, made it look easy. Does he do Judo or something?'

'Well Chris, just look at his dancing. All experts make things look easy.' Yes, Matt was handy, and indeed a black belt but not in Judo, in Tight Bond Glue or Tae Kwon Do or something. Won't be short of dance partners now! Little did the two twerps realise but Matt and Ruby trained together so they were on a hiding to nothing.

Keith shouted across to me laughingly, 'Perhaps you should put on *Kung Fu Fighting* next!'

'Or *Another One Bites the Dust!*' added Becky with a big grin on her chops.

One aspect of dancing – if you are doing it frequently – is that it keeps the pounds off and also keeps you reasonably flexible. And if you are doing Tap or Irish, it *really* keeps the pounds off! For those who are reading this and are, what they call *young*, 'pounds' is old dinner money for kilograms. Either way you'll be thinner if you tap – or should I say, you won't get fat. So, dancing is a win-win hobby, and Matt had just showed how nimble, fit and flexible you could be!

Poser.

I put *Crazy* on, then called, 'Keith, Becky – when this is finished can you gear up and do your *Telephone* routine?' Two thumbs up was the response. These two had made Lady Ga Ga's song their own with a special jive show.

Following the scrap, it didn't take long before Milt and another of his buddies came over to Matt, asking questions with back-slapping talk and similar banter. For five minutes Matt was king. There was no doubt about the outcome as far as I was concerned when it had kicked off. Eventually Matt managed to extricate himself from his new found 'groupies' and came over with Ruby.

'That was a first,' he said. This was true. We had never had to resort to, or get involved in, any fisticuffs during our gigs in the past. 'Probably got Viking blood in him or something.'

'I think it was beer in his veins, not blood,' said Ruby. 'Next time, please let me have a go!'

Well said Ruby… feisty.

The American lads came over.

'Hey boss, any chance – can we take a look at your bike now?' I was not sure who asked but it was an American accent.

Now was as good a time as any so both Matt and Ruby took a sniff from a flask first and then let me know they'd be outside for a few minutes with the bike, which Rubes had moved into a covered alleyway, almost like a small narrow garage where no doubt the council kept its tools, almost a general dumping area. 'Twas dark now. They opened the two small doors.

When Milt clapped eyes on it his face lit up and he whistled. In fact, he just stood there gaping at it as did Lou. They both looked at Rubes, then back at the bike.

'Jeez! This yours?' he said, looking at her again. He whistled in admiration.

'Yes, why?'

'A Triumph,' he eventually said, now looking at the controls more closely. 'What a beauty, is she fast?'

'Oh absolutely – too fast,' added Matt. 'I don't know what your Indian is like but she can do over 150.'

As the Yanks were totally absorbed looking at his machine, Matt leaned over and started it up.

'Hell, man – no kick start.' And straight away the lights shone onto the Range Rover across the yard.

'Holy cow!' Lou this time. 'What's that?' he asked as he moved away from the bike towards the Rover. 'A real fancy Jeep, nice and shiny,' he exclaimed.

'Jeep? That's our car, that's how Bob and the others got here. Ruby and I came on the bike remember. Want to have a look inside?' offered Matt. 'I'll pop back in and get the keys.'

He was out again in two shakes. The Rover lit up as it unlocked itself and Matt climbed in. He motioned to the other two to get in – which they did, tentatively, looking around like they were stepping into Tutankhamun's tomb for the first time.

'What's up? asked Matt, 'Not been in a Range Rover before? Just think of your Cadillacs. It's not quite like the *Enterprise* yet but they're getting there. They're quite high up aren't they – and very comfy, suits us just fine.' He fired it up. Hardly a whisper. Bob had asked him to do a quick check on the sat nav that seemed to have gone tits-up on the journey. Still static, no response. Frozen, but everything else lit up as usual just like the bridge on Star Trek – never failed to impress the team; none of this peering at black gauges with quivering, vibrating pointers they used to have in the 'good ol' days'. Then he turned on the radio… just noise. So he did an auto-scan: momentary silence as it scanned for a station, eventually settling for something completely garbled and scratchy. So he banged in a CD – nearly blew their socks off. 'Sorry about that, forgot I'd turned the volume right up,' he burbled as he turned it back down.

'Nope – still kaput Rubes, even the radio, but the CD's OK,' he said. Then he noticed the look on both the Yanks' faces. Not often you have quiet Americans with nothing to say, but their faces were faces of searching inquiry – like kids in a huge candy store or at Disney World, eyes wide open.

'Swell! Can I get the others in and show 'em?' asked Lou. 'They gotta see this, them seats are like in my Pa's front parlour.'

'Sure…' responded Matt half-heartedly. It's only a bloody car, he thought. Yeah – okay, there were some mods to it but nothing special. 'Hey Rubes – while we're out here can you just check the bike's sat nav please?' She was already ahead of him having wandered over to the Triumph. She knew they might as well check both.

'Same as before – no change. We must be in a real dead spot here or something's in the way,' she responded.

Then half of Barney's table turned up. 'Some of them dancing still,' Lou said. But immediately they were all over both machines – eyes agog, slobbering and dribbling in a kind of schoolboy rapture, all asking questions at once. Lou was looking at a couple of items in the console more closely. 'What are these,' he asked, holding up a couple of DVDs.

'Films – we always bring a couple along just in case.'

They continued to ogle. This worried both Matt and Ruby just a little. OK if it had been a Bugatti Veron or a McLaren, but this was just a run of the mill Rover… and a bike.

When they'd had their fill, Matt rounded them up and said they'd have to get back inside. 'Come on boys, we've dancing to do, we can talk more later.' They switched everything off and closed the doors. On the way in Ruby bumped into Chris Rawlings who was just coming out.

'Oh hello,' said Ruby. 'You've just missed the fun.'

'What fun? What's going on?' demanded Chris, his face conveying a look of suspicion. 'You mustn't be out here…'

Ruby cut in. 'It's alright Chris. We didn't let anybody in – it was just us showing those lads our bike and the Rover.' He was about to add something when he turned to look, his attention lingering on their vehicle.

'Is that yours?' he asked, but Ruby had already disappeared inside to join the melee.

Chapter 15

Uncomfortable

Back inside, back into the routine. Matt saw me on the mic saying something.

'What was that all about?' queried Matt.

'Two couples had bumped into each other and one of the lads fell over – just a few laughs, that's all so I said over the speakers 'steady boys'…which gave me an idea, and led me into another Bert Kaempfert record – *Steady Does It.* That's what I was announcing.'

'Deep!' exclaimed Matt.

Sure enough, when it came on the floor was packed, all of them bouncing away like no tomorrow. Bert was going down well tonight.

'Did they like the motor?' I asked, raising my eyebrows. 'Hope it wasn't too messy inside.'

'Fine,' responded Ruby. 'Actually, a strange fine.'

'What do you mean?' I asked, 'How strange?'

'Well… they didn't say much really. You remember the expression 'shock and awe'… it was rather like that – or at least the look on their mugs was.'

Yeah… who doesn't remember those words?

'But strange how?'

'Like kids in Toys R Us. Not how I expected them to behave.'

But after five minutes Ruby leaned over and whispered in my ear.

'Need to talk… away from this lot.' So we moved off, leaving Matt at the table.

'What's up Rubes?'

'I'm having the same uncomfortable feeling looking at and listening to this lot as Matt and I had when we were talking to those 'coppers' earlier on,' she said. 'The guys, the punters... they are all fine, but something's not right. Haven't you noticed anything... anything strange?'

'Almost like a time warp?' I suggested jokingly.

'Yes!' she responded, without smiling.

'Actually, now you have *me* worried in a vague sort of way... but then I thought it was just me. I, too, have had a kind of suspicion – the whole feeling and set up of this joint, I can't put my finger on it. But you have me thinking now. As a matter of fact, certain conversations, certain responses have just not been *right,* in fact have been unnatural. For instance, that woman over there requested Lionel Hampton; have you ever heard of him?'

'Lionel *who*? No.'

'Well there you go. Pretty certain he's a pre-war bandleader but not one of the usual suspects if you see what I mean. It made me wonder. How come a girl out here is asking for someone like him and not Madonna, Adele or the Sugababes? And they kept going on about the Andrews Sisters. Just give me a few minutes, we'll have a chat later, meanwhile you and Matt better go and be available, relieve Keith and Becks and... *Feeling Good* will be coming up. Ask Keith and Becky to come over as well please, Rubes.' I returned to the table and told Matt to go and join Ruby. I briefly re-engaged with the Americans – wanted to tell them that I was going to re-schedule the music. I made to move away but before I could a couple of Barney's crowd came over.

As we walked back to my hub one of them asked, 'Mr Temple, who was that you played earlier – the trumpet – the band... knocked my socks off – terrific... who was it?'

'That would be Bert Kaempfert... good bouncy orchestral music.' Bert again.

He is popular tonight... and yes, the sound he managed to achieve from his trumpet in *Dreaming the Blues* was out of this world... like it talked to you... in anguish. 'You're Milt, aren't you?'

'Yep.' Milt was watching me as I was messing around with my phone. I put it down. 'What *is* that Mr Temple?' he asked as he picked it up, a quizzical look on his young face.

'That's my...' I had to think quick, 'New recording device. We're giving it a trial. You can talk to it like a phone.'

'Phone? Eh? This… a phone – you serious?' he asked, looking at it. 'How does it work?'

'What do you mean how does it work?' I was just about to launch into an explanation of resistive and capacitive touchscreens and how they operated – my version – when suddenly I decided to shut up. A million thoughts had just caught up with me and were now racing through my brain, especially after what Ruby had said. 'Lads – I'll tell you later but right now I have a couple of things I must do. I'll be back soon, promise. Enjoy the music,' I said, retrieving my gear.

When I joined Keith and Becky I told them of what Ruby had said – and what I'd just been asked about my phone. 'Have you guys noticed anything unusual?' I asked.

'Do you know what? I can see why she said that… I'm wondering myself,' responded Becky and two things came off her lips straight away.

'First, they're mostly young, or look young, compared to what we normally get – which is usually most of them being at least 40, although their clothes make them look older, and second, they also look, well, there are few porkies amongst them, they are all slim, no slobs. Doesn't that strike you as odd compared to what we are used to?'

'Welcome maybe?' I added, raising an eyebrow. 'Actually, you're right – no muffin tops, no huge beer bellies.'

'Like back in the sixties?' said Keith with a chuckle. 'Mind you, they can't all be like me and Becks can they, but you're right. I've been too absorbed in the dancing and hadn't given it much thought – apart from the atmosphere. It *is* different, no two ways,' he added as he cast his eyes around.

I had not only been thinking about this but had also noticed the manner and conduct of the audience – the mood, the body language and individual mannerisms if you see what I mean, the smoking, the dress. Silly me. I'd not seen so much lippo on the girls, nor Brylcreem partings and slick-backed quiffs on the blokes since way back – since watching old black and white movies. Definitely no Kevin Keegans or Rod Stewarts here.

I took a pause… there were now several things that had happened and been said that gave me that cold feeling. The lads were mostly youngsters – twenties at most I'd say, with just a smattering of a more mature element. I was expecting more older folk but when I looked around and looked more closely, I noticed, just as Becky had already said, that apart from the old-style clothes they were wearing for the gig, they were indeed young, looked young, dressed old, a first in all the gigs we'd done. So – I too, along with Keith and Rubes, had a similar feeling of unreality and strangeness.

But seriously… I mean seriously? I had asked Chris Rawlings at the start when we arrived if this was some special dress party or something but no, just another evening dance as far as he was concerned – nothing special and no ticket occasion either.

How dim I am… so wrapped up in the music…

I thought on, and suddenly come over all hot this time – broke into a sweat.

A big penny dropped.

In a flash, I saw things that hitherto had been minor obscurities at the time, drifts of speech, quirks, everybody young, styles, all that smoking – things that should have guided me to the obvious conclusion.

It was the '388' that did it… so wrapped up was I thinking music, groups and bands, and sorting playlists, I never gave the number a second thought. But with everything else that had gone on, it clicked into place. I knew something about the local history. I immediately realised what '388' could actually mean.

It wasn't a pop group – *it was a bomber group*, a US bomber group, based probably at any one of the numerous bases in East Anglia. Then another penny dropped. Christ! Knettishall! Of course – their base – blindingly obvious! But this was bloody daft.

Now I felt queasy… but it explained why the Americans were here.

This *cannot be*, surely. I dashed outside just make sure my wheels were still there.

'Don't be bloody daft, Bob,' I said to myself. However, a simple solution quickly came to me – a simple test that would answer some questions without freaking anybody out, especially the locals. But I wasn't sure whether I – or they – would like the answers! I thought, 'Can't be happening to us… can't be.'

I carefully picked out four 'easy' tracks to play. Not The Pretty Things though – didn't want to frighten the horses just yet, and then brought my troupe together, out of earshot from anybody else.

'We all feel that something's 'off' right?' They nodded. 'Well I might have an idea what might be wrong and what we can do, how we can find out one way or another about what's going on,' I followed. I was really hoping I was wrong in what my imagination was telling me but we would soon find out. I told them about 388 and Knettishall – and what the connection was to our weird observations.

'I didn't want to say anything but I've felt the same – this lot are out of time – out of *my* time. Gives me the creeps,' said Ruby. Matt was nodding. In fact, they all were nodding again.

'Well I'm glad it's not just me then. So, let's try this… for the next track, each one of you take a partner and get into a conversation with them – and not about dancing. Ask them who they like music-wise. At the same time, I'll go round and ask for requests, you know, I'll ask, 'Shall we put on Robbie – or would do you prefer Adele – or Madonna?' See what response I get. Back here in about two or three tracks,' I finished. More nods.

'Good batting Thinkman,' said Keith.

Me

The first group I went to I opened up with, 'I'm Bob – no, not a builder.'

No one batted an eyelid… not a good sign.

'Remember I said earlier, you can make requests so you can make them to me right now if you like. What's your poison? I have over ten thousand songs I can play ranging from Glenn Miller (some nods) to Elvis, Robbie Williams, Queen, Adele, Lady Ga Ga… loads.' Quizzical looks were all I got from the last lot of names. 'Any takers? Got Frank Sinatra too,' I added lamely, now knowing I was fighting a losing battle.

'Ten thousand? Do you have Vera Lynn?' asked one local girl.

'Silly me – of course,' I responded. 'I know the one you mean,'

Yay – I'm now getting resigned to the possibility…

The next group just added to my misgivings. An immediate *yes* was forthcoming when I mentioned jazz and a suggestion for *A String of Pearls,* but no luck with The Spice Girls or Showaddywaddy. I tried one more table, getting a request for Duke Ellington but not a glimmer with the Beatles. When we met up again I already knew what to expect. 'Any luck anybody? Keith?'

Keith

'No. The girl I was dancing with had absolutely no idea what I was talking about when I mentioned *Strictly* nor when I asked her if she liked the Beach Boys. She asked if they were from Skegness or Southend would you believe; I laughed – couldn't help it, really made me chuckle, still chuckle when I think of the Beach Boys and Skegness… imagine Brian Wilson with a '99' cornet… but no, no sign of anything modern from the punters. You got *me* worried now.' He was tipped over the threshold – from a mild concern to, 'I don't like the look of this.'

Becky

Becky piped up, 'My partner was bold enough to ask *me* what *my* favourite music was. When I said that I liked ELO, he actually nodded – then spoilt it all by saying what a great singer she was! I reckon he thought I'd said Ella as in Fitzgerald. But I tried again with Bill Hailey. Nothing. I got Artie Shaw, Benny Goodman and Vera Lynn. I was beginning to lose the will to live. What IS going on guys? It's freaking me out.'

Matt and Rubes

'Like Bob said five minutes ago about Knettishall. And I'm feeling the same,' added Ruby. These people seem to be caught in some sort of time warp. Look at the frocks and hairdos – and the way some of them look at us. Intense looks. It's like The Midwitch Cuckoos.'

'Me too,' said Matt. 'All we need now is The Singing Postman to turn up. But look at them all – at least they obviously like dancing, no two ways.'

'Doesn't the world? Mind you, I don't think anybody comes here for parlour music and they seem to be OK with Doris Day right now.'

'Look – they've come for some fun and entertainment so that's what we're going to give them. What choice do we have anyway?' I added. 'And if you ask me, either *they* are in the wrong time or *we* are in the wrong time. I reckon it's us in the wrong time, I'm sorry to say. How it's happened, haven't a clue. Any ideas…?'

'I'm beginning to think that noise we heard on the way here has something to do with all this – remember that noise?' said Becky. Yes, Keith and I nodded together.

'What noise was that?' asked Matt, 'When?'

Of course – we hadn't told Matt or Ruby about our noise episode...why would we have done so? Anyway, we'd been too busy and they were late. When I recounted the episode, Matt chipped in, 'It's beginning to make sense now – those two coppers... we thought locals were having a laugh... they could have been real coppers – in the right time – and us in the wrong time. And the questions they were asking; no wonder they were all over our bike! It's beginning to make some sense to me now.'

'What questions exactly?' I asked. 'Tell us more.' Matt related what they had been subjected to from start to finish. Silence followed for a few moments. 'So you reckon they were actually real coppers – but from years ago?'

'Well... yes. They didn't behave like the coppers I know. When exactly, I don't know, but judging from the car, I'm guessing thirties or forties.'

'Has to be the forties – judging by the Yanks and those RAF types over there,' Keith added.

Then Becky asked the big question, 'So what year *are* we supposed to be in?'

'Slap bang in the middle of World War Two!' I chimed. 'Like it or not. Come on Becks, you tell us... look at what the girls are wearing... and the dances they are doing... and all that smoking... what year would you guess? Mine is definitely during the war don't you think?'

'You're right... I think the same, all those pullovers, long frocks and hairstyles.'

'This is ridiculous,' said Ruby. 'It might happen to Kirk Douglas but not us!'

'I'll be Kirk,' added Keith trying to lighten the mood. 'And better make sure there aren't any Japanese airmen around. However, seriously, we have to be careful. I've already noticed a few of the locals looking closely at some of our gear and muttering amongst themselves... might think we're spies or something. I have a worry forbode deep in the tumloader,' he added.

'OK – let's just do a bit more dancing while we ponder on a way out of our predicament, should our suspicions be confirmed. I just want to do a double check with Chris Rawlings. I'll be discreet. I won't give anything away.

I spotted Chris then sidled up to him and engaged in idle chat for a while with Albert hovering nearby – eventually talking about this being our first venture out this way. Did he get any trouble from the Americans or fights between them and the 'boys in blue', I asked him?

'No, not really, if there are punch-ups it's usually between the locals – some of the farm hands, maybe from the soldiers as well. But the guys from the bases, when they can, all flock to these dances. You can't blame them for going mad can you,' he added rhetorically. He then went on, 'But since they opened up that new army camp we've had a lot more pongos come here as you can imagine.'

'Army camp? Where – at Wattisham?' I queried.

'No – on the Newmarket road on the edge of town. There're soldiers everywhere these days.'

That would account for a couple of lorries we'd seen on the way in. Little did we know then…

The mention of bases, soldiers and going mad just added to the evidence. He pointed out a few in the crowd who were from Lavenham and a few fighter boys from Raydon. I must admit, I hadn't noticed any other flyers after getting into talk with Barney and his cronies, and Roland of course, just locals. I'd been too busy. Now I did, and could see the effect the uniforms had on the ladies. 'We get them from Rattlesden too which is just down the road.'

I think I had all I needed to know, although I couldn't come right out with the 65,000-dollar question – 'What year is this, what's the date Chris?' could I? Might call the police… or think I was an escapee from the local loony bin.

But I managed to find out by asking one of the Yanks, Joe, how long he'd been playing the sax. He actually volunteered his birthday –

'Started playing since '40, when I was sweet sixteen, although I tinkered before when I was real young. And that's when I started playing with Barney serious like, at school. Hell, here I am at twenty still learning – haven't managed to come far, musically speaking.'

So… 1944. And judging by the weather, similar month as when we set off – April. I told them. It was quite sobering – couldn't quite figure out what we could, should do.

'Better put some tape over the Panasonic logo to hide it… Japanese and all that – was Panasonic around then?' No one was sure, but just in case…

And of course, there was the elephant in the room… if we really were in '44, how the hell do we get back? We had only taken what we thought was a typical, everyday kind of journey to Bury St Edmunds. I could see this question forming in their faces – worried looks too. None of us had kids but we all had homes to go back to – hopefully. So I pitched in.

'We'll go back exactly the way we came. The time will be different but what else can we do? Just as well really if it's dark – they might have a fit if they saw our Range Rover in daylight. It would be like Flash Gordon to them.

Keith piped up, 'Well, the first thing I'd do is go and buy a couple of houses.'

'Eh?'

'I've got nearly five hundred quid on me,' he said with a smirk. 'Might even be able to buy a row of houses or a hotel at '44 prices!'

I suppose we managed a chuckle at this.

'Okay, okay. Let's just play on as if nothing's happened and leave when we have to, making sure we get near Six Mile Bottom before midnight – you know, keep it same day. Just in case,' I added.

'And another thing,' said Keith cutting in, 'We could, in theory, be bombed! I'm trying to remember if this place – this area – was ever targeted. I think it *was* bombed. Let's face it, if you're flying from North Germany or Holland, you'd probably come this way every day, besides, there are nice juicy bases every six inches in East Anglia,' he added.

That shut everybody up for five seconds.

'I knew we shouldn't have come here ever since that motorbike episode,' said Ruby.

'Bombing? Good point Keith; not thought of that. Anyway, we have a rough plan… the *only* plan we have right now,' said Becky. I detected that both she and Rubes were trying to hide the anxiety of the situation on how to get back. In fact for all of us I think our senses couldn't grasp our predicament just yet – in a kind of rebellion against the whole situation.

Matt was quiet, Keith thoughtful for a minute then offered a little light. 'I actually think it will pan out okay in the end as we go back. That's my feeling… it'll all come good.' He looked around and then added, 'We are where we are… and… we're here amongst pretty girls, cheap beer and good music. Life can be *so* cruel,' he finished with a laugh.

That lifted the mood. We had music to play, but then I thought of Grace. A sadness descended upon my mood. My God, I suddenly realised that the girl who had brightened up my evening earlier – she'd be dead in my time surely! Even her daughters would be in their eighties when we got back. This knowledge took the wind out of my sails. I resolved to have another dance with her… or two.

Chapter 16

Barney's table

'...and did any of you guys get to see his watch?' Lou said.

'No, why?' Joe said.

'It was pulsating!'

'What? What are you talking about – how do you mean *pulsating*? Don't be crazy Lou... that's the second hand just going around and around.'

'I'm not. It was kind of like a heartbeat – had like a beat, in the numbers as well as hands. Just have a look next time you're close to him; you'll see I'm right.'

'Sure will,' said Joe.

Barney cut in, 'But Joey, have you seen his stuff – his music gear? This guy's got some serious shit... just look and listen... have you ever seen stuff like that? I mean – just look at that film screen on the wall...how does that work for Chrissake?'

'Probably a projector somewhere?' somebody suggested.

'I dunno – no, I haven't. Where did they get kit like that? Who *are* these guys anyway...?'

'I ain't seen nothing like that,' added Milt, remembering the 'recording' device. 'He just seemed to touch it, moving a picture around like magic. And it was in colour too!' The craftmanship and engineering was beyond anything he had ever seen before – it was almost like a fine piece of jewellery. And don't forget the type writer an' all.'

They talked, bringing into the conversation the car and the motorbike.

'I don't like it Barney,' said someone. Just look what we do and 'hey presto' these limeys show up dressed funny...'

'You mean real cool...'

'Shut up Ricky!' Joe said. 'Then we see him – the old guy – talking to them other sumbitch fly-boys… them RAF fellas over there.'

'Which old guy?'

'Mr Temple old guy. That's who. He looks too old.'

'Oh come on man! You've seen some of the gigs we've been to. All the musicians look as if they've one foot in the grave already – even dressed in their funeral suits looks like… sometimes.'

'You're right there!' Walt said.

'They could be spies.'

That shut them up for a little while, ten seconds maybe.

'No way! Dancing spies dressed up and dancing like a bunch of Fred Astaires?! Who you trying to kid?'

'Hang on buddy… they might dance like him but they sure as hell don't look like him! And what was all that about the Andrews Sisters earlier. He got it all wrong – we didn't seem to connect, did we?'

'Yeah – it don't feel right to me,' added Ginge. 'Something stinks, something's not right. We could ask the boss man, the door man, who they are and where they come from.'

Nods all round.

'Well you might think they're strange but I think Mr Temple is OK,' said Barney, 'They're all OK. Sure – we don't know what these Brits have been getting up to over the last few years; remember, they've been at it a lot longer than we have. And we all know the Brits can be eccentric…mad even.'

He was cut off in mid flow by Lou, 'Eccentric as in old-fashioned I always thought, stuffy, old style. Not like this – not like that gear we saw!'

Nods again.

'But the Brits got some good shit; you know they have. Just look at the Queen Elizabeth liner; most people back home were shocked to find that it wasn't built in America. And we all know about the Spitfire – and that darn bomber that's as fast as the Mustang, the…'

'Mosquito,' chimed in Walter, cutting off Barney.

'Yeah, the Mosquito,' said Barney, a little cross that Walt had stolen his thunder.

More nodding.

'All right. Before we get heavy on this let's go over and talk, dig a little – do some sweet-talking like we did earlier, talk about football…'

'They don't play football over here… they play rugby and also…'

'Eh? Well – whatever they play. Cricket maybe? Motorbikes. Music. We'll soon find out something. We can ask them who made their auto,' said Barney.

'Is cricket a sport…?' Ricky said.

'Do you think their stuff could all be German?' asked Milt. 'The Krauts are boasting that they've got secret weapons and all that.'

'No. From what I saw on his typewriter it was all in English,' Joe said. 'But we could look more closely at the names on his equipment…and… let's start looking more closely at their clothes, their language – what they talk about. All agreed?'

Even more nods.

'Ain't we supposed to be enjoying ourselves tonight? All this creepin' about… pisses me off,' said Ricky to upset the harmony. 'I got my eye on some dames that need workin' on. All this could be a load of hogwash.'

…

Their earnest deliberations had not gone unnoticed. Nor had their sideways glances at me and my troupe. It was my turn to be nervous. My antenna was up and I was now looking out for any suspicious developments. Would we be rumbled and what could we say? What *could* we say?

'Yep – we're from 2012… how do you do…!'

Suppose they went to Chris Rawlings? Or was I just being paranoid, perhaps reading too much into what they might know – what they might be thinking? I shared my thoughts with the others.

'Keep a look out,' I said. 'And watch what you say – don't mention the war as in *Faulty Towers*. I'm already getting curious looks from them over there. They're definitely talking about us,' I said, moving my eyes towards the Americans.

'Have you considered that it might be this place that's out of time and not us?' said Matt. 'Remember the electrics we had to fix, their lighting and furniture. These people here aren't dressed the way they are for any festival – they are dressed the way they are because this is the way they actually dress in 1944!' A moment's pause followed.

'But that makes us out of time, surely.'

A pause… hmm.

'Yes, OK, we've established that somebody's out of time but I think it's us, not them,' I responded.

'Why so?' asked Becky.

'Because of the sat navs – no signal.'

'Oh Christ! Of course… and why there was no phone signal.'

'Sorry folks… it looks like it's us,' I added sombrely. 'Anyway, and for the moment we still have a job to do so back on your heads. I'll get some more requests in… but think up some plans too will you.'

'Well, when I get back I'm going straight down to the phone shop to complain,' said Keith.

'What do you mean, complain about what?' asked Becky.

'I'll tell them that my phone doesn't work in 1944 – and what are they going to do about it?!'

I knew that was coming.

'Good luck with that,' said Ruby, cuffing him round the back of his head, 'And what if he asks – 'how do you know it doesn't work in 1944…?''

'I'll think of something…'

I made the announcement for more requests with a suspicion about knowing what I might expect. I kept my eye out for Grace and her two daughters, hoping they'd pluck up the courage and come and see us – see me, but it wasn't to be, at least, not straight away.

The punters came up with a fair number of tunes – all of which we knew of, but difficult to find quickly in my collection. Some were complete blanks but we had requests for *A String of Pearls, Kalamazoo, That Old Black Magic, Jersey Bounce* by Benny Goodman, and a few others including *White Christmas* by Bing, to which I had to say, 'Sorry love, wrong time of year for that.'

It's still selling. Even today.

Amazing.

And yes, I could also source both Harry James and Tommy James and his Orchestra. I wonder if they were related, I mused? Don't think so. But Tommy Dorsey and Jimmy Dorsey were – we had a couple of requests for *Opus One* by Tommy, a nice slow smoochy number. Tommy Dorsey was RCA's greatest seller – until the king arrived... Elvis. But hold on... there can only be one king, so what gives?

It was all down to the so-called jazz royalty genre from before the war, a term encompassing the many great jazz musicians who assumed these aristocratic titles – The *King* of Swing, *Count* Basie, *Earl* Hines, The *Duke*. There was even a lowly baron. Poor bloke.

I also had, from what looked like a friend of Chris Rawlings, a request for *Stardust* by the great Artie Shaw so we had enough of the old stuff to keep us going, take our mind off things.

Without success, I have to admit... 1944 and all that.

But, unexpectedly, we also had requests for what was obviously modern music we had played earlier, of which they had no idea of what they were called.

'So what did it sound like?' I asked this geezer who'd made a request. I was scanning my list.

'It was very slow with a man singing and a lot of other singers – like a choir,' said geezer. 'My Bessie liked it... a nice slow song.' My thoughts went to *I'm Not in Love* but a quick look told me it was probably *Nights in White Satin*.

'Could it be like *Nights in White...*'

'That's the one! I remember those words he sung,' he interrupted. 'Would you play that one again please?'

'Of course.' He just wants another tight clinch with his bird. I'm good aren't I – keeping them happy.

Off he toddled, a happy customer. A good schmooze is a good schmooze no matter what year it is. I had to chuckle though when I saw where he went – she was ten feet tall, he was about five feet... his face would have been firmly embedded in her 'Bristols' during the dance.

The other request was for, 'That bouncy tune you played.'

'Man or woman singing?' I queried.

'Oh, no one, but there was a trumpet in it?' he asked hopefully.

I scrolled down – Bert Kaempfert... again, 'Is this it?' I asked as I handed him the phone and hit 'play'. At first, he was unsure what I was saying so I plonked a headphone up against one of his ears. It took a few seconds for it to sink in then his eyes lit up.

'Yes! That's the one.'

'In five minutes... and it's called *Melina*, by...,' I hesitated a moment before saying, '...one of my favourites.' Bert at his best, well almost because I already had another one up my sleeve, *Dreaming the Blues* was lined up, ready to go (again). Off he went too, another happy customer. Just to keep in vein with the prevalent tastes I also decided to put on a track from a film – a track called *Now You Have Jazz* from *High Society* featuring Bing and Satchmo, a Cole Porter song from 1956.

I spoke to Matt and Ruby and told them what was in the pipeline and what dances they might do.

'Good choice. That'll go down well along with the others,' said Matt.

'And see that couple over there...' I pointed, '...they look as though they need a hand with the moves. Can you sort them out?' You could tell quickly who could, and could not dance – who was struggling. And I was struggling with locating some of them old black magic tunes I'd been asked about.

I had it all mapped out an hour ago.

'Sure,' answered Matt.

'Keith, Becks,' I called them over. 'I've rehashed the tunes.' I showed them the new line up.

I was back on the mike making another announcement. 'Two real energetic numbers for you to work off some of that beer, then I'm going to play three songs you've never heard before... you'll love them, just listen, get on the floor and you can really melt into your partner's arms and have a breather. I did play them earlier.' These I lined up:

I'm Not in Love

To Know Him is to Love Him.

At Last

Years ago, I had literally clung onto my dance partner for dear life with these tracks at the end of a hard night's drinking... a saviour, especially *To Know Him Is to Love Him* by the Teddy Bears, always popular.

Then a little later…

'Ladies and gents… and are you listening Barney? …the first two… two tunes with the same title but by different artists – *In the Mood.* Check them out – one by some bloke called Glenn Miller and the other by an unheard-of group of lads, so here we go… let me know if you like both versions… especially you Barney! Keith – you and Becks do the modern one… give it the works?'

'Okay.'

Might keep Barney's crowd occupied for a while.

The group was The Alligators. No – me neither, but believed to be Dutch/Indonesian. A great rendition nonetheless, especially if you're into electric guitars – nothing brilliant technically, just a nice flow.

Sure enough, straight after The Alligators had finished both Barney and Joe were at my mixer.

'That was the electric guitar version wasn't it Mr Temple – terrific…that's what I want to do with my own guitar man. Who played that? Who was it? Where are you getting these new-fangled guitar records from Mr Temple?'

'Yep – it is a bit different from the usual bouncy, orchestral music; I'll come over and fill you in later.'

They had no idea…!

But after playing *Ladybird* I was confronted by a young bloke who asked who was singing – it is an old record and perhaps not up there with the Beatles and the Stones but we always found it popular… and for this crowd, probably just the ticket.

'Nancy Sinatra and Lee Hazelwood,' I answered. Wouldn't do any harm telling them – they're not going to know are they.

'Can you play it again please?' he asked. 'My girl liked it too.'

Perhaps I should be called 'Sam'.

Another one that went down very well, brought some questions and further requests, was *Stand By Me.* A great song and a great tune.

Yes… one of the best.

'What are we going to say to them?' I asked Keith. 'And just in case, we'd better make sure we have no incriminating evidence on us or on any of our kit.' We'd already taken some initial steps with bits of masking tape and pen-markers. 'Good job my laptop's not a 'Tosh' or a Sony,' I added.

'Dunno. Perhaps we should do a runner. Maybe not, but who do you think out of that lot we've met, would you consider not to throw a wobbly, or lose it, if we told them? I'm sure some of them are looking at us already and thinking there's something odd about us.'

'Yes, you're right, I've sensed it too.'

'Maybe we should try and find out who might be the 'sympathetic ears' and work on them… they obviously know that we're not the run-of-the-mill music troupe and that we are different somehow… and then take them into our confidence – if, and only if, it looks like someone's going to spill the beans. Otherwise we just say shtum 'til we have to leave. Just imagine,' and this is where Keith's imagination often came into play, '…it would be a surprise to get a cheque in the post when we get back – from 1944 – if we left in a hurry!'

'Nearly seventy years? Not bad, the post will have improved then.' Becky – her turn to joke.

'They don't know who we are or where we came from do they? Certainly not from Ipswich.'

'True. Shall we discuss this with the others? I need a drink!' Keith picked up his 'flask' and took a swig.

'Me too – and yes we should. But before we do, I want a dance with that nice lady over there…' I'd planned *Love Me Tender* for this dance I told Becky.

'The lady with the two daughters? Thought you might. I wonder what all the rest of the girls here actually do during the day? Today it would be check-outs in some mega-store but in '44 probably all in small shops – like shoe-shops, tailors, grocers and butchers, shops that that have largely disappeared from the high street.

'They could all be back on the till in one hour…'

…

121

I was back with the Americans, being friendly like and as unsuspicious as possible, hopefully more transparent, trying to keep their minds away from us and steering them towards the women, music and dancing. We had to tread a fine line as we didn't want to create any alarm or direct any unnecessary vigilance our way. An air of genial friendliness was required. But aren't I always…? In any case, our guard was up, and I was going to keep the focus on music when I chatted with the audience – in particular the Americans.

"Barney – Joe, as you guys are just as interested in music as well as scoring, I'll put something together for you shortly to listen to separately – music I just know won't disappoint you, music featuring some of the instruments you play. It won't take me long and you can listen with these,' I said, pointing at a set of buds. "Is that okay?"

'Hey man – it'll be chicks every time, no contest but…' Walt trailed off.

"Sure is, mad on music and chicks, eh Joe?' Joe nodded. "Like I said earlier, we used to play together before we joined up… guitar, sax." Barney continued. "What are these…?"

'Ear buds… one in each ear – not yet,' I replied. "But first let me ask you fellas about the music scene --- and what gets your attention.'

'Sure,' they all nodded, expectantly. I noticed that their attitude had changed slightly.

I marshalled my thoughts, trying to map in my head an order of things before talking… difficult. 'If I asked you guys right now who were your favourites today, what would you say? You're obviously closer to the jazz scene than me… I'm into the more novel, new stuff as you've probably realised by now. What tunes – what's your poison music wise?" I continued. As expected, Duke Ellington, Benny Goodman, Tommy Dorsey and Glenn Miller all figured.

'Well I guess *American Patrol* is one of my favourites – and *In the Mood*,' said Barney.

'That's Glenn Miller, right?'

'Right.'

'Joe…?'

'*Old Black Magic*, I reckon is one of my favourites as is *St Louis Blues*, and of course, I like just about anything with Louis Jordan in it – and Sidney Bechet,' said Joe.

'Louis Jordan? Who was he?' I asked.

'Saxophone, that's who... both.'

'I've got lots of good sax for you then – for later. I'll let you know when I do.'

'Like *Baker Street*... or Eta James and *Walk on the Wild Side*,' chipped in Keith. I nodded.

'What about you Milt, Walt? How about Ella or Frank Sinatra, do you like them?' I pressed.

'Who is Ella? Sinatra's the new dude ain't he,' said Milt. 'Yeah, he's OK. I like him. Good voice. He can hold a note.'

'He sang for Tommy Dorsey, right?' ventured Keith.

'Yeah, he did. Buddy Rich was also there. Great band.'

'Like Barney and Joe, I'm more into the jazzy side... with swing, you know – that's why I like the drums,' said Walt. 'I ain't into the singing too much... prefer faster stuff like that Bugle Boy you played earlier.'

'By the Andrews Sisters?' I let it slide this time.

'Yeah, like them.'

I must play them *Stranger on the Shore*... sure they'd like it.

They had some real knowledge on the old music scene of that era as you'd expect, which we were finding absolutely engrossing, particularly the early twenties music from the South and New Orleans which came about to satisfy a thirst for fun and dancing.

You see? Dancing has always been popular.

Guys like Paul Whiteman was, said Barney, 'The King of Jazz', (the other king) but it needed an infusion of some *indiscipline* – and needed black music too. Artists like Satchmo, Jerry Roy Morton and Fletcher Henderson provided it in the twenties. It was not refined; it was basic. My dad – who was also into jazz – told me that New Orleans 'ragtime' was probably the first kind of music that invoked the generation gap – with Benny Goodman and swing. The swing era went global.

'That's why I like The Duke,' added Barney. 'He somehow mixed them together; he brought the styles together. I love it... great music. *We* all love it. Things are changing man. Barney's version of our sixties I suppose. And we thought we were the first...

123

'Well we've all heard of Louis Armstrong, but never heard of the others,' I said. 'So, *what* about the jazz side of things?'

'Like you, swing jazz for me,' said Barney. They all nodded. Yeah, swing... to almost pinch an expression – 'Swing is in the *ear* of the beholder'. He went on describing how early jazz probably sprang from several places almost at once but that Harlem was what he remembered. 'Black swing' followed on from dances like the Charleston which developed into the Lindy hop.

'That's what I thought but wasn't sure,' I said. Barney went on and said that some swing era musicians had found that there was a call for more energetic music which became known as rhythm and blues.

Keith and I were beginning to get lost. 'Sounds complicated. I can never remember what *did* come first – and what followed what,' said Keith innocently. 'But like you, I do like the guitar.'

All we knew from where we were standing was that the old bouncy, brassy, orchestral stuff morphed into foot-tapping, finger-clicking music that grew into rock 'n' roll and eventually pop... and that was probably down to the guitar – the *electric* guitar, but we couldn't tell them about rock 'n' roll could we now.

'Hooray! You're my guy. Keith.'

'Glad to hear it.'

'I'm with you on that one too,' I chipped in. 'And we've got some treats for you too on guitars later.'

'We have to hear this,' said Barney excited. I was getting excited too, to tell you the truth; I just had to figure out a good selection.

I was taking a mental note of who, out of this bunch, you could take aside and confide in. So far Joe and Walter seemed the more quiet but savvy fellows with a measured but friendly manner. Barney was the obvious leader, an extrovert with a drive and very engaging, pleasing aura about him, no doubt extremely devastating with the opposite sex. I'd pick these three if I had to. The others were just, so far, nice, polite guys.

'Tell you what I'll do now that I know what you like; Keith and I'll download some great tracks with guitar, drums, sax – you name it; oh, and some just great tunes that'll blow your cotton socks off – including some electronic stuff. It'll all be swing, beat and magic.'

'Electronics...? I like the sound of that,' said Milt in a drawl. 'Must hear this for sure.'

I leaned across and whispered, 'Keith... would these people know about Doris Day?' I couldn't quite remember when she started her career but knew she was getting on a bit these days.

'Probably not... I reckon they are just before her time. They'd know about Frank Sinatra and Bing Crosby though... evidently.'

Chapter 17

The 'happy' couple

I was spooling up an old record when I casually glanced around the hall to see how many were on the floor. Matt and Ruby had just finished a routine and were sitting down for a breather. Both Keith and Becky were instructing local partners on the rumba with *Cry For Me* when I spotted a couple at the doorway: new faces. Must be chucking-out time I thought – or shift workers. They looked momentarily lost, hesitating and looking in all directions, probably for a friendly face.

Thought I'd give them a hand…

I was on the mic.

'I can see we have two newcomers… step inside love, come on over here. Say 'hello', everybody, to our latecomers,' I said as I motioned with my arm for them to come my way. A lame 'hello' rose from the floor as they all turned to view the new arrivals. The couple looked up, a little perplexed but, seeing me beckoning, they hesitantly moved in my direction while still looking around. She began talking animatedly to her consort.

I adjusted the volume as they approached.

'Hello. Who do we have here?' I asked them. 'My name is Bob Temple,' I said as I leaned towards them.

'Hello,' said the young man.

'Hello,' followed the young woman. She looked, I don't know – not cheerful?

A pause… shy maybe.

'You have names?' I invited with a smile.

'Oh… Wilf,' he responded. 'This is Mavis.' He was tall and had neat features, a slightly florid countenance around the cheeks, with a pleasant

126

smile and a lively keenness in his dark eyes. But his companion, medium height and well-shaped, on closer inspection had a look of what I could only describe as annoyance written on her face – no sign of a smile anywhere; perhaps they'd just had an argument, but she was unfortunate in that her mouth turned down at the ends making her look... well...miserable. Neither looked jovial nor exuded warmth, nor was there any acknowledgement in my direction, in fact she appeared to be looking intently at a handbag nearby, probably Ruby's, perched on the chair. Then finally a curt nod when he nudged her.

What is it with handbags and women, I asked myself?

'All right... just to bring you up to speed...' I gave them the 'gen' on what was going on and that they could request music – just come and ask, or come and ask for some dancing tips. 'So, what does Mavis do if you don't mind me asking?' I said, being polite.

'Post Office,' she answered. Still no smile, not a flicker of softness, just a stern picture where only her lips moved.

Yep, must have had an argument with her other half or something...sullen bitch. Poor Wilf. I could think of another name other than 'Mavis' – perhaps 'Grumpina' or something like that. I wondered if she was a distant relative of Dennis the Menace. She had that look about her.

'And you Wilf? What do you...' I broke off as I could see out of the corner of my eye Ruby gesticulating with her hands trying to silently attract my attention while shaking her head at the same time.

'Excuse me for a moment,' I said to the happy couple as I turned away. I moved over to Ruby who had turned her back and leaned in close. 'What's up?' I could see she was worried about something.

'Bob,' she said, keeping her voice down, 'I think he's one of the policemen Matt and I encountered earlier. That's why I'm facing this way – away from them. I'm sure it's him – not the sergeant but his young companion. As soon as I spotted him as they came down the side, I knew who it was – made my blood run cold.' I gently put my hand on her arm.

'Leave it to me. I'll check – we'll soon find out.' I moved back.

'Sorry. Where were we? Ah yes, so Wilf, what is it you do?'

'I'm a policeman,' he said proudly. So that settled that.

'On the beat – or do you get to drive a lot?' I remembered about the car.

'Oh yes, I drive,' he responded, looking pleased with himself. Still no smile from the Miss Misery.

'And what cars do you drive?' Please don't say 'police cars', I thought.

'Mostly Wolseleys, with the Guv'nor of course.' More proof.

'Where are you based – or where do you live?' I pressed.

'Ixworth.' Ixworth… just down the road.

'Go get a drink first if you like – park your bums somewhere and come back for a request any time.'

What a sour aura she had; no, not even ten pints would do it for me, even though she did have a cracking figure from where I was standing. There *are* people who have an aversion to the lighter side of life – and she was a definite candidate. Poor Wilf… she must be good in bed that's all I could think, but I could see why she had nabbed someone like him, someone in authority and no doubt with a reasonable income and probably a job for life.

Unlike in *our* time.

After they'd moved off both Ruth and Matt came over, she'd just told Matt about it.

'Yes,' he said, 'I'm pretty sure that that's him as Ruth says. So now what do we do? Mind you, they only saw us with all the kit on, the leathers, gloves…'

'Helmets…?' I butted in.

Ruth gave a quick grimace. 'We took them off for a breather, and before things became a little spooky, so he would have seen our faces – but not for long.'

'Ah, so they may, or may not 'make you' but who could forget a face like yours?' I said, attempting to cheer her up a little. 'And I suppose with all the sequins, tassels, and your chest rug and purple trousers Matt, they might not make the connection. It's a good job you had that scrap *before* they turned up. Do we have any routines where you could wear masks… anything like that? Perhaps all you need to ensure they don't recognise you is a bright green Mohican wig.'

'Might have one actually – but not here. We'll have a think. Let's hope they don't pop out through the wrong door and see our bike. He was drooling all over it earlier – now we know why, probably made them suspicious. Even if he doesn't see us but sees the bike, he'll come looking.

I think I'll try and cover it up. Tell you what – there's a loose cover in the back of the Rover… I'll cover up the Triumph with it.'

'Good idea… sensible,' I nodded.

We told the other two.

'We'll just have to keep our eyes on them but we can't suddenly not dance or hide away.' We decided to bring Keith and Becky more into the spotlight and relegate Matt and Ruby to only occasional dances.

I watched as Wilf and sour-face moved over to another group, falling into conversation with them, one of them being my previous acquaintance with the ear stud.

'Oh great,' I muttered quietly. That's all we need, Dennis the Menace's sister and 'weird guy' together – with a policeman… and they were talking with a readiness that argued a good acquaintance. Perhaps they all deserve each other.

'Let's hope the sergeant doesn't like dancing and pop in as well!' added Matt, trying to lighten the mood a little.

...

'Mr Rawlings!' called Barney. 'Can we have a talk?' Joe was with him.

'Yes of course. What is it?'

'Can we talk in there?' said Barney, indicating a door he'd seen Rawlings use a few times. Together they ambled over, Rawlings opening the door and beckoning them inside. Rawlings lit up a Woodbines.

Barney was hesitant before launching into the topic, looking at Joe for moral support.

Chris Rawlings detected the nervousness in these young lads and was wondering what on earth they were going to ask. Was there going to be another fight? Were they about to be busted by the MPs – the Military Police? Or were they about to make an offer on some shady deal? The Yanks had a reputation for using everyday goods which they seemed to have almost in abundance – but currently in short supply to the British – as a currency for luxury goods and favours. He'd been offered 'goods' before for free entry, or for getting lads fixed up with certain ladies. Fags, stockings, chocolate and other foodstuffs were always very attractive items, high on anybody's list of want. But Chris Rawlings kept a clean ship… he didn't want to be raided.

He needn't have worried. It was none of this, but the Americans' questions took him by surprise – initially.

'Chris – where do these music guys come from? Who are they?'

'Eh?' Rawlings looked at them. He was not prepared for this unusual question. 'They're from Bedford way I believe they said. Why do you ask?'

'Don't you find them a little strange, man? They look out of place. They *are* British aren't they… they're so different to the usual bands we get and we've seen a few haven't we Joe?' Joe nodded.

Joe then said, 'The guys are suspicious. The music they're playing is… I dunno – brash, weird, noisy, stuff we ain't heard ever, apart from some tunes…' he petered out.

'And we and the boys don't know nothing like their music machines they have Chris, like that typewriter with pictures. What is that? And that little gadget he carries about with him?' added Barney.

Rawlings held up his hand – a signal for a pause. He had to admit that although he himself was not a gadget man he too had not seen what the 'music boys' were using before and had been intrigued with their set-up. He just put that down to the music world and the arty types who always seemed to be able to lay their hands on all sorts of equipment.

'One thing I've learnt these last few years is not to ask too many questions. But actually, I don't really know anything about them – they just turned up more or less at the appointed time and seemed to know what they were to do…' he trailed off.

Rawlings thought back – those plugs they were wiring up after they arrived, and some of the idle comments made that sounded strange to him, and truth be known, he'd been surprised that Mr Temple had no musical instruments, just some peculiar record players and equipment that he fiddled with, somehow connected to the film screen. And how *did* the coloured lights work in unison with the music?

'Do you know – you have me thinking… but what's worrying you, again, why do you ask? They play music and that's what you've come for… no?'

Again, Barney and Joe looked at each other.

'Chris – they could be damn spies. That's what me and the guys are thinking, no kidding,' said Barney.

'Spies! Really?' This would be a serious matter. There was no doubting how different Mr Temple's group was – how different their clothes and mannerisms were. 'But one moment... they themselves are not actually suspicious are they – straightforward, pleasant, doing what they came to do, no dark furtive looks... no sneaking around.'

'But just look at their sedan, it looks like something out of Flash Gordon,' suggested Joe. 'Who makes autos like that Mr Rawlings?'

Mr Rawlings thought back. It was indeed a strange-looking vehicle, not the usual black colour; all cars were black, weren't they? Unless you were a millionaire. Not this one... this one looked silver grey but he didn't see its inside.

'And the bike. You ever see anything like their bike?'

'No, I haven't seen a bike. Where is it?'

They moved outside to take a look. What Rawlings saw was a thing of sheer beauty. He couldn't take his eyes off it. He knew what was new and what was old, but this – sleek wasn't the word. It positively gleamed and oozed in sheer good looks.

'Good God!' he exclaimed. 'So you think Mr Temple's lot are not what we think they are?' he said without taking his eyes from the machine. Apart from the wheels, he hardly recognised anything on it. Eventually he said, 'Look, go back inside and just carry on as normal. I'll get Albert to go around to the defence post. It's a good job he lives round here because it's bloody dark – no bloody lights, might take a little while. In the meantime, I'll try and get my boss on the blower. OK? Don't say anything or do anything to create alarm – and we don't want them alerted, do we, so just be normal.'

'But our buddies also think something's up – they know we've come to talk to you. They'll want to know what's happening too. We already told them, Mr Temple that is, where we're from... you know, our base.'

'Alright, bring your friends in on it but otherwise keep quiet – no blabbermouths. I shall not be doing anything rash – will just be playing along a while, watching.'

'Got it boss, mum's the word,' said Joe.

Their little sojourn away from the floor had not gone unnoticed.

...

I had been keeping my eye out, watching events.

'Keith, something's up. The Yanks and Chris Rawlings have just had a quiet chat in that room over there, and I reckon it wasn't about the weather. They also went outside, not sure why.' Events had been moving along – quick sideways glances, murmurings, close huddles – and I didn't like the little group that had formed with weird guy, Grumpina and our friendly copper.

We had a quick discussion on how to divert, or close down any suspicions the locals might have about us and *who* we thought we could approach to do this. It was agreed that if we had to, we would somehow take Barney, Joe and Walt to one side, and trust that we could contain the situation with the help of the three Yanks if we took them into our confidence. It might freak them out but we had considered the fact – brutal though it was – that these airmen were probably not going to last the war's duration and therefore the secret would automatically be taken care of. But it would certainly put a spring in their step, if we had to tell them who was going to win the war!

'We could make an excuse about wanting to fix something that was playing up in our kit, ask to have the use of a room to do it. We could even use the excuse, should anyone ask, that we knew Barney was into gadgets and have him join us for a 'look see'. Sounds good?' I offered.

'So, who's going to tell them?' asked Matt. I could see the same question in the eyes of the others.

'Me – and you two,' I answered, looking at Matt and Ruby. 'This will keep you both out of sight for a while from the copper while Keith and Becky can keep the ball rolling... 'scuse the pun. But we don't have to do anything drastic yet – no one has made a move so we're still safe for now, although we might have to make a quick exit.' We were originally booked until midnight with Andy Baxter but when I casually asked Chris Rawlings earlier, following the non-show of Mr Briggs, it was for 11pm – local rules or something, and we weren't going to hang around for payment!

'Christ! I'd love to be there when they're told. It's not often you get to tell someone that you are from the future!' said Keith, Becky nodding in agreement. They were all nodding.

I had to admit, 'Good point... yeah, you're right. Tell you what, I have a plan – and we'll all be there at some point. Could be a long conversation but as I've said, we are still alright for now and the show needs to go on. We don't want to precipitate a full-blown disaster.'

The plan... we changed our minds just a little bit about the tale we were to tell, and all agreed.

We had a quick discussion on tactics – we'd tell them the basic story and then Keith would pop out to keep things going in the hall.

Chapter 18

Our tall story

We corralled the three Yanks into the room on an agreed pretext....

'Barney... Joe, Walt – we felt we had to share something with you; we are quite aware that you and your boys are viewing us with some interest – perhaps with some suspicion. Am I right?' I asked on our behalf.

This opening took them by surprise.

Walt eventually started off, 'Yeah man. You guys aren't straight are you – you ain't normal people... ain't behaving or dancing like normal people or playing straight music... and your gear – where's it from? How does it all work? Not saying that there's no *good* music – just we ain't familiar with it. Our buddies are saying the same thing.'

All those *ain'ts*

'Straight?' I asked.

'Yeah – regular guys, you know, not dressing weird... you all look strange,' added Joe.

'That's because we're show dancers – well my dancers are – so we're bound to have fancy costume, but anyway, we want to tell you *really* why we 'ain't normal' as you call us,' I said to them.

I could see how we presented ourselves might draw comments – we sometimes get comments back in normal times, whenever that is!

'Well, here goes... we are from a new Technology and Arts academy that was set up shortly after the outbreak of the war, just north of London. It actually started off for entertainment reasons to boost the morale of both troops and civilians, headed by a guy who likes to keep out of the spotlight.'

Another pun... sorry.

'But purely by an accidental breakthrough in electronics, whilst trying to produce certain effects in sound and visual displays, the academy refocused the efforts of the team, set up by this... entrepreneur tyrant, for want of better word – a very rich, forward-thinking, no-nonsense man who had made his 'pot' before the war.'

I was reminded of Elon Musk today.

'His team were – are – eccentrics, weirdos, dabblers, radio hams, musicians, odd-ball mechanics and the like, plus some dodgy characters who, in retrospect, would normally be in gaol. But the bottom line was that they were all gifted in various ways in the arts and, importantly, in technical matters. The Chief – that's what we all call him, vetted them all at the beginning. His word was law. At first, he would brook absolutely no interference by anybody from outside – from the government or Ministries and especially the War Office. But word got out so, in order to pacify these people who always want a finger in every pie and like to control events, he offered them a glimpse just to keep them off his back – only a glimpse mind – of a small flat film display. This impressed them like hell and as they hadn't a clue how it was done, could not risk interfering. Then he told the men of the Ministry to go away – or he'd walk off. They promised to leave him alone.'

I could see we had their rapt attention.

''Just look at radar,' he had said to them. 'We could have had that a great deal quicker without the meddling,' and he threatened to shut shop if they asked too many questions. So, the academy was given free reign – mostly because the war, by then, was going fine and no one wanted to upset the applecart or ask for new funding.'

We all remembered about Sir Frank Whittle and how he was initially turned down with his jet engine... by Rolls Royce! Although these guys wouldn't know about that saga... yet. But they were all nodding vigorously – we were making progress. With officialdom, there was always that feeling to the layman, or 'average Joe', that *authority* was constantly against you – as Frank Whittle found out.

I continued...

'One breakthrough led to another... and another, that's what you see with us out there including, to some extent, the music we've played this evening. Even what we wear, and we'll show you some new free dances too that we've come up with. The development of better tapes – magnetic tape – and electronics enabled us to do strange things with music such as producing echo, and we've put it to use as you've heard. As for the car and bike outside – they are only prototypes because we didn't just stop with the arts... although you must admit, they 'look the business' don't they? We dabbled in mechanical design too. Everything under the skin on those vehicles we showed you is actually a bog-standard, current piece of equipment and chassis – but with the academy's designs covering them, a sheep with wolf's clothing... sort of. Conceptual.'

What a load of crap we were spouting! But yes, I could see we still had their attention – the ploy was still working.

'Does that answer any thoughts you may have had about the guitar music Barney, and all that other stuff?' He was momentarily lost for words.

'Gee Mr Temple...' he began.

'We *are* regular guys – and everyone loves entertainment and music; the whole world loves a good tune don't they... rhythm, pitch, lyrics, even a social context... music brings people together, right? And yes, we know, a lot of it can be crap too.'

'You betcha!' said Barney.

I carried on.

'With the music, we concentrated on small groups of musicians, no more than five men – cheaper and easier to control and move about than large orchestras. That's why, apart from a few exceptions, there are no big bands, the logistics were just easier. As for the guitar playing... this came about because, as you've pointed out, they make a lot of noise and something else you'll find – they pull the birds too.'

'Pull the birds...?

I could see the quizzical look on their faces. 'The chicks, the dames.' It sunk in.

'Ah – got you man,' said Joe and Barney, smiling in unison.

Matt cut in.

'And because all the young Brits were getting conscripted and others were doing essential war work, the Chief brought in some American talent – musicians and technicians – as they were not in the war at this stage. He just threw money at them, so they took the risk and came across. Not all were immune to conscription and industry but the Chief only had to show an enticing glimpse of what they were doing from time to time to keep his team largely unmolested.'

Matt was on message. A brief pause followed.

Then Joe joined in, 'How come we've not seen this before at other places and dances we've been to, with other bands?'

'Because this is the first time we've been over this way – all the bases are on this side of the country, and the other bands won't have this gear. There's only us working for the Chief with this kind of kit, and this is part of a 'field test' you might say, dancing and all,' said Matt.

'And it's the reason you didn't get Fred Briggs,' I added. I was wondering how long they would buy this, but so far so good. 'Even Rawlings doesn't know.'

'Anyway boys, we have a busy schedule and more music to play. We can meet up again later and talk some more if you like,' I suggested. 'I can put together plenty of 'new' guitar and sax stuff – and plenty of jitter-bugging tracks. I'll make sure I give you notice... and why don't you team up with Ruby and Becky; they'll put you right, I promise.'

Sweet smiles from the ladies.

'Cool, man,' answered Barney with a big grin. 'We have to hear this stuff don't we Joe, Walter?'

'So, when you get back please make sure that you pass the message around your guys OK? We'd appreciate, too, if you'd keep what we've told you, quiet – apart from your buddies of course... we wanna keep it low-key for a little longer.'

'Sure boss,' said Joe. Barney looked eager. Walt just nodded, saying nothing.

We wondered how long that secret would last. 'As long as it's for tonight I don't care,' said Ruby afterwards, 'We'll be gone by then – I hope!' We were thinking the same.

But it's true isn't it – partially, about the entertainment and communications industry? The 'go to' film studios for hi-tech films and special effects sought out by Hollywood these days are in the UK studios. The entertainment industry is now driving much of the Gucci developments we see today.

And reader… you didn't really think we were going to tell them that we were from the future did you…? Ha!

…Oh, and just a brief moment of your time – a comment on the Magnetic Tape.

This really enabled high-quality recordings to be made so that everything did not have to be 'live' on the radio as it used to be.

I didn't know that.

A German invention, discovered by an American officer searching a recording studio in Germany at the end of the war. He took it back, no doubt along with other Gucci bits of German kit such as the V2 rocket. The Yanks developed the Ampex tape machine and – with the help of Bing Crosby – changed the way music was recorded. Just look at – listen to – *The Wall of Sound* presentation by Phil Spectre for instance with *Da Do Ron Ron* by the Crystals. Just a snippet. Know who the lead singer was…? La La Brooks. Didn't know that either… must have been a lively Christening.

Just sayin'.

As for 'Ampex' – named after a Russian engineer in California. Alexander **M P**onietoff **Ex**cellence. Simples.

Bob, get back to the story.

Everything appeared to be ticking along nicely as we emerged and on the way back to our music post I looked at Keith and Becky and said, 'They might have swallowed all that crap for now but I wonder how long it will be before they really twig – or someone else does?'

'And you said it all with such a straight face too. Just another three hours – that's all we need. Actually, we could leave early,' suggested Becky.

It was agreed we may have reduced, at least for the Yanks, the atmosphere of suspicion. For a while.

···

Barney and his crowd were around their table giving them all the news about the talk. More sideways looks.

'You telling me this lot come from some 'advanced college' or something? I know magic when I see it and what I saw on his gizmo gadget he carries around all the time was magic – sommat special.'

'Well yes, of course it would be advanced – who knows what the 'backroom boys' are up to these days,' said Joe. 'Remember, these Brits have been at it for a hell of a lot longer than us so maybe they've had time to do this smart stuff. Actually makes me jealous.'

'Me too,' added Barney.

'Sounds like a tall story to me,' said Lou. Walt nodded in agreement.

'And I don't care,' said Ricky. 'Let's just enjoy ourselves – that's what we came here to do, guys. Just be careful, is all.'

'Yeah, I'll go along with that. And anyway, they did promise us some new music – guitar music,' Barney said.

'You an' your guitar. You still got your little gizmo you made?' asked Ginge.

'Yep – safely tucked away back at base.' Barney kept it locked up. The only time he took it anywhere was occasionally to fiddle with it in the workshop if there was no flying and no jam sessions… and he *always* took it with him on missions, no matter what. It was now small enough to be hidden in his gear… he didn't want anybody else laying hands on it if anything happened to the crew, made PoWs or something. 'But let's speak to Mr Rawlings and tell him we're okay with Mr Temple now – that he's explained the odd things. In fact, it might be a good idea if they told him what they told us. Like you say Rick, we'll enjoy ourselves but not be reckless.'

'I still reckon things ain't right,' Lou grumbled.

'Still not 100% convinced,' added Walt, nodding with Lou.

'Let's go and talk.'

'Really?' said Rawlings on hearing what the Americans had to say. 'So, you are no longer worried about them? Just as well, I can't raise anybody – but Albert's already gone to the comms post, not a lot I can do. If he comes back with anyone then I'll inform them that it was a mistake… but they take these things seriously you know. They may still want to talk to you.'

'Yeah, sorry Mr Rawlings. Why don't you go and see them – let them tell you themselves what they told us.'

'Yes – maybe I will when I get the chance.'

Chapter 19

Bliss

I was hoping that Grace had not departed as she'd hinted earlier so I looked around for her. She was nowhere to be seen. Nonetheless I cued up Elvis in readiness, but I must admit my heart fell. Grace had got to me. I wondered what she did, what work she was employed in; women were doing all sorts of work with all sorts of skills while the men were 'away'. They were building bombers, fighters, tanks – and the rest of the whole gamut of war materiel. Women could turn out a Wellington bomber over the weekend... amazing!

It had quickly become evident after the outbreak of hostilities that the typical worker in the war industries was going to change from 'Mr Cloth-capped man' to 'Mrs Headscarf'... and in huge numbers too. It had to be organised. So, women were enlisted through various acts: the National Service Act 1941, the Registration of Employment Order 1943, and the Employment of Women order 1942. This created the situation whereby all women aged between 18 and 40 could be conscripted into industry, but many volunteered anyway.

And here some of them were. Actually, quite a few. But where was Grace? I peered about for the daughters. Eventually I spotted Susan – or was it Cecily – and waited to catch her eye. When I thought she was looking my way I quickly raised my hand and made a beckoning gesture. This resulted in an obligatory giggle with lowered heads and side glances as she talked with a friend. I beckoned again. This time she stood up and sheepishly came over to me.

'Hello Susan – it *is* Susan, isn't it?' I asked, raising my eyebrows, making a bold guess.

'Cecily,' she responded – again blushing for England. Trust me to get it wrong. 'Susan calls you Mr Odd Couple,' she added.

Fancy that.

'Cecily, has your mum gone home then?' I asked tentatively, hoping she hadn't. 'I can't see her anywhere.'

'Yes...' said Cecily. My heart sank, '...but she will be back as soon as she's changed. We live close by and she didn't have time to change after work before she brought us. She doesn't normally come to dances I have to say.'

My world was suddenly OK again. 'Thanks Cecily – I'd like to speak to her when she gets back. I'll keep an eye out for her. Would you please let her know?'

Madness really – I mean, what future was there to be had with her? Perhaps to live just for the moment...?

A few minutes passed, a couple of songs, and there she was. My spirits soared as I made a beeline for her. She saw me coming but wasn't sure if I was coming to see her, until I was within a few feet.

'Grace, hello. I haven't forgotten that dance, remember?' I waited nervously, in case she said, 'get lost' or 'no thanks' or something. But her face broke into a lovely smile; how a smile transforms a person!

'Hello,' she answered with a quizzical look to go along with her smile.

I took her over to my mixer and then turned to Keith, introducing Grace.

'Keith, can you hold the fort for five minutes please while we have a dance?'

'No probs.'

I leaned over the table, scrolled to Elvis and hit the button while we both moved to the floor. Then we embraced or clutched into an awkward dance pose, not close together, copying what other couples had been doing. But Elvis soon changed that... as soon as he started to sing.

I slowly pulled her in closer and was immediately aware of her perfume – and her body melting into mine with a wonderful softness. What dance were we doing? Didn't care. I was lost in her gentle embrace as we moved to *Love Me Tender* and me cursing that the song wasn't half an hour long. Her hair was a chestnut brown tinting ever so slightly towards an autumn copper with an unusual short grey streak on one side, her skin a soft pink glow. Her clothes too, were gentle fabrics imbued with her fragrance. I was in a zen-like trance as we moved around the floor. I was in an enchanted place, didn't want to leave. I don't know about three steps to heaven – I was practically there in one.

I had to say something, we had to talk, I wanted to know about her. I opened up with the banal 'what did she do, where did she work?' – the usual preambles.

She was Mrs Atkinson, and she and her two daughters worked in a camera factory in town; I didn't enquire too deep but I knew it wouldn't be Nikon, probably something more specialised for the war effort such as photo-recce.

Then she asked, 'Who is that singing?' nodding towards the screen. 'What a lovely song – who is he? Is he a film star?'

I wondered how long it would take. 'Somebody called Elvis,' I answered. 'Yes he is – good looking even in black and white.' She must have been out when I first played it.

She eventually asked me what I did.

'This,' I answered, looking around. 'Playing music when I can. I'm semi-retired and widowed – and no one wants to employ knackered old geezers like me these days anyway,' I answered chuckling.

She joined in with the laugh then said, 'Oh – but I'm sorry about your wife.'

I didn't want to follow that up. As we talked some more I gently pulled her closer and closer. There was no resistance, our heads together now. I was in sweet heaven – totally beguiled. All sorts of thoughts were now rushing through my mind, daft, wild ideas.

I won't go home – I'll stay behind with her. No, don't be silly Bob.

I'll convince her to return with us tonight, take her home with us – but what about the daughters?

Shut up Bob.

It's funny how the myriad of thoughts quickly come, linger briefly and then fade as reality sets in. Three dances we had – three sublime events all rolled into one. My lips brushed her cheek and then hovered over hers with a brief touch.

She didn't pull away but whispered tenderly, 'No, no – it cannot be…'

Everyone knew that a stolen kiss is the most wonderful thing in the world – but it wasn't to be, not tonight, well, not yet.

There were so many reasons why 'it could not be' as she had succinctly said. And I had noticed one of the daughters looking at mum with a worried look.

'You are absolutely right of course,' I whispered, not without a little dismay. We pulled in more tightly in a wonderful squeeze before finishing the dance. On the way back to her daughters I said I'd see her later. This resulted in an almost imperceptible nod and smile – and then we parted.

'Becky,' I called. She looked up. 'I don't know what it is about her but I must be living in the wrong time – I just can't get her out of my mind. She drives me crazy just thinking about her. Even now I'm trying to remember what we've talked about already – things we said today, and that was just five minutes ago!'

Becky was my go-to person if I thought I was becoming embroiled with a woman – her instincts were excellent. In my job – or hobby – women were attracted to not only my dancers but also to me, the man fiddling with the controls, the man who played the music… even at my age.

Stop laughing

Becky would vet them, occasionally with Keith's help. I'd taken up with a few slappers in my past and although they knew what they were doing – I don't have to spell it out do I? – it's not what I really needed, or wanted. Some girls were good – nice – but none were like Grace.

'Remember Bob – you can't stay!' said this voice.

Chapter 20

Light fingers

'Bob, do you have your phone nearby?' asked Becky.

'Somewhere... why?'

'Keep your eye on that girl over there. I'm certain that she's thieving – just watch her and have it ready,' she said while readying her own phone.

It was her – you know, the happy one, the one with a face like a smacked bum, the ten pint girl.

'Yep... spotted her... I'll keep my eye on her.' We pointed her out to the others too.

It did not take long. Our 'girl' would find her target – walking past a half-empty table where the punters were busy yacking or ogling the dancers and, while walking back after a dance with her man, casually knock over a chair with a handbag on it, or accidentally on purpose brush a handbag or a packet of cigarettes off the table top. Profuse apologies would follow but it soon became obvious that with personal effects spilled out on the floor, and women trying to gather up their contents, our lovely lady would make off with something while seemingly trying to help. Maybe lipstick – but usually fags. It was simply, but nicely done. Then she would casually amble over to her den where – yes, you guessed it, 'weird bloke' was, sit down and with a make-believe fumble, spirit the goods into her own bag. Then you would see the victims looking around asking, 'Hey, seen my fags Beryl, I'm sure I left them just here...?' etc.

Cigarettes were a good 'currency' in these times.

'The sneaky little bitch!' said Keith under his breath. 'We'll soon sort her out.'

'Careful. She's with the copper remember,' Rubes pointed out.

...

'Hey Mavis... I've been watching those dancers, that woman over there,' said PC Wilf Robinson quietly, indicating towards Ruby who was dancing with somebody in army uniform. 'Have you seen her before? She looks familiar to me.'

'No, why should I? Hey, maybe an old flame is she?' a question accompanied with a suspicious inflection.

Robinson couldn't keep her out of his mind and was convinced she was someone he'd met recently but the way she was dressed just didn't fit any picture he had in his mind. She also had a sprinkling of sequins on her face. So he was quite content to just watch because, when all was said and done, she was a great dancer – a great mover. Then he thought perhaps he could ask her for a dance. Get closer.

'Oi!' said Mavis. 'Keep your eyes this way – you are not on duty now.'

'Yes, alright love, but there's something about her – I don't know what it is.'

'Like I said, you are off duty and if you keep your eye on her too much you'll be going home on your own,' she said acidly.

Wilf was the easy-going sort – was used to her tongue, so he decided to pacify her with the usual, 'Yes dear,' while knowing he would watch this dancer.

...

In order to keep Matt and Ruby under wraps' we'd reconfigured some dance routines for them wearing masks, or using heavy make-up... hmmm, scary. Then...

'Hey Mac, when are you going to do these new dances you told us about?'

I looked round to see Walt and Barney at my elbow. Then Joe joined.

'Ah! Tell you what, I'll just set the next tracks,' which I did, 'Come with me into the room again and I'll show you an extract on my magic typewriter with pictures,' I said with a 'follow me' nod. We moved off to the room where I set it down and quickly found what I was looking for. It was a way of keeping them 'onside' – not giving them too much time for cogitating about the tale we told them. The longer we could keep them away from any curiosity, the better. It was a gamble I took, but knowing of their all-consuming interest in music, dancing and dames, and not necessarily in that order, I decided to show them something that would really get their attention.

'Make yourselves comfortable,' I said as I motioned them to sit up to my laptop. I stood behind them, leaned over and hit the 'play', then moved round to observe their faces.

It was the Thriller video.

I'd thought about putting it on earlier before we knew our world had changed – now I was showing it to these guys and would gauge a reaction.

'Just watch for the dance routine later on. It's not long…' I said quietly. 'Enjoy.'

It wasn't long before the comments came.

'Jeez… look at that limo…'

Woops… I'd forgotten about the typical Yankee car – big and flash.

'Hey – they're black.' How un-PC.

'She's pretty. He looks weird… different… who is it?'

'Yikes…!' The graveyard scene.

The dancing started.

As the dancing progressed the looks on their faces were dominated by a mixture of sheer amazement and just a little horror… then questioning looks to me. Then it came to a close.

'Jesus Christ almighty!' said Barney. 'You guys came up with that…? Whose idea was it – Boris Karloff, Bela Lugosi…?' He was going to say more but I cut in.

'Probably,' I lied, but it would do. I'm glad *they* made the old-time, pre-war horror connection. 'And the dancing…?'

'I got to say man – that dude can dance,' said Walt.

'Well, there's a short version that we could play next door…'

'Who was he… where's he from, when did they do this??' asked Barney, interrupting.

'Somebody called Michael – I forget his last name but he's known for his dance routines,' I answered. 'The thing is, my dancers actually do the same routine – and teach it. Do you fancy trying it?'

146

Again there were looks of amazement – then the music ethos kicked in.

'Sure – yeah, you betcha!' responded Barney. The others were nodding too. 'Hey, that was scary!'

'Okay… as soon as we've shown it out there in the hall first.'

Some people have dance in them – some don't. Having watched the floor tonight I knew that these three, and probably the rest of their jitterbug gang, would do OK with modern rock 'n' roll, after all, it was the Yanks who brought the forerunner of the jive and rock and roll dances when they came across in '42. I wasn't sure about the rest of the audience and I had the feeling that most would be glued in front of the plasma when Michael Jackson came on – even for the short version.

'So, you go and tell your mates now… and we won't be playing the long version. In fact, there's a couple of other dance clips we can put on, so be prepared.' I was thinking of *Jailhouse Rock* and a few others. *Love Me Tender* had been well received by those who liked a good smooch.

I made the announcement about some brand-new dance routines which they could view on our magic projector screen – the plasma to you and me – and that if anybody wanted to try, my dancers would be only too happy to oblige.

'The first one is for you energetic types, as you will see from what Matt and Ruby are doing. It's called *Jailhouse Rock*. Take your cue from them. The second tune… well just wait and see.'

This dance clip really epitomised Elvis and his snake-hips – still impressive today. From the moment the clip started the punters just watched and stared wide-eyed while our two dancers went through their well-rehearsed routine. Even the Americans, no stranger to the jitterbug, watched in awe.

Barney turned around and looked at me; I winked in return with a thumbs-up sign – and a smile. A big grin appeared on his face. I mouthed, 'Great guitar,' to him.

'Now that you've seen the dance, I'll play it one more time so that you can all get stuck in,' I said. Then an RAF type came up and, before he said anything, I added, 'His name is Elvis,' to the expected question. 'And he's American.'

'Elvis? I have not seen him or heard of him – he is certainly a wiz dancer,' said our airman.

Wiz dancer? *Must* be aircrew.

'Becky here will teach you if you like… you up for it Becks?'

'No probs young man,' she responded and took our grinning young airman away. He was probably a cook.

Next it was Barney and friends again at my elbow all asking, 'Hey Mr Temple, where are these guys – these dancers – what's the dance?'

'Rock and roll,' I answered. 'But get cracking – I'm putting him on again.' They scuttled away. I had noticed the girls doing a little ogling at the screen while Elvis was playing. And while scanning the crowd I caught Grace's eye; she too had been watching, along with her daughters who had been doing most of the dancing, while she just watched. I flashed her my best smile. She responded with an almost hidden wave and a look of happy acknowledgement. That was good enough for me.

Elvis was really going down a storm with the Yanks, and quite a few Brits, doing Lindy hops and jitterbugs while others carried on with various versions of a quickstep.

Chapter 21

The jitter-bug pair

Here I am minding my own business, getting more nervous now considering what had passed in the last hour, when, just to take my mind off things, a couple approached me at my console, definitely local – could just tell. I looked up.

'Yes, how can I help?' Big smile.

They looked at each other, probably for encouragement. At the same time, another couple had joined them – obviously all friends together.

'Excuse me – you said earlier that you teach…' a pause followed. 'We would like to know how to dance better – like that dance those Americans have been doing. We've seen the dance before and try to do it ourselves but we were wondering if you dancers could help us a bit please,' asked the young lad. His partner gave a whopping great smile at me – a gorgeous smile. How could I refuse?

'Keep smiling like that, young lady, and you'll go far,' I replied, '…but of course we can. I presume you mean the jive – the jitterbug,' I quickly added. 'Just let me get my troops' attention.'

Poor choice of words perhaps. I motioned Matt and Ruby over and made the intros. While Matt made some small talk to them Ruby moved towards me.

'Actually Bob, we've noticed these two during the evening and they are in fact quite good, very enthusiastic, just unpolished, so it'll be a pleasure. Can you put on *C'mon Everybody* when I give the nod?'

'Will do.'

Matt and Ruby took them over to their table then said, 'We'll sit down and watch, while you dance. Okay?' Becky joined them at the table.

When the dance was over the two sat down with their friends. Technically their dance was just 'ho hum' and needed some pointers, thought Ruby, but she couldn't help thinking what an infectious look and countenance the girl possessed, obviously enjoying it all. All four looked attentively at Ruby who led the observations, explaining that their dance was not bad at all. Both Matt and Ruby were well aware that the genre of this type of dancing included Lindy hop, jitterbug, jive and of course rock and roll. Some called it the East Coast swing. In fact, when people did what they thought was jiving they were actually doing practically all of these dances, almost as a composite arrangement.

'So if you want to do what *they* were doing to *Jailhouse* then that's easy. When you do the flicks, just remember your feet are properly attached to your legs, right – not just lumps of meat that flop about… you have to point them. That needs tidying up. You are not flat-footed so that's good and your smile really carries the day – you obviously enjoy it; yes, it's a dance where you really have to look enthusiastic – bags of energy.

'I noticed you often miss or fail to link on your wrap-arounds and on the octopus – but that's down to practice. Practice and more practice – we'll have you matching up like a smooth synchromesh,' added Matt, '…and we'll show you one better than those lads over there with how to do the 'hip-hop'. But overall it was alright.'

Matt took Becky onto the floor whilst Ruby gave me the nod, then commenced with a running commentary on the dance to the young couples. I have to say that although a few years older than Matt, Becky could move. The next thing I knew, Barney and Joe where at my shoulder.

'Who was that?' Barney said, indicating the music. 'Can you play it again?' I'd noticed the Yanks doing their version while Eddie was on. When you hear the introduction to *C'mon Everybody*, some invisible force takes over and makes you want to make a fool of yourself. Well it does for me. Like I said, I like to twitch.

'No, we're playing *Stood Up* next, Barney. You'll like that just as well – and it's got guitar in it… big time.' Thumbs up from Barney.

Meanwhile Ruby was in full swing – if you'll excuse the pun.

'…and just so you don't knock your knees together when you are facing each other, just turn outwards a little, okay?' Matt and Becks demonstrated. 'See?'

The girl with the knock-out smile beamed, nodding at the same time.

'But a word of advice,' Ruby went on, now looking at Matt. 'Your clothes… if you're coming to a dance knowing you might be doing these moves – not talking about ballroom now – you have to be wearing the right clothing. Understood?'

Before Ruby could go on the girl asked, 'Where did you get those fabulous clothes you are wearing? You look wonderful.' Her friend was nodding along, the two boys stricken… girls' talk.

Not often Ruby goes red. 'Made them myself,' she lied. 'Now here's a truth, just look at the boys over there watching those girls with the Americans. It's inevitable that with all those moves you are going to expose yourself – show your legs and your undies,' said Ruby, pointedly looking at the girl. 'What do you think those lads over there are watching for?' It took a second or two before she went bright red. 'Exactly – they want to see your underwear and stocking tops when you twirl and jump around! Some no doubt wanting to see what might be in store for them later on…!' Even the two lads were going crimson now. Matt laughed. 'Watch, we'll show you… Matt, Becks?' They both got up and did a fast twirl, Becky showing everything but it was par for the course for her. The boys forced themselves not to look – but failed.

'Nice bum Becks.' Matt said with a large grin. This only embarrassed the youngsters more.

'You see, Becky's wearing a proper costume, so no problem, but when *you* get up onto the floor *you'll* be wearing a skirt, petticoat, knickers – white, we already saw – suspenders, belt, the whole paraphernalia, right?' Ruby was grinning, really enjoying herself. The two lasses didn't know where to look. The lads were embarrassed into silence. Then turning to the two boyfriends, 'Do you mind complete strangers seeing your girls' underwear when you throw them about on the floor?' They shook their heads, then nodded, then shook them again.

Poor lads.

'I thought not, but there again, you girls might enjoy flashing your fancy smalls to everyone. It's a good job you *do* wear knickers.'

What colour is embarrassment? The girls made a Ferrari look pale!

Ruby leaned into the other girl and whispered so that no one else could hear, 'We didn't see you dance just now… but you do wear knickers…?' A vigorous nod was the response. 'Good,' said Ruby. Both girls were now almost deep purple.

'So, what can we do about it? If you're not embarrassed about it then fine, but if you need a little modesty I'll show you how. Blatant flashing is too obvious and may earn you a reputation you don't want, so it needs to be minimised – the trick here is 'less is more'… a bit of mystery. 'See that

151

girl over there,' – it looked like one of Grace's girls, they all turned to see – '...she is wearing more or less what you're wearing, and when she spins... there you go, she has a slightly narrower petticoat that only flairs out so much. So, not a complete eyeful! Sorry Matt .../and you two lads.' They remained speechless.

'Nice legs though,' he said.

Both Ruby and Becky were fully aware that in their time some females turned up wearing trousers or spandex.

Cheats.

'Before we move on, just a final warning about clothing,' Ruby added. 'Don't ever wear thongs or G-strings. Ever. I think they're slutty – well, that's *my* opinion. You just can't beat proper pants, even if they are a bit naughty. Nothing worse than seeing a pretty girl stoop down exposing her string underwear – OK if you're going to floss while having sex. Otherwise avoid at all costs.' Matt was now laughing.

'Thongs?' said one of the girls with a quizzical look on her face. They could see the others were also puzzled.

Matt and Ruby looked at one another and realised that thongs were probably before their time.

'They are very skimpy versions of knickers,' said Becky to save the day. 'Another thing – these dances keep you fit. Nothing worse than sitting in front of the t... (whoops) by the radio all day. You'll finish up with a fat backside and bin... (whoops again) tombola wings,' said Becky. 'The jive will keep you toned and healthy. Get back to the floor again while we watch.'

Another twenty minutes managed to tidy up and remove some of the rough edges of their jitterbugging. Both Ruby and Matt were pleased with the progress but noticed that the girls were now very conscious when they spun, keeping one hand free to pat down their dresses and keep some modesty intact.

'They'll learn for the next time – when they come back,' said Ruby.

...

Chapter 22

Thriller...

The time came for *Thriller.* I called them all to silence.

'Everybody...'

I went on to tell them about the next dance routine produced from a short film.

'You will never have seen a dance like this before... it's a bit of a horror, it's new but just stand back, watch the screen and enjoy; in any case, I'm reliably informed that many of you are fearless... and that you can try this dance too, later.'

Barney had already given his buddies a heads-up and had now had them all grouped in front of the plasma expectantly.

The first few seconds of *Thriller,* as they walked past the graveyard, drew a few worried looks and quizzical glances followed by gasps and a couple of shrieks as the ghouls emerged. But the moment he suddenly confronted the camera with his staring, enlarged eyes, a huge murmur erupted from the audience, which then settled into fascination as Michael Jackson – and his ghoulish gang – performed his magic. Some of the women looked almost shell-shocked, hands to mouths, but they were all fascinated, truly.

Even I enjoy the dance routine... still.

A period of chaos followed when it finished. They all looking at me – probably asking, 'What the hell was that?' So I pitched up.

'Right... I told you so... great tune and what a fantastic dancer; shall I play it one more time... yes?' I asked as I was already keying it up. 'You can join in if you like – my dancers will be showing the way...'

Again, they gathered round the screens as Michael began his twitching once more, wanting another dose of this macabre dancing display. As I watched them all looking fascinated, I was minded about those horrible theme-park rides that scare you shitless and when you get off you say, 'I'm not doing that again!' but half an hour later you get back on, looking for the white-knuckle thrill for a second time.

Done it myself... haven't you? Go on, admit it.

Meanwhile Matt and Ruby were now doing the same routine with the Americans trying to watch both Michael and my dancers at the same time. Everyone was transfixed by the whole presentation and routine. Even Chris Rawlings looked impressed but I have to admit, its better when there's a crowd doing it as in the film clip. Now I was trying to figure out how to top that – what to play next. How about some line dancing, I suggested to myself? All five of us could do that and probably more in keeping with the audience's capability.

It's fair to say that after *Thriller* we were inundated with all sorts of 'who was...', 'where was ...', 'when was...' type questions with Matt and Ruby being asked for lessons, particularly by Barney's lot, no surprises really. But not to be outdone, a couple of local lads had somehow tagged along and joined in with the Yanks. Good. 'Come on you Brits, get going,' I said to myself.

Eventually we teamed up for the line dance with a couple of tracks to follow, nice and sedate – bit of a breather after Michael Jackson and Elvis.

...

Wilf and his Mavis had watched both Elvis and Michael Jackson with amazement, probably wondering 'how do you dance to that'; the waltz and quickstep were about their limit I reckon. They'd never seen or heard any of the music they'd just witnessed and Wilf, as a policeman, had seen many weird and strange things in his work I should imagine but he could not take his eyes off that girl dancer – our Ruby – much to the annoyance of his partner, while most people were glued to the picture show on the wall.

Several minutes passed watching Ruby and then suddenly he must have realised – when her hair moved with a toss of her head – *she's the girl with the motorbike!* Yes, he was sure it was her... the pretty girl that had roared away on the road leaving them in the dust – he and his sergeant both astonished, then angry.

'Mavis, Mavis, I think I know where I saw that girl before; she's got a motorbike and her dance partner was with her when we met on the road earlier on.'

'Eh – she got a motorbike... what, her? Are you pulling my leg? Don't be a twerp,' she said crossly. He told her the short story version of the earlier events on the road.

'No, I'm serious. The sergeant was there too, honest,' said Wilf, trying to steer her suspicions away from this pretty dancer. 'There's one way to find out... I'll sort her out just you see,' he replied.

Yes, for Mavis the green mist had come down. She had taken a distinct dislike to the women who looked like serious competition. If what Wilf had said was true, she would enjoy watching the stuck-up dancing bitch that seemed to have captured her Wilf's attention, not to mention the rest of the audience, becoming a cropper. She cast a jealous glance; her figure, even though she was older, was as good as hers. Yes, indeed, she was looking forward to the next ten minutes when the competition would be removed. Her glance followed as he wandered over towards the place where the man played the music – he was actually away doing some silly dance routine where they were all in a row. Again, she noticed that a lot of them were watching the dancers.

Policeman Wilf waited at the podium until eventually Mr Temple returned.

...

'Hello. What can I do you for – a request, it's Wilf isn't it?' I asked. I had seen the copper make his way towards my mixer – not without a little misgiving I might add.

'Yes, that's right; can I ask you a question?'

'Of course.'

'Does your dancer over there own a motorbike – yeah, and her partner?'

'Why do you ask?' I knew where this was going. 'Is there a problem Wilf?' I motioned Keith to come over – listening in.

'What kind of bike does she have?' Wilf persisted. Clever.

'I haven't said she has one... besides, what's it to you? Is it important Wilf?'

155

'If it's who I think it is, she committed a traffic offence earlier when she – and him – broke away from us during enquiries.'

'What offence? What inquiries?' Keith asked.

'Speeding, for one. But my sergeant – and me – want to talk to her about her bike and where it came from.'

Hmmm. This could be tricky, awkward. My mind was racing, searching for a way to respond, when Keith came to the rescue. He obviously had something on his mind.

'Come with me Wilf, I want to show you something… and you Bob,' said Keith, putting his arm around Wilf's shoulder in a coercive manner. Come on.' Very persuasive was Keith. 'Becky – mind the store would you please – won't be a mo.'

Keith ushered our policeman towards the door, then as we walked side-by-side Keith leant towards me and said, without lowering his voice, 'I have some great shots of handbags and fags.' I smiled in acknowledgement. I could see the plan.

'Handbags and fags – what about handbags and fags, what do you mean?' asked our policeman.

'Oh, sorry Wilf, that's just Keith and I talking – an old joke.'

We came to the door, opened it, moved inside and switched on the light after shutting the door – and there it was. Ruby's Triumph, covered up. Keith did a quick 'Ta – Daa' and pulled off the cover, revealing the bike it all its 21st century glory. Wilf gasped. Despite his copper credentials he just stood there, gazing at it.

'Nice eh?' Keith ventured.

'Yes… this is the bike. It is hers is it not?' responded Wilf.

'Indeed it is,' we both said more or less together. 'At first, I thought you were going to tell us it had been stolen.'

'Then I must talk to her and get her details, and then I must inform Sergeant Pugh,' he said while his gaze wandered back to the bike. Officialdom had come to the fore.

'Why? What will happen?' I asked. This could be interesting.

'I might have to apprehend them both,' he said, almost puffing out his chest a little while lowering his voice a touch. A bit of gravitas.

'Seriously? Really?' I exclaimed in mock horror. I noticed Keith had his cell phone in his paws. 'But we would be delayed; we have schedules to keep...' I said in vain while he interrupted.

'I'm sorry Mr Temple. Shall we go back inside?' said Mr Authority.

'But hang on a minute Wilf. What specific crime has been committed – can't we discuss this?' I ventured once more.

'No. My boss was quite angry this afternoon and I know he's been on the lookout for her... them. Easy to spot two on a bike – especially a bike like that, and the clothes they were wearing.'

Yeah, especially in 1944!

'Your boss... who's he? Is he a big cheese or something – head honcho, top banana?' asked Keith.

'Sergeant Pugh. That's who he is.'

I'm thinking Dixon of Dock Green...

I could just imagine what was going through his little official mind: kudos coming his way, slaps on the back, might even get an extra weekend pass from his boss. And he could bathe, just a little, in some tender embrace with Her Grumpiness. Poor man.

But he was serious.

He then turned to go. However, as he did, Keith held up his phone and said, 'Before you do, I have something to show you...'

Wilf paused. 'What's that...?' as his eyes closed in on the phone.

Chapter 23

The video clip

'It's a miniature camera,' said Keith. Couldn't really tell him it was an iPhone now could he?! 'Come and take a closer look,' Keith invited as he held it up to Wilf.

'Where did you get this from – that's not a camera? I know what a camera looks like.'

'Of course you do – you're a policeman, but this, it's a special – anyway that's beside the point, just watch. Watch closely,' Keith responded as he lay it on the bike seat with me watching on. Wilf moved over it to see what was happening and then peered into the screen to see the video play back. He appeared hesitant at first as if we were playing some childish stunt on him. A few moments passed as he watched then his jaw dropped, followed by a sharp intake of breath. His pallor had also changed. He looked sideways at us both then back to the screen. I hadn't seen it before either but could guess, and I looked anyway. Sure enough, as plain as it could be, there was the clip of Mavis moving round the tables with her well-practised routine, deftly picking out easily accessible objects from handbags, table-tops and, occasionally, the floor – after her 'minor' accidents.

'When was this filmed – how's it work?' asked our policeman, floundering somewhat and looking at Keith.

'Tonight, about half an hour ago, earlier – and like I said, it's just a camera. I'm also certain that my partner Becky has also filmed your lovely girl's exploits using her own 'camera'. Let's go and see her and then perhaps we should all then go and talk to Mr Rawlings.'

Panic spread on Wilf's face – his mouth twitched a little. I wasn't sure if he believed the evidence yet – the novelty of what he was seeing (even I'm still impressed) had affected his attention, possibly thinking, still, that it was a joke, a trap of some sort. If he thought it a trap, he was dead right but not the way he was thinking – Keith's trap was serious.

We walked back together into the hall. Becky looked up. I winked, with a gesture smile. Keith piped up.

'Becks – have you anything to show us… and can you show it to PC Robinson here please? Wilf, go and look at Becky's camera… go on… and yes, that's another special camera before you ask.'

He seemed reluctant but Becky placed hers on the table while he leaned over it to view. Becky's 'camera' was different to Keith's – bigger, and the picture movie was brilliant.

We watched and waited – Becky had taken more shots, there was more to see.

'This, too, was tonight and there is you in the background… see? No messing, no tricks. You tell us what you are seeing… come on… what is she doing?' I demanded.

The poor man had shrunk visibly and turned beetroot, 'The thieving little minx…' he muttered.

'She doesn't know, of course, that she's been filmed, so Wilf, are we still going to speak to your boss about Ruby and Matt… and the motorbike? Are we? Because if you are, our next stop is Mr Rawlings; I know what he will do without hesitation – this is his turf, his normal workplace. Now just have a closer look at the picture and you will see that your nice bit of stuff always returns to *you* and *your* table – where that weird guy sits too. Some could insinuate that you also are involved in what's going on. Your career would be over,' said Keith, connecting up all the dots for him.

Our policeman's brow was now showing beads of perspiration. He was obviously shaken. 'No, please wait…' said Wilf, holding up his hand.

Becky sidled up to us.

'While you were away, our lady in question paid me a visit and said – pointing at Ruby and Matt – that her 'boyfriend' policeman was going to make sure they were 'in for it' – that her Wilf would see to it. She actually used the words 'uppity show-off' about Rubes.'

'Did she now?' I answered. After what Becky had just said, I had an idea. 'Tell you what we'll do Wilf, let's go over to your table – she's there right now – and have a word in her shell-like ear. This could be fun. Bring the phones. You can film it too, into the bargain, so have your phone ready,' I urged Becky.

As we approached, Mavis looked up almost beaming. So she *can* smile I thought. Actually, it was more of a smirk. Then she kicked off first.

'What's going to happen to her and her boyfriend Wilf?' she asked with just a little malevolence in her tone – or perhaps a hint of smugness. 'Are you going to tell your boss now?' she asked expectantly. Then Mavis paused; she thought that her man should look more pleased than he was, but he didn't look pleased at all, his demeanour had completely changed. And from a look of almost happiness just ten seconds ago her face had reverted back to 'irritable face syndrome' once more. Suddenly, she didn't feel in control of the unfolding events.

'Hello Mavis,' I said pleasantly, 'I want to show you something – something I'm sure you'd like. Can I sit next to you please?' and I did so without waiting for approval. Weird guy was sitting on her other side. 'Just look at this,' I said as a laid the phone down in front of her, taking away my hand to reveal its display. There was just a flicker in her eyes, and the fact she couldn't take her eyes of it told us she was impressed. The sheer magic and sharpness of the colours, and the effortless movement of the pictures on my swipes had her captivated. Her eyes opened widened a little... something else she'd like to thieve maybe.

'Beautiful isn't it,' said Keith as a statement of fact, 'But pay attention.'

'What is it... what is...? Where did you get this from...?' she asked, looking up at Wilf before he cut in.

'It's a special camera... see all those pictures? Just look,' he said as we all watched me scroll through some group pictures.

'In this one, you can see those lads over there – those Yanks,' I went on, nodding in their direction. Keith *had* been busy.

She looked first at the picture and then over towards the Americans...acknowledgement that this was indeed a camera, a camera that was tantamount to a piece of jewellery, well, to her at least; I could almost sense her light fingers twitching.

'Now watch this little video extract – sorry, movie film. Tell me what you see – explain to your Wilf here what you see.' I started the sequence...

'Who is that?' I asked as I froze the picture pointing at someone on the screen.

'That's... me...' she mumbled.

'Yes, that's you. Definitely you Mavis,' said Wilf joining in.

Mavis was changing colour, first a pale pallor on her face then a burning red.

Keith hit 'play' again. It was fascinating to watch the various expressions as they crossed her face. At the same time, weird guy was also looking in. It didn't take long...

'What's this, some kind of trick – it's a trick Wilf!' she said, with rising vehemence but she knew she was undone, caught almost red-handed. And then the other phone was produced and plonked down in front of her – and 'played'. Same story.

'No trick. Just you caught with your hand in the till you cunning, light-fingered, sour-faced little bitch,' I said with a grin. I was enjoying this, as were my dancers, especially Ruby.

'Wilf! He called me a bitch!' she almost screamed, her face turning rigid, flushed with anger. 'He can't talk to me like that! Do something; you're not going to let these old farts accuse me like that, are you?'

Old fart...? I don't mind... really.

'You are definitely *not* a nice person, are you?' Keith responded matter-of-factly. Mavis started mouthing and uttering expletives, calling Keith and Ruby, all of us I suppose, shit-face and all-sorts of other nice things we'd heard a million times before.

'At least my parents were married,' responded Ruby.

It took a while for that to sink in as Becky clapped her hands together with a mouthed 'nice one'.

Even Wilf laughed, when he caught on – but only for a nanosecond, remembering that there was going to be no nookie for him tonight... or the foreseeable future. This made Mavis go bananas – big time – at her policeman, who was now beginning to assume the mantle of one, and then as she tried to get up he pushed her back down.

'You stay right there; I want to know where you've stashed your booty. Come on! Tell me.' But we already had an idea... our phones had it all. We turned towards weird guy, looking at him with raised eyebrows. 'Anything you want to tell us Stan?' asked Wilf.

So, weird guy was called Stan, and 'booty'? A long time since I'd heard stolen goods called that, but then I remembered where we were, *when* we were!

Stan slowly stood up and then said, 'It was her doing – it's all women's stuff anyhow.'

'What about the fags then? Are those yours you have there?' asked Wilf. 'I reckon she pinched the stuff and you kindly aided and abetted by flogging it off on the black market. I'm right aren't I?' Wilf then made a grab for her handbag but Mavis was too quick and managed to get her hands on it before it could be taken from her. An unseemly little tussle followed but the result was inevitable. Wilf then opened it and tipped the contents onto the table.

Ruby and Becky's eyes popped open as compacts, lipstick, Marlboro and Woodbine cigarettes fell out in a large bundle. There was also the odd lighter or two amongst the pile. Ronsons too – not bad.

'Christ! It's just as well they don't have the bags we have these days...' before remembering what Ruby was going to say. Now I remembered just after they had arrived, how Mavis had cast covetous eyes towards Ruby's handbag. No doubt the lure of visiting Americans with an almost endless supply of luxuries and fags was the reason for their attendance at these shindigs.

'You are the ones who are weird,' he said sullenly. 'It's them who are weird Wilf,' he said out loud to the policeman, imploring him to listen; this managed to get a measure of agreement from his partner in crime who frothed a little around her lips as she saw both Ruby and Becky smiling at her discomfort. Then we watched as a heated argument kicked off between the two thieves. No honour at all – each accusing the other but we had no doubt that it was Mavis who was the driving force in this little enterprise. And I was mindful of not wanting to attract too much attention – we didn't want Rawlings being dragged into this, we were not out of the woods yet. In this, and for other reasons, I'm sure Wilf didn't want that either.

'Us – weird? Hmmm – a compliment coming from you. Let me guess...' Keith went on, '...I suppose you two walked to school together eh? And no doubt you live at home with your parents, so why don't you just crawl back to them... if you know who your parents are.'

Weird Stan huffed a bit before he'd worked that one out. For a moment he looked as if he was going to throw a punch but Wilf's presence said 'no'.

I took hold of PC Robinson's arm and pulled him to one side.

'Wilf, I take it we're sorted as far as the bike's concerned, no need to speak to your boss and Mr Rawlings?' I gestured, holding up my phone.

He nodded... a look of resignation.

'You had no idea...? I gestured.

'No, not a dickie bird. I'll get these two out of here and make sure they don't get in here again,' he said as he turned towards his now ex-girlfriend. 'Come on you two, come with me... you are leaving and I don't want to see either of you darkening these doors again. You're lucky tonight as *only we* know about this little escapade – and that's the way it will stay.'

After they had left Wilf had collected up all the 'booty' and looked at me.

'Can you make some sort of an announcement to the effect that all this has been found scattered under the tables and around the floor due to enthusiastic dancers and fluffy frocks, and that they can come and retrieve their goods...?'

'I suppose I could.' Which I did, but we breathed a sigh of relief that's for sure.

Chapter 24

The whole nine yards

My mind was back with the Americans. I'd been thinking about what music might tickle their fancy without going over the top, basing my selection on the instruments they liked playing and probably what would be attractive to them. Much that we had would pass right over them, but we'd try...

I told my gang that we could relax a little, handed over the show to Matt and Ruby for a breather from dancing, picked up our modified ghetto blaster and ambled across to the USAAF boys.

'Guys, I have a plan – remember that music I promised?' Those still sat around looked up as I came up to them.

'Hey, what was going on back there boss – you guys having an argument...?' asked one of them.

'Something like that,' I murmured.

'Mr Temple, is this another one of your gadgets you made up at the academy?' asked Joe, looking at our blaster and smiling. 'Can I have a look?'

I anticipated this. 'Better still... here's the plan. You fellows, come with me into the room again.' A couple were still on the floor... they could join us later.

They didn't need asking twice. They all rose and followed me while eyeing the blaster. I thought modern electronics was supposed to miniaturise everything... the guys that made our ghetto blaster obviously didn't get the message.

When we were in the room I turned to them and said, 'I've made up a selection of songs for you to listen to... on this,' as I plonked the ghetto blaster down onto a table. 'You just scroll down the list of song titles – like this, see? This is how you get to play each one, how to stop, and how to 'fast forward', move back – and also move on to the next one. The volume control is here...' I said, pointing here and there, 'and I would like you to jot down what you like by the title you see. You don't have to listen to each song completely otherwise we'll be here all night...just sample each one. Play thirty seconds or so. Got that? I'm sure all of you will find something you'll like from drums, guitars, sax – the *whole nine yards.*'

They laughed – I think there was recognition with the expression I had just used which I can share with the reader.

The whole nine yards... we've all heard it have we not.

The most commonly offered explanation is that it refers to the length of aircraft machine gun belts that were nine yards long There are many versions of this explanation with variations regarding type of plane. But it is also used as an expression to convey...

'Give it the lot'

'All of it, full measure'

'The works'

'Don't hold back'

Etc.

And in May 1961, Ralph Boston broke the world long jump record with a jump of 27 feet and 1/2 inch – nine yards. So "Boston goes the whole nine yards" was the report. Prefer the machine gun belt myself. In fact, the expression was used way back early 1900s and was probably 'the whole six yards' originally.

...

Back to the ghetto blaster.

They had crowded round watching and listening intently at my instructions. There was an immediate babble as they put their talents to use to get to grips with *future* technology... 'Gee, let me at it fellas...' and so on.

'But I'll start you off. Barney – guitar? Just listen to the first five notes of this…' I said as I started *One of Them* by Jace Everett – then stopped it. Barney's jaw dropped. 'Don't worry – it's already on the list! As for the sax… well I've got a tune that covers both the sax and guitar, right up your… *Baker Street*. We'll check in on you – or Keith or Becky will. Any problems just shout, but don't be too long,' I said to them and left them fiddling and playing… and babbling like young schoolboys.

That'll take their minds off any talk of 'spies' and such-like… for a while.

…and back in the hall, dancing.

We had a few things to do before we started on some sort of an exit strategy and I was just a little worried that Chris Rawlings' errand boy – Albert – would come back anytime soon with half the British Army or with Dixon of Dick Green. I had to find Grace…

I looked around, caught her eye and motioned for her to pop over my way. She was with another woman at the time but disengaged herself and came over.

'Grace…' I could see a searching message in her eyes as she looked at me – like myself, a mixture of inquiry and sadness perhaps. Without looking too serious I said that I'd selected, no, dedicated, a song that reflected my feelings towards her, as we'd all be checking out later. 'I'd like you to listen to it – listen to the words.'

'Checking out…?' she asked, puzzled.

'Yes, leaving… heading home. Can you ask your daughters – and your friend if you like – to join us?' Her mouth opened then closed. After a pause, she moved off and when they were gathered I asked them to get with their partners for a dance to the record I had selected and was about to play… that they would surely like it. I called Matt over. 'Matt, would you please partner Grace here for the next song while I set up a special one for her when these are finished. Don't let anybody take her away.'

'Sure.'

Then, looking at Grace, 'Matt'll look after you then we'll dance, OK?' I added with a wink. A wonderful, wistful smile came back.

On went *Sleeping* by the Fab Four while I thought about an excuse for an early exit. Because I now knew that Grace was within sight with Matt, I relaxed a little as I set up the next programme of songs.

I watched intently. In fact, the 'floor' liked this simple tune – it was certainly one of those hidden Beatles tracks that most audiences liked and when it was finished, Matt brought Grace over to me whispering in my ear that, 'I think she's worried or upset'. I thanked Matt, looked at her, bought her round and sat her down next to me; her eyes were red. She moved in closer as I cuddled her. I wondered if this was to be the last time.

'What's up my pretty girl?'

'Will you be coming back? You said that you are leaving. Where are you going? Perhaps I shouldn't be saying this but I... I just feel... safe and content with you.'

That gave me an incredible, warm feeling I must admit. It was then that I realised *when* we were; Grace was probably imagining me being shipped off to some far flung, dangerous Far East outfit or the Med somewhere. I felt such a heel... but at my age?

'I'm too old to be going anywhere Grace as you can see, so in fact when we go we'll only be going as far as Milton Keynes, Bedford way – that's the area we hail from.' She beamed a little smile and relaxed. I followed up, 'There's no way I want to be too far away from you,' I said as she fumbled with her hanky to dab her eyes. 'Come on – come with me onto the floor. I've selected the next song just for you. I want you to listen to the song, listen to the words.'

'I don't know of Milton Keynes but we have a cousin in Bedford,' she replied softly.

Of course – who *would* have heard of Milton Keynes in 1944? The place was one of these new, made up satellite towns planned from well after the war had finished. Before that it had amounted to only a collection of houses and maybe some hall. They'd get a shock if they saw it today. But they're not going to, are they? Silly me.

So on went *Can't Get Used to Losing You* by our crooner Andy Williams.

We snuck in close. I didn't care where – or when we were. We had a silent language each time we looked into each other's eyes, or touched – I was in a kind of a dream, but a dream I knew was going to end soon. As we moved back to the console after...

'That was lovely. I haven't heard that before...' she broke off as she caught her breath because on impulse, I brushed her lips with mine fleetingly... and she responded lightly. Her voice was a soft and soothing caress.

'That track was just for you, princess,' I said. The beginnings of a smile brightened her countenance. 'And I hope your girls enjoyed it too.

By the way, apparently, I'm now known as 'Mr Odd Couple' according to Cecily.'

'Oh yes, it was Susan,' said Grace with a laugh, 'She wasn't sure whether you were referring to my two or something else... and they can't stop giggling about...'

'Tits and boobs?' I answered. She nodded, with a knowing smile. 'And 'Odd Couple'? A film actually.'

It wasn't long before 'the girls' came over, with partners, probably having seen mum now looking somewhat dejected and tearful. I left them together for a while but it had me thinking – about dad. I now knew why he was in Italy and what he would be doing whereas when she first told me much earlier on, I was thinking he must be over there on business... not up to his neck in muck and bullets.

The girls gathered round their mum. 'Gosh, that was so different, mum, to other songs... who was it, is it American? He had a very nice voice,' asked Cecily or Susan.

'Yes, he's American – a crooner... and yes, he does have a very pleasant voice. You won't have heard of him. Grace, you stay here with me for a while if you like – as for you girls and your partners, I'll put on a cracker of a record for you – a bit faster. Are you ready? I'll look after your mum,' I said, taking her arm and leading her away through the side door to our Rover. She came willingly.

It was quite dark in the side alley but as soon as the door closed I swept Grace up into an embrace and kissed her passionately. She was taken by surprise but – knowing we were completely alone – responded in like fashion. We came up for air after a minute or two, hanging on to each other, our arms and hands searching – but resisting that final intimate touch, until she said unexpectedly, 'You can touch me if you want to Robert... I want you to; I haven't been touched for years. Please touch me.'

I knew what she meant and slowly slid my hand down as she pulled in my waist... and I knew where this was headed. She was very moist and as I continued to fumble amongst her forties underwear, suspenders and suspender-belt she shuddered – and then reached for *my* belt...

But – she had upset the Gods because suddenly a door opened along the hallway spilling out a group of punters which immediately shut us down.

We kissed once more then intuitively headed back inside with me saying, 'At last – truly in my arms Grace – that was lovely – I hope you didn't mind – the kiss. Everything.'

'No, not at all, but such a shame,' she responded with a 'shush' motion, finger to lips, squeezing my hand until we were inside once more. And I'm sure her perpetual blushing must have given the game away to any observer, and I'm certain that had I pushed it and climbed into the back of the Rover with her... shan't dwell on that. We were gone for only a few minutes.

'Where have you two been?' asked Keith. 'On the other hand, don't tell me.'

'Just showing Grace the motor... not many people have cars do they so it was just a quick look.'

No matter how I said it I could not prevent myself from a little blush, to go with Grace's, and I could just imagine Keith thinking 'yeah, right'.

On went *Shot in the Dark.* More in keeping with the times and the orchestral theme; I just knew it would score well with the dancers as did both *Ladybird* by Nancy Sinatra and *Only Make believe* by Conway Twitty.

Conway Twitty? What kind of name is that, eh? His real name was probably quite boring, like Harry Jenkins or something. And I had to remind myself to call them songs or tunes and not tracks.

I kept my eye out for my dancers. It was good to see them explaining the niceties and intricate moves of the dances to the punters. My team knew their onions when it came to the subtleties of the different dance moves – the subtle techniques that changed an OK dance into a very good dance:

Keep the chin up, don't forget to rise and fall, heads back, and flow across the floor, fluidity – all these things to remember for the waltz, and more.

Whereas for the tango, the moves were sharper, staccato with upright postures, a tighter hold and 'don't stick your bum out too much'.

And the cha cha... straight legs with bags of hip action, finish moves in a clean way, don't plod – and keep bloody smiling!

Well, to me I could remember all of these techniques, but not all at the same time! I'd stumble from here to there – you know what I mean. It reminded me of playing golf. Don't move your head, don't look where your ball's going until after you've hit it and keep your arms and wrist 'just so' through the swing... plus a million other bits of advice. The safest place for anyone on a golf course when I'm playing is on the fairway.

When it came to the more energetic dances like the Charleston and the jive, my guys and girls were brilliant, especially Matt and Rubes. They had great timing with great swivels in the Charleston and for the jive, their 'New Yorkers' were just a blur. For me, I could just about master the move – but only slowly. I had plenty of enthusiasm although my flicks and kicks were sloppy. However, my robot dance was superb...probably because I was stiff anyway after getting off my chair!

So reader, you can see why I left most of the dancing to my experts. And because they were good, the audience were keen to emulate them which kept everybody busy.

...

'Right Grace – let us have another dance shall we?' I said as I rose from my seat, pulling her up with me. She watched as I keyed in *I'm not in Love* – another few minutes of bliss to look forward to, dancing to a haunting, almost ghostly, drifting melody. It took a while before everybody realised that the track had actually started but it did not take long before the tight clinches were in evidence – me included. I just lost myself once again in her arms.

'Where do you find these songs?' she asked. 'That was so... serene.' I thought back to *Only Make Believe*. If only I could tell her – real make believe! Just then I noticed the arrival of an unwelcome development across the hall.

'Grace... do you want to re-join your girls? I've just seen something that needs my attention.' Out of the corner of my eye I had just seen Albert come in accompanied by two soldiers and Dixon of Dock Green – Wilf's boss. I wasn't too alarmed – in these times there would no doubt be plenty of uniforms about, no strangers in get-togethers and dances like this. Additionally, I'd already been assured by our American friends that Chris Rawlings had been pacified as far as they were concerned regarding any 'cloak and dagger' goings-on. But I did motion to Matt and Ruby to colour up with a bit more make-up just in case Sergeant Pugh had a very good memory – which they immediately began to do. At the same time, I noticed Chris Rawlings and Wilf making their way to head them off at the pass before they got to me at the hub. A brief conversation followed and then they all turned and moved towards me. I partly closed the lap top, ready for some questions.

Could be interesting…

'Is everything all right here sir?' asked what looked like a staff sergeant – three stripes and a crown, didn't catch his regiment.

'But of course, Staff, having a great time… a real good crowd, aren't they Chris?' He nodded.

'Did you not mention that there were Americans here?' asked Sergeant Pugh, looking at Albert. 'Which ones are they?' They were normally not hard to miss.

I stepped in, 'They're in the room over there listening to some recordings. Do you want me to dig them out?'

'I'll get them,' offered Chris Rawlings and off he moved, just as the door opened revealing Barney and his buddies in animated conversation, coming out and looking around. I stuck up my arm. They strode across then slowed a little as they spotted the uniforms.

'So what gives Mr Rawlings?' asked Barney, looking at Sergeant Pugh and the army uniforms, then back to Chris. 'Hey, you should hear some of this music man – it'll blow your head off! We made a list Bob – and we got questions.'

'I bet you have.'

'Excuse me… is everything OK sir?' the staff sergeant asked Barney and co. 'Was there some trouble?'

'Must have been those tanked-up drunks earlier,' Barney responded as Albert nodded vigorously, beaming a little.

'You should have seen it, see how he…' Albert was in mid-stride when Chris smoothly cut in.

'A minor altercation – the usual causes… booze, but it was quickly dealt with.' It was only then that I noticed that having been attracted by the appearance of the uniforms and his boss around my console, PC Wilf Robinson had come over and was listening intently to the exchange of words, making sure that no fall-out from the light-finger Mavis episode reached his sergeant's ears.

'Ah – PC Robinson,' exclaimed Dixon of Dock Green. 'I see that we are enjoying the pleasures of dancing tonight, are we not? I have not forgotten – I still have my eye out for that flash bugger and his moll on that motorbike we saw earlier.'

Moll?

The new Bonnie and Clyde! Matt and Ruby'll love that.

And I saw a flash of recognition in Barney's features when 'bike' was mentioned, however Albert was not to be deflected about the fight... 'Yes, there were two of them. Blimey – right slobs they were, weren't they Mr Rawlings.' I kept thinking he'd call him Mr Grimsdale soon.

'Indeed they were.' And seeing that Albert was looking around to find Matt and to point him out, just as I was but for a different reason, to warn him, Chris knew Albert would keep talking about this all night, so closed down this avenue of dialogue, cutting in, 'Anyway Sergeant Pugh, can I get you and your two army colleagues a cup of tea or something?'

'We could do better than that,' I suggested, 'Something a little stronger?' My hip flask was already out.

'Just a little snort will do fine,' said Sergeant Pugh, nodding along with the army. 'Thank you. I know I'm on duty but life is too short and too hectic these days.'

Murmurs of agreement all round. Hectic? He should try driving round the M25.

'Gee – you're damned right sir,' said Walt or Milt – or was it Joe.

Life is too short. That could have come straight from my own lips – a modern expression if ever I heard one.

'Perhaps you'd like me to play a song of your choice lads,' I ventured to the uniforms. 'What does the army march to these days? Glenn Miller? Benny Goodman? No – tell you what, I'll pick something appropriate, to go with your drink break. But if you want Miller, I can oblige.'

Not getting an immediate answer I put on *Take Five* again, inoffensive, but catchy in a quiet way, and cranked it up.

Our new visitors looked around – must have seen similar scenes a thousand timed before. Youngsters enjoying themselves, making the most of today as, for some, there might not be a tomorrow. I was praying that Sergeant Pugh would not recognise my dancers who were amongst the dancing melee right now, nor ask too many questions about our kit. And there was no way I was going to put on ZZ Top... at least not yet. When they've gone perhaps.

It didn't take long before the eyes of Sergeant Pugh – and the soldiers – alighted on Ruby. I watched nervously but so far, Sergeant Pugh was not making any sign of a connection; there's quite a difference between brightly coloured leathers and a sequinned dance outfit. I looked at Wilf, with me making 'get him out of here' head movements. When you get older, you are allowed to have twitches.

'Gentlemen, while you have your drinks I'll leave you in the capable hands of Keith and Becky while I attend to the music and dancing, if that's OK,' I said as I turned to my console. It was going to be OK whether they liked it or not but I had no worries on that score as I had already noticed Sergeant Pugh's eyes move from Ruby and latch onto Becky – he was of similar age I guessed, and we're all human. One of the two soldiers was actually quite young – probably had flat feet or was 'scused boots or something… not at the 'front'.

The other soldier was close to me in age but not nearly as handsome.

Chapter 25

The list

I eventually turned back to our American friends.

'Sorry boys – where were we, what have you got on your list?' We all sat down. 'You can show me and then maybe we can play your choices to the floor if you want.' I looked at my watch… getting on.

They all wanted to be first so finished all babbling together, thrusting a sheet of paper in front of me.

'Cool it lads, one at a time. Just show me the list,' I interrupted as I scanned their choices. 'Oh, I see you've put your names against the songs. So what's Joe picked?' I asked out loud. I had taken a bit of time picking out tracks I *thought* they might appreciate but really, it's all down to personal taste and chemistry.

Before I could say anything he excitedly cut in, 'This one was cool boss – *Walk On the Wild Side* – you played it earlier, great sax.' In fact they were nearly all nodding along with Joe on this. 'We 'digged' this record Mr Temple, all of us. And there was no brass!'

Digged this record? 'Dug', surely. Hmm, I' would have to get my dictionary out and check.

'Yes… thought you'd like that one. I do too,' I added. As I looked back to the list I found myself nodding at their selections. Yep – *Baker Street* for both Barney and Joe – sax and guitar. Spot on. A beautiful guitar solo.

'I wish I could spend just five minutes learning with that guy on the guitar – a great sound, blew me away Mr Temple,' said Barney.

Shame they are no longer with us I thought.

Now I have to tell you that I deliberately did not have any pre-war music on the lists for them – what would be the point? It was all modern stuff.

Great word '*stuff*' – can be used to describe practically anything… but it's a lazy choice.

I looked at Milt, raising my eyes in invitation for his input.

'I really dig this song,' he said as he pointed to *Yesterday*. 'So simple man – easy on the ears too. Nice easy guitar work.'

The '*dig*' word again.

'You are allowed to say *like*,' I said.

They ignored me. 'Hey Milt – you getting at me and my guitars?' said 'guitar Barney' grinning. He went on, '…and he was in rapture when he listened to…' he fumbled with the list, '…this one – the broad singing *Move over Darling*, weren't you Milt?'

'No more than you were with…' he looked back at Barney's list, '…this one – *Wonderful Land.*'

'And me,' cut in Lou, referring back to Doris. 'Who is she – one hell of a voice? I think you played it earlier – she can sing me a bedtime story anytime!' Lou, a bass player, was also taken by *Walk on the Wild Side*. 'You got some weird music on that machine of yours… but that singer on *this* one, these barber-shop singers Mr Temple – he also has a top voice.'

Eh? Barber shop boys?

I did a quick check and found that I hadn't noticed *Moments to Remember* by The Four Lads was on the tracks, but he was right…somebody in there had one hell of a voice. Not sure they were actually barber-shop singers though. Not a track I normally played at our gigs.

I could just picture it. While you're singing, 'Short back and sides please'.

'What about the guy that sounds as if he's got a sore throat…?' They all jumped in on that one. '…real deep voice – almost like he's talking the mornin' after a hard night…'

'That would be *Wandering Star*, the guy that just growls his way thought the song,' I said. A real cool dude in my books, Lee Marvin, but not known for his singing that's for sure. 'You're right – and a very nice tune.'

'And this one was a real smoothie too – *Return to Me*,' said one of the Yanks' groupies. 'Who is he?'

Dino, of course. Nice choice. But knowing their penchant for the more exciting and faster moving music I had slanted most of the tracks towards the ability for jitterbugging which I knew they liked. I hadn't a chance to filter all the songs so I did ask that if there was anything they found strange, write it down.

'This was different but I could really dance to it, *Reet Petite*,' said Ricky (don't call me Richard). Yeah, you can't sit still when that's on, true enough.

'But anything you thought strange?' I tried again.

'Yeah, this one, real strange but actually, I did not dislike it,' Lou said. It was *Nike Town*. 'Punchy tune – catchy, whoever made that was on moonshine,' he added. Laughter.

He went on: 'And I would kill to be able to play like that guy in *Dreaming the Blues*. He makes that trumpet talk almost!'

'Sure was,' someone else said, but they were on my wavelength with this – I liked it too. Good job *Strawberry Fields* wasn't on the lists, I mused.

'How about this one boss – *Equinox 4*…? Is that how you pronounce it? Totally mad boss… sounds more like an engine than music,' said Joe.

'Yes, correct – and I know what you mean,' I responded. Good interpretation.

Barney came in again with *Red House*. So cool, so slow, by Jimi Hendrix. Mind you, I'm not sure Barney'd appreciated someone playing a guitar with his teeth.

'Join the club,' said Becky.

'Me too,' Keith.

'This… *Words of Love* – funny, thin voice but nice tune,' one of the groupies piped up along with someone else. Probably Milt. Must be the Buddy Holly rendition – not the Beatles.

'What made you like that one?' I asked – just for my own interest.

'I dunno – like he was talking to you, know what I mean, quiet like.'

A soft voice piped up. 'I liked this song,' said another of the groupies – Lou's girl I think. It was *Sealed With a Kiss*.

I suppose it is a bit of a girlie song.

'Don't forget the guy with the machine gun,' said Joe.

Machine gun?

'Yeah – called *Hound Dog*.'

I suppose you could make the connection. 'Okay boys, I'll leave you with some more while we get on with the dancing,' I told them.

But before I could get up Walt cut in.

'And this one too Mr Bob – this slow one... a real slow-ass tune. Me and Audry like it,' he said turning to the girl on his arm.

I peered at where his finger was pointing. 'Right – *To Know Him is to Love Him.* Yep, I like it too – a good schmoozer.' Seeing as Walt was the drummer in the crowd I might tell him later who the drummer was, how he became famous as 'Sandy Nelson', going it alone on the drums. 'I'll tell you a story about that record later...'

It turned out to be much, much later.

Chapter 26

Germany – 1944

A briefing

Major Ralph Vetter was standing at the back of Colonel Steiger's office behind other officers for a hurried brief that had been called. Steiger was conveying information for the crash investigation teams to be on the lookout for specialised bomb-aiming equipment the Allies might be deploying – perhaps miniaturised.

The Higher Command was not really interested in mundane aircraft parts such as wheels, engines, hydraulics and guns – what they desperately wanted was information on electrical, electronics, communication equipment, aerials, and bomb-aiming gear. But Vetter already knew this so all he remembered from the meeting was:

"No matter how small it is, we want to know about it! We need to know exactly what the Allies are doing, what new technology they might be using – anything! So we will do any investigations. Just bring what you find interesting or unusual to us. Do you understand?"

Many pairs of heels clicked together in unison.

He had terminated the meeting with, 'We are expecting the weather to clear in the next two days so we all know what this will mean – more bombers, more raids, busy times ahead for you all. Dismissed!'

Major Vetter was one of the newly appointed 'Science Officers'- part of an assembled group of 'grounded' ex-flyers and engineers who used their experience and expertise to keep an eye out for anything new on Allied aircraft by examining the wrecks of downed aircraft – the team usually knew where to look. A great deal of intelligence could be gained, and there were many wrecks to examine. Too many. With Sergeant

Schneider, his accomplice, they were just one of many small two-man teams looking over these crashes across Germany, most revealing nothing new – only the gruesome aftermath of those poor souls who did not get out.

At first, and like most Germans, Ralph Vetter thought some winning, mutual arrangement would be the outcome of the war with Britain even if they were not able to invade across the channel – the RAF had shown themselves a strong opponent. He thought perhaps that eventually, German scientists would come up trumps with weapons that would force the English to sue for some kind of co-existence, leaving each nation to go about more-or-less as before as long as Germany controlled Europe. Britain could look after its Commonwealth with its powerful navy.

He believed that Hitler knew what he was doing... initially. And then he invades Russia – and he declares war on the US too!

Idiot!

He felt the impact of this straight away. Valuable materials, spares and personnel were suddenly no longer available like before – diverted to the Eastern Front where, just as in France, Belgium and Holland, the war was going Germany's way. But Vetter felt uneasy. Russia was a vast country...Britain was only 500 miles from top to bottom. In Russia it could be 500 miles between one city and the next, however, even then he still had faith in the final outcome – victory for Germany because they could at least neutralise the Bolsheviks. But another factor that began to worry both he and his aircrews: he thought that Britain would sit back after the air battles of 1940 and slowly rebuild their forces without threatening Germany too much. But the RAF had other ideas and began to go on the offensive in limited fashion... and as soon as the USA came in with the Allies, thanks to Japan and Hitler's declaration, Major Vetter had thought 'that was it' – Germany could never win now. Why did Hitler go and spoil it all and attack Russia? German forces were now fully stretched with the quality of fighting personnel and materials falling each day.

When the bombing was heavy Major Vetter and Sergeant Schneider would sometimes attend up to three crashes a day. They'd often been asked by their colleagues if it ever affected their appetite.

'You just get used to it,' they'd replied, but it was the tiredness that really got to them because not only was there the constant mass bombing raids, the Allies were now in the habit of flying Mosquito fast bombers into Germany each night, separate from the heavy bombing, just to trigger the air-raid sirens, so nobody had any sleep. How he longed for just a few days rest back with his wife Miriam and baby son but life was so hectic;

only when there was a break in the bombing could he snatch a day or two back home – and this nearly always depended on the weather, so he'd pray for low cloud over Germany to keep the bombers grounded, no point in flying for many hours only to find the target is completely hidden by cloud.

...

Sergeant Schneider, Ralph's NCO accomplice, was an ex-He111 bomb-aimer, or bombardier as the Americans would say, now grounded. He was badly injured over the channel having tangled with a Hurricane after only six missions; his pilot was lucky to make it back to crash land in France. He was *sure* it was a Hurricane that got them – and killed his gunner – but one of his colleagues swore it was a Spitfire... there was always a weird pride in being taken out by a better class of aircraft. He very quickly began to hate his position in the bomber once operations started over England. He felt so vulnerable sat behind a plastic glass dome with British fighters coming at them head-on; he'd had a few close shaves before he was put out of action. In any case, his flying days were over, he now had a limp as a result of his left leg and could no longer raise his right arm above his chest without pain.

Major Vetter was also an ex-flyer, a pilot, but had managed to survive flying longer than his Sergeant. As a 109 pilot, promotion came quickly in 1940 and '41... losses were high. He, like Schneider, knew only too well how even the Hurricane could be a formidable foe. Although not as fast they seemed to be able to turn quicker than 109s and take more punishment than Spitfires. He had 'mixed it' with both types over the months in France and managed to claim one of each on a single day. My God, did the wine and schnapps flow that night! A few months later, fate took a cruel hand when he was returning to base after a routine defensive patrol over the Channel. He selected his wheels down – locked, everything seemed OK, until he touched the ground. His 109 sank one side then flipped over.

Vetter woke up in hospital with a fractured skull, two broken legs, a jagged cut on his right arm and some very nice attention from the nurses. When he asked what had happened his boss told him it was as a result of sloppy maintenance; when the undercarriage came down, the operating jack fell apart and one of the legs collapsed, a bolt had not been fitted properly – had worked loose over several days.

'What was responsible?' asked Vetter at the time.

'You mean 'who' – Unteroffizier Bossen, who is no longer with us!' said his boss.

'What do you mean by that... no longer with us...?' Vetter again.

'You know... posted. Anyway, why should you worry? He nearly killed you; you're lucky to be alive.'

'Where to? I liked Corporal Bossen. Diligent, or at least he seemed to be. He was always busy being run ragged and I often saw him working on aircraft late at night in the most foul of conditions. You are telling me the truth aren't you – you haven't had him shot have you?' asked Vetter.

'No no – just posted. In any case I think your flying days are over.'

Vetter pondered his luck – grounded by an accident! Still, it was a fact that nearly half of their losses were due to accidents and not by enemy action. He was pretty sure that it was the same for the Americans and British; young lads, both pilots and ground crew thrown into the deep end with High Command always demanding more regardless of the weather – and the odds.

Vetter suspected that the Corporal was not personally responsible, but was hard pressed and had relied on someone else to ensure it was all checked out, with Bossen putting his name to it. Such was the pressure. Very few days passed without allied fighter-bombers coming across the Channel and strafing their airfields. All this went on while ground crews struggled to maintain and arm the aircraft. Bossen... nice lad, always had a happy face, was always cheerful.

He would remember his name – and just imagined him now struggling somewhere on the Eastern Front.

Chapter 27

UK – Bury
Walt not Happy

In the side room Joe was back running the show and keeping order, getting the choices written down. He was smitten by the sheer simplicity of the gadget record collection and how you could move it all around. It reminded him of fancy ticker-tape machines he'd read about – except there was no paper. He had also seen some hi-fallutin' recording tape machine at college. 'These boys must be good at that fancy joint where they made this,' he thought to himself. He imagined himself working there when this war was all over. 'Wow, you would just love coming into work every day playing with gadgets like these guys have.'

They group was talking over each other, making comments, fiddling with the controls and then standing back while the sounds sunk in. Faces were pulled – or lit up – depending upon what they were listening to.

Walt had also been swept up with the story Mr Temple had given them – and these 'toys' they were now playing with... and who made them.

But...

What he was seeing was too much 'adrift' from the possibilities of what was sensible in his view – what was achievable according to his *own* engineering know-how, thinking and practical senses; what he saw was surely not possible – but there it was. And Walt had imagination – oh yes, he could dream about wild ideas like the best of them. This backed up his doubts. He still harboured suspicions of this dancing troupe – they were definitely odd, strange. He couldn't think of other words. Yeah, he knew that they were now in a different country. A foreign one, albeit on the same side, same language, similar ancestry, fighting the common enemy, but it wasn't making sense to Walt. These guys were too... clinical, ultra-modern, completely unstuffy. This was the first country he'd ever been to outside of home in the US so he didn't have a great deal to go on. He'd read, and been told by Uncle Sam and the USAAF, that the British were different... polite but tough, behind the times maybe, reserved, basically old-fashioned, not 'with-it' like his buddies – square even – but contradictory. Now, after meeting these British dudes, talking to them and watching them organise the music and seeing the dancers, he now felt like *they* were old-fashioned – and that *they* were the ones who were 'square'. But the others, the audience? Nw they behaved as he expected and what he was used to so far with the locals.

One of the first observations he'd picked up on when he first saw them was their shoes – no laces. The men had some kind of wrap-over strips with flashy-coloured basket-ball shoes... bright blue – but no laces! Everybody had laces, didn't they? I mean, how do you keep them on he wondered. The other guy had bright green ones with purple streaks on his, until he put on his fancy dancing gear. And notwithstanding the so-called 'academy' the demeanour and mannerisms of these Brits was... just too relaxed, even by his standards. They were *too* cool, *too* confident, *too* knowledgeable, all unnatural and out of place in his opinion. Yes, that's what was bugging him – they were clever, *too* clever. He'd met some real characters in the USAAF but not like these guys. Although they were obviously older, *they seemed superior...* totally different to Mr Rawlings, someone who Walt thought *was* like a typically British Brit. All this bothered him. He wasn't totally sold on what they'd been told by the guy in charge, Mr Temple – not even about the technology. But it was the behaviour, style and the way they acted and talked like young guys – it was all left-field to him.

He wasn't convinced.

So what could it be – what could explain his uneasiness? Nor could he believe that they were German spies using advanced equipment... I mean, he thought to himself, they are so blatant and relaxed about what they're doing for Chrissake. So right now, his senses were in rebellion against his imagination. He wondered if it was just him and whether his buddies also had misgivings – what he'd seen so far was overwhelming.

To reinforce his doubts, earlier on, he had also noticed something while they were fiddling with the music, an observation that made him wonder – an idea he thought preposterous, bizarre, plainly impossible. An idea he couldn't share with the crew else they'd think him 'crazy man'. He had noticed the number '2012' at the top of one of the lists as happened earlier when he's asked Mr Temple about his appointments, thinking it was a time – twelve past eight. He just thought it might be a recording time – but the same *time* twice? Why not just 2000 – eight o'clock or 2100 – or five thirty? Why 2012? He went cold – then hot.

Who could he share his suspicions with amongst his crew – who would tell him he wasn't crazy? Guys had been kicked off crews and flying for showing signs of delusion – some had even used it to *get off* flying.

So for now he wasn't going to say a word – not yet.

But in his mind, a little voice was telling him that the number 2012 wasn't a time… *but could it be a year?* When he considered this, the more he considered this, it actually made him feel more comfortable because, quite simply, it addressed his doubts; it provided answers, it explained the unexplainable. Out of this world technology that performed as if it was magic – some kind of trick, which is what had immediately crossed his mind when he'd first seen that phone. Magic.

But then… what if that voice was correct? What then? How would you explain this away, how could it have happened?

More questions. It could be them, or it could be us who is in the wrong time. They could be thinking right now it's us who's strange and that the cockamamie tale they told us was all lies. He looked at them and thought they were playing it very cool with, apparently, no care in the world – except for their music. He had not forgotten a comment made by that Mr Temple when they talked about Norwich and that dance club, about it being closed down long ago – and yet it was still going strong last week apparently. Walt picked up on things like this – odd at the time, but would make sense if that little voice was right.

Part of him hoped he was wrong and that everything would revert back to normal. Please God.

Chapter 28

Walt, Barney and Joe

Serious

'Hey Barney.' Walt had waited a while but couldn't hold on any longer; he needed to share his anxieties without going too far into detail – especially about 2012, so to hell with it he thought. Barney suspected Walt wanted to get something off his chest by the manner in which he sidled up to him. Walt went on...

'Did you buy what he said to us earlier about all his fancy gear – I mean, you're an engineer and I'm an engineer but I can't see how it could happen... not in my mind anyhow? It's like magic... that stuff is like dream-world.' Walt was sounding Barney out but was afraid of taking it to the next level. 'It sure don't feel natural to me.'

Excited and impressed as he was with the tale Mr Temple had told them, Barney had to admit that what they'd seen was too slick – beyond expectations in his wildest of dreams. Maybe Walter was right. Just maybe.

'But what else is there Walt? What explains it all... some big con, a big lie, a big trick? Let's get Joe in and hear what he thinks. Are you worried about the Germans again?'

'Funnily enough, no... it's way out of their league, even for them,' responded Walt. This surprised Barney.

'But he told us what happened...' He was going to continue but suddenly said, 'Let's get Joe over.'

Walt's answer had made him think... not the Germans. So who... what was worrying him?

'What do *you* reckon Joey – what Mr Temple told us, do you buy his story?' asked Barney in a strong whisper. 'Walt's having second thoughts. The more I think about it I have to say that I'm not totally sold, much as I like the whole idea. I was even thinking that when this pesky war is all over, asking for a job with these guys! Imagine working with all this? Anyhow, anything in particular that's got your goat Walt? Something we've not noticed?'

Joey threw in his penny's worth, 'I'm just amazed by it all – haven't even thought about any other reasons or possibilities. I guess the only thing that kept crossing my mind was me trying to tell our buddies back at base about all this and trying to convince them.'

'See!' exclaimed Walt. 'No one is going to believe us for obvious reasons if you tried to tell them.'

Both Joe and Barney could see that Walt was quite vexed by it all.

'You'll think I'm crazy – but I'm worried that I might be right with what I want to tell you. You have to promise me that after you've told me how stupid I am, you ain't breathing a word to anybody else. You have to goddamn promise… promise? But I might just be able to prove it too.'

Joey and Barney could both see how serious Walt was, his breathing becoming heavy, beads of perspiration appearing on his now-troubled brow. They looked at each other.

'Sure Walt, sure… we're buddies, right? Sure.'

'Well… you know those lists we were playing and those numbers we saw – those numbers that were repeated on a few pages, did you notice them? The number 2012?'

'Yeah. No. What about it?'

'…and I saw on his little fancy phone gizmo earlier the same number come up,' added Walt.

'Which number – 2012? So what?' said Joe. 'What's so special about 2012? That's a time isn't it – like on our raids.'

'Yes – that's what bothers me. He was looking up on his calendar for a meeting or something. That number was at the top. Big too. Not like a time but like a date… 2012,' said Walter.

'A date…? What – like a year…?' Walt watched as Barney's face went white as what he had indicated slowly sank in, momentarily lost for words. Barney took in a breath as if to say something but paused before saying. 'God. Please God, let it not be true,' knowing in his own mind that it supplied the answers. Then a rational streak of thought asserted itself.

'No, no, surely not! And how Walt? You saying…'

'Shush,' interjected Walt. 'Not so loud. Don't want everybody hearing...'

'So... you saying that these guys are from the future... 2012? But that's over sixty years ahead. And *how* in any case?' But his mind was already telling him it was a perfect fit – but impossible too. Or was it? 'Joe, what do you think?'

'Oh Christ, I feel sick. How did they get here then? *Why* are they here?' Can't be spies 'cos they'd be way ahead of us man, I mean their cars would be... oh shit! That explains that machine outside!' Their mouths dropped – Joe had provided, had reminded them, of some *proof...* that sparkling, shiny vehicle by the door – and the motorbike. It was all adding up... plus the limo in that scary film clip.

'Are they the ones who are in the wrong time or could it be us?' asked Barney in a panicked tone. They all looked at each other, then slowly looked over at Mr Temple who had caught their look, giving a thumbs up. 'Yeah, but hold it man,' Barnet went on, '...that means they know who won this goddamn war!'

'We're winning it hands down already man,' said Joe.

But the answer to Barney's question came almost immediately – the unmistakeable sound of an air raid siren.

Chapter 29

The siren

I'd been thinking about bringing on a little dance competition, something we occasionally had depending upon if the punters were up for it – get a few couples to take part doing waltzes or jiving etc. The quickstep and foxtrot were clearly being put to good use as you could imagine considering the date, however, we already had a good collection from previous gigs already set up. All I had to do was make the announcement telling them that my dancers were the judges – and play the music. Matt and Ruby usually took care of the more energetic moves while Keith and Becky looked after the more sedate arrangements. As a prize, we normally had a bottle or two of something for the winners but it crossed my mind of course that just about all bottles will have a date on them – somewhere. Wouldn't do would it. 'Hey Molly, nice wine this, I wonder what year it's from…? Let's have a look.'

But there again, who drinks wine in 1944 – in England? Even the boss drinks whiskey – the big boss, you know, the PM.

'We could promise the winners some special coaching – one on one – in any dance they wanted,' suggested Becky.

'Or a day out at Blackpool,' added Keith, '…sorry, even Great Yarmouth.'

Blackpool? Great Yarmouth?

Shaddup!

'Nice idea. Okay that's what we'll offer, some coaching,' I responded. As I leaned over to the mike, the eerie but unmistakeable sound of a siren interrupted our train of thought.

Now it so happens that earlier, when we were desperately thinking of some kind of escape strategy from our so-called 'time-slip' predicament, an air-raid did not even figure in our plans. For some reason I'd thought that towards the end of the war the Germans had more or less forgotten about sleepy-hollow market towns in its bombing strategy and only concentrated on the big joints – and military targets such as airfields.

But Bury…? Surely not.

I looked over to see Chris Rawlings making his way over to us. I raised an eye-brow in question. As he approached he spoke up.

'Probably a nuisance raid Mr Temple but we have to remember that East Anglia is on the way to London if you're coming from Holland and Germany. However, there is RAF Rougham nearby and it has been attacked before and Bury was directly attacked last year. We have to take shelter… follow me and Albert… or go with Wilf. We usually nip over to my Aunt's house just around the corner by the square.'

'What? Your Aunt's has an air-raid shelter?' exclaimed Keith.

'No – but she has a sturdy table under the staircase – and its nearer. Come on!'

'Right behind you Chris – we'll follow,' I called out.

A quick double take showed people moving towards the doors – obviously in a well-practised fashion, no panic and no doubt headed towards the nearest public shelter. I whispered out loud to my dancers, 'This is our chance to get going guys… what do you reckon? By the time Chris has noticed we are not with him any more it'll be too late.'

'Absolutely… tailor made! We'll help you load up as soon as they've legged it out the door,' said Matt. A crashing sound drew our attention…one of our tables had been knocked over in the exodus with glasses, cups and fags everywhere. A young airman – over-exuberant – fell backwards from his Lindy hop attempts and rush to exit, and barged into the table we had sat at; iPods, car keys, phones and paper went flying. We quickly gathered them up.

'Are you OK…?' I asked.

'Gee, sorry Mack – got carried away,' said the Yank staggering towards the exits. This was followed by laughter and guffaws from a nearby table.

'Hey, Eddie – been drinking milk again!?' shouted someone from across the floor, '…can't take him anywhere!' More laughter. Had to be Barney's lot.

They all seemed to know each other – well at least all those dressed up in USAAF gear.

189

'It's before midnight – remember what we said,' I reminded them. 'We knew immediately that we had to act reasonably fast – we weren't sure how long these raids might last before the 'all-clear' sounded. Bags, plasmas, laptops, music mixer, lights and the rest of our so-called gig-pack were to be gathered up and thrown into the Rover. Well, almost thrown… but we weren't going to be too delicate – not tonight. Frantic packing, ultra-quick loading – a quick look around to make sure nothing missed – and we were out. Matt and Rubes probably did the fastest change into leathers ever done.

'Where's my phone? Did you pick up my phone Rubes?' asked Matt.

'I saw Bob chuck a load of stuff into his bag in the panic. Pretty sure it was in there somewhere along with mine.'

'OK.'

Most of those on the move had not cast us a second glance – they were only interested in getting out but there were a few stragglers who watched fascinated as we dismantled our show in record time. I did catch a brief glance from Grace who quickly raised a hand and a smile in acknowledgement as she disappeared through the door… a 'goodbye' wave? I turned back to our packing.

'Are you coming back…?' asked a hopeful.

'Yeah… in about seventy years' time,' Keith shouted on his way out.

Before we actually set off we agreed to retrace our steps and meet up at the same pub. But we had to take it easy – no point in being flagged down by some military type armed with a Thomson machine gun. We agreed that we'd have to drive without lights… or only with sidelights if we were desperate.

We'd been on the move for only ten seconds when we realised we needed the sidelights – and then 20 seconds later…

'Listen!' exclaimed Keith. Sure enough, there was the sound of aircraft engines. We lowered the windows for clarification. 'They sound quite low,' he added. I was so involved in looking around in the semi-darkness that I nearly ran down a woman hurrying along the street with a masked torch. I quickly swerved to avoid her.

Grace! My God – it was indeed her.

'Grace – get in quick!' With the sound of aircraft engines filling the night she quickly looked at us and with me leaning out and recognising me, she didn't need any further encouragement. Grace scrambled in beside Becky.

'Oh, thank you. Thank you,' she said a little out of breath and looking at each of us in turn. I could see she felt relieved – and safe. 'I was looking for my girls. I can't find them. We only live nearby – that's where I was going. They were with another group I think,' she said. 'But where are *you* going...?' she said as she looked around the Rover, seeing all of our jumble in the back and on our laps. 'Are you leaving Bob? Where are you going?'

I nearly cried out. I could see Keith looking sideways at me with a look that said 'You can't do it – you can't take her with us. You know we can't.'

'Bedford and Milton Keynes. It's not worth going back and setting up again but we can keep you safe for now – and then we'll drop you off back home which is, what, just back down the road... is that okay Grace? We have time.'

Keith whispered under his breath, 'Don't forget – there might not *be a tomorrow* Bob. There might not even be a 'here'. We have to be careful.'

'Yeah – don't I know it,' I said quietly in his direction.

A whispered voice from the back said, 'Yes please – thank you.' I turned around to Grace and gave her a smile adding,

'I'll look after you Grace – and I'll make sure you get home safe...don't you worry.' For some reason I relaxed – I wasn't worried any more, nothing else mattered but Grace. I'd known her for no more than a couple of hours or so and exchanged less than a few hundred words. It was then I noticed her beginning to take in her surroundings – our car, the seats, lighting and I was just a little disconcerted when Becky had said, 'Come on, we have to get you belted up.'

'Belted up...?'

'New rules Grace, sorry,' I added.

'Look at me Grace, look straight at me,' said Becky as the phone flash went off for a snap. 'I'll explain later... we'll *all* explain later when we have a break and meet up – I need it.'

'Hear, hear,' from the rest of us. 'A little further and then we'll pop back.'

'Hope you had that in video mode as well,' I added looking at Becky.

A million thoughts now began working across my mind – and I kept looking at her reflection in the mirror; she was constantly looking at me in return. I no longer had to fathom how she felt about me – that passionate kiss, snatched in the alley, her acceptance to trust in me said everything... but we were 'out of each other's time'.

'Look ahead guys,' said Keith. 'Is that our bikers pulled up over there on the side? Yes it is.' As we were only doing about thirty in any case – trundling along in the dark – I only had to turn in, stopping behind Matt and Ruby who were standing by their machine.

Keith and I climbed out. 'We'll have a better look and sort out our stuff when we get to the pub – too dark here.'

'OK.'

Matt and Ruby came up to the Rover. 'You *did* pick up our phones I hope?' asked Ruby.

'Pretty sure I did, just scooped up everything that was knocked onto the floor plus some gear on the table – threw it all into my bag,' said Keith.

'I think that this is near where we encountered the police car we saw earlier – we noticed the other lay-by just back there – we think,' said Matt, pointing up the road. Rubes nodded. Then she did a quick double-take looking into the car.

'Who's that with you...? Oh my God, is it the girl you were dancing with, Bob?'

'Yes, but don't panic – we just happened to pass her right in the middle of the raid. 'Damsel in distress' and all that. We're taking her straight back to her home in a minute – it's not far. Sounds like the planes are going away now,' I said, noticing the initial look of alarm in Ruby's face. 'You two carry on and we'll meet as arranged – if the pub is still open. We'll see you there one way or the other, open or not.'

Grace was listening intently to what was going on with her looking from one to another as we spoke but her glance kept returning to me...me, now realising that very soon, it will be the last time – ever – that our glances would meet... the last time my gaze would fall on her captivating and beguiling eyes, her gentle smile. And of course, *she* would not know that shortly, it would be forever. I opened the door. I felt such a fraud as I bent down to give her my best smile – and a brief touch of a kiss, as Becky looked on, watching both of us intently.

That kiss... Grace smiled back.

'Right then, we'll set off and catch you later,' said the bikers as they picked up their crash hats. As Keith and I turned towards our motor, Becky let out a scream.

'Oh God... where has she gone? Becky was moving away from where Grace *had* sat... but pointing frantically at an empty space. The inside light had given it all an eerie semblance. Grace was no longer there – she had simply vanished. During these discussions, we suddenly found ourselves back on a busy road with speeding, noisy traffic, in modern times – but with no sign of Grace; she has simply disappeared – gone from our lives.

We all stood in shock, staring at the empty seat in the Rover. Becky clapped her hands over her mouth, her head shaking. 'She was just there... just sat there... and she's gone!' she said, pointing again at the space. Keith got in beside to comfort her. I could only think of the fading sight of Grace. I was already desperately willing for her to reappear...to reappear anywhere. I looked around then looked at the others.

'She's returned. She's back in her time. Or we are. My God. Did she say anything Becky?' I asked, desperate for anything.

'No – nothing.'

That bit of news didn't do me any good at all.

The road had become busy – normal lighting, cars flashing by. Our dusty lay-by was now a proper parking area.

'And yes, so are we!' exclaimed Keith.

Matt and Rubes cuddled each other, 'Thank God for that,' he said. 'I need a bloody drink!'

'Don't we all,' I remarked, still in shock I had to admit. 'Let's go in first pub we see!'

As we cruised away, our minds in turmoil, Becky said, 'Christ! What happened just then? What a night!'

Now that it had all sunk in we were quite stunned by events.

We left Bury behind.

My mind kept returning to those few seconds ago... where had she gone? Was she now trapped somewhere – in some no-man's land? How was it explainable, I mean, I'm a technically savvy bloke, can change a light bulb, wire a plug. Can't do a Haydon Collider just yet – but what had we just witnessed?

It transpired that no, we had *not* picked up all the phones; we'd left one behind which had us all thinking of the possibilities.

'Bloody hell – let's hope nobody finds it. What do you think *they'll* think it is?' Matt asked later.

'A piece of junk if the battery's flat,' said Keith. 'It was 'on' the last time I remember seeing it. Might find that some distant relative of Steve Jobs has picked it up or something… it's *too* nice not to be picked up.'

'Now *that* would be interesting…' Matt responded on a lighter note.

PART 2

Chapter 30

Where's mum? A delivery

Susan and Cecily were becoming increasingly worried; they'd eventually reached home after a few cuddles and kisses from some local farm-hands only to find their house locked up.

'Mum!' they shouted at the upper windows, 'Let us in!' It soon became apparent that no one was at home so they had to scramble around in darkness fumbling for their own keys. The house was empty.

They hadn't heard any bomb explosions during the raid so they were at least unworried on that score. After two hours of frantic knocking on doors of friends and relatives, their mum had turned up and when they saw her in the kitchen light they gasped. She had practically turned grey overnight – and was distraught.

Grace told them she had been given a lift in the middle of the raid by the music players shortly after leaving the hall, and that when they had stopped out of town before bringing her back, she had suddenly found herself sitting on the ground – the vehicle and everybody in it had simply disappeared along with the two bike riders.

'Oh mum, they didn't 'interfere' with you did they… they didn't hurt you?' cried Cecily, almost crying and noticing her mum's dishevelled clothing.

Grace was completely shaken. She wondered if she'd been the subject of some elaborate trick; she had briefly noticed – for less than a second – the musicians' faces melt into nothing… that's when she realised she was sitting on the ground and now completely on her own, in almost total darkness. But she reassured them.

'No, no, no… nothing like that – they were charming but I remember that it was a strange vehicle with strange coloured signs in it. Mr Temple was very nice, they all were, but they simply disappeared like in a magician's show. I can't explain it… they just vanished!'

'But you've turned grey. Something must have happened mum!'

'Please don't ask me about this, girls,' she had begged on returning, 'Let me get some sleep.'

After the shock of finding herself all alone at the roadside Grace had seen two houses nearby and made her way towards them. She managed to tell a story of being stranded and eventually, because one of the occupants worked at the newly built army camp, managed to get back to her home.

As she lay in bed that night her mind went over and over the evening's events. She began to worry that she may have fainted in the vehicle and that they had simply taken her out before continuing on their own journey – she had fainted once before when she was pregnant; one moment she was about to order her meat in the shop, the next she was laying on a makeshift bed in the local school with her neighbour fussing around her – it must have been the smell she said. She'd lost nearly five minutes. But no… Bob would not have done that, not.

When she could she would discreetly enquire from Mr Rawlings where Mr Temple had come from exactly. Surely he would have a proper address – she had never heard of Milton Keynes but one of her neighbours worked in the post office. Maybe she could help.

The next day brought an awful realisation that although she was married, it had been two years since she had last seen her 'man' – and that Mr Temple had completely crowded out all thoughts of Sergeant Jim Atkinson, her soldier husband – the father of Cecily and Susan. He was somewhere in Italy. Pangs of guilt swept over her. She was hoping that her two girls had not picked up those invisible feelings and thoughts that had passed between them last night when they were dancing. And that brief kiss… she could never forget that kiss…

In the back of her mind, something all women had to get used to in this war, was the knowledge that the dreaded telegram might one day drop onto her mat. She had no idea what dangers her Jim faced each and every day except to know that he was not infantry. 'I man the tanks,' was all he would say, proudly. The girls, of course, being girls, would laugh and giggle through the days listening to the radio and helping their mum when they could after working in the army food distribution warehouse, which seemed to be stockpiling an awful amount of goods. God knows what for. Grace often wondered if they thought at all about what Dad was doing – what dangers he faced, and when he would be coming home. Her guilt returned whenever those moments from that evening were recalled. Then one day the girls came home saying the warehouse had been emptied – emptied practically overnight – completely stripped bare. Grace had made

198

the connection even if the girls hadn't, it was shortly after 6th June and the papers were full of it.

'Remember girls – the army marches on its stomach, and you played your part! Everybody is working for the war, even with simple jobs,' she had said. It was palpable how the general mood had brightened up. All her friends and neighbours were suddenly more chatty – more friendly. Maybe the war was going to end sooner than they all thought. Nevertheless, Grace's thought would always return to Bob, wondering where he was and what he would be doing.

Susan saw him first as she walked towards her front door – and shrieked. Cecily was following and hurriedly caught up with her throwing her hands up to her mouth when she too saw the buff coloured paper in the hands of the man at their front door. They knew what it meant.

The three women of the household sat there all night – the girls inconsolable. Their father had died of injuries sustained in a skirmish. Thousands were dying in Northern France every day, and yet her poor Jim met his end as a result of some small battle over in Italy, away from the main battle. Grace was numb for several days but, as was usual in their small town, people gathered round, helped out, provided what comfort they could until they could cope once again. That's how it was.

...

Chapter 31

Germany 1944

The Find

Major Vetter's mind came back to the present. 'Sergeant Schneider, I think we should return to base now,' he called. 'There's only this that may be of interest,' he added, holding up the unusual object they had retrieved.

Some parts of the B-17 were still smoking and there remained the all-pervading stench of a gasoline-soaked earth. 'It'll be some time before anything grows here again,' thought Vetter. And it was not just Allied planes that were crashing – accidents were happening too often – in the next field only a few hundred metres away was the wreck of a Messerschmitt 109, an accidental crash apparently, no enemy action, the pilot just lost control and did not make it… only eighteen years old he was informed.

Major Vetter's thoughts floated back to his last squadron – to a close friend and colleague, but also a hot-head. He'd never forget the day when his friend, Ernst, returned over the airfield from a mission having shouted down the radio that he had bagged two – you could tell by his voice how excited he was, according to control. Ernst was a brilliant marksman and already had five British machines painted on his cockpit. He came roaring over the dispersal. 'Just keep it calm,' thought Vetter, watching him, 'Don't get silly.' But Ernst was having none of that. He flew low over the hangars – upside down – showing off, which then brought him down towards the end of the landing approach area, and where the other returning aircraft were already lining up, wheels down to land. Instantly, Vetter guessed exactly what his friend was going to do.

'No! No! Don't do it,' he shouted out loud.

As if he could hear!

Of course everybody was now outside watching. Ernst saw the closest returning 109, and thought he could do a quick, sharp turn and drop down in front of it, to avoid having to go round again to join the queue. Yes, he did the turn but Vetter could see the inevitability of it all – the turn was too sharp, the speed too slow, wheels and flaps already down. He stalled and spun into the ground, the aircraft cartwheeling with an almighty *crump*. Amazingly there was no fire but Vetter knew, as he sprinted to the crash, knew that few would survive that kind of crash. Ernst was still strapped in the smashed cockpit which was on its side and on its own – the engine, wings and tail were thirty metres away. He was still moving – still breathing – but broken when Vetter reached him. Blood covered his face and flying jacket.

'Why, oh, why?' he shouted at his dying friend. '*Why* Ernst?' Others came running. Vetter leaned in closer to his friend.

Still conscious, he mumbled – whispered through his shattered, blood-soaked mouth, 'Herr Kapitan... Ralph, put a bullet in my brain, I beg you... I know I'm finished.'

Ralph Vetter looked closer into the cockpit. The rudder pedals were unnaturally close to the seat; Ernst had practically lost his legs. And Vetter realised too that his friend's head was sitting at a strange angle. No part of his body was moving apart from the laboured breathing. This man, a man so full of life, joy and vigour – this man un-complaining every day at the number of sorties and battles he fought with the enemy, now lying shattered in the wreck of his beloved, personalised 109. What a waste. Vetter wanted to scream out loud – even strike his friend in sheer frustration for this needless waste. The fire truck was just then approaching with noisy sirens. He looked up from the cockpit, took a sniff – no fuel smell. He reached for his pistol, brought it over the side and placed it against his friend's head. He leant back in. Ernst slowly nodded, knew what was coming.

'I salute you Ernst.' And he pulled the trigger.

Chapter 32

Germany 1944 – bomb sights

He looked again at the wreck. How was a small item like this going to change the course of the war for the Allies? A German *wonder weapon* maybe, but this?! He admitted to himself that it was probably something associated with electrics – not hydraulics or landing gear. There was not enough bulk to it and was that glass that was part of its construction? He wasn't sure – it needed cleaning up.

The American B-17 was a large bomber with a crew of ten. Some in the Luftwaffe referred to it as 'Four Motors' but Vetter preferred to use its proper name.

HQ was always interested in radio and radar developments, for something special or different, a new bomb aiming device perhaps. There were also rumours of an auto gun-laying system, and that something might be being developed at Thorpe Abbots with the 100th Bomber Group and also of a special bomber squadron – even knew the number (101) operating out of Lincolnshire that might have counter-measure equipment, especially radio counter-measures… yes he knew about these outfits.

He now had a practised eye in spotting items of interest even though what he looked for was usually bent or broken, or if it wasn't broken, it was usually burnt, often beyond recognition. He also knew where to look… he was always on the lookout.

They were both quite conversant with the Luftwaffe's own bomb-sighting systems including Lichtenstein and were now very familiar with the American Norden bomb sight. He had even retrieved intact mechanisms. Not every crashed plane hit the ground nose first although he knew that aircrew, before bailing out – if they could – had instructions to put a bullet into the bomb sight before jumping out. Amazing! Vetter had come across only a few of these – let's face it, he thought, who is going to spend precious seconds doing this when they were always desperate to get out, their lives at stake... and when most airmen thought the crash would do the job for them?

He certainly knew about the Oboe and H2S systems the British were using, could do with finding one intact, particularly H2S – a system that mapped the ground's features using radar. The British relied on a combination of tactics and technology to improve their bombing accuracy – 'Pathfinders dropping marker flares' for the bomb aimers to target spots backed up with Oboe, although that only had limited range and H2S – not every aircraft was equipped with it. Germany quickly caught on – the air defences would light up fake markers and flares to fool the main bombing force.

Perhaps it *was* a piece of aircrew kit he was looking at, its size saying so. American airmen had a reputation for being well-equipped when it came to personal kit. He looked back at the tangled mess from where he'd retrieved the item but it was not typical of bomb sight parts he'd seen before, and it was covered in an oily, dirty layer – maybe acid contamination, a common occurrence.

As an ex-pilot, he knew that nearly all instrumentation was generally round, dolls' eyes and dials, and even after a battering, he could guess what shape they had been. How often he'd seen the last register of a pressure, the final speed, the bomber's attitude at death... even the time.

Although slightly twisted by impact, he thought this item was rectangular-shaped and quite certain that it was originally flat, like an old battered cigarette case.

Command often showed its displeasure and made angry calls when it was presented by bits of junk that someone had thought interesting; what they wanted was something tangible on radar, radar-assisted bombing systems and guidance mechanisms.

This did not fit the bill in Vetter's opinion; he considered discarding it but changed his mind, placing it onto a trolley just for the moment, belonging to the salvage team, with the intention of looking at it more closely when they had finished.

Fire always brought its own dangers – some materials produced deadly toxic fumes. Batteries were a particular danger – he knew of crash investigators who'd been burnt by acid, it could drip onto you from anywhere. However, this wreck was now only smouldering in parts, with the rest of the scattered plane lying there, awaiting their attention.

Have you found anything Schneider – anything…?' They'd been looking for about twenty minutes already and they usually knew where to look first.

'No, nothing yet sir, apart from the three bodies reported earlier by the first crew… and some tags. I am still looking.'

It was then that Schneider discovered three crumpled tin helmets in the same place in what was left of the front fuselage part – he called over to Major Vetter. Pointing at them he said, 'These are the sort of helmets soldiers wear, not aircrew Herr Major… and not our soldiers either; I think they're British.'

'Really? But it's an American machine.' The Major walked closer to have a look. A mystery he thought – British soldiers' helmets in a crashed American bomber…?! Maybe they should pay a little more attention to this wreck. 'OK Sergeant.'

He wondered – just three bodies. Some of the crew must have made it, must have escaped, thought Vetter. The B-17 crews numbered ten – *usually*. But three tin hats too…? 'Thirteen in a B-17… what's going on?' he asked himself – impossible for thirteen. And in any case, the initial recovery team should have dealt with dead crew members, not them. But why the tin hats? He'd never seen that before. In any case, whoever was wearing them, if anybody had been, they'd be as crumpled and bent as the helmets.

'Still no idea what this item might be…?' asked Vetter, referring to the object again. Schneider looked at it for a while, intrigued, turning it over,

'It looks like nothing, too small but it is telling me something special. It is not obvious to me, Herr Major, what it could be… perhaps personal equipment.'

'I think so too.'

Chapter 33

UK – Bury
Mum Resolves

As the days drifted into weeks, Grace began to think more and more of the mysterious encounter with *that* Mr Temple at *that* dance. What might he be doing right now? Was he safe? Surely he must be because he was too old to be involved in the war effort. And yet he *wasn't* old, not to her at least. The way he walked, talked and conducted himself, his mannerisms, that youthful gleam in his eyes told Grace that there was some hidden story – some mystery about him. It was the same when she recollected her thoughts of that evening, about his dancing partners – they too were of a different mould to other people she knew. When she thought about men Mr Temple's age at her factory, they were the foremen, the janitors, old gents, and the big bosses… ancient, all getting on. It showed in their carriage, language and approach to life – real 'pipe and slippers', not a spark of youth in them at all. Finished. Just biding their time.

Bob had been different.

As the memories of Jim faded, Grace once again considered approaching Jim Rawlings, who she knew 'at a distance' as they say, but she would have to make up some little white lie to maintain the innocence because people talked… they were naturally nosy and word would soon get around on any juicy titbits.

'Mr Rawlings, my girls have said to me that the staff at their work want to organise a party or dance and they were wondering if you would give me the telephone number or address of those dancers you had in the Town Hall a couple of months ago. Do you remember? They would like to see them again, especially the dancers.' Grace didn't know why, but she was embarrassed just asking – as if the white lie was plastered all over her face.

However she had been dismayed to be told that it was not he who had booked them at all… they had just turned up! His original booking had been lost or something, so he had no idea where they had come from – apart from the leader saying they were from Bedford way, some place he hadn't heard of. In fact, Chris Rawlings went on, '…the Americans at that dance were suspicious of them – as I was at first. They thought they might be spies with all their fancy equipment and odd music. We even summoned the police but Wilf – remember Wilf? – said it was nothing to worry about, that they were OK.'

Yes, she remembered it well.

But spies? Bob a spy?

There were unusual aspects of what she had seen that night – and heard. The music was mostly new or strange but Glenn Miller was Glenn Miller. And who was that strange boy singing they had danced to? She was not totally ignorant of what was played on the wireless as it was constant all day long courtesy of the BBC, both at home and at work. And she had worked in the post office briefly, knew what a tele-printer machine was, but Bob's machine he played his music on – the peculiar typewriter – and that cinema screen he had hanging on the wall, well, maybe Bob moved or worked in different circles to others. In any case, she'd been pleasantly struck by the amiability and forwardness of Bob when they had first approached him for a request.

But a spy? No… almost laughable

However, Grace kept coming up against the last, unbelievable experience – when they were all together in the car, then *suddenly not together*. What had happened to her – where had Bob and his partners gone? She had kept quiet about this mysterious episode. Only she and her daughters knew. Nobody else, apart from Bob – and what was her name… was it Becky?

Perhaps she had been slipped a drug, this was all she could hang onto to provide a sane explanation of the events, but she knew it to be unlikely.

Grace resolved to write a letter to Bob in the hope that it would find him… somehow. Bedford was not that far away really and the surname *Temple* not too common, so she enlisted her close friends to ask around for anybody who might have contacts that way, such as the address of a local post office – and also near Milton Keynes which she remembered. She daren't tell Cecily and Susan what she was planning to do – they were still struggling to come to terms about their Dad. That they would eventually overcome their sadness, Grace was sure and then she could pick her time to explain. Life had to go on. Bob was not young but she imagined that even five years with him would be better than a long life alone.

Post office addresses were found and a neighbour's cousin who had once worked in the vicinity that way promised to make further enquiries. Grace sent letters to these distant post offices and even to a *Temple* in the area that had eventually been found. Her heart sang when the one reply she received was from a sister of a 'Bob Temple', unfortunately, a Robert Temple serving in the Far East... and only twenty-one years old.

She stepped up her search.

She had tried initially looking for Temples in her local area to see if it was a common name and was surprised to see that there were only two listed... but Bury was small place. Bedford, she knew, was bigger and likely to have several Temple families. Her friend eventually informed her that she had no luck and was unable to find any trace of any 'R Temple' – but there were a few 'Templetons'.

Grace did not give up and sent many more letters, widening the search area in the region, however, she realised after a while that her search may have been compromised by the chaos of the war and the many disrupted or destroyed postal facilities. Communications remained haphazard and people were constantly on the move. Her search and chance of success was made more difficult by the lack of any street name and house number, so it really was a scatter-gun approach – just a surname and a town or village and relying on the well-known initiative and resourcefulness of postmen. Letters had got through on a great deal less information when sent to the fighting forces on the front lines. So she was hopeful – there were many hamlets and villages covering a large area over that way, far more populated than in Suffolk. She had decided early on to write the same short letter starting with,

My Dearest Robert,

I hope this letter finds you safe and well. I shall never forget our short time together – and when we danced... etc. etc.

The months passed with only a few kind, but unhopeful replies. *Mr Bob Temple* seemed to have vanished into thin air. As time passed both Cecily and Susan had noticed a sadness envelope their mum as she slowly retreated more and more into her house, going out only when she had to – never attending any dances or social gatherings such as tombola meetings like her daughters did often. And now both were married and the only enjoyment Grace had was with her daughters and grandchildren.

Then one day Cecily and Susan said, 'Mum – we're taking you out to the flicks – you need cheering up and there's a good film on at the local flea pit. Margaret is babysitting for us so it's just us three.'

'No, I don't want to go out – I can look after the children, you don't have to ask Margaret, you know I love looking after the kids but thank you all the same... you go.'

'Sorry mum, we're not taking 'no' for an answer,' said Susan. Eventually they persuaded her; Grace agreed as long as her neighbour friend could come along too.

'What is the film we are going to see?' asked their Mum.

'*Love Me Tender*.

Chapter 34

Bury

At the Flicks

Grace kept wondering. A little bell was ringing in her head about the film – the name seemed not unfamiliar and Cecily had told her that everybody was going mad about this new singer who was a master of the new rock 'n' roll dance all the youngsters were doing, and that he was real dishy mum' into the bargain.

But she became disturbed when, during the film, the young star made his appearance. No… surely not, but she could not get out of her mind that this boy, Elvis Presley, she had seen somewhere before.

'Susan – Cecily,' she whispered hard, leaning towards them in the darkness to get their attention. 'I'm sure we have seen him before somewhere. Was he the man we saw dancing in a jail, when we all went out together many years ago, remember – here in Bury?'

'Shush,' was the only response. Elvis had their complete attention along with the rest of the cinema. Then she thought perhaps that this young lad may have made appearances as part of the regular morale-boosting forces shows that were always on the go in the war, alongside people like Bob Hope, Bing Crosby and the Glenn Miller band. But it was the voice that captivated her. No one else that she knew or heard had a voice quite like this boy starring in this film. With her thoughts in turmoil she just could not relax and enjoy it. This film was new. It was now 1956 so it was very doubtful he was singing all those years ago. He looked about twenty years old – if that!

Then he started to sing.

Love Me Tender.

Within ten seconds, Grace was numb. She listened a short while longer then let out a despairing cry, 'Cecily! Susan! Oh dear, oh no! It's the same song,' and rose to her feet scrambling to get out of the cinema. The daughters made desperate apologies to those nearest and scrambled out after her, Cecily already crying. They found their mum just outside sobbing and gasping, 'How is it possible? I don't understand.'

It had suddenly dawned on Cecily too – her mum was right. Only a few moments ago into the singing she recognised the soft tones of a song from long ago, and yet here it was again, in a new film... or maybe a very similar voice but the tune was unmistakeable.

'It has to be a coincidence,' offered Cecily as they tried to calm their mother down. 'It must surely be someone who sounds similar replaying the same song mum,' she said hopefully. Susan could only vaguely remember the night in question and could not recall the song, although she did remember the young good-looking man dancing in a jail.

But Grace was certain, it was one and the same man, no mistake. That voice – you could *not* forget *that* voice... and Bob had played it for her.

It was not long before another friend came out to join them wondering what was going on. 'What's happened? What's happened Grace?'

'I'll explain later,' Grace responded, knowing she would not be able to. After a minute or two they went back to their homes.

'I'll look after her,' her friend had said to the two girls.

At home Grace made a cuppa for them both and then sank into the settee, explaining that she was upset because she had been saddened on hearing an old song that brought back memories.

'What, from the film?' she asked, '...an old song?'

Grace nodded.

'But this is a new film,' her friend replied.

'That's what baffles me.'

She was now wondering who Bob Temple was exactly, and where he had come from – and where had he returned to.

The next day she sat down and resumed her quest for the mysterious Mr Temple, writing several more letters to previous post office addresses – and to some new ones. It had been several years now since she last wrote. Bob would now be twelve years older. Would he still be alive, and what would he be doing now? She had managed to see Mr Rawlings again in the past and asked for details of orchestras, bands and other musicians in the hope that they moved in similar circles and might know of the elusive Mr Temple. But no one had. Now, hearing that tune again had hardened her resolve to continue the search.

Chapter 35

Germany WWII
A B-24

At the wreck.

They had found nothing else of interest so he went back to the trolley and looked again at his find. Part of its casing was fire damaged; the rest of it looked intact but with some dirt on it. There seemed to be what looked like faint markings around the remaining edges. He could only make out one letter – 'V' and possibly a 'W'. He shook it; it made no noise. Usually when he shook broken parts, something would rattle or fall off.

The salvage team had already informed them about three bodies they had found and removed.

'Sergeant Schneider, inform the local authorities and the clearance party that there'll be allied aircrew scattered or hiding somewhere close by – probably up to seven or eight of them,' commanded Vetter. Unless the rest of the crew were in a part of the wreckage they hadn't seen yet, but in this case it was unlikely. It was not unusual for some of the bombers in their terrifying death throes, plunging to earth with major parts wrenched off and finishing hundreds of metres away from the main part, but the fuselage, all of it which contained the crews, seemed to be here. Tail-gunners had been found in their positions in broken off tail sections many metres away from the main crash site, dead but whole – almost serene, unlike the horrible fate of those found crushed or dismembered in the main part of the aircraft.

'Of course, Herr Major!' said Schneider. Vetter thought that the locals were probably already doing just that; they were well used to these situations by now – a twenty-four hour routine almost. The only respite they got was when the weather was bad and the enemy was grounded.

He had known of an incident involving a B-24 on its way to target, fully loaded; the bomber had been hit so badly that the whole machine was a fireball after thirty seconds. The crew obviously knew what the result would be – they didn't hang about, two were out while it was still level. The aircraft began to roll and oscillate. Several seconds later, the fighter pilot reported, a wing came off, the B-24 did a short cartwheel and went down like a weather cock with the remaining wing keeping the doomed machine on its side doing a corkscrew. Another two made it from the bomber while it was in this position and then, to the amazement of the watching pilot, the other wing came off. Mesmerised, he watched the wing, in flames, flutter downwards. But his attention then switched to the plummeting fuselage, still on fire, dropping like a missile gathering speed with only the tail acting like a shuttlecock, giving it the nose-down attitude. 'Surely, if there's anybody still inside then they are finished,' thought the pilot. It looked as if the fire was now out.

Such was the speed of the fuselage, the fighter couldn't keep up with the fuselage projectile and yet, incredibly, very close to impact, another body came away from the B-24. The pilot had to pull up then, and lost sight of the crewmen but he did see the crash, no explosion – just a spray of dirt… and then nothing. He flew around looking for the last man but could not see anything initially, until he saw an open parachute on the ground. He took note of the approximate location and, on landing, made enquiries on the crews that had survived… but he was only interested in the one who had dodged death by seconds – wanted to meet him, to meet this *blessed* man. Yes – he was safe but quite badly injured having hit the tail on his way out. It was an emotional meeting – the survivor was twenty-nine years old and actually married – a rarity for aircrew. They talked for nearly an hour. The fighter pilot made sure that he would get good treatment and personally ensured that a message would be sent quickly of his miraculous survival to the Allies.

The reason Vetter remembered this crash was because the authorities, on discovering which machine it was from its tail serial number and eventually the wings, had reason to believe it was specially equipped and that the wreckage – all of it – *had* to be retrieved. Eye-witnesses on the ground had reported a silver, bullet-like projectile plunging down at terrific speed, then a crunch and that was it, no fire, hardly any wreckage. When the recovery team arrived, apart from B-24 tail-plane, they could see no wreckage at all – just a crater, like a small pond. They left it, assuming that in the absence of any other wreckage, or bodies, the tail had somehow become detached during its plunge. It was only when the boffins told them about this wreck they realised they had a job on their hands.

The fuselage, with bombs, was found *under* the crater, several metres down, compressed into a three metre tin coffin, containing the cockpit...everything... and more bodies, although it was difficult to accurately describe how many. The bombs had provided the energy and were found deepest.

...

Vetter and Schneider were still wondering about their find with no idea as to what purpose it might serve.

After a short discussion, 'No – I have no idea Sir,' said Schneider again shaking his head. 'I'll go and collect the camera from the car and take a picture of where you found it in the wreck.'

'Yes, of course... and the tail number and squadron motif, if it's still visible,' responded Major Vetter. Squadron markings and tail numbers were usually recovered with few problems on the larger parts of remaining structure; the difficulty arose when all the pieces were either too small or totally burnt out, but they nearly always found *something* to provide its identity... sometimes even on aircrew briefing notes. When they had started doing this job they actually had trouble recognising even what kind of bomber it was at first, whether it was a B-24 or a B-17 but it didn't take long... number of fins, fuselage shapes, types of engine and engine cowlings, and even colour. And if it had crashed in the day it would be American – night time, the RAF, which usually meant a Lancaster or Halifax, perhaps a Mosquito.

Major Vetter looked around then said, 'Let's get back Schneider.'

There was a light breeze and spring was in the air. Beyond the immediate fields, Ralph Vetter could see a small hill and a few trees now devoid of foliage as a result of fire, like some featureless mound, a barren convexity; especially in the summer, the civil defence teams were often kept busy preventing fires spreading caused by crashed aircraft from consuming vast forests and whole villages.

The two of them were just about to turn back to their vehicle when, while they were looking again at the object in Vetter's hand, it made a noise. He dropped it immediately, both of them running quickly for cover, shouting to others. They weren't taking any chances.

'What was that? What was that Herr Major?'

'It's my turn to say, 'I have no idea'. Maybe something inside had worked loose when I turned it over – I did shake it before, remember – nothing.'

Both of them knew it wasn't a rattling 'loose marble in a tin' kind of noise; it was almost a soft crunch. He wondered if soil had got inside and was just moving about. Still, they gave it fifteen minutes then wandered back. It wasn't smoking, ticking, hissing or showing any signs of life. Vetter picked it up gingerly, looked at it closely again – no heat, no smoke, no fire, nothing had changed. Nothing else of interest materialised in the rest of their search so they decided to call it a day. They squelched their way back. They both knew from experience that at any crash site the ground was nearly all churned up, usually muddy and more than likely saturated in either oil of fuel so they always wore good solid footwear. But occasionally, Vetter would put on rubber boots. The only places where they didn't have the soggy ground was when they'd been to crashes near the Sennelager area – the soil was so sandy everything just sank through.

'So back to base Schneider... and when we do, I'll contact the initial crash teams. I would like them to search all bodies of any dead airmen they recover in future, especially Americans, for any unusual personal kit. Make sure I don't forget!'

'Of course, Major.'

Ralph Vetter reflected; there's no way he would encourage his son Hans, who was only two years old, to join the military – he'd seen too much. That's if there was to be a military after Hitler's war.

On their walk back to their vehicle, it did it again – made that noise. They quickly placed it on the ground and moved away but this time retrieved it after five minutes when nothing happened. There must be some spring or clockwork in it winding down or something, thought Vetter.

'I'm wondering if it's some sort of barometric device,' Vetter said out loud as they ambled to the car. They left the crash site in the hands of the clear-up gangs and the medics who'd also have to clear up the Me109 next door, when the B17 was finished. What a horrible job, he thought – theirs was bad enough but he couldn't do what they did every day. He then put his find into some soft wrapping from their essential recovery kit.

Following a closer examination back at base, Major Vetter was surprised to see that his object of interest was indeed electrical, or at least partly electrical, from two visible small wires or contact connections but unfortunately, they were compacted with dirt. On closer examination, he also realised that it was partially made of a light alloy. He now wondered if it was a clever, very small sensing device operated and controlled by miniature switches and he suspected that a part of it was the remains of a very small battery. Closer examination of the carcass had also revealed two letters, a 'V' and a 'W'. There were other letters but were indecipherable, obscured by damage. The letters meant nothing to Vetter. He thought against trying to clean it up in case he caused more damage…it looked fairly delicate.

At base his boss was as intrigued as Major Vetter and sanctioned him to contact Area Command, indicating that there was something they might just want to see from the B17 and where greater expertise might be able to provide a better evaluation.

Having described it over the military network, they were ordered to travel to Area Command as soon as possible: they were interested.

'At least we might get some decent food out of this,' Vetter said to Schneider. 'We might even have real coffee!'

Chapter 36

Germany '44

Mohn not Impressed

'Who will I be reporting to?' asked Vetter. He liked to smooth things out as far as possible before he went anywhere... transport and communications were becoming increasingly chaotic. 'Who exactly...?'

'Oberst Mohn, Herr Major,' replied the clerk.

'Damn!'

Vetter knew Colonel Mohn – an officer who had been one of his bosses a couple of years ago. He wasn't looking forward to this as Vetter remembered him to be erratic in temperament – and usually difficult. Turning to Sergeant Schneider he said, 'I hope this damn thing is worth the trouble otherwise the colonel will give us a hard time – well, he'll give *me* a hard time that is for certain.'

Schneider smiled. He knew that his boss was largely un-fazed by bullying autocrats and stupid diktats – they seemed to have no effect upon him at all. Schneider was an experienced technical airman and had occasionally clashed with others in crash parties on the diligence needed when searching for specialised equipment. Vetter would often deflect any criticism of his NCO side-kick and tell anybody if they had any complaints about Schneider that they should go through him first.

'If anybody is going to tell him off or if any shouting is to be done it'll be me who does it. Got that clear?' he would say.

As always, an Intelligence Officer was to give them a quick briefing before they set off to tell them what routes were open, which ones were not – it could change daily after bombing raids. Canals were particular targets and roads were often flooded from bombed-out water-ways.

'...and if you are on the roads, if you are attacked from the air you must quickly get under cover. Just get your vehicle off the road! Get behind a wall, into a farmyard or into some trees because if you are attacked or buzzed, you can guarantee that his No 2 will be called in to finish the job; you will have no chance... you cannot outrun them on the road.'

Loud and clear.

Their plan was for them to fly to the closest airbase to HQ, where they had been summoned, probably in a Storch aircraft or whatever was available, and then make the rest of the way in a staff car that had been arranged for them. This suited Major Vetter. In his current role, he had been able swing a posting not a million kilometres away from his home area and planned to make a short diversion in the car to see his wife, Miriam, and son, Hans. He was also thankful that his village house was not in any town of importance, he'd seen the aftermath of the huge bomber raids: utter destruction, and it was also the outlying areas that suffered too as bombing – Norden or no Norden – was still in its infancy, a hit and miss affair... villages close by had been wiped out. If the main target was not visible due to bad weather, the bombs would be dropped 'in the general area' – they were not going to take the bombs home!

As it turned out, it was a Storch aircraft for the first leg of their journey. After a few vibrating minutes in it, flying low, Vetter thought he could drive faster! As he looked at the horizon he could see the results of the last bombing in several places – huge pawls of smoke many, many miles away, probably from last night. When they landed, there, on cue, was the vehicle waiting for them – with driver. The Intelligence man had advised them to travel during the daytime – it was just impossible at night, no lights, few signs but they ran the obvious risk during the day from Allied fighter-bombers carrying out target-of-opportunity attacks. These days, not every Allied aircraft over Germany was a heavy bomber.

Vetter did not pay particular attention to the driver, only the vehicle – he was just thankful it wasn't raining, the vehicle was an open-topped typical utility machine, a German Jeep – their version of the famous American Jeep, a VW Kübelwagen. Every army had their own version of a basic utility vehicle. Still, it was only for thirty kilometres, and Marian would ensure that they would both be given a welcome break, even if it was for only half an hour when they called. They could stop off again for longer on the way back maybe. Snatched moments.

His real worry was the fine weather which also meant the threat of random air attacks. These were increasing every week, reaching into the heartlands of Germany. He turned to the driver

'Your name, private?' commanded Vetter.

'Obershutze Meyer!' he replied, proudly.

'Relax driver, don't be so stiff. So – you have been promoted from private to private *first* class, eh, good,' said Vetter looking first at Meyer, who he thought looked like a child just out of school, then at Schneider with a slight shake of his head. He was obviously thinking the same. They're getting younger... but as long as he can drive. Both Vetter and Schneider were tired, the work never-ending... just too many wrecks to examine and too many forms to fill in. He might grab a quick nap on the way there. He continued, '...but just take it easy Meyer – get us there in one piece, no pot-holes, no ditches, you understand! And just because we're in Germany doesn't mean we're not in danger from the air, so watch out,' said Vetter to both men. He continued, 'From England, Mustangs can fly all the way to Berlin and back – it's ridiculous – so watch out driver.'

'Of course, Herr Major, always!'

Just after they'd set off, Meyer asked, 'Your pardon Herr Major, my colleague asked if you were in France at the beginning of the war? His name is Unteroffizier Bossen. He wants to be remembered to you. He saw your name on the roster and wondered if it was you.'

'Yes, yes, it was me; yes – I remember Corporal Bossen; how is he?' asked Vetter. He was pleasantly surprised to hear that Bossen was not in fact battling it out on the frozen Eastern Front against the Russian hordes. 'Is this what he's doing now – driving? What happened to his work – his engineering?'

'Today, Herr Major, he is still an engineer but on vehicles – and he also has to drive as well. We do not have enough manpower for all the separate jobs.'

At least he was safe, thought Vetter. 'Please say hello for me when you get back Meyer.' When Major Vetter had been told he was to report to Colonel Mohn, he'd had misgivings: 'Anyone but him,' he thought. Yes, he knew Oberst Mohn from previous; his reputation came before him – a difficult man. He could be bombastic one moment, accommodating the next. His first name was Maximillian, his middle name Oscar but Vetter thought they should really be 'sarcasm' from what he remembered; this was his default mood, his style – part of his autocratic management technique. His face always appeared to be constantly decorated with a latent anger, but Colonel Mohn produced results. Genghis Khan would have been proud of him.

If he was in a mood, and you questioned anything he said or argued with him, he'd just ask you in a loud voice where you wanted to be buried, then laugh... off-putting for those who did not know him. Some of his subordinates quailed in front in his presence; he was both feared and respected, most disliked him. Nevertheless, his men were loyal and although he'd shout at everybody, he couldn't delegate, he needed control, a finger in every pie. Vetter remembered him as someone who nearly always had a complaint or criticism on his lips about what had been done – like a 'universal' mother-in-law, and any compliment – these were rare – usually had a sting in its tail. In previous 'spirited' discussions, when he had been his boss, Mohn had sometimes not shouted or even raised his voice but his manner had carried all the menace of a creature about to strike. Clearly, he expected to have his own way. On the other hand – and this is probably why some of his men liked him – God help anybody who dared criticise *his* men, it was tantamount to being personal. He would defend them resolutely. In a way, he was like 'mother' and if work was ever slack, he'd expect you to go out there and 'kick backsides'. Vetter surmised that when the colonel took leave, God would stand in. But over time, when Vetter had got to know him and knew his ways, he had come to like him in a way... his bark was definitely worse than his bite, at least to Vetter. When he had been posted – had gone away – you never forgot him.

...

'Come in Major – OberFeldwebel Schneider can wait outside,' said Colonel Mohn. Not a good start – he liked to put people in their places. 'How are you these days, how are you liking your role as a Science Officer? Better than flying eh – especially these days.' Mohn laughed. Flying might have been fun when the war started and everything was going their way, but now... 'A desk job is the safest job these days, eh Major?'

'Very well thank you Colonel – and yes, my present job has its moments, but nothing beats flying,' responded Vetter. He had flown since sustaining his injuries but only as a member of a Junkers crew. Not quite the same. The usual pleasantries continued then Mohn abruptly changed the conversation, wasting no time.

'Show me what you have Major. My staff said the way it was described sounded unusual when you phoned so I'm intrigued. I too used to fly and I still retain great interest in technical matters. Let's have a look at this American object you've brought us – if it *is* American. I hope it's worthwhile!' Colonel Mohn hadn't changed much, was always smart, buttoned up… and loud. Vetter couldn't imagine him scrambling about in a wreck with his gleaming boots though.

Vetter was getting a little worried now – he was prepared for a verbal bashing should Mohn be disappointed and say, '*Is that it – is that all?*' A report was always written up following each crash search – usually very brief, with comments such as, '…nothing to report… wreckage buried too deep… totally destroyed by fire…'. In this case Vetter had produced a full page on the official documentation with photos to go with it. When Vetter took the bag out of his briefcase and laid it on the table he placed a pair of light cotton gloves alongside for Colonel Mohn. Vetter had always been fastidious in his handling of unknown and unusual equipment.

'What's the matter – don't you trust me Major?' said Mohn on seeing the gloves. He quickly put them on, his eyes narrowing as he picked up the bag and removed the item. He was awhile just staring at it – turning it over in his big paws. No explosion from him… no castigation. Must be getting soft, thought Vetter. His wife must have been good to him last night… or a promise tonight!

'Have you already fiddled about with this?' barked Mohn. 'It looks like a lot of fuss about nothing! It's too small to be of any consequence surely!' said the colonel eventually. 'Where exactly was it found?' he asked.

'In the main fuselage, front part – it's all there in the report Herr Oberst, and photographs too. It has no obvious or immediate technical characteristics to indicate what it does or to which system it belongs; Sergeant Schneider thought the same Herr Oberst,' he continued. 'I was thinking perhaps that it might be part of a miniature atmospheric or pressure device – one controlled electrically, but I did not want to fiddle too much. It's not big enough to take too much rough handling. It looks too compact, too delicate.'

'Indeed. You could have at least cleaned it up Major. Just look at this horrible mess on it. What is it?'

'The result of a combination of oil, dirt, fire and who knows what, I imagine. As I have said, I did not want to interfere too much Colonel…you see it more or less as we did when we first found it. We have indicated all aspects in the report Herr Oberst,' Vetter responded.

'Yes yes – so you have said, but let's get it over to our little workshop and see. I have important matters to attend to meanwhile. To be honest Major, I was hoping for something really juicy – and all you bring me is a silly little object. It looks too small to be anything that would contain valves, pumps or radar – just look at it. I have no idea what it is for… the only aspect is that it *is* unusual.' Vetter wondered if Mohn was actually talking out loud to himself for a moment. 'Look, off you go and get something to eat while our technicians conduct their investigation – see if they can crack it open,' said Colonel Mohn, '...but I cannot see there being much room for anything of technical interest inside this, it's too small,' he said again shaking his head. Vetter was wondering now whether they should have bothered – quite a distance travelled, for what?

The outcome was that Mohn had actioned his staff to carry out an immediate, but quick initial look at it while Vetter waited; the Colonel had no idea as to what it might be and was pessimistic that it would amount to any value. 'I think you have wasted our time Major... you just wanted a day out didn't you,' he chuckled.

Vetter was about to say something in his defence when Mohn started waiving him out of the office, a sign that the meeting was over.

Two hours later they were summoned back to the colonel's office to be told the lab technicians had given it a cursory examination but due to it being partly encrusted with debris, and its small size, were both unable and reluctant to ascertain what it might be – they, too, did not want to destroy it while carrying out the investigation. It needed deeper skills and equipment, and like Vetter they were sufficiently intrigued, so recommended it be taken immediately to the specialists at the Siemens factories. They had already contacted them to let them know. And they had added an annexe to Vetter's report on what they'd attempted to do, and their opinion on possibilities.

'The Siemens factory – at Siemensstadt colonel?! But that's in Berlin,' said Vetter, now feeling better for having raised other technical interest in the object with the workshop technicians.

'No, no – one of the closer units. It will only take a few hours,' responded Mohn. The colonel was angry that such a little object should consume this much effort and attention. He informed and ordered Vetter to continue their journey and then report again on the way back to let him know personally what had been found out about this piece of equipment – and they were to leave first thing.

God! Another day's driving – and in the wrong direction. Vetter was not pleased – he wanted to call in again that day to see Miriam. Now it would have to be the day after. They had had only a few minutes on the way and he'd left saying they would call in tomorrow on the way back. Still, better late than never – they were treasured moments spent with Miriam.

However, while the pair of them had been waiting Vetter was more convinced than ever that the object was something to do with either personal kit or something the Allied aircrew used to interact with the bomber's bomb-aiming equipment and thus had an idea, an idea he discussed with Sergeant Schneider, who also shared his major's view on its function. So they went back to the colonel before disappearing on a wild goose chase to the Siemens factory. His only worry as that Colonel Mohn would not be interested and that Vetter should do as he was bidden, but surprisingly he invited them back into his office − without too much shouting. Lunch must have been agreeable.

Chapter 37

Hut 14 – Germany

'What is it this time?'

'Colonel – I have an idea that may save time for all of us. Not far from here there's a prisoner of war camp…'

He went on to describe what their thoughts were about the object and that by a little trickery they may discover its purpose and function quite easily – and swiftly.

Colonel Mohn had listened and agreed – 'You're a sneaky one,' he had chided Vetter afterwards on hearing of his plan, '…but I like your idea. We are, of course, always spying on our Allied prisoners as no doubt the Allies are with our own airman.' He had spoken to the camp commandant to notify them of the visit. 'But if you are unsuccessful then I expect you both to do as originally instructed and continue onto Siemens… are we clear about this Major?'

'Absolutely Herr Oberst,' as they quickly came to attention. Neither Vetter nor Schneider indulged in the stiff-armed 'Nazi Salute' – it wasn't mandated yet. In any case Vetter wanted nothing to do with The Party and its politics – few in the Luftwaffe did, as long as they kept their noses clean with respect to the insidious 'Subversion Law'.

'What is it that you wish to do Major? Your colonel only briefly described the purpose of your visit.'

Vetter, without going into too much detail, described what they did day-to-day and the situation they were in to the camp commandant, '…and it's the American airmen with whom we'd like to talk particularly. If it's at all possible I would like to have them not spooked, have them relaxed as much as possible – nothing official you understand.'

'Then it'll be hut fourteen.'

He barked out orders and twenty minutes later they came to hut fourteen accompanied by a single guard who, they were told, was on good terms with the inmates.

'Everybody stand to attention. Fuhrer Fritz is here!' shouted a voice with an American drawl. They all jumped up and stood to attention – then collapsed in laughter as the guard, with Vetter and Schneider behind him in the doorway, glanced at his visitors ruefully.

'Always joking these Americans, Herr Major,' said Fritz.

Vetter and Schneider were well aware of the Americans' views on authority and their approach to life – they had seen quite a few Yankee movies before, and even during the war. Ralph had always thought the Americans a sloppy, disrespectful, ill-disciplined bunch of hillbillies, but his view had modified – there was obviously a spirit, skill and bravery that enabled them to climb out of bed each morning and clamber into their bombers, knowing what was waiting for them over Germany. Shouts came from the bunks.

'Fritz – are these your friends? I didn't know you had any. What have you come for this time?'

'Go away Fritz,' said another, '…and give Adolf my regards.'

'Where's that camera you promised me…?'

'Forget that Polski, what about my pencils…?'

'…and that Luger pistol...?' More hoots and shouts.

'Hey Sullivan, ask him where your leather trousers have got to?'

'Shut up Martinez!' said Polski.

'What is it this time – need some stockings for your wife – your sister – or for your girlfriend?' More laughing. Major Vetter stopped on the threshold, looked at Schneider and grinned.

'They like you 'Fritz'!' remarked Vetter, smiling, and invited him to take them right inside.

Guard Fritz held up his hands to try and bring them to some order.

'Gentleman, gentlemen – this is not an official visit. These two officers – they are like you, flyers, and they want to see that you are well treated, ask some general questions, that you are OK. It is not an interrogation so please, just for me, cooperate with them. Will you do this for Fritz, your favourite guard?'

'Fritz – Mein Fuhrer, just for you,' said the hut spokesman. 'What do you reckon boys?' More hooting with nods.

They had not come empty handed – Schneider had American cigarettes in his deep coat pockets which he brought out and placed on the table. They all looked up at this but before anyone could move the spokesman said, 'Hang on guys, fair shares now! Don't be greedy.'

Vetter then moved onto the main business with general talk about conditions. Eventually the major asked to sit down to take some notes and moved to get his notebook out – and proceeded to remove more tobacco along with 'the item' which he placed innocently alongside the cigarettes. He made great play of struggling to extract his book.

'Ah, here it is,' he said, then looked up at Schneider, who had been watching the PoWs' faces closely when his boss had produced the object, to register the slightest sign of any recognition. The cigarettes soon vanished leaving the item on its own.

'Hey boss, what's this? Man, looks busted, kaput, real kaput. What is it…?' One of the Yanks picked it up to get a closer look. He then quickly put it back. 'What's this crap on it?'

'I know what it is. Fritz… it's a new cigarette case, right?' said Polski.

'Nah, nah… I *know* what it is,' said Sullivan. 'When we've finished with Hitler and we come for you Fritz, you'll have one of these to keep your cyanide pills in, won't you Fritz?'

Schneider looked at Major Vetter with an imperceptible shake of his head. No one had showed any sign that they knew what it might be – no recognition whatsoever. Another PoW picked it up turned it over – even took a sniff before returning it to the table.

The talk drifted onto other things.

'Fritz… hope you don't mind but we've put a picture of Betty alongside the camp orders on your notice board.' Everybody looked around to get an eyeful of Betty Grable.

'Ja – it's OK as long as you take it down before each time the commandant carries out an inspection.'

Major Vetter and Sergeant Schneider left twenty minutes later. It had been a failure. Perhaps the item retrieved was a one-off, experimental piece of equipment known only to the crew of the crashed aircraft, which might explain why none of the PoWs in hut fourteen recognised it as anything.

'Cyanide pills eh Schneider? I never thought of that,' he said chuckling to his sergeant.

...

Chapter 38

Germany '44

The Mosquito

Both Vetter and Schneider had looked at the annexe Mohn's staff had added to the original report. Their view partly coincided with Vetter's – except they had added the possibility that it could indeed be some personal kit like a beacon. They had similar misgivings about its robustness and also did not want to delve too much apart from a partial clean-up. There were no bolts or obvious clasps that might indicate how it came apart – or what held it together – nothing. And partial damage and contamination were probably masking from view a simple method of access. As for material – they could only assume that it was a newer kind of paxilene and glass. In any case, all work had to cease when they were interrupted in their endeavours by the air-raid siren. An hour and a half wasted before the all-clear came.

Vetter had contacted Colonel Mohn about the results from the PoW camp so the colonel had ordered Vetter to leave straight away without any further investigation. 'I have more important things to attend to Major Vetter. I can't waste my time on a frivolous, meaningless investigation. Take the damn thing – whatever it is – straight to the company. Let them fiddle with it!'

It took all the next morning just to travel a few kilometres because of diversions, sirens, unexploded bombs, military convoys getting priority and general mayhem – always increasingly encumbered by troops, tracked gun vehicles, support trucks and all the other unending impediment of an army and civil forces under movement.

'I do not want to be here,' he muttered to himself. It was unusual to be sent beyond Command HQ... they were the ones who usually did the leg work, meanwhile there was bound to be a backlog of wrecks waiting for them on their return. He hoped that somebody else was dealing with these. They had to get a move on.

Eventually on the move and making up for lost ground, it was mid-afternoon when Sergeant Schneider and Meyer cried out in unison – both had spotted at the same time the unmistakeable front, head-on view of an Allied fighter-bomber coming straight at them – a Mosquito, guns blazing, strafing the road and their vehicle with cannon. Most missed but some found their mark smashing into the front of the wagon, forcing Meyer to swerve off the road. They hit the side of the ditch, catapulting both Vetter and Schneider out. The vehicle, already on fire, came to rest upside down on top of Major Vetter. Schneider, flung against a stone wall, was killed outright.

The diver scrambled out and saw immediately that Sergeant Schneider was beyond help; no head can be at that angle, eyes open, staring as in surprise, and still be alive. Then he heard Major Vetter groaning. Meyer scrambled back under the vehicle trying desperately to drag the major out and away from the wagon and away from the flames. They were both lying close to the ditch. Meyer was injured but he could see the major was in a desperate way, seriously injured, choking, gasping, mumbling words.

'Meyer, make sure Schneider gets my case, takes my case to… to… to… continue to… make sure…' There was a pause then, 'he'll know where…'

'I think he is dead Herr Major… he is dead…' said Meyer. Seconds passed. Meyer tried to support the Major's head.Vetter was now really struggling, gurgling…

'Dead… dead…?' Seconds passed with laboured breathing, Meyer trying to make him comfortable. Eventually he rasped out, 'Meyer, my wife – you know where she lives – on the way we came, you know…' More seconds passed. Then another effort from the major, 'Make sure she gets this… she'll know what to do with it… there are… I told her…' These were Major Vetter's last words before lapsing into silence. Another two minutes and his breathing stopped.

Meyer looked around now in dire need to move away from the wagon as the fire grew in intensity. He saw the briefcase and picked it up. Then he scrambled behind the wall for protection just in case the Allied plane returned. He realised that he was bleeding badly from his arms and head, cuts from flying debris and broken glass. The vehicle continued to burn before he heard the inevitable explosions as fuel and tyres exploded. He moved away and waited. It was not long before another military vehicle turned up – a truck. They yelled at him to get in quickly – they did not want to hang around and become a target themselves. A nearby forest beckoned. Meyer had already stuck the briefcase under his coat before he was hauled onto the back of the lorry; he did want to invite too many questions.

'We will come back for them when it is safer,' shouted one of them, nodding towards where Major Vetter and Sergeant Schneider lay. Intelligence was right. From the safety of the woods they saw the Allied aircraft carry out another run, confirming the kill – and looking out for more targets.

...

Corporal Bossen was shocked when he was told about what had happened to his friend Meyer – and of Major Vetter's death. What a tragic end for a good man, a true leader – someone he really looked up to, not one of those arrogant party-liners that now seemed to be everywhere.

Major Vetter had had no time for these people. If he thought some bumped-up party hack, some wet-behind-the-ears officer idiot was getting above themselves and criticising the efforts of *his* staff, he would step in and ask them, with his eyes boring into theirs, if they'd ever seen any action – anywhere – already knowing the answer.

'Well I can soon arrange a transfer for you. That way your combat experience will catch up with the medals you are wearing!' They usually turned red, followed by bluster but in the end they'd back down, slink off, and he wasn't afraid to do this no matter who could hear, even in front of the troops. He could spot these hacks. They were like professional bureaucrats, with un-calloused hands, un-muscled frames, neat hair, no tans. Indoor people. Office folk.

Major Vetter always had time to stop by after sorties to see how his ground engineers, him included, were coping. He would listen and was not afraid to make noises further up the food chain to ensure the ground crews were not neglected, or left short. But Major Vetter realised it was almost a hopeless task, even back then, how hard-pressed everybody was. All the spares and equipment his squadron had were snatched away for the attack and push on the Eastern Front, which Vetter believed was an error of the greatest magnitude. When Germany was initially doing well against the Russians, he just knew, as did Bossen, that it would not last. He was right, and now he's gone. Corporal Bossen remembered all this about his old boss.

But Meyer had conveyed a garbled story to him about the major's briefcase and that it needed to be taken to Major Vetter's wife.

'To his wife – really, why to his wife?' asked Bossen mystified. 'It's an *official* briefcase – shouldn't we give it to our own major and let him deal with it?'

'He was quite specific, poor fellow. He did say *his wife...* perhaps there are personal effects in it.' Neither of them knew the nature of Major Vetter's journey or what was really in the case, although Meyer did take a peek. He did see documents but he also saw some knick-knacks that looked personal.

'I'll take out the documents and pass them onto our security and if either of us should be in that area again, we can give Mrs Vetter his briefcase,' said Bossen.

'Shouldn't we give it all to security?' asked Meyer.

'No. They will only lose it; you know what they are like – always poking their noses into everything. I'll take care of it.

Bossen never had the chance to remove the documents; there were too many distractions, too many air attacks and bomber raids, too many things to do. It was forgotten. By the time surrender came, the briefcase was still lying at his brother's home where he had taken it on leave, gathering dust. By then it was all irrelevant.

Chapter 39

Germany '44

The Flood

Frau Vetter woke suddenly. It was pitch black – two explosions in the distance, stray bombs from the RAF no doubt. It was nearly midnight. She waited awhile, praying for silence and for the bombers to go away. A minute passed, nothing more. Silence. 'Good,' she thought to herself, no further danger. She drifted back to her troubled slumbers; she had still not recovered from the devastating news of her beloved Ralph's death a few weeks ago... her life now grey, miserable and aimless. She was weary at heart and despondent – life seemed a dreary struggle, a dreary emptiness. But her mother was her salvation, looking after the young Hans while she slowly recovered – just like a lot of wives right now who were losing their men. Mother was going to be joining them soon to sit out the war as soon as Frau Vetter had got both her house and mind in order. She could not bear to leave it with all its memories.

She woke again... still dark. There were voices close by in the street – and the sound of water, a gurgling noise and an unfamiliar smell in the room. 'What on earth is going on,' she muttered? She pulled back the bed covers, swung her legs out and plonked them down onto... water! She shrieked, got up and found that there was now nearly a foot of water in her bedroom... and rising. Frau Vetter grabbed her coat and when she sloshed her way into the next room, it was just the same.

Her bungalow was flooded... and getting worse. Nor was there any electricity, just the sound of rushing water, raised voices and the steady but diminishing drone of more bombers in the distance fading away on their way back to England. When she opened her front door, more water poured in from the village street – it was like a river. The bombs she had heard before had landed less than two kilometres away, destroying a major water channel that linked two nearby towns. Her village was in the way. The water cascaded downhill, down the village street, flooding houses on both sides. Torches were being used by struggling neighbours. Otherwise there was now complete darkness and panic.

A side street offered sanctuary – it was uphill and dry but of course no one knew at the time how long this chaos would last. Frau Vetter ventured around the corner until she came to a friend's house – an elderly couple who, like her Ralph, had two sons in the Luftwaffe. They hurried her indoors, welcoming and warm – and waited. Further sleep was now going to be impossible.

The flooding had subsided when dawn arrived. No one had wanted to look around outside until they could see what was going on but Frau Vetter feared the worst as she trekked around the corner back to her house. The street had come alive with people rushing around pushing brooms and wheelbarrows with sodden rubbish, carpets, clothes and, in some cases, old folk in them. When she turned up at her front door it was already open. On seeing her, someone shouted to other villagers, 'It's alright, Frau Vetter is safe – she's here now.' Her neighbours had already been into her house looking for her. Her heart fell when she stepped in; everything had moved including her prize piano – the marks on the wall indicating how high the water had reached. Apparently, the rush of water lasted less than two hours before the civil guard and engineers stopped the flow... but it was enough to flood and devastate the village.

In a moment of panic she looked around for her photographs in her bedroom – her treasured pictures of happy memories with Ralph, all gone, or lying ruined on the floor. She cried out then wept, stumbling from one ruined room to the next, looking for something to salvage. Her walisische kommode – her wonderful Welsh dresser – with all their ornaments, porcelain, momentos and other pictures had been lifted by the water and toppled.

She crunched her way over broken pottery and sodden cushions to the bay window hoping to find at least one unaffected treasure – her wedding photo or the picture from their very brief honeymoon near Detmold where they visited Hermannsdenkmal. A wonderful, all-so-brief break, with captured moments of love and tenderness. When he was with her she always felt safe and secure. Now she was devastated and heartbroken, both pictures were gone from the bay window but the glint of metal on the floor drew her to a frame, intact, as was the sodden photo inside it. She picked it up, taking great care to preserve the picture. A quick glance around the floor did not reveal anything else to save. Perhaps she would look again after getting changed into dry clothes; she was still only wearing her *unterhosen,* nightgown and a coat she grabbed in panic on the way out. She quickly found clothing on the top shelf of her bedroom wardrobe that had survived. Now the damp smell of everything, and God knows what else, was becoming overpowering, pervading every room.

Later, the full force and implications of what she had been left alone with – only one picture of her dearly beloved and memories – began to sink in. Maybe mama had a memento or two but Frau Vetter didn't think they had sent any photos – but she could hope. The mail system had been chaotic.

She met Ralph when he was on a training course – she was still at school nearby and saw him on her walk there and back, catching a glimpse of him just now and then, but Ralph was unaware and she daren't say or do anything until after her last day when she could say she was no longer a school-child. He wouldn't look twice would he! Then she joined a local family's bakery. He came in one morning for cakes; she immediately turned beetroot red. He would remove his glasses, wink and smile every time he came in and bought something. She would just blush more, crumble into acute embarrassment and stumble over her words. What a figure he cut – smart, handsome with a wonderful crinkly grin, a ready, open smile.

One day early in the morning he had bought his usual bread and then left. Ten seconds later she realised he had left his glasses behind.

'What should we do?' she asked the manager. Well he could see right into her obvious crush for this airman and suggested she go after him before he got too far away.

Panic.

She dashed out through the door and was about to catch up with him before he climbed into his vehicle when he stopped and turned around to go back. They almost collided. She was already holding out his glasses for him, now breathless from her short dash. A huge smile spread across his handsome features. He thanked her but all she could do was remain mute in his presence, then her world changed forever, because he asked her to walk with him when she finished work – to take her home. My God! She could not concentrate all day, bursting with excitement and happiness in anticipation. As the time approached she could not contain herself... her heart was in her mouth. What would her friends say when they saw her with an officer on her arm?

She was absolutely stricken when he failed to turn up... crying all the way home, furious, frustrated and despondent. 'I cannot go back to the shop,' she said to herself. 'How would I face him if he came in again? I'd die!' She managed to stumble back to work the next morning in a daze, her mind flitting from one thought to another, her emotions in turmoil.

She had lain awake all night worrying about the reason. Had he been injured? Perhaps he thought she was too young – but how cruel for him to play with her heart like this. Didn't he know how she felt about him? Was he blind?

The shop owner was always there one hour before proper opening, making preparations and ensuring that the cakes were laid out as he liked them to be, to entice his customers – times were difficult. She could see him moving about as she approached. She had already decided to ask to work at the back as she would not be able to face him if he came in.

Miriam walked in and almost walked into the back of a man wearing a uniform who was talking to her boss. 'Oh, excuse me...' He turned around... it was HIM! He gave her a huge smile – and a present of chocolates.

'I'm sorry my little princess, the Allies kept us busy yesterday.' Her heart soared as she broke down in tears. Ralph stepped forward and swept her up in his arms. Miriam didn't care – she was in heaven. A month later they were engaged, then soon married... you had to grab your happiness when you could in the war. Now she was alone once more, with most of her memories destroyed...one soggy photo.

Later, Ralph had said from the start, that if the war goes badly – and it was going badly now – she should stay put in their house, closer to the western borders. And if anything happened to the house, his brother Harald was always a possibility for providing sanctuary. He too was in the Luftwaffe, working in *Intelligence*. Or there was Pa Vetter who lived near Krefeld, a place called Wegberg where he was involved with the local defence and repair parties like most of the older men in Germany.

'You do not want to be in the east or going to the east no matter how things are turning out on our western borders. The western Allies at least have a culture about them that separates them from the animals of the Red Army,' he had said. 'So stay here, stay near your relatives and friends – and if, God forbid, the Red Army come this way before the Allies, move towards the Americans and the British. Get to them before the Russians get to you. Promise me, yes?' She promised. She did not need reminding – Goebbels was frequently on the radio reminding the German nation of horror stories and atrocities against German women and children by the advancing Russians on the Eastern Front.

Chapter 40

Germany today
The Notar

Karl looked through what he thought was all of his father's effects. Hans Vetter had died three weeks ago from a heart attack. It was not unexpected. Karl was almost relieved when Papa eventually went to the big 'beer hall in the sky', having watched him slowly deteriorate following previous attacks. His father was a big man and had – as did many Germans – faced hard times following the war, being brought up by his mother and elder sister, and *his* father, Ralph, had been killed in an air attack in 1944. Now here they were, several days after the funeral with the family Notar.

Where marriage was concerned, Hans was a disaster area. He was on his third when he died. During his later life – and as a result of his women troubles – he took to drink; his money had drained away. He reclused himself. Karl had drifted apart from his father and they were never to become close. It was only when Grandma contacted Karl, telling him that his father was not doing well, that she feared the worst, suggesting they should find out what – or if – Hans Vetter had anything of material and sentimental value that the family didn't know about... and to make arrangements for the inevitable.

Hans had proved uncommunicative over the years and was usually drunk in any case, so Miriam had resorted to asking a family-trusted Notar to look into the matter. This proved to be very timely as it was only two months later that the heart attack occurred. Karl, just like his father Hans, had taken up engineering, starting as an apprentice. He successfully moved up the company ladder and eventually finished up in South Africa with the firm, spending many years there. Now he was back in Germany.

The family notary, Mr Geller, had set matters in motion making most of the arrangements including this family gathering. He had things to discuss. From these it was apparent that Hans Vetter had squandered more or less everything he had and would normally refuse any help, but for Frau Vetter she was more interested in the possibility that there might be some information or momentos associated with her beloved Ralph.

'Mr Vetter, are you aware of what your grandfather did during the war? Several weeks ago, and in your absence, your grandmother had asked me to look into the matter, which I have done, and tell you as much as I have found out,' said Mr Geller addressing Karl.

'Not specifically… only in vague terms, no real detail, but I **do** know he was in the Luftwaffe and was killed later on in the war,' answered Karl.

'Yes, well indeed, he was a fighter pilot at the beginning of the war operating in France but had to retire from flying due to injuries sustained in an accident. But your grandmother, Mrs Vetter…' Geller nodded towards her, '…could only outline what he did following his accident and of course with no details. I found out why details were scant… this was because he had taken up a post as a technical officer, a rather secretive position at the time, whose task was to examine crashed American and British bombers in order to determine whether they had, or were making, any technical advances or breakthroughs etc. that might be giving the Allies advantages. Those words I'm quoting are straight off an old document you understand. These 'technical detectives' were not allowed, of course, to share any information outside of their own clique. Did you know this…?'

'No, not at all,' answered Karl. It was also the first time Miriam Vetter had heard of this role that her long- departed, dear Ralph had undertaken.

'Well…' Geller continued, '…from what I understand looking at his records that were sent, I managed to glean the fact that just before his death he had, along with a working colleague, indeed 'recovered' an item from a wreck that had attracted their interest and further investigation. According to a report, an initial, cursory examination was unable to enlighten anybody at the local Command what it might be; he was therefore ordered to deliver the object by road, to a Siemens factory in fact. It was on this journey that both of them met their deaths… yes, the sergeant was also killed apparently, according to the driver who survived, at the hands of an Allied fighter-bomber. Both died at the scene – although Major Vetter, your grandfather, was able to convey a message before he died.

A sob came from Mrs Vetter. Karl reached for her hand in comfort. He too was hearing these details for the first time. When this had all actually happened all those years ago, details were hard to come by for

Mrs Vetter – and often inaccurate – due to the existing war circumstances, but since then, and owing to typical German attention for keeping records – and the fact that the wall had come down releasing hitherto vast amounts of hidden records from the former East Germany, Geller and his 'snoopers' had traced many particular details concerning the major.

Geller went on, 'The driver of course had no idea of the nature of the journey nor that the major was delivering anything... but Vetter had, as I said before, obviously conveyed a message to him who had the presence of mind and duty to take the major's briefcase and keep it out of harm's way... any car wreck was good for looting – money, personal effects, disgusting as it sounds but items like tyres and fuel were extremely valuable then, they were always in short supply! Anyway, he in turn managed to get it to a former colleague of Major Vetter's who apparently used to work for him when he was in France. Due to the turmoil of the war, the briefcase was lost – or its whereabouts not known for a while; everything was in chaos as you can imagine. It was only in 1946 that Mrs Vetter received a visit from an ex-Luftwaffe airman who handed over the briefcase, explaining vaguely how he'd come in to its possession. It was quite battered even then but as Mrs Vetter will tell you, there was nothing in it of a real personal nature.'

Miriam remembered; she had been bitterly disappointed having found nothing in the case of a personal nature – no photos, photos he may have kept of them together somewhere from years ago. No, there was only a bag and some technical documents... Luftwaffe documents. She had desperately hoped to find a picture, any picture of her husband in it but sadly no, so she had not taken any further interest in it after that. She had put it on top of an old cupboard and completely forgotten it. It was only when Hans had peered into it years later and had suggested that one day they should take proper time out and look into it all that Miriam had remembered it contained *something*. Of course Hans had done nothing about it, as usual, too busy chasing women and getting drunk. So when it was obvious that Hans was quite ill and unlikely to return to any semblance of rude health, Mrs Vetter had asked Geller to look into the matter. Although she retained a sharp mind, she was too frail now to physically take on such a task.

'So, this briefcase and its contents – where is it now?' asked Karl.

'I have it here with me – but before your curiosity gets the better of you regarding the object that was found, let me tell you that it still has not been properly examined, even after all these years. What we did do, Mr Vetter, is to replace the old paper bag with a transparent plastic one and to place the old documents into modern plastic wallets. The original materials are retained in their own separate plastic bag in the case. The object in question is still wrapped in its original cloth material as it was obviously dirty. There is mention of 'contamination' in the documents so it would be unwise to meddle yourself.'

'Really? But that was over sixty years ago... may I please take a peek?' asked Karl Vetter. Geller gingerly handed over the briefcase to him, watching the astonished and expectant look on his face. The clasp worked flawlessly, popped open with a dry click. Karl reached into the case and took out the plastic bag, then unzipped it.

'Before you go any further,' said Geller, '...before you feel that you must tamper with it, I advise that you leave it well alone and let the experts deal with it first. When we transferred it into the new bag, it felt to me quite... well, sticky, dirty. Someone in the past has covered it completely with what looks like an axle grease; remember, it's had seventy years of accumulation of 'God knows what' on it and I believe the major indicated with his last words to leave it alone – not to touch it, leave it to the experts. And from the old original report, it seems that what you can see on it, or in it, is probably dirt... or something. It was obviously partly damaged by the crash too, according to the documents that are with it.'

'Axle grease? To preserve it perhaps? It looks like it might be made of some kind of plastic, glass – oh, and metal too,' responded Karl, '...and it all smells!' He looked at it inside the bag for several moments but could not see it clearly as it was double bagged, only a dark outline. He added, 'You are right; I think I will let someone else get their hands contaminated as I'm wearing my suit. I wonder what it is – quite flat isn't it,' he said almost to himself.

'Again, I have taken the liberty Mr Vetter. I have already established a contact for you, at a Siemens industrial unit in anticipation that you would take my advice. Here are the contact details for you. They sounded quite intrigued when I gave them the background to it all – imagine looking at an old object after so many years, an object that started the interest at the time.'

'I bet they were, aren't we all, well – at least I am... aren't *you* Grandma?' answered Karl. She nodded. 'I shall attend to this right way.'

After thanks and apologies, Karl took his mother back to her home at the old people's residency.

Chapter 41

Germany

A Hoax

Following the meeting with Mr Geller, Karl undertook to speed matters along with respect to the briefcase and its contents, taking the details of the laboratory contact established by the Notar at a new Siemens facility. It was a Mr Kurtz he needed to talk to. Indeed, as intimated during the meeting, Mr Kurtz couldn't wait to see and examine this seventy-year-old object of history; anticipation was high.

The phone rang.

'Herr Vetter... Karl Vetter?'

'Speaking... is that Mr Kurtz?'

'Yes. Peter Kurtz from the laboratories – I took the liberty of making first contact. I hope you don't mind. Apart from brief details we do not know what to expect but we have set aside a small decontamination area to clean up the object as Mr Geller tells me that it is a poor condition with grease and dirt. If you like we can dispatch our own courier to collect it as I know this must be a difficult time for you. Would this be acceptable? In fact, would you like to be present?'

'It is – and is much appreciated Mr Kurtz. I will ensure that the briefcase is itself bagged and then I'll put it in a box for you – I believe you already have Mr Geller's address, that is where it will be for collection. Thank you for your offer but I'm just too busy to come over – but thank you again.'

It was collected the next day.

Initially, Karl was only mildly intrigued by the possibilities contained within the briefcase but now he had to admit to himself how he was looking forward to the results, if only because of the sheer length of time and that maybe, just maybe, there might be some personal family effects hidden amongst the contents. Mr Kurtz had assured the family that all contents, everything, would be dealt with correctly and deferentially.

He wasn't sure of the significance of the object in question, something made back in the forties and found in a wrecked American bomber, but no doubt Mr Kurtz and the laboratory would be enthusiastic and excited for the chance of pulling apart a piece of old technology – a departure from the normal, mundane work activities. The only clue that Karl had was that it was a cigarette-case sized object. It might be an object considered totally mundane in this day and age... but yes, he was interested nonetheless.

As for his grandmother, he knew that she might be getting her expectations up and hoped that she would not be too disappointed. Whenever she reminisced about her beloved Ralph there was always happiness mixed with sadness – there were few personal effects and only a faded photograph, a sad reminder of how little there was left of her dashing husband. Karl had obviously seen many photos of German WWII flying aces such as Adolf Galland and he had to admit, they looked smart in their uniforms... but he had not seen anything resembling these pictures of his grandfather.

The next day, his life was turned upside down. The phone rang...

'Herr Vetter, it's Peter Kurtz here.'

'Speaking... hello Mr Kurtz. Please call me Karl.'

'Karl, look, regarding the briefcase – the object – I don't know how to tell you this but you and your family has been the victim of a hoax.'

'What? A hoax? How so? What do you mean?'

'Well, the object in the case is a modern smartphone Karl – yes, a cell-phone! Damaged, but there is no doubt. It's a modern phone... a Samsung, they told me. I'm afraid your time and our time have been wasted. We are so disappointed, but the documents, including the old photographs – quite faded now – are indeed from 1944. It seems that someone is playing some kind of an elaborate joke on you and has placed a battered cell phone in with a report of another object. I have to remind you that today it is a simple matter to digitally change photos to give an ancient appearance and the only photo of the phone – which of course is in black and white – shows the broken phone lying on the floor, on the ground; that picture could have been taken anywhere – there is some faded writing on the back of it. Apparently, there were other photos taken according to additional reports written back then. I think that – and it has to be recently because of the year this phone was produced – the original item was perhaps lost and to avoid embarrassment at the time, someone has put this in its place, covering it with grease.

Karl was stunned – lost for words.

'Is this to believe… really? All this for nothing? Who could have done this?' His immediate thought was his father – his father looking for money or anything he could pawn to fund his drink and his women. But no, he dismissed the idea… he wouldn't have had a clear mind and been sober enough to do something like this. The last few years had reduced him to a stumbling, shuffling old man. 'No – I can't believe this Peter, there must be something wrong. There has to be another explanation surely. What kind of phone was it – an iPhone?'

'Oh sorry, no, as I said earlier, it's a Samsung,' answered Peter. 'If you would allow us to go ahead we can wire it up and see what's on the phone and SIM card – assuming it still works; after all it belongs to you. Can we do this? We might even find a clue who has perpetrated this trick. That in itself could be interesting.'

'Yes, please do – and of course there might be some photos too. I feel frustrated and saddened to be honest. It will be a huge disappointment to my grandmother.'

'Well, we are sorry too, but no 1940s cell phone I'm afraid! Now *that* really would have been a talking point! I'll ring back, probably tomorrow, to tell you what we find.'

'Thank you, Peter, goodbye.' Karl was wondering how he would tell Grandma. He decided he would wait until the weekend.

Chapter 42

Germany

Further developments

A knock on his office door. Peter Kurtz looked up at the young man in a white coat whom he recognised as one of the laboratory technicians dealing with the 'Vetter' briefcase.

'Hello Konrad, come in,' he beckoned. 'What is it... any news?' he asked as he stood up with an expectant look on his face.

'This is difficult to explain – we seem to have some kind of paradox Mr Kurtz. The best way to explain – to demonstrate it, is for you to observe it first hand in the laboratory where it is set up and where we can perhaps better convey the situation we have, and in a secure area, away from others,' added the technician while inviting Kurtz to follow him.

'Away from the others... secure...? Hmm, what is going on? This sounds interesting.' Kurtz immediately moved around from his desk, 'You certainly have my attention – is there something wrong, a technical problem; we have not damaged any of the items have we?' asked Kurtz, not without a little tension in his voice now.

'No no – absolutely not, nothing like that... we will show you. You will come to understand why shortly.' Together they made their way away from the offices down to another level and then into a laboratory. 'Please sit here in front of these screens and we will take you through what we have discovered from the download from the phone's memory – from its gallery of photos. We did have some trouble in getting it going – we had to use an alternative battery source that we've slaved in as the original was completely and utterly dead Mr Kurtz – totally useless. My wife does the same with hers sometimes – she has two, and forgets where she leaves one of them for weeks on end and wonders why it's flat! But this was in a different league... really flat.'

Peter Kurtz nodded, 'OK, interesting. Please continue,' noticing now that all the blinds were drawn. There were three lab technicians in the room with him and he could see the briefcase on one of the desks.

'We're going to take you through the photo gallery on the large TV here, in the order they were taken, from start to finish, okay?' Peter Kurtz nodded.

'What do we have... holiday snaps?' he asked before realising that his staff looked serious, with no immediate answer.

'Right – number one, the first picture... what do you see?'

Peter Kurtz looked at the screen – then more intently, putting on his glasses. 'A small garden wall – and in the background a village scene in...that's not in Germany, is it? That's in England looking at the car plates and the post-box – if I remember correctly.'

'You are right – we checked with the British – these are British number plates. It looks like someone's proud of a new wall they've just built.' The others nodded, smiling.

Kurtz motioned with an approving nod – they are thorough!

'The second photo...?'

'It looks like the same place – with a couple standing by a motorbike... ah, yes, you could just see part of the bike in the previous picture if I recall; probably the same house.' The first picture was brought back; sure enough, part of the bike was there.

'They look happy – must be theirs I think. Taken this year,' added Konrad. '...and I'm guessing that this phone, therefore, belongs to them too.'

'But how does their phone finish up here in Germany, eh?' asked Kurtz out loud to no one in particular.

'A moment Mr Kurtz. Now we have picture number three...'

'Hmm – it looks like a party... no, not a party – a dance.' Peter pondered the photo a moment before adding 'A fancy-dress dance! Just look at the styles – all like Hollywood, don't you think? Oh, what wonderful styles. I wonder where *that* is?'

'We have an idea – but there was no editing. Do you notice anything unusual...?'

Kurtz intensified his scrutiny but he was lost, he couldn't spot anything unusual.

'Everybody – well most of them – is smoking. You don't see that normally; we are not allowed to smoke anymore unless, of course, this is some illicit gathering so we thought that it might be from a film set or a new TV programme Mr Kurtz. And look at the posters over there on that wall… you will notice between those posters there are window black-out covers, therefore it has to be a programme they are making in a studio, to go to all that trouble.'

Yes, quite plausible… logical thought Kurtz; he could see the poster – a World War Two poster, 1940s vintage, English posters. 'It looks like a good party, a party or a movie being made in England,' he murmured. There were many uniforms amongst the dancers.

'And number four: more dancing only this time you can see a group of people dressed obviously as American flyers – and – in the corner Mr Kurtz – the DJ! Notice the laptop and his music console…?'

'But that would spoil the film, wouldn't it?' said Peter. 'What do they call it – a 'continuity failure' or something; like Moses wearing a watch?'

They moved to the next.

'A nice close-up photo of a woman in this party – just head and shoulders, very pretty; well, it looks like the same event looking at the background,' the technician went on. 'She is also dressed in the old-fashioned style for the party.'

'Now in this one you can see a man nearby to the left who is obviously dressed in modern style – you can tell by the jeans and footwear he has. He also looks older than most of the others and is standing next to the laptop, so he is likely to be the DJ… maybe the organiser? Notice the two next to him – see their clothes? *They* are proper dancing clothes I suspect… shoes, everything.'

True thought Mr Kurtz – they looked the part, but he interrupted…

'However, they are *not* dressed in old style are they – I have seen these clothes on TV. These are modern dancers. But what is the mystery?' he asked, 'What are you showing me? OK, so we have a dance or a party – or even a film set-up in a studio somewhere in England… so what?'

'When we saw these two dancers we thought they are the same two from the motorbike earlier – we are pretty sure about this.' They flicked back.

'Yes, I think you are right, they do look very similar…' said Peter Kurtz. 'It must be them… definitely in England then.'

'Ah, but we have not finished yet Mr Kurtz. I'll move it along...'
They flicked through a few more photos before the lab man said, 'This is
where it gets extremely interesting. Look at the next picture.'

The next one flashed up and, like the rest, it was in full colour.

It took just a few moments, then Mr Kurtz froze – a close-up picture
of a crashed aircraft appeared. All the lab technicians were now looking at
him intently. The picture was not of anything in particular in the wreck
but unmistakeably, it was an American bomber, the picture unfocussed in
parts. The implications of what he was seeing suddenly dawned on him.
He looked around at his lab staff – they were still looking at him
expecting him to ask the obvious question, instead he said, 'Please show
me the original black and white photographs from the briefcase would
you...' With the photos in his hands he looked up and exclaimed, 'But
this is the same bomber – look at the letters on the side. How can this be?
And is that part of a uniform we can see at the bottom left?'

'Yes, Mr Kurtz – probably an accomplice; it would seem that both the
old and the new pictures are of the same aircraft, an aircraft nicknamed
Tail-heavy Betty, but look at the next picture...'

Up on the large TV screen came another photo, only this time it
looked like a random shot. But there, plain as daylight, was a face of a
Luftwaffe officer looking slightly to his side, perhaps in conversation with
someone else. Could the officer be... 'Who was the officer taking the
briefcase in the report...what was his name...?'

'Major Vetter... Major Ralph Vetter, Luftwaffe – and we believe that
the other man, in the next photo, is likely to be Major Vetter's colleague
Sergeant Schneider.'

Peter Kurtz suddenly found himself sweating. 'This cannot be – you
know the implication of this,' he asked softly. 'It means that somehow this
Samsung phone has found its way back to...' he looked back at the black
and white photo to confirm the dates, '...back to 1944! This is ridiculous!'
He quickly glanced again at the other briefcase photos.

They all shifted uncomfortably.

On the back of one, quite faded, were the words, 'Three helmets' –
British Tommy helmets?! Kurtz looked once more and yes, he could make
out the three helmets. One was intact, the others partly crushed, but
interestingly, attached to something, possibly what looked like a piece of
board. Even he knew that they were definitely not WWII German army
issue. 'This does not make sense – British 'tin hats' in a crashed American

bomber,' he said, looking at each of the lab staff, hoping for some answer. They all shrugged as one.

'This is why I used the word paradox earlier,' said Konrad. 'We have no idea how this has happened… it is a complete enigma to us all.'

Peter Kurtz has never entertained the idea of ghosts, goblins, phantoms, and other stories of the paranormal and his mind was now working overtime to explain this. It was all very simple two days ago. It was a hoax then – he was so certain of it, and easily explained by the fact that during the passage of time, the briefcase had never been kept in a secure area, just somebody's bedroom; opportunities for a prank or even fraud were many. But this turn of events had suddenly altered the situation. However, he still thought that must be an obvious, simple answer, then Konrad cut across his thoughts.

'Peter, there have been stories, many well documented, of people stumbling across strange scenes in modern times as if they have temporarily moved into the past only to find no trace on subsequent investigation. People have reputedly heard war cries on ancient battle sites. There is a wealth of information available of such tales, some difficult to explain away… the holiday family who stopped overnight at an old farmhouse on a drive down to Spain, only to find that on the way back, when they wanted to stop again at the same charming old accommodation, it no longer existed – but the foundations of the building were still evident from over two hundred years ago. And the extraordinary tale of the two English ladies in Versailles in 1901 who thought – they were convinced – that they had travelled back to the time of Louis XVI.'

'Really? What do you think all of you?' They were all shaking their heads. 'Are there any more pictures?' asked Kurtz, suddenly remembering they had paused during the slideshow.

'Yes, one more.' This showed yet another crash site snap of poor quality, almost entirely out of focus but in the background, was the blurred outline of a small tracked vehicle behind parts of the wreckage.

'What is *that*?' asked Kurtz pointing at it. 'It looks quite strange; is it a motorcycle…?'

'We think that is one of those general purpose haulage, towing machines called a *Kettenkrad*. It has the front end of a motorbike with the body of a half-track. They were originally designed to be light weight and for being air-transportable, but in fact were used as general utility towing machines. It looks like the one you can see might be pulling a trailer full of debris.'

How peculiar it looked, thought Kurtz. He'd never seen anything like it – didn't know such machines ever existed. His mind came back to the subject matter of the photos.

'Does anybody else here know of this... about these photos?' asked Mr Kurtz, looking around at his lab staff. They all vigorously shook their heads. 'You are absolutely sure? I'm serious now.'

'Absolutely sure Mr Kurtz, no one else knows – nobody.'

'Then we must keep it that way, understood all of you – until we discover some explanation.' He was about to go on when...

'Mr Kurtz – we did some additional investigation. We managed to obtain some fingerprints from the brief case, the old photos and the documents and two from the actual phone, although these, unfortunately, did not match any of the others. But some of the others matched, ones on the old photos and the report did match ones from the briefcase. We did this while we had the opportunity.'

Indeed, his crew were thorough.

'I believe they would be wearing gloves in any case, which may explain no matches to the phone.'

'Thank you, I was about to say that what I'm going to do next is to invite Mr Vetter, Mr Geller the Notar and Mrs Vetter, if is she is up to it, to our facility and show them what we've found but before we do, I'd like us to have session to ensure what we think we have here isn't complete and utter nonsense. We need to go over it all once more, and I think that the man in the photo... is, could be... Mrs Vetter's husband! I will tell you about that later.' He realised of course that his lab-rats were only vaguely aware of Vetter family, and the connection to all this, so he told them the story about the original WWII investigation. 'In the meantime... utter silence on this. We are a professional company involved in serious research in a very competitive market – we cannot have our reputation undermined by silly rumours of the paranormal: our funding would cease. Understood?!'

They all nodded vigorously.

Later, they reconvened going back over all the photos, studying them more closely and discussing the possibilities. Whichever way they looked at it, a smartphone from 2012 had found its way to this 1944 crash site... into the hands of a Major Vetter.

How?

'We need to find the connection,' said Peter Kurtz. 'It is impossible, stupid. There must be a sensible reason. In the meantime, I'll have arrangements made to bring the Vetters here.'

One thing that exercised their minds in a following discussion was the mention in the original 1944 report of two 'letters' reported by the Luftwaffe officer when they initially tried to identify the object, the letters 'V' and 'W'. They now realised that in fact the 'V' could be an 'A' – when they looked at a phone they realised that the second letter in *Samsung* is left uncrossed and that the 'W' could in fact be 'M'. But, of course, this would just undermine any attempt to bring common sense to their predicament.

Then one of the lab technicians posed a question that they hadn't considered at all – what if the party pictures and the dancing were also taken in 1944? They all sat without a word for several seconds.

'No! There are the British number plates don't forget,' said Konrad. They momentarily relaxed.

'...and the laptop,' said another.

'But... the first two may be true, but all the ones after may not be,' continued the technician.

'How?' they all asked almost together. The talk descended into thirty minutes of argument and counter-argument before Peter Kurtz eventually said:

'Look – let's give it a rest for today. Something has obviously happened for which we have no proper answer but I am certain there must be something we are missing... a logical solution.'

Chapter 43

Frau Vetter sees

Karl Vetter's phone rang. It was Mr Kurtz from the laboratory.

'We believe we have something quite interesting for you to see – we can come to you or you come over to us and we can explain it all; we will take care of the travel arrangements if you wish.' He went briefly over the situation about a party in England found on the phone without going into any of the intriguing aspects – or saying anything about the B-17. That would wait.

Karl decided they could do with a nice day out for them all – especially Grandma who never ventured far these days, so two days later found them all together – the Vetters and the Notar with Peter Kurtz and his staff in an office adjacent to the laboratory. The atmosphere was pregnant with anticipation.

After introductions, the lab staff more or less repeated the sequence of events from before, with Peter Kurtz leading.

'These have all been downloaded from the cell phone. Apart from the first two pictures the ones you are going to see now are of a dance or party somewhere in England, and if you look at the styles it is probably a themed party – they are all dressed from the forties, we think. Frau Vetter was looking intently, nodding slightly.

Karl looked at Mr Kurtz and asked, 'These are from England?' Peter Kurtz nodded and informed them all that the UK had confirmed the vehicle number plates as being British as he clicked onto the next series of pictures. They all seemed fascinated by the dance scenes.

'The ladies do seem to have a great deal of lipstick on don't they,' commented Mr Geller.

Peter let them dwell on each picture before moving on to the next. He was wondering what their reactions would be when they arrived at the crash scene photos but decided not to give any warning that events were about to change. He could hear a few words spoken between Mr Geller and the Vetters – Frau Vetter seemed captivated by the dance and the dresses, a little smile forming on her face.

'Wonderful dresses, wonderful fashions,' she managed to murmur, nodding slowly.

As before, when the first crash scene picture appeared there was an audible intake of breath, the Vetters and Mr Geller trying to fathom what they were looking at. The dancing was already forgotten. Peter Kurtz could see their looks of puzzlement but before anyone could interject, he went straight to the next picture. There was a gasp.

'Ralph!' gasped Frau Vetter. 'Oh Ralph!' Everyone turned to look at her. Moments of silence followed.

Karl was transfixed.

'This... is he your... husband?' asked Mr Geller, 'Really your husband?'

'Oh yes – yes! Oh, that's my Ralph!' said Frau Vetter gasping. 'Ralph! Where is this? When did this happen? When was this picture taken... it's in colour. Oh wonderful,' she trailed off having spoken her words slowly and softly.

They were all stunned, especially Karl and Mr Geller who suddenly realised what was happening – and the impossibility of it all.

Peter Kurtz was also shocked. So it *was* Major Vetter! He had been hoping all along that the whole saga was some sophisticated fraud or hoax – some strange set-up. Konrad looked shaken too.

'But how is this possible Peter? Surely there is a simple explanation?' he asked as he turned to his Grandma, but Frau Vetter was still looking at the huge picture of Ralph – the biggest and best picture she had ever seen of her beloved, all in glorious colour on a very large flat TV. What a handsome man he was. She was now totally absorbed in the picture, totally unaware of the paradox.

'I need this picture,' she said quietly as she slowly stood up and shuffled closer to the huge TV screen. 'How can I get this picture?' she asked as her eyes moved to Karl. 'Can I have a picture... please – a big one?'

'Absolutely you can,' responded Peter Kurtz, looking at Konrad. Konrad nodded and was quickly out through a side door into what was a printer set-up. Moments later he was back with several A4 pictures which he tentatively gave to Miriam Vetter. She gently took hold of them as if

251

they were the most precious objects she had ever held. 'We can do better than this later – a proper print picture that can be framed.'

Karl was open-mouthed. 'This is too much for me – I do not understand,' he said turning to Peter Kurtz. Is there an explanation for this? Last time you mentioned a hoax… is this part of it?'

'I wish it was,' responded Peter Kurtz. 'The camera dating confirms that it was taken very recently, not in 1944, I can assure you. This is no hoax – just look at the black and white photographs from the 1944 report…'

Karl looked at them – and then back at the TV again. 'Peter, I don't believe in these things… but what can I say? It is all unbelievable.' Mr Geller was nodding in agreement. 'I hope that one day you can tell us all how this has occurred. And I, we, must thank you for what you have done for us.'

'I promise we will,' responded Peter Kurtz. 'There may well be some more pieces of the puzzle to come!'

'We will also provide you with an electronic version for you to take back,' added Konrad, but Frau Vetter was a long, long way away now, lost in memory as she stared at the picture. She began to weep. This signalled the end of the current presentation with Peter Kurtz recommending that after some refreshment they would talk and discuss matters. But what about, he was not entirely sure.

What is the link, he wondered? What ties all these events together? He thought back to what Konrad had said earlier about events occurring out of time.

His only brush with strange, unusual situations that had shook him was quite recent when he took his family, including the family pet, on holiday. They had visited an old Schloss. The tour guide had taken them around with the inevitable stories of battles, pillage, plunder, and hauntings. Peter had rolled his eyes at the family when the guide had mentioned that in the past, some poor unfortunate resident had met a sticky end and was supposed to 'walk the corridors' and a nearby garden; he was not having any of this nonsense. Ghosts! But what shook him – and frightened his children – was the reaction of their dog when they approached the corner of a room. It stopped and would not move no matter what Peter said or did – it just snarled at the corner, staring at some invisible object, its hackles raised. What was wrong with him? And then the tour guide, taking in the dog's behaviour, looked over to Peter and said.

'He *knows*…!'

'He knows what?' asked Peter.

'That according to records this is where the unfortunate victim met his end – in the corner. Animals can sense all manner of things humans cannot.'

Peter and his family had been really jolted by this event. Could the dog see the 'unseen'? Something had upset it – something beyond Peter's comprehension.

His mind returned to the phone.

Now he wasn't quite so sure about his physical world.

Karl Vetter was both mystified and pleasantly surprised; initially shocked, he had overlooked the obvious and unfathomable circumstances but seeing such a clear, wonderful picture of his grandfather instead of the usual faded black and white photos one normally had of relatives that far from the past had overridden all thoughts of the conundrum.

They all spoke around the issue and then realised, after being reminded, that the photo detail from the phone had recorded the picture as having been taken in modern times… both time and date.

'There must be some explanation – even I know that this cannot happen and if I told anybody about it they would probably think I'm losing my marbles. I deal in finance with large corporations. Any suspicion of me being involved in stories of silly time travel and they might assume I was on drugs. No, I cannot understand it – except to say that there has to be something obvious we have overlooked,' said Karl, probably echoing the thoughts of others around the table.

'But the aircraft number tallies – we checked – it is *Tail-Heavy Betty,* and there is Major Vetter in all his glory – looking young, not 90-odd,' Peter pointed out. 'Look – we cannot unravel this mystery today so I suggest we close our meeting for now. We will continue to delve into this. In the meantime we'll contact the experts in Korea and also look back at the war records. We will also try to track down those we have seen in the other pictures from the dance.'

'But the dance could *also* be from 1944 – what then? They would all be dead now!' said Konrad.

'What? You think that it, too, is part of the conundrum Konrad? But wait a minute… what about the first few pictures? The brick wall – the motorbike?' added Peter.

'Yes… of course!' shouted Konrad. 'I'd forgotten about that. From the car number plates, we might be able to track down the location – and perhaps the owner of the phone!'

Even Peter was excited about this possibility, his excited smile spreading to the other technicians – including Karl Vetter and Mr Geller. They were all nodding at the prospect of solving this mystery.

When Peter Kurtz returned home that evening, he realised that regardless of what transpired, even if they tracked down the owner, the paradox remained – it would not be solved. He thought back to his dog…

The next day, Mr Geller phoned him. Another shock.

'Peter – sad news. I am afraid to inform you that Frau Vetter passed away in her sleep last night.'

Peter was stunned. He told his staff. They sat there in his office in silence for at least a minute, until one of them said,

'She died happy. She had her picture – and her memory. She was reunited.'

'I think you are absolutely right,' said Peter, endorsing the thoughts but with mixed feelings – both happy and sad for the Vetter family. 'I have some calls to make. I must pass on our condolences to Karl Vetter first. Tomorrow we will think some more. I'm sure that you, like myself, would like to get to the bottom of this, so please do some thinking.'

When he had eventually contacted Mr Vetter he had said that although he could not understand the circumstances surrounding the photos from the different years, he was quite sure that his grandma was simply happy – and at peace – to have had the picture, a wonderful picture of her long-lost husband.

'When we get to the bottom of all this we'll let you know,' promised Peter Kurtz again.

Chapter 44

Gunther explains

The next day…

'OK, so what do you think links all this together, what is the common denominator?' Peter asked his staff.

One of the technicians, Gunther, put up his hand. 'I think it's the Americans. It's an American bomber, Americans at the dance…' he said tentatively.

'Yes… go on…'

'Well, we saw some American 'flyers' at the dance did we not. My thinking is that they are a 'real' crew – but the unfortunate crew members of the crashed bomber we see in both Major Vetter's report, and from the Samsung phone.'

'But how did they get the phone?' This was the 65,000-dollar question Peter pointed out. He was allowing them to do the speculation and brainstorming.

'Well… we also saw at the *dance* the older man with a laptop… so whether the dance is real or not, those guys presenting the music including the modern dancers – we counted four dressed differently – *were modern* and *must* have had cell phones. You may be able to spot one in the other pictures. I also saw on the wall a TV – it looked like a plasma and over there, I'm pretty certain that they are LED lights.' They were all rapt with attention now as Gunther pointed his finger at the presentation.

'Carry on,' invited Peter. He didn't want to ask the obvious question just yet – how did the 'modern' element get to be with the 'old' element. He need not have worried… Gunther continued.

'…therefore I believe that the owners of the phone were at the same dance and that the Americans have stolen the phone, taking it with them when they left – to eventually finish up in the wreck.'

'That's a stretch,' somebody commented.

His audience sat still for at least ten seconds while what he was suggesting sunk in. 'But *how* are they together – *how* are they at the same dance?' asked Konrad. 'I mean, who is in the wrong place, the man playing the music or all those dancing – all those dressed in old styles?'

They all looked again at Gunther who was beginning to turn red now. But he was getting into his stride.

'It is the part where we depart from normality. In my opinion it is the musicians who are 'wrong'. I don't know how but they have stepped into the time of the dance. I'll explain... at the dance, everyone – there are no exceptions – is dressed in old style. They cannot be faulted. I have looked at all their clothes, footwear, even their watches where they are visible... nothing, nothing is modern. I can go to any dance today and there will always be *someone* wearing Adidas, Puma or Nike trainers – I guarantee it.' He was emboldened now, really had their attention and he could see from their expressions that they *wanted* him to solve it. He continued.

'Somehow, these modern people you can see in the picture here have stumbled into 1944! I did warn you about departing from normality and reason,' he said, pointing at the screen. 'But how? Please do not ask me that – I cannot answer that, but it must have happened! I believe that this is the connection, the modern people at the dance, the Americans – and the bomber.'

Peter was impressed – impressed at Gunther's thoroughness and logical thinking.

'Thank you, Gunther.' Peter looked around at the others. 'Any questions from anybody?'

'Yes. How did the phone manage to survive all these years?' asked Konrad.

'There's not much in a modern phone – hardly any moving parts really – and it was smothered in something that gave it protection if you remember. We did have to exhort to some desperate measures to resurrect the power source and of course a memory card... well, there is nothing to it. They are quite durable. Even if it was damaged in the crash, it would seem that the officer had activated the camera without knowing it – after all, he wouldn't have known what he had, would he? It was just another piece of wreckage as far as he was concerned – different perhaps, but maybe that is what made him curious as you can see from the original report. However, if we could somehow trace those in the first pictures...' Gunther trailed off.

'But of course... that's it! We must trace them if we can. Fascinating. Who *would* believe us?' Peter paused, 'I wonder if they returned...' he looked around and could see them all expressing the same question on their faces. 'Yes, this is what I will undertake to do – to get some answers.'

'But Peter, to trace them should not be difficult. If you look a little closer you will see in the front space of the that house here across the street – the front garden...' he walked up to the screen to point at it, '...you can see there is a 'sale' notice; it looks like 'Moffat and Moffat'. This will be the name of the agents,' said Gunther. 'Find them and you will be close to the motorbike owners. The same street.'

'Well done Gunther – I hadn't noticed that. Excellent, this must be our lead,' said Peter Kurtz finishing up. He was now really excited and wondering where the investigation trail would take them. At the same time, he wondered if in reality, they had 'made it back' to the present – and weren't wandering about in some limbo-land, frightening people... and dogs.

Chapter 45

UK Today
Pondering

A couple of weeks had passed. Here I was at home trying to concentrate.

None of us could get our heads round what had happened on the Bury gig. There was simply no rational explanation and I could now begin to appreciate those many stories I'd heard about time-slips… holiday-makers and disappearing accommodation; battle sounds from fields. Yes – I'd looked it up, I mean – who do you tell? Who *wouldn't* laugh at you, at least behind your back?

And yes, I too had read about the holiday family – Versailles – and of many others.

Images of Grace kept floating into my vision while Matt and Ruby were imagining some country hick – or maybe one of the Yanks – getting to grips with their cell phone if that's where (and when) it was. Keith and Becky were reliving the 'Miss Light-fingers and her PC plod boyfriend' episode.

'Did it all really happen? Did it? I have to keep pinching myself,' said Becky.

'Well, we actually have pictures to prove it all happened, have we not?' added Ruby.

'Yes, we have – and you took the last snap in the Rover, of Grace just before she vanished,' I said.

We had pooled all of our photos onto a file and backed it all up on a remote hard drive. Now I had a fabulous, full-sized, colour picture of Grace, framed already, sitting in my living room. Weird but wonderful.

Matt and Ruby had returned to their house after some shopping, Matt casting a glance, as he always did, towards the phone. Yes – the light was flashing. Could be another booking. He pressed 'play'…

'Hello, it is Mr Kurtz here, I am speaking from Germany. I wish to speak to Mr Boulton. I will call back this evening if that's OK – early evening as I'm travelling right now.'

Hmm. Germany eh? Mr Kurtz? Don't know him, thought Matt.

'Know anybody called Mr Kurtz Rubes… from Germany?' he called out loud. No.

'Now why would anybody be calling us from Germany?' pondered Ruby, listening in to the message. 'I'm certainly not going all that way for dancing,' she added with a chuckle.

That evening the phone rang. Matt could see the same number in the display from earlier.

'Hello?'

'Mr Boulton?'

'Yes, Matt Boulton here. How can I help you Mr Kurtz? We were out this afternoon.'

'I believe I may have something that belongs to you…' For a split second Matt thought that he was getting a cold call and nearly put the phone down; cold calls don't come in from Germany, they usually emanate from either Outer Mongolia or Timbuktu.

A slight pause. 'Really? What might that be Mr Kurtz?'

'A cell phone. Have you misplaced one recently?'

That made him sit up.

He put his hand over the phone. 'Hold on a moment Mr Kurtz. 'Then he shouted, 'Ruby! Ruby! Quick, get your bum down here sharpish.' As she came rushing to his side he gestured her to listen, putting the phone on 'speaker'. She perched herself on the edge of the sofa. 'Just listen,' he said.' Ruby's eyes were wide open with concern. Then back to the phone Matt invited his caller to carry on. 'Sorry Mr Kurtz, you say you have a phone, please continue.' This brought Ruby up to speed.

'Yes, Mr Boulton, I have a Samsung cell phone – have you lost it?'

Ruby nearly fell off the arm of the sofa.

'Where did you get it from?' Matt responded without making any reference to losing or finding anything. He wanted to see where this was headed first.

'Mr Boulton, please call me Peter. The phone was found in Germany in very peculiar circumstances. I wish to talk to you about it – but not over the phone… that is if the phone *is* yours…? Some pictures on it convinces me that it is… and I will *not* send them. I have to show them personally.'

Matt and Ruby exchanged looks. Again he'd nearly put the phone down until the words *in very peculiar circumstances* were spoken.

'Okay Mr Kurtz… Peter. I'm listening. Yes, we did lose a phone but why can't you tell me about it now while we're talking?'

'I'm sorry but I assure you it is for the best. I work in telecommunications – this is my background, my work. I want to come to see you in England and tell you – explain face to face. I often travel to the UK and I can make the visit as part of my work.'

Pleasantries were exchanged, loose arrangements made, but Matt and Ruby were stunned.

'How the hell did the phone end up in Germany, babes? This is creepy. I'm going to tell the others. '

…

A few minutes later Matt rang me.

'Bob – just had a strange phone call…'

'I wish I had one or two… not one of those dating agencies…? Okay go on…'

'Some guy in Germany phoned me. He asked if I had lost a phone recently.'

'Eh? Are we talking about your phone and our gig in Bury?'

'Yes, that one. He had traced us from a picture on it.'

There was a pause of several seconds.

'How did he do that – how did it finish up with him anyway? Who is he?'

'It was found in Germany… some guy from Siemens called Peter Kurtz. He wants to come and see me – and Ruby. He wouldn't tell me over the phone – he actually wants to speak in person about it. Well – after what happened I think we all should be there.'

The conversation became stilted with lengthy pauses as we both tried to solve, while talking, how this could have happened.

'Absolutely – good call.'

...

Bloody hell. Found in Germany? I'm just getting my head round this. We'd thought the whole episode was going to quietly fade, although not totally – you could never forget completely an experience like that. We hadn't untangled the mystery and common sense told us all that it was some kind of aberration; none of us touched drugs and other mind-bending crap – leave that to the spaced-out dope-heads. My mind was only allowed to be bent by a good old-fashion Gin and tonic. Oh, OK, maybe a vodka or two – or six. So we were still unsure what had happened. And believe it or not we had unconsciously steered away from that area for any new bookings.

'Don't fancy coming across any black Wolseleys again,' Matt had said.

But Matt's phone in Germany eh? Fancy that. I just sat there in silence for half an hour thinking about it all going over and over as much as I could remember from that night.

It was duly arranged – Mr Kurtz was due in a fortnight, coming in at Stanstead, and he'd come as my guest for the first two nights.

Chapter 46

Hello Herr Kurtz

I met 'Herr' Kurtz – a genial, pleasant looking fellow, not quite as tall as me, mind, but stockier. The usual introductory pleasantries followed. 'But I have *seen* you before Mr Temple – I'll explain later.' Straight away he added, '…and please call me Peter,' explaining that if I didn't mind, he'd prefer to tell the complete story when we were all together, so the talk on the way to my house was all about jobs, airport queues – and cars; women can talk about handbags, blokes about cars… usually… agreed reader?

'As you requested Peter, we've arranged my little studio for your 'presentation'. Later we're gonna hit the delights of our local village for a few gallons of Dunkel Bier followed by Britain's favourite dish, Tikka Masala.'

'Excellent – it sounds very agreeable. I love dark beer even though it's not cold. We have some dark beers in Germany but not as many as in England. But what is this Tikka Masala… is this the famous curry we hear about?'

'Well technically, it's not really a curry I'm told, but we don't have to have it too spicy in any case. And yes, there has been an explosion of new 'bitter beers' here in the UK – very popular now. In the seventies many people stopped drinking normal beer and started on lagers. Probably the very hot summer of '76 had something to do with it. Now the pendulum has swung back to traditional beers, I'm glad to say.'

Keith had said, 'Perhaps he'd like to try a pint of Spitfire – or maybe not.'

Peter told me that later on in the week he was off to one of his favourite past-times – walking, hiking, particularly in the North West of Scotland.

'I often come to Scotland to explore, and I have some days owed to me so I can kill two birds with the single stone – is that how you say it?'

'It'll do,' I answered smiling, '...but you have the majestic Alps on your doorstep, wonderful views, so why Scotland?'

'Ah, yes, the Alps are very nice but that is a different kind of beauty, almost like a chocolate box picture. In the Scottish Highlands, even though they are not as high, they are awesome, rugged, forbidding, unique... almost mysterious to me. A magnificent solitude. I often find it ghostly... if the weather is not cooperating!'

I knew exactly what he meant having travelled extensively 'up there'. The Highlands are special as Peter said and I, for one, often asked myself when taking in the view from some unpronounceable crag, how this could be the same piece of ground, the same piece of earth – albeit four hundred miles removed – as that of my boring home town.

He went on, 'I always remember the first time I travelled there – it was on a whim. My first visit, and my first surprise was when I went into the hotel bar. Behind the bar all I could see was whiskeys, from one end to the other! When I asked if they sold anything else the barman said, "We try not to!" There seemed to be distilleries everywhere, every kilometre it seemed to me Mr Temple.'

'I also noticed that the men at the bar were drinking both together – a sip of beer followed by a sip of whiskey. I could not imagine how they could afford this and I also wondered how they managed to do any work the next day! How do they manage this? Are they mad?'

'Some are,' I said laughing, having known a few.

'And when I went to a place called Glen Coe – is that how you say it? – I could not believe that people actually lived there hundreds of years ago and you can see the old ruins of their houses. Unbelievable – truly unforgettable. It was the same when I was looking at another ruin called Urquhart castle – I saw it from the other side of Loch Ness...' he trailed off shaking his head. 'I understand that Loch Ness is very deep, is this not so?'

'Yes, very. I think it is about...' But I had to do a quick conversion as I still operated in old dinner money... nine hundred feet. '...about three hundred metres Peter.'

'And is it true what they say about a monster?'

I wondered how long it would take to get around to the subject.

'But of course it is Peter,' I replied laughing.

My fond memories of being in the Scottish Highlands always brought back memories of the occasional rumble you would hear, somewhere close – or in the distance – just to remind you that there was a more serious side to the Highlands as a training ground for the military, and I shall never forget while passing over a bridge on the A 82, in the middle of nowhere of course, my colleague shouting – while pointing – at a Phantom coming straight at us in a shallow dive. Didn't know it was there. Nearly blew me off the road.

'Good job my ticker's okay,' I had said at the time.

'This time will be my sixth visit to Scotland and I shall be going to the Isle of Mull.'

'Good fish there I'm told.'

Peter Kurtz soon settled in, then I called up the rest of my gang to come over. There was no doubt that they were all intrigued, if not a little nervous, about what was to take place.

When Matt and Ruby turned up and entered my 'den', Peter immediately stood up and exclaimed, 'Ah yes, the dancers! Pleased to meet you.' Again, introductions were made with both of them looking at me with a questioning look. How did he know that?

'He'll tell us in a minute,' I said. This was all repeated when Keith and Becky appeared and again, Peter introduced himself like he was some long-lost friend, with Keith and Becks registering not a little surprise.

This should be good I thought.

Here we were now perched in front of both Peter's laptop and my TV. Peter opened up his briefcase and, from a soft pouch, produced a phone.

'First – I will tell you about *how* the phone has finished up in my hands later, so I hope you'll bear with me on that point. 'Is this your phone?' he asked as he put it down on the low table in front of us. We all leaned forward for a closer look.

'Bloody hell... yes, it looks like mine. What happened to it?' asked Matt, noticing the state it was in. 'I *think* it's mine,' he added, taking a closer look at it.

'Yes, it's a right mess,' added Ruby.

'But it's difficult to tell with any real certainty,' added Matt while turning it over in his hands and then looking at Peter Kurtz.

'Good. Well, this is when I can tell you, that now that I have seen you all in the flesh that I am convinced it *is* yours. The phone was damaged in a crash and explains why it is damaged like that.'

'A crash? Must have been a serious one for it to be like this – unless it was run over, maybe?' Keith pondered out loud.

Peter continued, 'Amazingly the memory card survived so we extracted all the details as far as we could and I now have it all on my laptop, and it is the pictures you took that I want to show you; but perhaps it would be more convenient if we could transfer it from my special 'stick' into your TV.' Peter was obviously a whizz with IT and soon had it plugged into my big Sony, ready to go. He had us intrigued as you can imagine.

The gig in Bury was once again brought back to be fresh in our minds – all laid bare, and how Mr Kurtz had tracked us down from the first two pictures in the phone that had an estate agent's sign stuck in a neighbour's garden. But it was the dance that had us all in animated discussion.

'But hold it Peter. 'I nodded to Becks who came prepared, pulling out her own phone. 'Becky here also took some snaps that night. Just have a look at these…'

We connected up to the laptop and crowded around, giving Peter the best view. Becky flicked through some photos.

'Oh, Mein Gott!' He exclaimed, 'This is incredible – little did we realise that there was another phone *from then.*'

'We?' I asked. '…from *then*?'

'Yes – my technicians and I had wondered what we had stumbled into – something unique, unexplainable.'

'And I, too, have a phone from *then* – as you call it,' Keith chimed in.

'And me, Peter.' I didn't want to be left out.

We showed him the extra variety of shots from our now strange gig in Bury; he was fascinated and marvelled at the individual pictures we had taken – innocent pictures at first, but then pictures taken for other reasons including Miss Light-fingers.

'Now Peter, perhaps you can enlighten us as to how the phone finished up in your hands,' I prodded, the gang all nodding along. 'You mentioned a crash…?'

'This is where it becomes truly interesting,' he said. Just as his lab team had gone through the pictures with him in order, he repeated the procedure. 'Watch closely please…'

He carried on through some more dance pictures – then I shouted 'Stop!' on a picture of 'my' Grace amongst the dancing. I just gazed at it – then nodded for the show to continue, before coming to a totally different scene – black and white photographs that had been scanned in, showing the wreckage of an American bomber… and there, literally in black and white, was one shot of a cell phone lying on the soil – Matt's phone, close to where it had fallen out. Peter detected the intake of breath.

'Before I continue, am I correct in assuming that you had a strange experience that night with these people – something inexplicable?'

We all nodded.

'We sure did, but when was this?' asked Keith. 'What crash?' Then as the other black and white pictures were flashed up, it began to dawn on them. These pictures, judging by the background and uniforms they could see, were very old.

'Okay then – so it wasn't a car crash,' Keith said.

Peter, in anticipation of the questions about to hit him, raised his hand…'Indeed not. Just a moment – before you ask, these black and white ones are *not* from your phone, they are just old photos taken at the time and added by me with some scanning, however, we shall now continue with the *remaining* photos from *your* camera, thus…'

More intakes of breath as the colour snaps of what appeared to be…the same wreck!

'Is this the same crash Peter?' Matt asked – already knowing the answer.

'Yes, it is, as you can see by the numbers on the side of that piece of wreckage. They match, but the pictures are not professional – we believe the camera was operated accidentally by the officer you see here. His name is Major Vetter, of the Luftwaffe.

'How did my phone get to be in this wreck? And *when* was this crash…?'

There was a moment's silence, then Peter said, 'I think you already know – am I right?'

'1944.' It was Ruby who eventually answered in a whisper, her voice straining, getting louder – 'The Americans! The Yanks… it's their plane!' she almost shrieked.

'You mean Barney and his crowd,' added Keith.

'The crash must have been in 1944 then,' I said… no point in beating about the bushes.

'You are correct Bob – and I can see that it probably comes as little surprise to you all. As for the mystery of how your phone ended up in the B-17 – that's what the aircraft was by the way – you have already identified the link, as we did when we were first trying to unravel this mystery in our laboratory – the link being the Americans. One of our technicians, Gunther, made the connection and… one of the Americans somehow managed to obtain your phone that night. *Somehow* – please do not ask me exactly how – *you entered their time*. Because we had no idea, my team were fearful that you may have not managed to 'return' from that evening, and yet here we all are thankfully. So, you can imagine how we felt in the lab… am I right?'

'You have no idea Peter!' My thoughts flashed back to that night.

Then I asked the obvious question – 'Did they survive the crash?' The girls waited for the answer in breathless anticipation, mouths open, but we all wanted to know the fate of our boisterous American flyers from just a few months ago – *our time*!

'I'm afraid not all of them. We did obtain a list of the crew – and those who managed to survive the shooting down but it is back at work. I can easily have my team send it to me right away.'

'Oh dear… I'm worried now,' said Becky solemnly. 'I hope they are alright…'

Must admit reader, I've never been so engrossed in anything like this since I watched *Alien*. Now I'm wondering who 'made it' – and who didn't. We then decided to go out as arranged – and to let it all sink in over a few beers.

They did not all 'make it'… the two pilots, nor did Ginge (Lenny) and Richard (Ricky). The girls were visibly upset but I suppose we spent most of our time that night with Barney and his closer buddies and were relieved that they hadn't come to a sticky end as far as we knew. Peter told us they all became PoWs for the duration. One of them had not only taken the phone that night, but had also taken it with him on this final mission with Major Vetter picking it up from the wreckage.

'I wonder who nicked it,' mused Keith out loud. 'And I wonder if any of them are *still* alive…? Probably close to your age now Bob…'

'Thanks mate… not.'

Peter took us through the saga of the Mr Vetter and the phone – what was intended for it after its retrieval from the bomber. 'You see, the major had no idea what he had picked up – only that he thought it unusual. An initial inspection was carried out before being instructed to take it to a proper lab. But unfortunately, he was killed shortly after. His briefcase and its contents, including the 'object' – well, somewhere along the line it all went missing, with the report and those old photos you have just seen.' He went on to tell them about Frau Vetter and the 'accidental' photo… 'taken on your phone.'

Ruby spoke. 'So the poor old dear got to see a picture of her husband who had been killed all those years ago…? Aahh – so sad. And you say she passed away shortly afterwards…?' Poor Ruby looked so upset.

It was all completely mind-boggling.

'It sounds just like that story, or film, called *Brigadoon*,' said Keith. We explained briefly to Peter about this charming old movie – even Matt and Ruby didn't know about it.

'And of course, we all know about the Kirk Douglas film don't we?'

But the most engrossing aspect of conversation was Peter asking us how we felt – how did we find out, or when did we realise that our situation was 'miss, what gave it away, what clues? He was absolutely fascinated by our experience and suggested we contact psychic research organisations to relay our story.

'You have the pictures as proof,' he said. 'They are logged by your phone with the date and time – this is evidence, this is proof surely!'

'Yes, but unfortunately, not the 1944 date – only the *current* time and date. So they'd probably suspect some tampering or some hoax,' I said, chucking in my penny's worth.

Another hour passed. Eventually Peter asked how far away was this place where we had had our experience and was it possible to see it? 'I am not going to Scotland for another two days yet. Is it possible to visit this town hall?'

'Peter, sure we can – just for you. We can take the day out tomorrow to Bury. It's within striking distance,' I said.

Then, looking at Matt and Ruby, he said, 'But first – I must return to you your nearly-seventy-year-old cell phone – what a life it has seen, what a story it can tell! While I am in solitude during my walking, I will have plenty of time to think about this strange happening; before I came to England I was told by one of my lab technicians, Gunther, of another strange event that occurred in Versailles – apparently, he said it was quite famous, so I took time to read about it. After my experience with our pet dog, and your experiences, I am no longer as sceptical about these matters.'

'Yes, us included Peter,' we all muttered simultaneously.

Well, in the end it took us all day… some sight-seeing in Bury plus a pint in one of the smallest pubs I've ever been in – 'It is amazing Bob, I could not get even two of my drinking friends to fit in here!' – followed by lunch at one of the oldest and continuous drinking establishments in the county… so I'm told, nearly six hundred years old! That *is* old. Mind you – it's about time they changed the wallpaper.

As Peter and I sat right outside the hall in Bury, we just stared at the building wondering about the ghostly account we had uncovered – if only it could speak…!

'There it is Peter, in all its glory… your bog-standard town hall with, for you and my team, an unexplained mystery.' We walked round it; Peter took a couple pictures for his team 'back home'.

He departed the next day after a brief trip to see Matt and Ruby's famous 'wall'… not quite as famous as the one in Berlin.

'It is just as we pictured it,' he said, '…and how we tracked you down I see that they still have not sold that house over there!'

Hadn't noticed that.

…

On the way back I thought more about Bury – totally different to my thoughts from that night months ago having now seen it in daylight. Yes, I liked it… small compact, interesting.

It now had a 'pull' on me.

Bury St Edmunds.

Did it have a mega stadium? No.

A premier soccer team? No.

Shopping mall? Two! Well, one and a half actually I'm told.

Theatre? Yes

Cinema? As well.

Train station? Naturally.

Brewery? YES! Double points.

Usual clone shops? Obligatory.

Museum? Yes.

Speedway? Not in town… somewhere else.

Mega theme park? No.

Skyscrapers? In your dreams.

Cemetery? Yes… people will keep dying.

Small places? Yes – the pub.

Old places? Yes – mega! Cathedral, abbey… loads. Pub (the other one).

Factory? Sugar – mega, with knobs on.

…and somewhere, my phantom lady, Grace… somewhere.

I must find her.

So, all in all, I liked Bury, not too big, not too small – think Peter liked it too, especially the beer. I'll speak to the gang and we'll arrange a day-time visit.

Yes, a special place to me.

Peter Kurtz returned to Germany with a few more pieces of the jigsaw puzzle in place. He too realised the difficulty of trying to find a rational explanation for what had happened – except to accept the fact that one of the Americans at 'the dance' had probably picked up the phone during the chaotic last few minutes when the air-raid siren sounded, and then had kept it with him on a mission over Germany.

'You can just imagine what he must have thought when he saw such an attractive item,' he had said. 'We do not know, unfortunately, which American took it – I hope he survived the mission. In fact, we found out a few of the crew were saved as we said previously.'

When he had mentioned this it gave me an idea which I parked onto my imaginary 'to do' list – yes, who were the survivors of 'Tail-heavy Betty'? And where might they be *now*?

No doubt dead I would have thought... or close to it.

Shortly after Peter had returned from his visit he phoned me to say 'Thanks' – and also to tell me the sad news he'd not mentioned on his visit, that Frau Vetter had passed away previously, shortly after having seen the pictures and apparently, clutching her picture of Ralph.

'I reckon your lab technician was right Peter – that she 'went' happy.'

Which made me think of Grace... again.

Chapter 47

An old letter – UK Today

'Please tell me more,' I said.

'...he's my father, his name is Raymond Temple. I'm Paul Temple,' he said to me as I listened intently on the phone. 'We've had to put him in a home as he couldn't cope on his own anymore. We'd been intending to clear out his house for ages. We actually did some of it just a few years ago when he came to live with us but he needs more care these days than we can give him, so we moved him to a proper place. When he was still capable – while he had his marbles – we went through all his bits and pieces together; this included old letters from dear old mum, God rest her soul, and this letter that I have in front of me now. It *is* addressed to a Mr R Temple but it has no house number or street on it, just our village. My dad says he received two or three of these letters over a period of time years ago from the same person, a lady, but not meant for him as you can see from the contents – they were for a *Robert* Temple, not Raymond, somebody looking for someone in the past I imagine... you know how it was during the war.

'As they weren't for him he took the first one back to the post office then chucked the second one away, but after the third one arrived he became intrigued, so held on to it. He told me some time ago that if he found time he would attempt to follow it up as it is like a 'lost person's' kind of letter, someone who wasn't giving up, important, so he hung on to it. But his mind began to deteriorate – and now I have it. Mother said it must be from some poor lady, perhaps from many years ago, searching for a lost relative. There were many such situations after the war if you think about it. The date on it is 1955 or 6, can't see clearly. Anyway, I've looked at the 'R Temples' in this area, and here we are. Is it you – how long have you lived here?'

'Fifteen years or thereabouts,and yes indeed, I'm a Robert...Robert Temple.' You don't have to be hot to break into a sweat, but I was suddenly sweating.

'Fifteen? Oh – so it's unlikely to be you then. Hmm, sorry. I'll keep on looking if I have time.'

'Hang on, hang on… just tell me how it's signed at the bottom and the address on it if you would please.'

'But it might not be meant for you… it would be wrong. It looks very personal.'

'Alright then, is it signed by someone called *Grace*? And has it come from Bury St Edmunds?' There was a pause and I could hear the rustle of paper. My heart was in my mouth.

'Yes, it is. How did you know that?'

So, I went through hot and cold in quick cycles. Beads of perspiration were already on my brow. Then an involuntary sob escaped me.

'I think it was meant for me – if I told you a story about this you would not believe me. Where are you? I'll be straight round if you don't mind… I would love to see the letter. Is that OK? I'll be fifteen minutes.' As I drove, there were tears in my eyes – I don't remember the journey at all… getting soft in my old age.

We were sat in his kitchen with a cup of coffee.

I looked over the envelope he'd given me and then gently pulled the single sheet from within, casting my glance to the address. The franking on the outside was illegible but the date shown at the top was indeed 1955 or 1956, I couldn't quite make it out – a 'five' or a 'six'… and from '2 Brewery Cottages, Rattlesdon Road, Bury'. And there at the bottom was her name, *Grace*.

'Do you know who it's from…?' he ventured, now realising how cut-up I was. I found it difficult to control my emotions and I daren't read the letter – not yet. I wanted to do it in the privacy of my own place.

I nodded, 'Yes. May I please have this letter Paul?' I asked.

'Sure you can, and I'd like to know of the story if you are able to tell me if you don't mind. My dad often wondered who she might be; now I'm also intrigued.'

'I will do, and many thanks.'

The return journey was the same – a complete blank – with my heart almost bursting with all sorts of expectations. What had she written? *Why* had she written?

The car managed to find its way back to my house and park itself because I don't remember doing it. In a jiffy, I had poured myself a stiff drink and then plonked down into my favourite swivel recliner. I pulled out the letter, paused, took a deep breath and began to read the flimsy paper, the ink somewhat faded.

Dear Robert,

I apologise for not having your correct address but I hope this letter finds you safe and well – and please do not think me forward for writing to you, but I cannot forget those tender moments we shared together, oh so briefly that night... and how we parted.

I was able to speak to Mr Rawlings and the policeman about your address but neither could help me, only telling me roughly where you were all from. Besides, they were very busy I think.

Not long after that evening, we had very sad news that my husband Jim had been killed fighting in Italy – we were distraught – but it was particularly hard on our girls.

As time passed, my thoughts would constantly return to you and our dances together – I had felt that there was a mutual attraction and I have to admit to being in heaven when I danced close to you. I feel embarrassed thinking of this now but you were so... amusing and just different Robert. I cannot explain how we parted only to say I was completely shattered.

Today my life is empty... all I wish for is to be in your company – to see you again, to talk to you and hear your voice, to gently touch you. I'm terrible, aren't I, saying these things?! But I hope that should you receive this letter you will reply and give me your news – that you are safe and that one day soon you will return to Bury. There is much news I would like to tell you so I pray my poor scribble manages to find you.

Missing you – always in my thoughts

Grace xx

I flopped back. I didn't realise but I was perspiring and I found it difficult to hold back tears that had begun to form right from reading the first line.

So Grace had tried to get hold of me/ The sadness and hopelessness of it all brought on more tears – a lost love, for I too had found myself in

274

Cloud Nine when we had danced, both before and after we (my troupe) had discovered our impossible situation. And so cruel on Grace, not knowing any of this and not knowing of our own predicament.

My team was astounded when I told them and showed them the letter. Ruby had tears in her eyes as she read it. A letter from just a few months ago… or sixty-eight years!

'How dreadful – how sad Bob,' Becky said. 'It makes me want to cry, especially as I took that last picture in the car before she…' She had struggled. 'Sorry. It's brought a lump to my throat… before she vanished.'

'I only spoke to her once – she was a nice girl. I reckon I was the first to see that she carried a torch for you Bob,' Ruby added.

'Yes – it's difficult to realise that she was 'a girl' as you call it – and also a mother with two daughters! I suppose she must have been in her thirties… late thirties… forties? To me that age is quite young but her style – the style of dress then made her appear older. But to me she looked great.'

'…as we noticed. So, what are you going to do Bob. I don't suppose there's a great deal you *can* do is there?' said Matt.

'Probably look at the historical records, see what happened to her and her daughters. But I'm not sure I want to know.'

'I feel the same,' said Becky.

I noticed the others nodding along but I had a feeling that my curiosity would get the better of me and that I would be looking eastwards sometime soon. Another idea – another follow-up, another task. Something that I valued being left behind, unsecured.

Chapter 48

Where did you get to?

'I'm thinking of going to see an old pal of mine – Micky – in the States,' I said to Keith. 'He's retired so it doesn't matter when I go. I'll only be gone two weeks or so, haven't decided yet but it'll probably be when we have a gap in the bookings. And then when I return, I'll make that trip back to Bury.'

'Right. You really want to go back there to Bury. It's got to you Bob, hasn't it? We know we can't explain what happened back then, so what's up?'

'I don't know to be honest... it just bugs me, but I did some background work and found that one of Grace's daughters remains in the area – in a home there.'

'It's going to be kind of weird is it not; you – three times her age just a few months ago, and now she's older than you...! She won't remember you. If she does I'll show my ass in Burton's window, or whatever they're called these days. Anyway, pass on my hellos to Mick when you see him.'

'Will do Keith.' Mick was an old friend who both Keith and I knew some time ago before he had become fed-up and emigrated.

'Place is going to the dogs,' he would say.

'And,' I said continuing,'...if I get the opportunity I'm going to follow up a few leads that Peter Kurtz gave me on the B-17 survivors.'

But while I had been looking up on history with Grace's family tree, Peter Kurtz from Germany sent an e-mail about *Tail-Heavy Betty* and the survivors. In the e-mail Peter had provided a couple of links with US veteran's associations, so I suddenly became very busy again tracking down the names Peter had furnished. We already knew of course that the two pilots didn't survive nor did Richard Simms and Ginger-nut, but what of the others?

Walter was closest to where I was going in the States. He was in a vet's studio compound, where they lived in self-contained units.

I had arranged with the Vet's Association for a visit early one afternoon: I was quite surprised that these guys were actually quite busy – they were not allowed to vegetate in a chair plonked in front of a TV watching *I Love Lucy* reruns all day. They could if they wanted to, but generally they were kept occupied with all sorts of organised visits and entertainment. I told 'those on the desk' from where and when I'd known Walter – everything tallied, but that I wanted it to be a surprise... please don't tell him who I am, that it had been many years and that I'd wanted to surprise him.

So far so good.

A staff helper took me into a pleasant, airy room, a fan churning the air.

'A visitor for you Walter...'

He was sitting in a large, comfortable armchair. As I walked in with a nervous smile on my face, he looked up then studied me intently. Ten, twenty seconds passed before...

'Goddammit! Goddammit! I knew it! I was right all along. You slimy limey!' he exclaimed with a huge grin on his face slowly struggling to his feet. Then in a whisper with almost a choke in his voice, 'Holy Moses... I don't believe it.'

He paused again then added in almost a whisper, 'I knew it – I was right all along... I wondered when you'd show up...! I knew you'd come one day.' His eyes were now rheumy, his hand shook as he offered it to me but his voice was clear.

I was totally overcome for two reasons. One, that he recognised me and secondly, how the hell did he know? I struggled to find the right words.

'Walter, it's a pleasure to meet you again – *after such a short time*! Please don't try to get up.' He continued to stare at me – almost as if I was some kind of deity. 'Look. Like you Walter, I don't understand what happened back then either, yet here we are.'

He was having nothing to do with staying put and already standing, he turned towards a cabinet. 'This calls for a stiff drink... a real stiff drink. What's your poison? Just remind me your name?' His memory was good but not *that* good.

'Bob Temple. Just call me Bob.'

'That's it! I remember now. Darn it, it ain't what it used to be... my memory. And looky you! You're the same. To this day, I still remember almost word-for-word what you said – all that crap and my arguments with, umm, with, with... Barney and Joe. Sorry, I forget names. You sold it to them... yes sir, you sure did. It took a goddamm lot of talking-to for me to convince them but I pulled them round. And then you were gone! Yep, I knew it,' he said, shaking his head and smiling. 'All that horseshit! They did not want to buy it. I knew... I knew...' he repeated, looking at my slightly. 'Couldn't fool me... well, just for a while. You don't forget things like *that* in a hurry!'

'Walter, how the hell do you think *we* felt with all those furtive looks and whispers especially from you Yanks? When we all realised our predicament the two girls were quite worried... worried that we'd all be rounded up and shot as spies... "It's okay officer, we're time travellers just having a good night out".'

Walt chuckled, shaking his head again.

'We couldn't tell anybody... who would believe us?'

We sipped our drinks and pondered awhile in silence. He could not stop shaking his head from side to side.

'Talking of Barney, what happened to him – and Joe? I remember them like it was yesterday.'

'Okay, Joe Tutucci – I liked Joey; after he got back he took up a Flight Engineers post with a small airline in the emerging aviation scene after the war. For those who had flown in the war, you either wanted to carry on flying, or made it the last thing you did! He finished up still doing it when the first jumbos came along. He actually got to pilot himself, you know, little Cessna to go into the mountains fishing or over to Florida. And yes, he still played... actually took up with some jazz musicians – off and on.'

Good ol' Joe.

'He's not quite the Joe he was, slowed down a little. Based over near St Louis, still is, but the last I heard was that he'd broke a hip followed by a slow recuperation. Otherwise happy... and on his fourth wife too! A real sucker for punishment!' he cackled. 'No... he was happy. We send cards... in fact you've reminded me.'

'And Barney – the guy who wouldn't pipe down, always laughing...the guitar man? What about him?'

'Now then... he left right after the war and wanted to get into the entertainment industry. Didn't start well – tried all sorts of things. He was real impatient I remember and we actually met up one weekend for a session shortly after, like we used to, and wanted to form a band.'

'Really?' I said arching my eyebrows. Mind you, I could imagine that.

'We couldn't do it Bob – it's okay when you are all thrown together like we were with Uncle Sam so we parted with just a promise to keep in touch, and we've done that more or less – or we did.

Uh, oh... sad tale coming up.

'Short story. He managed to get in with some musicians, did some playing in Nashville and if I remember correctly, was going to hook up with er... think it was Lonnie Donegan...? Not sure if it was him... but he was always *with* somebody or with *some* band, always on the move. As long as he could play. But he did manage to get a licence – yeah, for flying so that he could do shows around the states. I'm sure he was mad. But like me, his hearing went. Actually, mine's not too bad but his really went south, so he more or less had to give up on the music – not completely but no longer as the 'day job'. As his eyes were okay he managed to get a job fire-spotting – flying a light plane over some of the local national parks.

'One day he didn't come back like he should. They found his wreck in a wood – ironic – he nearly set a whole forest alight! But he was thrown clear. Doc says he'd actually died of a heart attack at the controls – probably.'

'When was this?

'Eighty something...? Ninety something?' Walt replied with a little sadness in his voice. 'Not sure exactly. And he was on his fifth wife!'

'Bloody hell,' I said. 'Some get all the luck... or all the pain!'

'He was always one with the dames that's for sure. Lost track with rest apart from some brief news from the vets about Milt – that he had shacked up with some dancing girl down in some plantation in South America – Joey reckoned it was Brazil because he really had a love for Latin American music. Not a molecule of Latin blood in him either – said he traced his line back to Norway or something. Nothing since.'

'Yeah – the Vikings were renowned for their Latin music,' I said trying to lighten the mood. 'And you – what about you Walt?'

'I was a waist gunner on a B-17. What good was I to anybody? There was no call on the DC6s or 707s for waist gunners – or tail gunners come to that. I mean at least the Russians had bomb-aiming positions on their first passenger planes! Imagine that? So I hung on for a year with the Air Force while I trained up.'

'What as…?' I liked the string of humour that ran in his conversation… and yes, the Russians did still maintain a place for a bombardier on their passenger jets. Paranoid lot.

'Well, I knew about guns – became a training guy with the local police force. Then I married Cindy. She could talk Spanish and French, so I soon picked up the lingo and there I was – able to speak three languages and playing with guns, not quite the 'nought point fives' but good enough. I got promotion and finished up running my own weapons training establishment. I was tempted at one point in applying for an Air Marshall post but it meant too much travelling. I was done with all that.'

'Good for you Walt.' The boy had 'done good' as they say.

'And I was a single-gal guy too – stuck with Cindy. No kids Bob… can't complain. She passed away three years ago.'

I don't know about you reader, but I always well up when I'm told these things. What *can* you say?

'Sorry to hear Walt – know exactly how you feel, same with me, now single – my 'gal' also passed away nearly ten years ago now Walt. And no kids either.'

He nodded slowly, pursing his lips.

I related my story: ex-forces, travelled around doing engineering jobs – everything was going tickety-boo for many years until I lost my wife. I was at a loose end for a while so I took up teaching for a year or two but it became boring so I took up dancing… and music, which I've always loved. 'Just like Barney,' I added. 'And there we are at Bury with you guys!'

'Yeah, let's drink to that. How can you explain that one away!? I just wish I could move around like I used to – like on that night. Don't get me wrong, this is my place and I can come and go as I please. The staff are good – I'm just glad I have my marbles! I seen places where they look after those poor old farts who don't know what day it is but could probably remember that they won ten dollars at their local bingo hall back in 1952!'

'And I'm supposed to be in a rocking chair on the porch – remember that…? Who said it – can you remember?'

'For Christ's sake – yes! I remember it being said, but I thought he was cheeky… could have been Lou who said it. Me…? Not guilty

M'lord,' he said in a posh English accent, laughing. 'Now you see, I can remember that night but I can't remember last year Bob!'

One day somebody'll invent a system where you can plug into some USB port just behind your ear or some place and retrieve all you past information. All of it… "Bloody hell – don't remember doing that" or "Nah… didn't take her out – did I? Must have been pissed".'

One day.

'Did you ever tell anybody about us – about that night and your suspicions?'

'Do you know, we did talk about it. At least I did with Barney and Joey but what could we say to the others. They'd think we weren't right in the head or something; did you ever see the movie *Stalag 17* and the poor lad who was injured – got soft in the head. Remember that? I thought about that when I first saw it. We didn't want to give anybody any ammunition to have us put in some Kraut mad-house. But we didn't forget that's for sure and we would speak to each other out of ear-shot.'

'Well Walt, let's refresh your memory,' I said as I reached into my pocket and pulled out my phone. I moved round to Walter. 'Get yourself comfortable and realise that the last time you saw this phone – yes, this one – was back in 1944.'

It suddenly dawned on him what I was saying. 'This one… what, from that night?' he asked looking at me.

'The one and the same.'

I shan't bore you with too many of the details of the next hour. It was flash-back time.

I told him the story of Matt and Ruby's phone; tears came to his eyes as we scrolled through. We drank some more and when he saw *Tail-heavy Betty* both in colour and black and white, spread out over a German field, he wept. I did too – don't know why.

'Skipper's in there somewhere Bob.' So I told him that in fact their bodies had already been removed. He just sat there staring at the phone.

'I'll make sure you get a download Walter.' His only response was a slow nod. I couldn't imagine what was going through his head right then, however he perked up and was thrilled to see some of the snaps taken that night with some good shots of the boys – him included.

'Why were you taking photos?' he asked. I told him we always did as part of our routine adding that on that particular night, what had gone on with the handbags. He was fascinated.

'Sure hope you nailed the bitch.'

'We did – all thanks to this,' I said waiving my phone about.

We eventually descended into talking science fiction. He, like me, had an interest in the subject and how it might be linked with the paranormal.

'I had absolutely no thoughts on it at all until that night and could never shake it from my mind... 'cos you guys just vanished – went away. We couldn't prove nothin'. Barney had asked, when we all trooped back in the hall – "What happened to the music? Where are they... where have they gone Mr Rawlings?" He was as perplexed as we were. That's when I told Barney I was right all along, "See, told you Barney – I knew they were up to no good or something". Nobody would believe us today would they Bob,' he said rhetorically. Not like the moon landings. There are guys out there still think it was faked.'

'Well it was... wasn't it?' I responded, laughing.

'Don't you start! Pour another drink you damn limey!'

Eventually I had to leave – get a taxi to my motel. Both of us were slurring and I was just a little unsteady on my pins. Before I finally left Walter managed a, 'Damn good fun Bob – pleased as punch to see you old chap,' mimicking a posh English accent once more.

'Remember Walt – *you're* the old chap this time, not me!' was my parting shot. A cackle followed me down the hall as I left.

Walter... with his marbles still intact... and I never did get to talk to him about The Teddy Bears and Sandy Nelson.

As far as the others he hadn't heard from were concerned, Walter had tried but thought they'd all 'bought the farm' – 'popped their clogs' as they say. When I arrived back home I told my gang all about it, gave them the debrief and showed them Walter in as he is today.

'So Barney is no more,' said Matt solemnly. 'He was so keen on his music – almost fanatical. Wonder if managed to sort out a guitar?'

'Actually, I will ask Walt when I send him a Christmas card; he probably did judging by what Walt told me because he spent a lot of time on the music scene.'

All sobering.

Chapter 49

Ivy's care home

After spending a great deal of time searching the usual sources I eventually decided to pay yet another visit to East Anglia.

I had a few leads, the '61 Census amongst them – plus cemetery information and a list of care homes in and around Bury.

Apparently, Grace had moved in with Susan and her family. She hadn't remarried and was not in the '71 census. Cecily, the elder of the two daughters, had married someone in the RAF – East Anglia was littered with RAF bases at the time – and moved away from the area.

Grace had passed away in 1966 and was buried in the main cemetery. There was a little part of me that thought I should have stayed that night – I could have had twenty-two years with her.

Stop it Bob.

And if records were right, Susan was still around but now on her own – I'd found that by marriage, her surname was now *Kelly*. I managed to track her down to 'Ivy's' Care Home' for the elderly in Bury. She hadn't moved far in all those years. Well if she had, she'd come back.

I had great difficulty in getting to see Susan as the staff were unsure of my motives – I could not convince them that I knew her from the past. It was only when I mentioned that I also knew her Sister Cecily, and her mother, Grace, that they allowed me to see her.

'They are in self-contained apartments within the home Mr... what was your name again?' asked a nurse or helper – I wasn't sure what her role was.

'Temple.'

'My apologies... Mrs Kelly – Susan – has hardly any visitors these days, only an old friend of hers who occasionally comes to see her and a relative. It's the relative who comes more frequently... and I have to tell you that her sight is not so good – one of the reasons she is here. Plus other things; nor is she that mobile, otherwise she's alright. Can I ask, when I pop down and tell her she has a visitor, how she might remember you Mr Temple…?'

'Believe it or not, I'm a dancer – or used to be. Tell her I play music and that I played for her and her sister Cecily… oh, some time ago now.'

All true.

She returned in five minutes, signalling that I follow telling me that although mostly confined to a chair, her mind was still as sharp as a pin. My heart was in my mouth. I hadn't paid too much attention to Grace's daughters except remembering them as being both pretty and giggly. I wasn't sure what to expect.

As I walked in my eyes immediately focused on the little old lady sat in one corner and because I'd seen her as a young girl *recently*, I immediately detected a trace of the physical attributes that we saw in the *younger* woman and now carried forward after all these years – for her: for me it was only a few months! She looked up. Her hair was almost a snowy white but her skin in excellent condition. She perhaps had a slight stoop but I couldn't easily tell with her sat down.

I went straight to her, knelt down and said, 'Hello Susan – what will it be – Andrews Sisters, Lionel Hampton or Maurice Winnik…?' I said putting on my best smile.

It was a long shot.

She showed no sign of recognition and remained silent as she cocked her head to one side as if to invite me to say something else. I continued.

'I played music for you a long time ago – a long, long time ago, for you and Cecily, and your mother, here in Bury one evening.'

She continued to look at me for a while then said slowly, 'I don't remember you young man; you say you played music? It must have been a long time ago.'

I leaned up close to her and, as the staff member was present, whispered, '1944, when your mother – Grace – took you and Cecily to a dance here in Bury. Remember – The Andrews Sisters, those Americans? Or Lionel Hampton or Maurice Winnik – you requested them?'

I'd been told that her mind remained sharp and as I gazed at her it was obvious that she was processing my words and perhaps trying to retrieve her thoughts from long ago.

Then I took a punt and said, 'Odd Couple?' and waited. The 'Odd Couple' episode was still fresh in my mind. Then I suddenly realised that I might be able to *really* jog her memory. I took out my phone and fiddled a bit until I'd located some photos from that night, one of which had both her and Cecily in it, and which included some other people dancing in the background. I handed it to her but with not too much optimism – and let her digest the dancing scenes. In the meantime, I took off my coat and waited, watching Susan studying my phone intently.

I was about to continue when she made a movement, turning her head back towards me while raising her hand, almost pointing at me. But she remained silent. But something was churning in her mind I could tell; however I was beginning to wonder if it was beyond her faculties and looked across at the member of staff who had remained in attendance, shrugging my shoulders, almost as a question such as, 'Am I wasting my time?'

But Susan then coughed, a small imperceptible cough, raising her arm even further, inviting me closer, before she uttered the word 'tits' in a whisper.

That stunned me. Yes – I can easily remember our brief conversation that night, but for me it was not long ago; for Susan, it was a lifetime – yet she remembered! They say that about old folk can't remember yesterday but *can* remember their first ever job interview fifty years ago. The beginnings of a smile appeared on her face and on mine too. The staff member looked bewildered, glancing at me with a quizzical look, a question on her lips.

'Brilliant! She remembers me,' I answered and was about to blurt out loud 'tits and boobs' before I realised where we were.

Then she followed up saying, 'Odd Couple... you are Mr Odd Couple.' Another link *had* triggered her memory.'

'*The Odd Couple*?' mouthed the staff attendant looking at me with a question in her eyes. 'The name rings a bell.'

'A film – and a TV programme, before your time,' I answered.

Susan spoke again.

'Yes...' she said slowly. She continued in a clear voice, 'I always remembered those two girls. They made me laugh and then I had a troubling thought at the time – why did they sound so familiar to me, it was if I knew them all along and that someone had told me about them. But I could not think who... it was you wasn't it? How would that be possible?'

I nodded, 'At your service.'

Another pause.

She went on… again slowly but clearly, 'Amy, this is someone who I met a long time ago,' she said looking at the nurse, then back to me. But a silence came over her once more before she eventually spoke. '*Are you that man…?*' How could I respond? Susan was obviously struggling with this, 'But… I recognise your voice,' she added.

They say that if you lose one faculty, another often becomes sharper. Her voice became stronger and more clear the more she spoke.

'Yes Susan – and doesn't time fly eh?' I continued, trying not to dwell too much on the obvious passage of time. Besides nobody would believe any silly or strange ramblings from an old lady.

'Are you married, do you have any children?' asked Susan, now speaking with more confidence.

I shook my head, 'Widower – and no, no kids. I'm all on my own in this big wide, wicked world,' I added with a hint of a smile.

'Oh… I'm sorry,' she trailed off softly.

The nurse joined the conversation as I had mentioned on the way in about Susan's mother. 'Her mother was also here a long time ago I believe. Let me check with my boss.' A few words on her phone and two minutes later an elderly lady stepped into the room. I reckon she was older than me. That's old. We made our introductions.

'I knew Susan's mother – she was here too?' I asked the principal.

'My my – that was a few years ago! Yes, she was. It's when I joined here as a young assistant – my mother ran this home then. Now I run it, with my daughters. You weren't here then Amy. Grace? I remember her as being quite a dignified lady with a soft voice and a melancholy air.'

That hurt me, struck me directly in the heart. It was also when I found out that Grace had been buried in a cemetery within Bury. I made an excuse that I was 'over this way' on some errand and therefore could make a visit to the cemetery as I was already here.

'Near West Road, I believe, if you want a name,' said the boss. 'We know it well don't we Amy,' she indicated as a statement. 'But these days, not so much back then, many are cremated…the crematorium is a little further out.'

Either way, probably common destinations – eventually – for those who were at Ivy's Care home. I also found that Susan had children and grandchildren, nearly all scattered to the wind – Canada, Spain and the US. Only a few of the clan remained in Britain.

'And Cecily?' I enquired.

Susan slowly shook her head. 'She went to Canada. She died many years ago from cancer.'

I don't know but I just felt so saddened, and I knew that shortly it was going to get worse.

Susan and I continued to talk with Amy now leaving as alone, but the conversation became difficult, stilted. I had the distinct impression that her mind was telling her impossible things which appeared to be interrupting her flow and slowing down our talk. Otherwise she was well.

'I will stay in touch,' I said as we made our goodbyes. I took a last look at Susan, took a couple of snaps and then I popped down to the office to say, 'thank you'. I gave them my contact details and then left for the real difficult part of my visit – the cemetery.

Chapter 50

The stone

You can tell the passage of time and plot locations just by looking at how the headstones weathered. Bright shiny marble slabs told me they were this year or last year, or recent, so I moved along looking at the dates in descending order, praying that her stone had not faded into unreadable script... or that it was even there.

I'm at the eighties now. One stone made me gulp... a two-year-old, a life taken so young; had she lived she would be in her prime right now probably with kids and enjoying holidays with them. I just stared at it with tears in my eyes – a complete stranger to me but I was upset.

Can't help it.

I was getting nervous now. I could just quit – go home because I knew she was here... so what more do I need to know?

She's gone Bob.

I'm looking... looking... and here we are in the seventies... back track to the sixties, next row back.

It was the second from the end. Of medium size, a simple stone with no adornments and in remarkably good condition. I don't know why but I could only gaze in the general direction, unfocussed, looking for her name without wanting to read anything else – I wasn't really interested in the dates. Of those I was already aware; Grace had passed away in December 1966. Eventually I took the plunge.

GRACE FLORENCE ATKINSON

Sadly missed by her family and all who knew her

A place of peace, my searching over...

Searching...? Searching for...? They must have been her words surely. My mind raced for many seconds conjuring up a myriad of possibilities...and then I recalled that faded letter...a letter written decades ago, sent in a forlorn hope of finding happiness...of wanting to belong to someone. Was it for me – or for someone else – or God?

What despair! I had to crouch down and cover my face in my hands...I just cried for a while. What a cruel fate – like ships that passed in the night only these ships briefly encountered each other...to go on their separate ways afterwards...both longing to meet up again...somehow, somewhere...

Perhaps she has...now looking down on me – and waiting.

I hope she's waiting.

I took a picture or two and returned to my car. I must have sat there for twenty minutes picturing in my mind a funeral many years ago, with Susan and Cecily weeping besides the graveside, when my phone 'peeped'.

'Who wants to talk to me?' I asked myself.

No, sorry reader, but it won't be *that* which you may be thinking...don't be silly now.

'Hello?' I said not recognising the number, but it was Ivy's Care Home.

'Did you leave a pair of glasses behind Mr Temple when you were here earlier?' asked the voice. 'Amy found them under the chair in her room.'

I fumbled in my jersey. No glasses. 'Dark blue case...?' I asked hopefully.

'Yes, we have them here...they'll be at reception if you would like to call in – I hope you are not too far away.'

'Sokay – I'm still in Bury. I'll call in...and thank you,' I sniffled. Before I switched off the voice hurriedly added...

'Please come around to the rear Mr. Temple – you must have started something...it's quite rare for Mrs Kelly, Susan, to have more than one visitor in a single day; well one of her children, sorry, grandchildren, has just turned up out of the blue; parked where you were. She is popular today!'

'I promise I won't get in the way,' I offered. Must clean myself up – my eyes were red and I looked as if I had a cold, sniffing away as I was still thinking about Grace and her gravestone.

I hadn't enquired too much into the family tree, only as far as Grace's daughters were concerned and if they were still alive, where they might be... only to be told that Cecily had passed away. Now I hadn't even thought about grandchildren and beyond, but of course, life goes on as they say. Some mental arithmetic told me that her daughter would have been in or around her sixties as Susan was in her eighties, perhaps approaching ninety... I couldn't recall. Therefore, any grandchildren would be, what... maybe in their forties?

I took my time returning to the home but as I began to draw closer, I speeded up a little; I realised that I needed to see the descendants, no matter how far removed they were from Grace. I could be discreet – I could view from my car or just go right in there to pretend to say 'good-bye' once more to Susan. But there again, I didn't know what car they were driving.

I drove in as instructed, noticing the car that was in my previous slot – a red Jazz. They all seem to be red, don't they? I walked back round to the front of the building only to almost barge into a young woman who was just leaving through the door.

'My apologies, so sorry,' I said, ever the gentleman, even though she had a phone clamped between her head and shoulders, yacking away, oblivious.

'My fault, my fault – sorry,' she answered hurriedly. But my attention was then distracted by the Jazz and somebody else who had just come out and had opened the rear, another woman, struggling to lift a few items out but succeeding only in dropping a cushion onto the ground.

I had seen the cushion beginning to fall in slow motion and had immediately tried, unsuccessfully, to catch it before it hit the ground. The result was me stooping down and then looking at the woman who briefly glanced sideways at me as she too crouched down at the same time, seeming to struggle to pick it up. She wore tinted glasses and the light breeze flicked her hair across her eyes.

'I'm sorry, what a failure I am! I was never any good at cricket – couldn't catch a thing, but please let me help,' I said with a smile as we both slowly stood up behind the car. She then quickly stepped away, realising our closeness.

'Oh, thank you,' she answered almost in a whisper, so I helped with a couple of her bags into the hall. 'Thank you,' she repeated.

But before she moved off down a corridor I added, 'Please let me guess, you must be Susan's granddaughter?' Her mouth popped open. 'It's okay, I was here earlier visiting her. I came back to collect my glasses.'

She looked relieved, 'Oh... Amy told me that someone had already visited. Yes, I am her granddaughter,' and before she could say anything else I ventured further.

'Tell you what – and if you don't mind – may I come along after I've picked up my glasses just to say a proper farewell to Susan? I'll bring the other bags along. I won't intrude, promise... just to say goodbye. I won't get in your way.'

A pause. She seemed uncertain, and then flashed a smile.

'Yes, of course. Please do. Thank you. Oh crumbs, I'm forever saying 'thank you' to you.'

Chapter 51

Granddaughter

'Crumbs'? Unusual term these days.

I liked that. But my heart had skipped just a little beat, because she looked quite familiar.

Because of the change of light from outside and then into the hall, I had been unable to get a really good look at her, or a profile view, but what I had seen so far, her pale thoughtful face, made me ask, – had I looked into those eyes before? This woman, as yet unnamed to me, reminded me of someone I used to know or had seen recently. She was moving away now when I remembered… glasses, don't forget my glasses! So I picked them up then almost trotted along the corridor towards Susan's room.

Steady on Bob.

The door was open. Susan was in the chair where I had left her much earlier. However, when I looked at the other lady, the jazz lady, she was bent down facing away from me, attending to Susan's shoes.

'Nice view,' I said, grinning. She bolted upright at my voice, turning around to me, a crimson flush across her face. 'Sorry, I just could not resist,' I added cheekily.

She looked up too to meet my gaze, not wearing her glasses now, a little smile beginning on her face. But my smile vanished. I was stunned – her poise, her shape, her eyes, the tilt of her head, the colour of her hair and the kindly expression on her face that had captured my heart during a dance just a few months ago, I could now observe more clearly; it held me in check, because here in front of me with modern clothes, modern hair style with just a few curls not quite reaching down to her shoulders, was the essence of her great-grandmother, Grace. And a similar age if I was not mistaken.

This wasn't a chance meeting; this was almost like a reunion.

Well reader, that's how she appeared to me. It was my turn to go red, really red. I suppose she should perhaps share some resemblance, after all, she *is* a descendant therefore a genetic link might be obvious, but to me this was rather more than just a genetic link – there was something else at work. It was uncanny – I couldn't take my eyes off her until…

'Mr… Mr Odd Couple is here again,' Susan said. This produced a quizzical look from jazz lady.

I strode over and introduced myself to the new lady. 'Bob Temple,' I said, taking her hand, briefly putting my other hand on top – almost at the same time as the two ladies chimed in with:

'Olivia – pleased to meet you,' as she pulled her hand away.

Susan said, 'This is Olivia, my granddaughter.' She then turned to look directly at Olivia and said quite without warning, 'He's not married you know, Olivia. He's single. He told me.'

Wow!

I heard the gasp, 'Oh Nan!' cried Olivia, who looked at me not without some embarrassment, changing colour. 'You mustn't say things like that. Oh, I don't know what to say… I'm so sorry Mr Temple.'

That *was* a surprise from Susan. I was *not* expecting that at all!

I laughed out loud and held up my hand. 'It's completely okay. Please don't be embarrassed on my account. Susan… you are a naughty girl,' I said turning to her.

My, this old lady was direct…! But they don't have anything to be fearful of, do they? Old people, that is. My mum would occasionally say outrageous things, even nasty outbursts in public. She didn't care.

But in truth, reader, I didn't care either – just looking at Olivia I was headed towards Cloud Nine. I could not take my eyes off Susan's granddaughter. There was something about her – that essence of Grace.

Then, 'What's your game Susan – you trying to fix us up?' I added, wagging a finger at her, grinning again. 'She's trying to marry us off,' I said to Olivia laughingly.

We then settled into general and polite conversation – 'call me Bob' and all that. Olivia's voice held me captivated. When she spoke, she did so in a soft tone all the time, dropping a note as she finished her sentences – wonderfully relaxing just listening to her, almost dream-like. Her whole demeanour was soft and unhurried. I would never have any trouble at all falling asleep if she told me a bed-time story and she could have explained

Einstein's Theory of Relativity to me and I would have been held in rapture. She was also in the habit of turning her head away slightly to one side while talking to you, and while still looking at you. Peculiar, but captivating.

Then out of the blue, shaking me out from a trance into which I had lapsed, that soft voice.

'Have we met before Mr Temple – I'm sure I know you from somewhere?' she asked.

'The police station? Crimewatch? McDonalds? Another time – another place?' I offered trying to lighten the atmosphere.

But oh yay! I was thinking exactly the same about her reader. I had seen those eyes before, surely.

'Strangely enough, I was thinking the same about you, but I know your grandmother,' I answered lamely after gathering my wits.

Perhaps there is a God up there after all.

Susan was watching me intently.

And Olivia continued to look at me, then she went on.

'How did you get to know my nan?' It was a question I had anticipated, and it had duly come.

'Through music and my job,' I explained. 'We were at 'an occasion' across this way and that's when I met your nan.'

'When was this, at a festival? It must have been some time ago,' said Olivia looking at her grandmother.

'Yes, quite a long time ago.' This was stretching it a bit – no time scales mentioned, no deliberate lies. Not yet. I quickly changed tack. 'Where's *your* mum Olivia?'

'She lives in Spain – she lives over there now with her family,' Olivia replied.

'Doreen upset me when she moved there,' muttered Susan to no one in particular.

'Doreen?' It was her daughter's name, and Olivia's mother.

'Actually, she lives in Majorca,' Olivia added.

The water in… Shut up Bob, not the right time.

'Really? Good for your holidays then,' I ventured. I was almost afraid to ask the next question. 'And what about your family,' I asked quietly, holding my breath and trying to give the impression of polite, casual interest. 'Where are they?'

I was on tenterhooks.

'She hasn't got a family,' said Susan, cutting in again. I glanced at Olivia. She had turned deep red.

'Oh, no children you mean?' I said, still hopeful but still anxious.

'No – she never got married,' said Susan again butting in, almost as a criticism. Olivia looked embarrassed.

'Nan! – please don't be rude. Mr Temple doesn't want to know about our lives. Besides, I can answer for myself thank you.

Oh... but I *do* want to know, and I managed to wheedle out from Susan – without her realising – that Olivia 'came along' in 1967 as she put it. Again, Olivia was not too impressed with her nan and gave her a stern look. I could see she was becoming agitated and my mind was beginning to imagine things.

'That was just after your own mum passed away... I saw it this morning when I visited her grave. Were some of those *her* words on the gravestone Susan?' I quickly explained to Olivia the reason I was here, that being this way on other business, to see Susan and her mother's grave as I knew her too – briefly.

Which was true.

'Yes, I think they were. I can't remember exactly,' as Susan's voice trailed off.

It was then I noticed Olivia's left hand, when she had momentarily raised her hands to her mouth in response to Susan's funny, but rude, outburst. I had wondered earlier why she always had something in her lap when she sat down, why she always seemed to be carrying a scarf over her arm – and why she fumbled with the cushion she had dropped outside.

Her left hand was deformed.

It was not withered in an unsightly way, just not properly developed. What I could see as she sat there was what looked like the absence of two fingers. Her left arm otherwise looked normal. And she caught me looking, turning her gaze away from me and changing colour whilst trying to hide her hand once more. I was equally embarrassed for being caught staring. Was she resentful that I had spotted it, I wondered? And was it the result of a natural birth defect – or of an accident? I didn't think she was old enough to have been affected by Thalidomide, when all that had occurred.

Actually, rather more mundane I think – the result of birth, a condition known as *syndactyly*. Who knows how these things happen? Corrective surgery was probably conducted when she was young; now you would hardly notice a thing unless you looked for it, but she was obviously still conscious of her condition.

If she was in her forties Olivia looked well for her age although I noticed an unusual streak of grey in her hair on one side. She was above medium height. The more we talked the more I detected an element of protectiveness, an endearing vulnerability about her... that she was wary of something, something beyond her obvious physical infirmity. It resulted in a presence that gave her a mysterious facade. I began to observe her more closely, trying not to make it look obvious, taking a keener interest in her features, studying her hair – yes, that tinge of grey – studying the way she moved, her poise – as you do. When she stood up to rearrange her gran's cushions I was able to observe that she carried herself well and my guess, when I had first saw her, would have put her in her late thirties, not in her forties because her skin was flawless. But the way she moved... had she ever attended a Dork school I wondered?

She was built with more curve than bone – not too much, just puppy curve, with just a hint of padding on her backside. Yes, a very nice backside as I had seen already. Her legs? Not thin, no stick-like legs here, no PoW thigh gaps. From what I could deduce under her cardigan, her bust was ample enough with her tummy not quite flat... a small pod, but flatter than mine! So, no hourglass shape but at least she *had* a waist – overall a very pleasing picture nonetheless. And there was something about her eyes – slightly turned up, and her right eye – odd. But these attributes, combined with her slow-spoken speech, her poise, presented an image of an attractive softness... and desirability. My old heart fluttered.

Then I asked Olivia about her job. What might she be doing to keep herself off the streets? She smiled at this but I must admit I had no idea just looking at her what she might do for a living. Maybe a legal secretary perhaps by the way she was dressed – a relaxed smartness, a dress or skirt to just below her knees, a blouse and cardigan. She was definitely no shelf-stacker. She also asked me to call her 'just Vi' – as in vee. She didn't like the whole 'Olivia' nor Olive'. Just Vi – a nickname she became stuck with from school. But what a surprise when she told me of her job.

'So you are involved with an organisation that looks after memorials – local stone memorials, both civil and military and other old representations,' I repeated by way of acknowledgement.

'Yes, I am. Well, it's not just that; we are also involved with various care homes and organisations for certain ex-armed forces members as well as their upkeep. The monuments... these are the not-so-well-known monuments you see scattered in almost every village. I travel around a bit in the local area, around this area here – and we have many voluntary workers too.'

'I bet you do – you must be very busy! East Anglia must be full of them,' I answered. 'I must admit I've often wondered about some of these old stones and monuments that you see every day on the side of the road. What an unusual job. Do you enjoy it?'

'Yes, very much. We rely very much on charity donations.'

'Olivia, you must be quite proud,' I said as I slowly stood up, standing up in mock attention, smiling at her, 'I don't know whether to salute you or kiss you!'

Perhaps I shouldn't have said that, because up piped Susan.

'Kiss her! Give her a kiss! She could do with one!'

Outrageous!

Olivia gasped and put her hand to her mouth. The shock on her face. 'Nanny, stop it! Why are you saying these silly things? Oh, I'm so sorry Mr Temple,' she said but could hardly look at me. For a moment, I thought she was going to yell at Susan – she looked hot and flustered.

'I wouldn't mind actually, but I'm sorry, it's my fault Vi. Grandparents! What can you do with them eh?' I ventured, in an attempt to cool things down. Besides, who'd let me kiss them? 'Susan, you are being naughty again,' I said, wagging my finger at her once more, smiling. It was then that I noticed, when I glanced over to Olivia, that I had caught her looking at me. She quickly averted her gaze just as Amy the nurse knocked at the door to come in with the menu for tonight.

Susan spoke again. 'You want to watch him Olivia – he was chasing my mother around the dance hall, took her outside,' she said just loud enough for us all to hear, including Amy.

I didn't see that one coming either. So she had seen us sneak out too, on that night!

'Nan... please stop it...' She was trying to admonish her nan with a little dignity.

Even the staff nurse Amy picked up on it and smiled.

'It's alright – my secret's out at last... guilty as charged. Yes, I chased your mum around the floor – couldn't keep my hands off her,' I said chuckling, knowing that nobody would take a blind bit of notice of the old lady's ramblings. But two of us in the room knew that what Susan had said was true. She knew and I knew. A fleeting smile crossed Olivia's face but I could tell she wasn't entirely comfortable with the way the conversation was going.

Perhaps it was me. But I was totally beguiled by now. Smitten. Done. Finished. I surrender.

Then I suddenly remembered...

'As it happens, I actually have a picture of your mum, Susan,' I said reaching for my phone. I fumbled away until there she was – the picture of Grace, the one taken by Becky. I had others too, just in case. I moved to Susan and showed her. 'Remember when we first met a long time ago, you showed me the pictures of your mum and Cecily. Now it's on my phone,' I said stretching the facts, mingled with a lie or two.

She stared at it for a short while. 'Lovely... mum... fond memories,' was all she said quietly, a glimmer of recognition but also of sadness in her eyes.

'Indeed she was,' I mumbled.

Then over to Olivia. I sat down right close to her as I gave her the phone.

Did I detect her pulling away from me, just a fraction, as I sat down...? There was an intake of breath as she looked at it. 'Oh, what a lovely picture. But it's in colour; it looks so fresh – how did you get it on your phone?' she asked. 'I've only ever seen photos from those old times in black and white.'

Little did she know.

'You youngsters!' I said with a chuckle now looking at both Amy, who was young, and Olivia. 'Not everything before 1960 was in black and white. Just look at *Snow White and The Seven Dwarfs* – that was in colour, *The Wizard of Oz, Micky Mouse...* and it's amazing what you can do these days with IT. ' Then I leaned in just a little closer and deliberately looking intently at Grace's picture, I said in a much lower tone, 'It just goes to show what a good photographer can do. What a very attractive lady she was, just like her great-granddaughter.' Now I was looking straight at Olivia when I said that, who turned to look at me – and just as quickly looked away with embarrassment.

'You're close enough now – go on, give her a good kiss!' Susan said again.

Another intake of breath from Olivia, and I saw Amy's open mouth too, with a look that asked, 'Did she just say that?' For a moment, I thought Olivia was going to cry – her cheeks were flushed. I was still close to her. It was then that I saw the reason why one of her eyes, her right eye, was ever-so-slightly turned up, producing an unusual attractiveness in her face. She had a scar close to her cheek and right eye. It was cleverly hidden by make-up but it was this that I had noticed earlier. It had the effect of changing slightly the whole shape of her eye and that part of her face. It looked like some past accident to me but it did not detract from her pleasant appearance, in fact I thought it gave her an unusual, attractive aspect. I gave absolutely no hint that I had seen it but she must have *known* I'd seen it.

Olivia had registered a strange feeling when this Mr Temple had sat down right next to her and looked directly into her eyes. It was if he was gazing into her very soul. Who was this self-deprecating man who readily laughed at himself and who had attracted her interest? She was quite certain he was familiar to her but could not imagine from where, and she could sense that he was not un-attracted to her, but with men it was difficult to tell. And she was worried her nan was not helping matters.

Chapter 52

The row

'Please excuse me ladies – I shall just make a short visit to the big boy's room, it happens when you get to my age,' I said and stood up to leave the room, following Amy, who also thought it good idea to make herself scarce for a while. She must have been witness to these kinds of goings-on in family gatherings many times before. I reckoned a couple of minutes by themselves might help – but something was definitely 'going on' in that family. Amy left the door open.

As I moved off and entered the corridor I caught the tail-end of – 'What are you trying to do nan... why are you doing this?' drifting down the hall. Olivia's voice was stressed. I paused a second, stopped walking, even back-tracked a few steps. Now I'm eavesdropping. Not so far away that I can't pick up the thread of a conversation, Susan's voice was now quite strong for one of her age, quite audible and sounding angry.

Why, I wondered?

'You silly girl Olivia. How many men-friends have you had and you let them all slip through your fingers, eh? What's the matter with you? Can't you can see he's smitten?'

'Smitten? We've only just met – and he's old enough to be my father! Why are you always trying to do this every time a man appears and trying to get me fixed up, it is humiliating and no doubt very embarrassing for him too. I want you to stop it nan, please, or I shall leave. And we don't know him. Besides, he probably thinks something's wrong with me – I saw him looking, he knows. Just look at me nan... he'll think I'm a freak! And I'm fat too! You just keep embarrassing him. You'll frighten him off!'

'Ah, so you *have* taken a shine to him. Too old? Pissh – I don't buy that argument. Besides, you said it without any conviction my girl.'

'No I haven't. He's too old and we know nothing about him.'

Olivia fat? No way – not even close. And me old…? Only three score and… well, that'll do.

'Oh, are you sure of that? You may be surprised young lady. Olivia, get out of your silly cocoon, you'll finish up a spinster – don't be such a prude. I know he's not Rock Hudson but he appears to be a nice man, and he's not that bad looking really, is he? He carries himself well – he walks 'young', looks fit, vigorous. You could do much worse. Just because of what happened to your sister doesn't mean all men are like that.'

'Nanny… stop it!''

Oh dear, so there is some family history here. I felt ashamed listening into this as I could tell Olivia was not taking it well.

And Rock Hudson? A bit better looking than me I suppose, taller too – but bad example.

Susan could readily recall the fall-out from the rape episode involving her daughter Laura and the subsequent attack on Olivia. It had affected the whole family badly and was one of the reasons Laura had moved to Spain. But Olivia had remained behind as she had a job she liked, working in a flower shop – at the back, making up arrangements away from the public gaze… and it was Susan who picked up the job as 'parent'.

When Olivia was younger Susan had quickly noticed that she rarely took up with any boyfriends. Susan surmised that she was psychologically damaged in some way and even suggested she see 'someone'. Olivia absolutely refused to see any shrink. But one day Susan had found out that Olivia had a date arranged to go to the pictures. Susan prayed that it would work out and when she next saw her asked how it had gone. She knew it had not gone well as there was never any further mention of the man again. It took some time to find out but when Olivia finally explained, she had said that during the film he had suddenly put his hand on her thigh. She'd froze, pushed his hand off and couldn't wait for the film to end – and to leave. Several times Olivia had made arrangements or dates to meet people only to cry off at the last moment.

Then there was another liaison about which she managed to wheedle information from Olivia – another failure. She had been taken to a pub and while in there, several of his friends came in. It didn't take long – when he went up to the bar to get drinks, she saw the sidelong glances, with one of his mates clearly moving his fingers and all of them turning to look… and then talking to her consort. When he came back he asked her about her hands… he had not known! She was mortified, humiliated – as was he it seemed. They left.

When they returned home he tried it on, pulling her towards him with his hands everywhere. She stopped him, simply opened the door and left, not wanting to see him again… nor did he try and contact her any more.

'When they realise that I'm like this,' she had said, showing her hand and pointing to her head, '…all they want is to get their hands in my knickers and have sex with me, then leave. I don't trust any of them nan.'

But Susan continued to look out for her as she considered Olivia to be not unattractive and surely well-shaped for any man so she never passed up on any opportunity to play Cupid if she spotted a potential suitor who worked in or about Olivia's sphere. But to no avail so far.

Yet here was someone from out of the blue who had done something to Olivia's senses and brought a reaction. A spark had occurred – a flame ignited. Of that Susan was convinced.

'How can he be smitten ? We've only just met. It's impossible, it's silly.'

'He's smitten in just the same way you are smitten, young lady. Oh yes, I can tell!' Susan continued, 'Stop being so prim and proper – wandering around like a church mouse all the time. Don't let your sister's episode stop you at least trying. Come on, tell me, when was the last time you laid down with a man, eh my girl? Answer me Olivia. You can't remember, can you? I'm beginning to think… oh my Lord! Please don't tell me you are still *intact* – or still wetting yourself?' I heard a cry, and some rustling. Susan went on, 'For God's sake, just look at the way he's been looking at you. Are you blind? And I've seen you peeking too. I'll tell him when he comes back. I will.'

Intact – what kind of language was this?

'Shush nan, be quiet – he might hear you, I could never live it down if he heard you saying these things and talking like this… it's personal. You mustn't say anything… he doesn't need to know. Don't you *dare* say a thing. I'm quite happy the way I am.'

Vi thought she could never live down the shame and embarrassment of someone like this Mr Temple knowing of her intimate frailties and what had happened all those years ago – it would totally destroy her self-confidence once and for all.

'I'll tell him.'

Christ! Time to leave. She was talking to her as if she was a child. Then I heard Olivia's voice saying something but couldn't quite make it out, but I could tell she was upset once more.

302

And tell me *what* exactly – that she might be a virgin? Oh come on Susan! A desirable woman (in my eyes) like Olivia still a virgin at her age? No. I couldn't imagine that. And Susan using Biblical terms…? And wetting herself…? What *do* we have here…?

A woman who is psychologically flawed -

A scarred face.

A deformed hand.

Possibly frigid.

Possibly intact…

And so desirable! I just felt an overwhelming urge to be protective towards her and to make her mine. She'll do for me! I was sold…

Because *she was different – and because I thought I knew her.*

This was getting heavy. This family has issues and I could only guess at what they might be. I was feeling more like a dirty snooper listening in like this – probably the reason I was burning red.

Don't get involved Bob… just say goodbye and leave, said a little voice.

Which I ignored.

I slunk away and then, while standing there peeing in drips and drabs, my mind was all over the place, trying to fathom what the situation was here. What was going on? Olivia's mother was not around and so Susan had taken on that role, but not closely it seemed. How could she, stuck where she was? Perhaps I could help in some way. I had noticed the looks I'd caught and also recalled Olivia's imperceptible move away from me when I sat down next to her. Was *she* conscious of her scar being discovered, or her hand – or both?

As I trudged back to Susan's room, humming loudly to announce my return to give them warning, I noticed that indeed, it had all gone quiet. I walked into an atmosphere you could cut with a blunt knife. They were both sat there mute, stern-faced, Olivia looking at the floor.

'What's happened?' I asked the room. 'Been arguing again?' I asked cheerfully

No answer, at least for ten seconds.

'I told Olivia that when you came back I was going to tell you something.'

I could see Olivia stiffen.

'Did you know – ' She was cut off in mid flow when Olivia suddenly stood up and shouted.

'Stop it!' as she sprang up in mingled annoyance and embarrassment, collected her bag, and stormed out in a sob without a sideways glance.

I could hear her crying all the way out.

'What on earth were you about to say? No, please don't tell me – will she be coming back? Oh Christ, I'd better get to her before she gets away.' But I was too late. She'd gone.

I panicked then went back inside.

'What happened Susan? How has all this happened – and where has she gone?'

'Home, young man.'

'Will you tell me what happened while I was out?' My world was beginning to look grey. Olivia must have been so upset to have left without so much as a 'goodbye'. I looked at Susan, 'Oh Susan... I've only known her for half an hour and already I think she's wonderful!'

'Yes – I could see that, and I told her so. She's an idiot.'

'But why did she go...?'

'Because she was afraid I would tell you something else.'

'But you haven't told me anything, so how can there be a 'something else'?'

'Something else that she and I were talking about while you were out.'

I didn't ask but I could guess what it was. Then I noticed she'd left a carrier bag behind in her rush to leave so I dashed back out, indulging in an anxious hope that she would come back for it. No such luck. As I returned inside I saw Amy, who told me she saw Olivia leaving – and in tears. I continued on to Susan's.

'Where does she live then?' I asked hurriedly.

'I'm not sure young Mr Temple, honestly. I never send any mail anywhere.'

'Don't you realise what you've done...? I haven't a clue where she lives, don't even know where to start looking. She could be anywhere. I don't even know her surname! You must have an address somewhere here surely.' I was determined that there was no way I was going to let *this* girl slip through my fingers... this girl, I was convinced, I seemed to know.

Then Amy reappeared, not realising exactly what had taken place and asking what had happened and why Olivia had gone. 'She was in tears, Mrs Kelly, when I saw her.'

'Do you know where she lives Amy?' I asked in quiet desperation. Amy didn't know either, but said the boss would have an address – but was away 'til tomorrow.

'However, I remember her mentioning both er... Rigby and 'thorpe' – could be Burthorpe...?' she offered tentatively. 'I live on the other side of Bury so don't know that part very well.'

It was enough for me. I could track it down, but before I bade 'Susan The Troublemaker' goodbye and promised that I would be in touch, she held up her arm to me and said, 'But there is something I need to tell you Mr Odd Couple... you need to know. Please let me tell you – please listen.'

I sat down beside her. 'What is it Susan?' There were tears forming in those rheumy eyes.

'Olivia is a good girl. When she was much younger and after she had left home, she was beaten up quite badly I'm afraid to say. Her sister's boyfriend...' Susan's voice trailed off. More tears. 'He was a nasty piece of work.'

'The scars on her face...?' I remarked. She nodded.

'She can get frightened – gets afraid, panicky with men around sometimes. She can't forget *him*... his face. She will often leave a room or shop if she's in it on her own with a man she doesn't like the look of.'

'What the hell did he do to her?' I was becoming concerned now. 'But is she okay Susan – in good health?'

'She may be a bit fragile... but there's part of her mind that remembers only too well what happened. She told me her neighbours keep an eye on her as she's on her own... poor girl, it's not her fault. Please be mindful of that won't you Mr Odd Couple?' I nodded. Susan paused. 'Because she keeps herself to herself and out of harm's way she has the sentiments and feelings of someone much younger, sometimes like a child.'

'Surely not. She looks and sounds fine to me.'

'There's something else… no I'd better not…'

'Susan – you can tell me later, right now I'm on a mission,' I said, and set off, looking for a red Jazz in some small out-of-the-way village in the middle of nowhere, just praying that it wasn't hidden away in a garage by now.

Chapter 53

The search

My heart was in my mouth. 'Rigby' could be Risby. As for Burthorpe? Same direction – both headed back towards Newmarket. For a while I searched these hamlets finding nothing and despairing, turning this way and that and sometimes finding myself back on the same road again.

Hamlets are supposed to be small, right? No, not always... clusters of homes hidden away behind trees – or just around the corner, all in the same village. Well after giving up on these two places I ventured out and further away, further into the countryside and off the beaten track, realising the day was getting on. I was cursing Susan – a combination of anger and chagrin. I turned into a lane with a row of 'two-up, two down' cottage houses on only one side. Some vehicles were parked along the road in a line. A quick squint – no Jazz, just a normal line of cars and a big chunky SUV, one of those custom jobs with over-sized wheels. So I paused; I was beginning to lose the will to live I think. I'd looked long enough and this must be the last lot of dwellings in the area. Nothing. A part of me thought, just for a nano-second, to get out and knock on someone's door and ask, 'Excuse me ma'am, or sir, but do you know anybody who lives locally called Olivia?'

No, won't do that.

I also felt like going back to Ivy's Care Home and Susan – it was my only link. Then a blast from a horn behind shook me up. I had stopped in the road in my search not realising I was blocking the way – the way to *where* for God's sake, does this road actually lead to anywhere... really? I held up my hand in acknowledgement and moved further forward onto the verge while pulling over to let a Land Rover pass. I was on the point of doing a three-point turn to get back into civilisation – I had to look up over my shoulder to do it, and suddenly, a car hidden previously by the SUV came into view... a red Jazz! I came over all hot and cold, saying, 'Yes, yes,' because how many red Jazzes could there be? But they are all red, aren't they? I Just knew it was the right one.

Knew it.

I parked further along around a corner, got out and walked slowly to what I thought would be the house that belonged to the Jazz. I felt like a young teenager on my first date... and yes, a neighbour's curtain twitched.

All the houses were set back from the lane with a ten-yard front garden and a path taking you straight to the front door. This house had, set on one side of the door to the right, a wooden bench seat with a boot-scraper on the other side. That's how old these houses were. I opened the gate and with due trepidation, crept up to the house. I stood there for ten seconds, listening. I didn't hear movement but I knocked anyway.

Silence. Nothing. I knocked once more. I considered that if it *was* her house then Olivia might not be in the mood to speak to anyone, least of all me. But, as I said before, I'm not letting this one go so easily. I knocked again, harder, standing flat as I could against the house so that if she was peeking out of her front window, she'd have difficulty making out who was there.

Then I heard two locks unlatching. The door opened... but only a little, to reveal Olivia, no doubt expecting me to be the last person at her door. Her eyes looked full of trouble, her face slightly puffed. Just a fleeting glance was all I had of her before she quickly and firmly closed the door. From what I had momentarily glimpsed, she was a mess.

'Please go away!' were the words she uttered. Then more forcibly, 'Go away!' My God, she sounded really upset from what I could hear through the door. But why?

'No! I'm staying put Vi. I'll camp out here if necessary. This bench looks comfortable enough.'

It looked terrible.

'I don't want to talk to you Mr Temple, *please* go away.'

'Took me ages to find you so I'm not leaving. You've given me real heartache. So, what *did* your nan say to you Vi... please tell me. It must have upset you as I can see.'

'It's none of your business. Please go,' she said again, more sternly this time.

I tried the door but it was firmly shut, locked up again. For five minutes, I sat there and thought perhaps she had issues, and a family rift with Susan that was ongoing. But I thought I'd try another tactic.

'Okay Vi. I understand, I shall go, but do you know what? I've only known you for a little while and think you are delightful, wonderful – and you are right, I think we have met before, somewhere, don't know where. I… I wish you well and hope you find happiness… so goodbye, give my regards to your nan,' and I walked up the path, slammed the gate without going through it as I hurriedly retraced my steps back towards her door, then quietly sat down on the bench… and waited.

About twenty seconds it took. A quiet scramble at the door inside, locks and chains moving again, the door opening, and Vi hurriedly moving straight out and up the path looking left and right down the lane, holding her breath as she went… not seeing me.

I heard her mutter or whisper something but couldn't catch it as she realised she couldn't see where I had gone. Another sound broke from her lips as she cupped her face in her hands and stamped her foot in anger. Her face was a picture of turmoil, some tears came to her eyes, and of course she wouldn't have known what car I drove. She still hadn't spotted me – totally unaware of my presence.

Then she turned.

Chapter 54

Two sore ones

'Hi Vi, looking for me?' I said meekly with just a little wave. If only I could have filmed that moment.

Vi let out a gasp when she saw me, as I stood up slowly moving towards her. I held out my arm as if to say, 'this way'. But she was motionless, staring at me. Then...

'Very funny,' she said without humour.

'Come on Vi, your door's open, let us go inside.' I went up to her and gently placed my arms under her elbows and guided her back through the front door. She was trembling just a little. I half-closed the door as we moved further inside.

'What is going on Vi?'

'I don't know you Mr Temple. You're a stranger; we've only just met,' she said hesitantly, dabbing her eyes and trying to control her emotions.

'Not strictly true – even you thought earlier that our paths may have crossed before, in any case, that's what I want to change. I'll tell you a story one day. But come on, please tell me what has happened; did your nan tell you I was just a wicked, dirty old man or something?' I asked with a hint of a smile. 'And I don't care if I *am* old enough to be your father, just please tell me what's happening between you two.'

Her look changed. 'How did you know... old – were you listening to what we were saying?' Her tone had changed to one of suspicion, an edge to it.

I ignored what she said, not realising the danger signs.

'I'm not leaving until you tell me, and by the way... because I want to keep my eye on you, I'm staying the night.'

That'll put the cat amongst the pigeons.

Her hand went straight up to her mouth, 'You're so rude! No, you can't stay, you must go – get out please.'

'And why not?' I interrupted.

'You are rude… so presumptuous,' she said trying to control her voice, but before she could continue I gently took her arms and pulled her closer. She was still trembling – and resisting, trying not to be coerced. I remembered what Susan had said.

'Are you frightened of me? Okay, I might be a gnarly old man but am I *that* bad…?' I had to ask… what was it about me I wondered? Or was it just her take on men?

'I hardly know you… or what you want Mr Temple,' she replied, still gently resisting and pushing at me.

'It's Bob, and it's to get to *know you*…that's what I want… in a nice way Olivia.' That sounded lame. 'I'm no slimy pervert, I just want to get to know you better.' I waited for her to say something. 'Okay look, if you don't want this to go any further then tell me now Vi and I'll leave,' I said as I turned ever so slightly towards the door.

But I detected uncertainty both in her voice and body language, that she wasn't sure, so I turned back. I was beginning to understand that whatever had happened in Vi's past was affecting her – a more serious history than that indicated by Susan's titbit comments. At first I hadn't attached too much importance to, or known how seriously I should take, the tales Susan had related to me before I left the care home. I pulled her closer to me, slowly.

'Look, no matter what happened to your sister and how it's affected –'

She took a sharp intake of breath, pushing me away and stepping back. 'You *were* listening! You were eavesdropping on our private conversation weren't you – about being too old and all that… you were… spying on us? Oh God! And now you've come here…' She was stumbling over her words now, pushing me harder, '…using it as some excuse to get into my house to sweet-talk me and take advantage,' she said, her voice rising.

The thought of him hearing what Susan had said about her private matters… total humiliation.

'Eh? No Vi, that's not –'

'Go on, get out – please leave. Please get out of my house. You're all the same – deceiving us!' She was angry now.

'Not true Vi, please let me expl–,'

Even louder, 'Get out you sneaky, you sneaky… pig… you, you… just leave!'

Whoa! There was something here I did not understand; something that she withheld. Had I stepped over some invisible boundary and frightened her? I tried to hold her hands, moving closer to try and calm her down but she threw her hands up to her shoulders in a 'keep away' gesture, a move that resulted in me touching her chest, purely by accident.

She jumped, 'Get your hands off me!' she almost shrieked, pushing harder against me. 'Don't touch me.' I was beginning to appreciate her grandmother's advice. Something had gone completely wrong in the space of about twenty seconds… a line had been crossed.

'Sorry,' was as far as I got before an arm grabbed me from behind and a gruff voice said, 'You heard what she said!' I momentarily struggled with my unknown assailant, turning him round to my front before there was an explosion between my legs – a massive kick from behind by someone else, another attacker, that propelled me head-first into the wall before crumpling into a heap.

'That should stop him!' said the other. Then there was a third voice joining in the melee.

I was collapsed to the floor in sheer agony, unable to breath, curled up in a ball. I may have fainted, I don't recall, but I do remember a couple more blows, some voices asking, 'Are you okay Missy Dawson – and Who is he?' and such like. I also heard the words, 'Thank you,' uttered by Vi. Had she called them? But then I vaguely remember her telling them to stop… I don't remember, but the door had been left open. I also remember being hauled to my feet – there was no way I could walk – and being dragged outside then thrown onto the path after hitting the scraper. As I couldn't get up I was assisted to the gate with a series of pushes and more kicks. I heard Vi imploring them to stop now. Was there a genuine and natural concern for me in her tone…?

Just as one of them was about to take another good punt at my ribs, I held up my hands in supplication, saying in gasping tones, 'Okay, okay – I get the message,' as I slithered through the gate on hands and knees. Once through, I propped myself up against the small garden wall, still trying to breath properly. Then I was sick – the pain. After ten minutes, I attempted to stand up, still gasping, the wall helping me so that eventually I was up leaning over it almost. I was in agony and my face, head and side hurt too.

Then it began to rain lightly.

I looked around to see if the coast was clear. It was, but a movement of a curtain caught my eye and a figure behind – Vi must have witnessed the whole saga including my ignominious removal. And I noticed there was blood everywhere – all over my face and on my clothes. I must have looked a total mess, like one of those Saturday night A & E cases. It was a nosebleed – it hurt, but not half as much as my ribs and my jewels. And mentally I was devastated. I was wounded, defeated, crushed and baffled. As I stumbled back towards my car – I had to stop every ten yards – I looked back once and saw Vi back out in her front garden looking at me. I shook my head and moved to my car but stumbled, trying to breath.

As I approached my car I fumbled for my keys, tottering, falling to the grass verge. The fall resulted in a stab of pain that stopped my breathing momentarily. I attempted once more to locate my keys. Although I still had my wallet I could not find my keys, must have dropped them – they were not on me. For a brief, few seconds I looked around on the grass while trying to get up to retrace my steps, falling back to earth again.

...

Olivia spotted the keys as soon as she went into her front garden the next morning to straighten up some flowers that had been damaged in yesterday's fracas. They must be his, she thought, but now she was concerned; she had seen the state his was in as he staggered away. 'I hope they are not his keys,' she mumbled to herself, 'and that he returned home.'

But she knew. She knew they were his. Who else? Now she was fearful. Donning her shoes, she turned both ways, looking for a car she did not recognise while bleeping the fob. None answered so she walked in the same direction she had seen Mr Temple go, around the corner further up.

There were two cars parked around the corner, one of them a police car! A policeman was surveying the immediate area. The other car, a Rover, flashed in response to Olivia's efforts which, of course, stopped the copper who looked up.

Olivia's mind was in a sudden turmoil, in some panic. What had happened? She rushed forward towards the policeman, in acute alarm.

'This your car ma'am?'

'No – but I think I know who it belongs to,' she replied, beginning to realise the gravity of the situation. Olivia was devastated... what had happened to Mr Temple?

'A man was found lying here last night, injured. An ambulance was called.'

Olivia steadied herself against the wall, 'Oh no, no, no...' The policeman was on the radio which was crackling away.

'Are you okay?' he asked as he approached, looking concerned.

A voice on the radio announced, 'Doctor said not a *hit and run*. Probably a punch-up or a domestic.'

'Roger that.'

Olivia eventually told the copper who he was and blurted out that it must have been some random fracas he was involved in after leaving her house last night, forgetting his keys... and why she was upset. She hadn't actually seen him drive away. The policeman then told her he's under supervision in the local hospital, but not seriously injured as was first thought. He didn't know how long for, he told her.

Olivia was now terrified, appalled. What should she do – what *could* she do? Her sense of responsibility and desperation was overpowering. What must he have been thinking as he was looking back at her? When he came back for his keys, as he surely must, what could she say to him? But more terrifying – what is he going to say, or do?

She slunk back to her house and waited. Was he in hospital for one day, two days? The 'not knowing' was a torture – and should she go and see nan?

I woke up in a hospital with two medics looking at me, blokes unfortunately.

'How did I get here... when...?' I asked as I noticed a copper nearby, only vaguely aware of some painful trip in an ambulance.

Long story short... earlier, a dog-walker almost fell over me at night where I had fallen on the verge right next to the road. At first, she thought I was dead but I was only unconscious. Although she couldn't see it, I was covered in blood. She phoned the police thinking it was a 'hit and run' incident, but an ambulance took me to the hospital. There was no mention of a car.

They checked me out, tidied me up and kept me in overnight for observation. I just told the copper I could not remember anything. They knocked me out with pain killers. But the next morning I was just one big hurt. The goolies were subsiding, my head ached, my leg was sore but it was my side that really hurt… and my pride.

'Your ribs…' the doc had said, '…not cracked as far as we can see, but certainly severely bruised. And you were lucky – it was cold last night. Good job they found you when they did.'

Then my mind started to get back on track. How the hell do I get back to my car? And when I fumbled for my keys… nowhere. Lost! I suddenly remembered – I could only surmise that they had fallen out of my pants during the scuffle. I didn't even know where I had gone to see Olivia – where exactly she lived, no idea the name of any street or village; but fortunately, the policeman told me from where I had been picked up.

Believe it not, the copper took me back and dropped me off right by my car. Nice bloke.

I searched for my keys where they had found me, but no luck so I slowly back-tracked towards Vi's house still in a lot of pain, praying I'd find them outside – I didn't want to see her again, at least, not looking like this. Still no luck. Once again, with even more trepidation – and anger – I shuffled my way to her front door. I hadn't bothered to check out my appearance but I knew I was a disaster. I caught a brief glimpse in the copper's car – a black eye and swollen nose with traces of caked blood here and there.

I definitely could not give Rock Hudson a run for his money right now.

I didn't have to knock – the door was opening as I approached. Vi looked shocked, her mouth working but before anything came out I said, 'Vi, if you don't have my car keys in your house I'm in real trouble.'

She said nothing – just retreated into her hallway and on return duly produced my keys, blurting out as she handed them to me, 'Mr Temple, I'm so sorry, I didn't mean this to happen… are you… okay?' I had the impression she wanted to do something as she stood there with uncertainty apparent in her poise. 'Would you like a cup of tea Robert?'

So, it's 'Robert' now. I shook my head and turned to go but stumbled over the edging of a flower bed, falling on my backside. Wow that hurt…not my backside, just all my current injuries being shaken up with a vengeance. I winced, then I heard laughter. It was the 'chuckle brothers' from next door – dad and two sons – the ones responsible for my pain, who had been drawn out of their house by my arrival. It took me a moment to recover my breath.

'Zac!' Vi shouted, 'Stop it!' she admonished him across the low fence. She came forward, crouching down to help me. 'Was that ambulance last night for you... were you there all night...?' she asked haltingly, with a look of concern.

My face was close the hers. 'Probably, no thanks to you and your 'friends'.' She shook her head in contrition. She said nothing further as she crouched close to me before I stood up.

I continued, 'Vi, Vi, listen to me – I think you need help. Get yourself sorted out. I must go now – goodbye Vi,' were my last words to her as I limped my way down the road to the car. I could not look at her in the eye – I did not *want* to look at her. I was just too broken. I wanted to forget. As I rounded the corner I heard raised voices and remonstrations between her and her goons.

Me and women...

The journey home was the most miserable I'd ever made. What had gone wrong? My mind kept returning to the altercation. One minute fine, marching up the hill, happy, the next I'm called a sneaky bastard. Yes, I hold my hand up – I was guilty of eavesdropping, but only a little, and everything I had overheard in the corridor, Susan had more or less repeated on my return... I think.

I'd only known her for a few hours but was absolutely captivated, however, I now realised that she came with baggage, with a health warning... something that was no longer going to concern me. I'd seen the look in her eyes – a look of hate or fear, or both. I'm not sure.

'Becky – you're right, I need a woman... but not that one!' I said to myself as I whimpered home – with two new sore things, a sore nose, painful ribs and a dead leg.

But something that I valued was being left behind, unsecured... over in Bury.

Chapter 55

Commiserations

Another day passed.

As soon as Olivia walked in to her room Susan knew there was something wrong. Without any hellos or talk about the weather she asked, 'Did he find you then Olivia?'

'I don't want to talk about it nan,' she answered quietly.

'Oh dear. What has happened? You must tell me something. What did you do? He was nice chap – you did not turn him away did you...? Oh no, my dear girl, come on – you must tell me. Before he left here he was telling me how much he liked you, that you were somehow special to him. You've messed it up, haven't you?'

'Oh, that's typical, I'm automatically getting the blame – as always. For your information, I had to ask him to leave but he wouldn't, so my neighbours threw him out.'

'Threw him out... threw him out?' she said again with emphasis. 'But why – how? Oh Olivia...'

'Did you know he'd been eavesdropping on us, on our private conversation nan? He had listened to us arguing when he was out because he told me about Laura, and then tried to take advantage of what happened to her to stay in my house. I felt so humiliated to think that he heard those words you uttered – I couldn't face him. He tried to deny it too! He's just like all the others nan, just as shallow. Then he had the cheek to say he was staying the night – I was angry and shocked.'

'Can I –' but Olivia cut in.

'It's a good job Zac next door was there – they helped get rid of him.' Susan could see Olivia was getting more angry about it the more she spoke.

'Did they hurt him...?'

317

Olivia didn't answer. She sat there staring at the floor shame-faced.

'They hurt him, didn't they?' asked Susan, looking intently at her granddaughter.

Olivia nodded. 'They thought he was getting fresh with me nan, that's why. Yes, he was bleeding...' she trailed off. 'He went to hospital... he is okay nan.'

'What?! Hospital! Oh Lord! Poor fellow... he's not a young man either is he – and your so-called 'friends' beat him up! I despair for you... you've done it now girl. Well for your information, young lady, let me tell you something – he didn't spy. It was *me* who told him all about your sister when he came back... I told him the story.' Tears were now forming in Susan's eyes as she realised what had happened. 'Oh lord! It was *me* you silly, stupid head-strong girl; what is the matter with you? He saw your hands – saw your injuries but he did not care! Not a bit! That's why he came to your house.'

Olivia sat there horrified, speechless, trying to form words to say, trying to breath – now realising the awful truth. This man, the only man she'd ever met who had caught her attention, who had produced a spark of hope in such a manner as he had done, who had come after her despite her 'infirmities' – an innocent man – was now gone. Probably forever.

Seconds passed.

'Nan... what have I done? What have I done...? she asked, trying to catch her breath, tears forming, her lips trembling.

Susan beckoned her over to sit next to her as Olivia buried her head in her shoulder, Olivia's convulsive sobs shaking them both. And Susan began to weep as old folk do, but Susan had never seen Olivia cry like this before. Never. It was a flood. Over forty years old and behaving like a stricken teenager.

It could only be love... something she had never experienced before.

Eventually...

'Where has he gone?' asked Susan.

Olivia shook her head, having recovered some of her composure, 'Home I suppose. Oh nan, when I saw him he had blood all over his face. He was hurt. He must have seen me – I could see the anguish and pain on his face as he left. I don't know where he lives. Oh God, I feel awful. Then he was found lying on the ground, cold and bleeding, and I didn't know! He could have frozen.'

'It's probably gone past that stage now young lady, the way he's been treated… and I don't know where he lives either. Sometimes you only get one chance.'

Those words led to another five minutes of tearful self-recriminations.

'Just tell me Olivia, what if he had stayed, what would you have done?'

'I know, I know nan what you are getting at. He would want to get close to me wouldn't he. I don't know what I'd do, but it's all immaterial now. I didn't know you'd told him those things.'

'But why was it such a big issue?'

'Embarrassment nan! Because I thought he'd probably overheard you say something about me being a virgin or being unhinged or wetting myself.'

(Susan hadn't told me that exactly.)

'And if he had… so what young lady?'

'It's very personal, that's why! I don't want everybody knowing, certainly not a stranger.'

'But he still came after you. Just remember that.'

He had, hadn't he?

Another minute passed.

'Do you think he's gone forever?' Olivia asked sadly.

'Yes, I do. As I said, sometimes you only get one chance, but my God – you're only in your forties young lady. You never know what might turn up.'

But Susan hadn't given up on him just yet.

Chapter 56

Back home

'So how did it go Bob?' was Keith's first question.

My looks and appearance conveyed a message almost in answer. 'Becks, I think it did not go well,' Keith added turning to her. 'Are you going to tell us about it – don't have to if you don't want to.'

I told them.

I had Becky in tears. I tried to explain how I felt when I'd first seen her – that she was somehow familiar and she had said the same to me, as if we already knew each other.

'Oh, I feel sorry for the poor girl Bob – she could just have had a panic attack. You may have spooked her. And are you alright with, you know – your whatsits?'

Good old Becky… while Keith gave a grimace.

'Still sore… all of them.' My attempt to lighten the mood.

'Eh? How many have you got boss?'

Just for a moment I had them.

'Just the two,' I said as we all laughed, '– but not quite the same shape as they used to be.'

But my gang had noticed on our next outing that I wasn't the same, not spontaneous. 'Morose,' said Ruby. 'Too quiet,' said Matt. 'No patter,' added Keith. A listlessness had descended upon me and Becky felt sad for me.

Woe is me – miserable.

'You have to go back, Bob, otherwise you'll always regret it. There must be an explanation for what she did surely,' suggested Becky.

'Yeah, but she's nuts,' I said. 'You should have seen the look on her face. I'll get over it.'

'You didn't try it on did you – get heavy or creepy with her?'

'I didn't think I did, no. In fact, I actually wanted to do the opposite.'

'Wow, that's a first,' said Becky, 'A bloke who actually wants to keep it in his trousers…!'

'He must have been feeling ill at the time when he said that,' was Keith's answer, looking at Becky with half a smile on his face.

'Actually, I did say I'd let Susan know what happened so I will give her a ring. But Olivia? No,' I said without conviction.

'Susan probably knows already – I'm sure Olivia must have told her by now, and put her spin on the story,' said Becky.

'I'd not thought of that,' I answered. 'In fact, I've not thought straight for days. I'm all over the place thinking about her – does that make me crazy?' I asked them.

This bothered me just a little as Susan too would be worried about those events.

But Becky… she's right again; I need a woman. And here I am, reader, over sixty, pining. I stared at my phone expecting it to ring, knowing it won't. And I still found myself reminiscing about Grace and our short time together – those magic moments captured only a few months ago and that crazy girl who has taken her place.

Definitely lonely.

'It's no good Becky, Keith – can't get the woman out of my head. I'll just have to make sure she's okay, fragile creature that she is – and I'll do that with a phone call to Susan.'

'Ahh, are you not going to see her then Bob? See Olivia?' Becky again.

'No. I won't be able to help her – she really needs help.'

'Buddy, the help she needs is you… I don't know anybody better than you who could provide it,' said Keith, putting his arm round my shoulders. 'She didn't get the chance to get to know the real Bob Temple.'

'Yes… dead right,' said Becky.

I thought about this, and what they had said.

Two weeks had passed. I picked up the phone and dialled.

'Ivy's Care Home…' etc.

I told them who I was and asked to speak to Mrs Kelly – or Susan, as she might be known by. It was a bloke who was talking so I asked if Amy was there to speak to.

In the background, I heard a voice calling out for 'Amy'. You know how it is reader – scratchy noises, muffled sounds, clatter of objects, pages being turned and then…

'Hello, Amy speaking.'

'Amy, remember me, Mr Temple – just recently visited Susan when her granddaughter was here. I'd like to talk to her if I could?'

'OMG – Mr Temple – yes, who could forget!?' Her voice dropped, 'I shouldn't be telling you this but Susan's been in a terrible state on account of her daughter –'

Red Alert!

'Granddaughter, you mean. What's up – something wrong?''

Yes, I think so. I will tell her… now. I won't be a moment. Please hold Mr Temple.'

Sound of receding footsteps and swinging doors. She was soon back.

'Mr Temple, Susan was overjoyed when I told her you were on the phone and begs you to come here at once as she's terribly worried.'

'Is it about Olivia?' Now I was worried more than I ought I'd be.

'Yes.'

A song suddenly came into my mind, 'Get me a ticket for an aeroplane, ain't got time for a fast train…' You know the one?

I was in a hurry.

'Amy, tell Susan I'm on my way. I'll be two hours.

Chapter 57

Back to Ivy's

I walked to Susan's room in some haste and when I knocked and entered she looked at me.

'Oh, Mr Temple, thank you for coming; please, please – you must go and see Olivia, I'm worried about her. I think she is avoiding me, she was terribly upset when she left me last time. Please, just for me, go and see that she is alright. Tell her I'm sorry. Try not to be too hard on her – she's not like other women; you understand that, don't you?'

'Yes of course I do, I've had first-hand experience of it, haven't I? Call me Bob, okay.'

'And, young Bob, I can see that you have eyes for her – but I *know* she has eyes for you too, so please, don't take advantage. Her mind is like a delicate flower sometimes.'

Poor Susan. 'Don't worry, I'll tread very carefully… best behaviour.'

'It's not where you are putting your feet that bothers me young man, it's where you might be wanting to put something else that I would be worried about… I've seen the way you look at her.'

'My God Susan – what kind of books are you reading eh?'

'Look… let me tell you a few things about her to put you straight so that you don't do the wrong thing – and you must promise not to let her know I told you about this. I just don't want her hurt because in certain social experiences she's far behind, totally innocent and sexually immature.

'When they were young, particularly Olivia, they were happy girls – they laughed a lot and were inclined to look on the good side of people, to see only good… until *that* happened. Now I'm afraid to say, Olivia distrusts or is suspicious of all men, after all, she herself has had nothing else but trouble from them. Her only contact with them is in her job and they are usually older men in any case. As far as I know she has rarely dated from when she was young – she is not interested in any dating agencies or whatever they're called these days. I'm not saying Olivia is a recluse, but she does keep herself to herself when she's away from work, looking after her garden and reading. And you certainly won't ever see her – or pictures of her – in a swimming costume.'

'Really?' I interposed. 'Tell me, what came first to start the nasty ball rolling – the comments and all that? Was it the hands…?'

'Yes – the hands. At school. Kids could be so cruel. Then adolescence. While Laura was able to go out and be free and easy, Olivia couldn't – she soon picked up on the sly looks and sly comments about her hand so she went out less, and when she did, it was normally with her sister.'

'Poor girl.'

'Then the 'incident'. The whole idea of sex – and males trying to get close – makes her quite uncomfortable. She doesn't like talking about it when she comes over to visit, doesn't like smut and crudity. But I have hope; importantly, I have never seen her look at a man… *until I saw the way she looked at you.* It only took me a minute to realise when she came in that something had happened… like some veil or barrier had been removed… and because of this and what happened to you, she is absolutely petrified now. She feels completely lost.'

'Why me – I'm no oil painting, and why should she be petrified Susan?'

'In case you never want to see her again. She said she feels a kinship with you – and now believes she has lost you. But you are going to see her again aren't you, to see that she's alright? Please tell me you are; it will put my mind at rest.'

'She sounds really screwed up but I have to admit to strong feelings for her, a real spark – and a spark of recognition the moment I saw her, but yes, of course I'll go.'

'Bless you. If you do fall in together then you'll have another problem… with all her sex issues. She told me a long time ago that she would have a real problem with getting too close – and intimate. She's lost twenty years of love and companionship because of that brute… twenty years robbed, when she could have had a normal life.'

'Cross that bridge and all that Susan…'

'So – there you have it. Either way she needs protecting, she will hide herself away and become withdrawn, won't face up to anything. And don't try it on – she'd have a fit. Besides, she's probably dry as an old crone by now.'

'So – now she thinks it's just for peeing through…'

'What…? Oh, so crude… but I see what you mean now… probably. Yes, headstrong? I was like that – so was Cecily, and my mum too when she was arguing with dad.'

'I've noticed the headstrong bit. Just to make sure Susan, Olivia's not a lesbian, is she?' I asked, probably knowing the answer already.

'Pissh. A lesbian? Nonsense… I'd know if she was. It always makes me wonder that – at least men have got something to use and play with but women? They've got nothing to do anything with. Silly.'

Susan – definitely old school!

'They would probably argue with you on that point Susan; anyway, for Vi I suppose it's all down to what happened. I will be careful. Promise – I don't want to be duffed-up again.'

'That was disgraceful – she couldn't stop crying about it when I put her straight about her sister.

'And me…?'

'Yes. She is smitten – she sees something in you, something unusual. As mum did… oh yes, I remember!'

'Before I go, one other question – when was she born?'

'Olivia...? April… er I think April the seventeenth. Why?'

'Nothing… I had a notion earlier… but it's not what I thought…'

Chapter 58

A shade of pink, not grey

Once more I approached her front door not without some trepidation. How would she receive me? Surely not a repeat of last time. I wanted to make peace, to reassure her I was fine and confirm whether she was okay or not, that it was all the result of a misunderstanding and that everything and everyone is forgiven. Then probably, knowing of her 'issues', would bow out – would say my goodbyes and leave.

I'm not convincing am I…?

I knocked. There was no immediate answer so I waited a few seconds and knocked again. I felt like a schoolkid standing outside the headmaster's study, about to accept my caning.

Instinct told me that someone was at home, perhaps round the back, so I retreated to the corner of the lane and decided to walk along a small path that ran along the edge of the back gardens – the rear of the houses faced open fields. I didn't have to go far before I heard the activity of breaking twigs, metal moving soil and over the rear fence – it was a low hedge actually – there she was, standing by a bush, tidying it up. I would not describe her look as 'happy' but what surprised me was what she was wearing – gardening while wearing a dress and bloody slippers!!

Who does gardening in their slippers?

And her dress had seen better times. Working togs I reckon, plus an apron. I could see the French windows open giving her easy access to the garden so she must have spotted something and just popped out to attend to it.

I observed her through the top of the hedge.

Moving a gardening cushion into place, she dropped onto her knees, crouching down to retrieve some pegs from the flower bed, facing away from me. She was wearing a floppy top with her sleeves pulled up. Beside her was a bag of compost and a trowel. I couldn't see what she was doing exactly so I decided just to watch from the margin of her hedge. Then I discovered that there was in fact a rear gate further along so I moved to it and stopped. I now had a much better view and I could hear her breathing.

For a minute or two I watched her in silence, admiring her, salivating just a little I have to admit, but I had to do something before anybody saw me and wondered what I was doing – an old geezer looking over a hedge at a woman, you know how *that* could pan out…!

Then suddenly, she leaned forward and momentarily over-reached herself in picking up a short rake. This movement caused her dress to ride right up her body.

I nearly choked. She had exposed half of her bottom, displaying her underwear, totally oblivious to my presence. And why shouldn't she be oblivious? It's just open fields where nobody should be. It was only for two or three seconds before she sat back, but it really made my pulses run… fast.

As I began to make a move, she paused, looked up at the house keeping quite still, motionless, then stood up. Her pause had also made me stop. I waited another few seconds when she suddenly froze, turned around and let out a cry when she saw me.

'Wow! What a wonderful view Vi,' was all I could think of right then, just as before. 'You shouldn't be gardening wearing that!'

'How long have you been there?' she asked, her hand flying to her mouth, and turning red again as she desperately tried to pull down and smooth her dress.

'Long enough to see that you are wearing pink knickers,' I said with a glint in my eye, perhaps being a little too bold. 'It should be a criminal offence Vi, what you did… I could have had a heart attack.'

Actually, I was trying to inject some humour – I was referring to her displaying her underwear to an old man, but she read it wrong, probably remembering and referring back to our last encounter. But seeing her like that – well – my blood was up!

Flame red was the colour she turned then. 'Oh, Robert,' came from her lips quietly, softly as she stood there motionless trying to explain I think. 'I… I'm so sorry. You must be angry… I didn't want that to happen. I didn't want them to hurt you – they just heard my voice they told me… can I –' was all she said before I interrupted, cutting her off. …

'Shush, be quiet Vi.' I opened the back gate and walked towards her taking her hand saying, 'Come on. We have some unfinished business.'

'What... what are you doing... where are you taking me... I'm all dirty...?'

'We're going inside Vi. After what I've just seen, all I want to do right now is take you inside... do I have to paint a picture?' I said as I pulled her along with me. A hot red mist was descending upon me... well, I'm a male and I had no defence.

'No! Robert, stop it, stop it. Why...? Oh don't, please don't.'

The French windows were open as I pulled her inside, quite surprised that she was trying to reason, and not struggling that hard. 'I know you are angry with me but please don't – I didn't want it to be like this Robert...stop... stop it!'

Yes... there was a little anger in me, but also a deep, hot desire.

Desire was winning.

Chapter 59

Another disaster

The next thing we are inside with me pushing her up against a wall, my hands pulling up her dress – my hands on her bottom, clawing at her underwear while she was struggling and almost shouting, 'You are punishing me aren't you… for what happened…? Oh, please stop it. Please stop! I didn't mean it!' For a brief moment, I actually thought she was going along with the play with token calls for me to stop. Was her guilt making her pliable? I thought it was.

How stupid of me!

But she had no chance. I was too strong and powerful and she was pinned helplessly by my weight. In the space of twenty seconds it was all over… nearly. I was about to commit that vile deed – about to drop my jeans when I stopped as she cried out:

'Go on then – get it over with but don't hurt me,' she sobbed… '…is this what I am to you – a piece of meat you put up against the wall so that you can have your dirty way…?'

I felt her go limp and begin to slide down the wall sobbing convulsively. I had stopped, but it made no difference: to her, she had been violated.

The worst twenty seconds of my life probably, when I realised the magnitude of my terrible blunder, just for the sake of a few seconds of lust. 'What have I done?' I asked myself. Oh, if only I could reverse these last moments of madness – and Susan's words of warning totally forgotten.

Olivia, now crying almost hysterically, just slowly slid down the wall and collapsed in a ball, knees up on the floor trying to protect herself, her clothing in disarray.

Distraught wasn't the word for it.

I yelled in rage at what I had done. Immediately I bent down to help her up but she cringed away saying in huge sobs, 'You pig, you sod... oh dear God, what's happening to me... I feel... dirty... horrible – WHY did you do it?' she shouted. 'WHY? You have destroyed my dreams – I had put you on a pedestal, now you have broken my faith in you. You are no better than *him*. You bastard!' There was steel in her voice that I had not heard before.

Him?

And I just stood there observing this pitiful scene, unable to do anything other than feel completely wretched, knowing I had committed a terrible, unforgivable act from which there would be no chance of recovery.

I tried again to help but it was of no use – the looks of loathing I caught each time she flashed another outburst of anger at me said it all. 'You scum – go away, go away,' she repeated. 'You hurt me!' Her crying had now taken on the form of deep sobbing while she remained on the floor. Eventually it became almost silent weeping and still she made no effort to get up. Somehow during the very brief struggle her lip had been cut and was bleeding.

'I misread the signals,' was my pathetic attempt at some form of justification, 'Please forgive me Vi --'

'What – because I didn't struggle hard enough, because you are too strong? You assaulted me deliberately! I feel disgusted, violated... I hate you. Get out of my house.' Her voice was now more controlled.

Once more I offered my hand – this time she grabbed hold of it, and came up willingly, I thought, only to be caught completely unawares with a girlie punch in the left eye, before she stumbled upstairs, groping and uncertain, clutching her clothing, crying once more, mumbling incoherently. I noticed her nose was bleeding... had I done that? The crying and sobbing continued for another half hour before there was quiet. But I felt compelled to stay, to not leave her on her own. I dearly wanted to comfort her to show it wasn't entirely naked and that I had truly blundered.

I waited awhile then took the decision to go upstairs – I desperately wanted to make sure and to see for myself how she was coping and to still try and reason with her. I also wanted to know how physically hurt she was. I just could not leave it like this, so I crept upstairs and headed towards the low moaning sounds she was making. Had I physically hurt her more than she said?

I thought the door would be locked but it wasn't. She had apparently flung herself straight on the bed so I walked in quietly. She suddenly turned, looking up. 'No no, go away,' she croaked. The light from the doorway showed the misery and fear in her eyes.

I slipped onto the bed and before she could move away I put my arms around her and held on tight. 'I just want to hold onto you Vi... I realise I've made a terrible mistake. I won't do anything else, just please stay with me – just for a while, then I'll go.' I clung onto her as she attempted initially to move away, still trembling and weeping as she lay with her back to me. Eventually silence descended – I guess she must have fallen into a troubled silence or slumber, just as I did.

...

I awoke in the dawn. Vi was no longer with me so I carefully went downstairs to find her sitting motionless, staring at the floor. She looked as if in shock – totally numb.

'Vi,' I ventured, looking for suitable words of consolation.

'Don't say anything to me. Just leave,' she said in a monotone voice. 'If you don't go immediately I will call the police and my friends next door. I don't ever want to see you again. I don't want you visiting my nan either. I will call the police if you do and tell them.'

Vi knew that she would never bring the police or any other outside agencies into this, who would just ask embarrassing questions and want intimate details for something that wasn't rape.

I didn't know that of course, so once more – and with yet another 'shiner' – I set off home feeling completely wretched. Why did I do it – how did I lose control? On this innocent flower, I had inflicted both physical and spiritual violence, their effects magnified, I suspect, from events of the past of which I had only scant details.

I had blown it yet again and it was definitely all my fault.

How do I come back from this – or do I just give up?

Chapter 60

Grandma & granddaughter

It was several days before Olivia had the courage to visit nan again because she knew she'd have to explain – Susan would know something had happened.

Susan was shocked, shocked that it had taken place and shocked that it was him, Mr Temple.

'He said he would not do anything like that before he left me. Are you going to call the police my darling – or is it too late?'

'No, I'm not, but I told him that if he came back to my house or came here then I would. He was like an animal nan.'

'Oh – it's a crying shame my dear, I am sorry. Whatever it was, I'm so glad he stopped short. You were right… but are you absolutely sure that there was no silly misunderstanding like there was last time? Remember – you were convinced then weren't you. You didn't – you didn't perhaps do or say something that made him…'

'No! Nan, you are taking his side again. I did nothing to encourage him!' She deliberately omitted to mention the incident immediately before when she was gardening, knowing it would just provide further ammunition for her nan's argument. 'He just dragged me inside and put me up against the wall.'

There was silence between the two for a few moments.

'Well – I have to admit I am disappointed, I thought that he was the one person for you. I thought he saw your light hidden behind that defensive guard you have… the real Olivia.'

'What he saw in me was sex, probably that I'd even be grateful for it – that someone was willing to try…'

'But that can't be right surely. Just think… why would he come all this way for some funny business when he could – a man like him – have fun at home? Why come this far? I still believe he carries a very large torch for you.'

That made Olivia pause. Yes, why come this far? Do I give the impression that I'm easy meat, she wondered?

'It was for sex nan... he was very rough... I couldn't stop him.' She paused a few moments. 'I was sick afterwards... and he hurt me too. I could have killed him, I really could.'

'Well in that case you should contact the police.'

'No nan, you know what will happen – they'll blame me and ask all sorts of personal questions. I've already decided not to pursue the matter. I just want to forget it all – and him especially.'

Susan, astute, knowing her granddaughter, detected that Olivia was ninety-five percent convinced. She'd try and work on the remaining five.

Chapter 61

Becky suspects

I said nothing to the gang, only so much as to indicate that as far as Olivia and I were concerned we weren't really compatible and had decided to part on friendly terms. It wasn't until I looked into my rear view that I realise I had a black eye to explain. I was fortunate that we didn't have any gigs for at least ten days.

I'd lie low for a while.

But as usual, a few days later, Becky guessed that matters had been more complicated – she could always tell just by looking at me.

'Come on Bob, tell Becky. I want to know it all, scalps on the bed-post, warts and all. What happened *this time*?'

I told her straight. I did not give any embellishments for any excuses I might have had; her jaw dropped as I went into the details of the events of that fateful day.

'You complete and utter idiot! Oh – the poor girl. I'm sorry Bob but I'm right on her side on this. I know you are no monster but were you wearing ear-muffs or something – didn't hear what she was saying, or couldn't you see her face…? You twit – you asshole! You complete idiot,' she said again.

Wow – that was strong coming from Becky. 'Bum' is usually her strongest word. I was in trouble even with Becky which does not happen often.

'It was the garden incident that did it for me, Becks… you don't realise what a woman's rear-end does, especially **her** rear-end, to a bloke when she's bent over like that, and when its only covered by a pair of panties… in full sight! I'm afraid a mist came down – I lost it; as you can imagine, straight away I felt terrible afterwards.'

'What would have happened if she had called the police?'

'She won't – she's not like that. I already know that she's too private a person to want to go that far. She won't.'

'She really has got to your heartstrings hasn't she – is there *any* way back Bob… any?' she then asked. 'You will have to say sorry… somehow.'

I shook my head, 'I don't think so. I feel that I've done her… that I've betrayed her in a terrible way. There is part of me that wants to go back and lay myself prostrate at her feet so that she could mete out some punishment.'

'Yeah – stomp all over you wearing stiletto heels, it's what you deserve!'

'Hmm, I might like that…'

'Temple… you are impossible! If you'd tried that on me you would be dead.'

'Wow… but what a way to go!'

'Seriously Becks, this girl is in need of protection and I know I'm the one who can provide it – given half the chance; yes, I know I blew it but something tells me she knows it was out of character.'

'Oh yeah and how would she know that? So far you've had two disasters – on only two visits – great track record so far Bob!'

I knew what she meant. However, every time I'd looked into Vi's eyes I had seen some deep connection between us – that she *knew* I wasn't bad, that I wasn't a monster.

...

Curiosity and simple guilt had the better of me in the end and I had a hole in my life ever since Bury, a hole that required some attention for my own peace of mind. My daily routine suffered, and more than I should be, I was short-tempered with my gang. I knew Keith and Becky looked out for me and wanted me to be back to normal but they realised – certainly Becky did – that the source for this lay east in a quiet little village near Bury.

It was a record that brought me up sharp to remind me, *Heartbreak Hotel*. Often when you listen to a tune the words can be lost or not matter because it's the tune you like. Well I listened to it *and* the words thinking, 'That's me'. I did not need a hotel to be miserable – I was doing fine all by myself. "Oh woe is me yet again!" and my imagination and curiosity were working overtime. What would *she* be doing right now? Probably sticking pins into an effigy of me, Mr Bob Temple, no doubt, but I could not just sit still. I had to find out – I had to make amends.

And I wanted her back.

I phoned Ivy's Care Home.

I wish I hadn't.

I eventually made contact with Amy. 'Yes, Susan is still here and of course is her usual self, Mr Temple – only more bad-tempered.'

I then asked, 'And how is her granddaughter? Does she still visit – I hope she does?'

'Yes she does but I believe it won't be for much longer, I think she may be going away Susan told me.' Then her voice lowered, '...going into Holy Orders or to Spain Mr Temple, I'm not sure which – fancy that eh?'

'WHAT? To become a nun – into a nunnery?' I said almost shouting down the line. 'Oh God no... no no, she can't be. Since when?'

'Since soon.'

Shit shit shit... double shit... bollocks – with knobs on.

I drove in sheer panic calling first at her home but nobody was in – no parked Jazz, but there was a 'For Sale' sign in her garden. Another bad sign... if you'll excuse the pun.

So I pressed on towards Bury, to Ivy's, and slotted into the first space I saw, ignoring everything as I hurried through the entrance.

I knew the way.

'Oh Susan, Susan, please tell me it's not true,' I kept muttering to myself as I moved towards her room. And another part of me was thinking, praying, 'Becky, Becky – please guide me through this with your common sense'.

The door was closed. Deep breath. Knock on the door.

'Come in,' came Susan's voice. It was then I noticed I had tears forming in my eyes.

Perhaps I should have taken more notice of the cars in the car park because sat right next to Susan was Olivia.

Silence followed for five seconds and at first I did not know where to put myself or what to say. I looked at Vi but she deliberately turned away, avoiding my gaze. Eventually...

'Please tell me it is not true Vi. Please tell me you are not going to be a nun... tell me that you are not going into a convent... or going anywhere else.'

Vi said nothing.

'Yes, it's true,' Susan answered. 'And all thanks to you mainly. You let me down young man.'

Then Olivia spoke, 'Nan – will you ask Mr Temple to leave,' still not looking at me. 'And please tell him I do not wish to speak to him at all.' This could turn out to be a real difficult meeting if it continues like this. 'I shall go nan, if *he* doesn't,' Vi added.

'Vi...' I implored, but she would not engage my eyes. 'Can you not forgive me... please... I'm so sorry.'

'She can begin at the end of the month for initiation and you will not be welcome where she is going, just as you are not welcome here young man, so please will you respect her wishes... and leave.' Susan was quite stern.

'What... begin so soon... how is that possible? Surely it can't be like going to join the army, it takes time doesn't it... probation, discernment, initiation and all that?' I knew sufficient to know that the process was customarily quite a long drawn out affair.

And still Vi ignored me, staring at somewhere to the side, so I crouched down to put my face right in front of hers. She simply turned to face the other way, remaining silent.

'We do have nuns come here to the Home occasionally,' Susan responded. 'They have provided the contacts and the help.'

'Nan – please ask the staff to come and make him leave,' she said in a soft monotone. '...or I will call the police.'

I was prepared for this. 'Go on then – call them,' was my response. 'Go on... I'll just wait here. I don't care any longer.'

Olivia knew it was checkmate. She would never want to revisit that day when I had almost stripped her nude.

'Nan – please inform him that I'm going, and that I do not want him following me.'

'You heard Mr Temple,' but before she could continue...

'Okay, okay. I shall be going – but please let me say this so that there is absolutely no doubt with either of you.' I moved back to Vi, knelt down even closer in such a way she could not get up and slowly placed my hands on her chair as gently as I could and speaking to her quietly asked...

'Do you really want to hide away your lovely face and shining light from everybody Vi? To deny someone the pleasure – someone who dearly loves you – of ever seeing you again?

'Do you really want to deny yourself the tender embraces that could be yours, the soft caresses and the gentle kisses... the wonderful brief touches – do you want to deny yourself that?

'Do you forever want to lock yourself away so that each time you dress and undress, only you will see you and no one else will ever cast their hungry eyes over you as I would, as I want to, to appreciate you.as I did when you were gardening?'

Susan looked up at that.

'Will you not want someone – someone like me, who sees your beauty and your inner softness and vulnerability, to be desiring you and wanting to excite you?'

'And do you not want to love another, and be so loved in return, with gentle cuddles or passionate embraces – to be with someone who cannot live without you? Do you really want to remain shut away for the rest of your life, to be lonely? I have seen your scars. I have seen your hands Vi – I know of these things which you should not hide, that you should not be ashamed of, because I love you V and I think you love me.'

'Oh my Lord! Where were you when I was young?' exclaimed Susan, looking at me. 'Did you hear all that Olivia – did you? Did you hear that? He loves you!'

I had noticed that Vi had started to colour slowly, her face first then her neck. Her mouth was moving, her lips quivering. She began to shake, her colour displaying some inner turmoil and still she remained silent. I felt I was wasting my time. Whatever battles were taking place in her mind, I eventually stood up. 'Big-boys' room,' I indicated, '– and when I come back, well, as you now know how I feel, I'll be off.'

As I walked out I caught a momentary glimpse of Susan's face, a look of alarm spreading across it as she looked towards Olivia.

On my return, I asked again. 'You won't consider changing your mind?' I said pointedly at Vi, wondering what they may have discussed in my brief absence.

'Nan, if he does not go now, I will.'

'Did you call the police then…?' I asked, already knowing the answer. With that, Olivia stood up, collected her bag and began putting on her small coat.

'Oh Olivia, don't go,' implored Susan while casting me looks of annoyance. 'Please tell him why – tell him your story. You owe him that at least as it's been the cause of all the misunderstandings. Please tell him,' urged Susan with some passion in her voice.

'No. It's none of his business.' She stood up and brushed past me. 'Are you going to leave now or is it me who has to go? Ask him nan.'

'I'm staying Vi, but there's just one more thing I have to do before you go. Are you watching Susan – remember what you said when we first met in this room, what you told me to do twice…?'

Vi looked at her nan. 'What *did* he sa–' but before she got any further, and taking her completely by surprise, I took her in my arms, pushed her against the wall adjacent to Susan's chair and gave Vi a kiss that lasted several seconds before she struggled free; it was a kiss, it was no snog.

'You said, "Give her a kiss", remember? Well now I have and it was magic!' Susan looked shocked at first then her face broke into a smile. 'I'm sorry Vi but I've wanted to do it since I first saw you. Now I have and oh my goodness, it was lovely.'

Olivia, on the other hand, spent a few seconds in a kind of fluster, bringing her hand to her lips then looking at me. Eventually a choking sob came from her before she regained her composure.

I continued, 'Notice she didn't push me away at first Susan…because she was enjoying it before she realised she wasn't supposed to. Now are you going to go like you said…?'

But she had already picked up her coat and stormed out of the room then had stopped to retrieve her scarf that had fallen from her arm.

Chapter 62

The 'M' word

I had to think quickly while she was still in the corridor. I remembered how the sound carried but I had to be fast so I spoke out loud, knowing my voice would carry.

'Well Susan, if she's made up her mind about the convent, shall I ask this girl to marry me?' I said in a deliberate way, but unaware at first that I had said *not quite* the right words.

It was definitely said loud *enough*, I thought, knowing from experience how voices would carry. Susan quickly guessed the ploy but nevertheless my move had surprised her. She gazed at me in astonishment with the beginnings of a smile forming. I made one woman happy I suppose.

I waited. *We* waited, nervously. The receding footsteps had slowed, then stopped. I continued talking out loud. 'Anyway, I'd better be going – it's a bit of a drive so I'm off…' After all, Susan's hearing was okay, but not *that* good, so I had an excuse to be loud. And if Vi didn't come back…? Well, I knew where she lived, all bases covered.

Then quietly I said to Susan, 'I think I overstepped the mark there when I kissed her – a little. I Just went from madness to badness, couldn't help myself but the 'M' word has been uttered. I wonder if she heard it?'

She *had* heard – she had *caught* the word 'marriage' but not quite all of what was said. It had given her pause. It was an unexpected development. Marriage was a commitment above and beyond – after all, men would say fine things just to get you into bed wouldn't they, then be off. She already knew this man lusted after her, but was this a sincere expression of his deeper feeling he had alluded to just a few minutes before? Could she trust him? Some of her work colleagues had been victims of the smooth talker who promised to leave their wives to be with them, suddenly finding themselves cast adrift after being bedded. And if she was honest with herself, she had to admit that it had been an impulsive move weeks ago following his groping attack, to decide to get away from it all and join the Sisters – or join her other sister. She was angry with the world; all she wanted was peace and solitude, no prying eyes, no awkward moments, and no fear. Suddenly she wasn't so sure – and time was running out.

Now there was the 'M' word she had just heard. But was it for her...?

He had said *this girl*: he hadn't said 'her' or Olivia, so who was he talking about? Did he actually have another girl he was seeing and he would marry her instead if she disappeared from the scene and went off to Holy Orders? What was the meaning here – why should her world hinge on two words? Surely he wasn't already playing footloose and fancy free with other women, this audacious, insolent, fascinating and worn-looking man who kept popping up in her mind, like *someone from the past.*

She stood there wondering if this was going to be the moment her life changed – irrevocably. Should she continue down the hall to the exit – or go back? And what would she say if she did go back?

What should she do? Why was life full of so many difficulties, so many decisions to make? Her mind wandered back to her humiliation that day weeks ago. No, he had shown his hand. And now he had just said he was going. She then remembered a bottle of wine at home, unopened; a period of oblivion beckoned, somewhere to hide for just a few hours.

On her way back her driving became slower, her mind desperately trying to recall all the words she had heard – or thought she had heard. Again, she wondered how sincere his words were earlier when he had knelt beside her.

And then the word *marriage!*

Was it aimed at her she asked herself yet again? She came up to a roundabout and considered going all the way round and going back to the Home to ask who was he talking about. Was there another girl on the scene? But she could not bring herself to do it. She was crippled by indecision and potential humiliation.

That bottle of wine looked even more inviting.

Back in the room.

Susan and I waited, but we heard her footsteps resume, quickening down the hall, probably running, leaving. I knew she would be upset. Susan motioned for me to stay put. 'Leave her for now Mr Tits. She'll come around when she finds herself alone in the house. Wait awhile.'

341

We spoke about the next steps and Susan was telling me how worried she was about Olivia going away for good and about the 'M' word.

'Are you serious about that? I hope it wasn't just a frivolous, throw-away line to trick her. I would never want to speak to you again if you were not serious young man.'

'I was serious – serious with a capital 'S'.

'Well, it's for you to follow this up without any help from me. You're on your own.'

'That'll be a first.'

After a while…

'She should be home by now; it's not often I ring but we'll see – she will be really worried about what happens if you turn up, she's not expecting you… oh, it's ringing.' Some moments passed. 'Oh, it rang but she put the phone down before I could tell her. She's terrified, I can sense it… she cannot see past what you did to her.'

'I understand completely Susan; I will treat her as sensitively as I can but I'm not giving up, she's not going into any convent if I can help it. I'll change her mind and I promise I won't do anything that frightens her – nothing is likely to happen anyway the way she feels right at this moment… you never know.'

I waited half an hour, talking with Susan before setting off.

Chapter 63

Tom

Here we go again, back to her place, hoping she had gone straight home. Didn't need my sat nav, knew the way. I looked at it to switch it off.

Me: I know the way Tom.

Tom: I'll still guide you there.

Me: I'm okay thanks – no need.

Tom: You know she's bonkers, don't you?

Me: Yes, but she drives me crazy. I'm must be bonkers too.

Tom: She's unstable. You'll be hurt again.

Me: No I won't – but I can't let her go into a convent... or to Spain.

Tom: She's determined.

Me: Something happened to her. She hasn't told me about it yet but she will.

Tom: She doesn't want you to know everything – have you thought of that possibility?

Me: I'll sprinkle some of my magic dust over her to change her mind about me.

Tom: She's doing this to spite you.

Me: I'll find out, just you wait and see.

Tom: She's not Grace you know.

Me: She's close enough – just a bit wonky that's all. I'm not giving up that easily.

Tom: You only have three weeks before she leaves.

Me: Don't I know it.

Tom: We're nearly there...

Amazing what tricks your imagination plays with you.

Chapter 64

True feelings

The phone had rung earlier. Vi hesitated then picked it up, holding a glass of wine in the other hand. It was her grandmother.

'Is he still there?' she had asked.

'No, he's going home now –' but the phone suddenly clicked. The line went dead before she could say anything else. Susan was about to add, 'But he's on his way to your house first'.

Stupid girl. She tried again. Engaged.

Strong-headed, stupid girl.

Vi had put the phone down but off the mount. So that's it then, he's actually slunk off home. But it was the 'home' word that made her think – nan had already pointed out, 'Why come all this way just for a bit of 'how's-your-father'?'

Yes, why?

'He's come for YOU my dear – warts and all! Can't you see that young lady?' her mind said.

Olivia nursed her drink, thinking about this point with her mind continuously going over the words. She had heard both those intended and those unintended and that blasted word 'marriage'.

As she looked around she began to realise her heart ached. The house was quiet, still, empty and cold. What had she to look forward to? On her own, drinking wine without enjoying it – the proverbial 'drowning her sorrows'. A single, lonely woman. How *sad,* she suddenly thought. Perhaps she should have gone back into Nan's room after all for a decision to be made one way or the other. But it would have been a devastating humiliation if it turned out he had been thinking of another woman.

At least she had been spared that.

Again, her mind drifted back to that event in the garden and when initially he had put her against the wall. There had been an element of excited panic when he had grabbed her hand and taken her indoors. She saw the passion and determination written on his face and felt the strength of his manhood as he leaned into her – something she had never experienced before, ever. A small part of her made her realise that yes, *she*, Olivia, had excited him and this in turn had briefly pleased her at the time, until he had lost control and she had freaked.

And… and that kiss an hour ago! Once more she had 'felt' him – just a little satisfaction that she had this power. His feelings for her; he had come all the way here just for her. She had excited him and just for a brief moment, he had excited her too. But do all men turn into animals like he had do they always have to be rough? It scared her.

But he's gone. Gone, maybe to someone else. A choke escaped her followed by another sip and another.

She cursed herself, 'Bugger, bugger, bugger; sod it,' she muttered. Now she couldn't have him or see him again. After all those words he had uttered, the more she thought the more she wanted him. As she stared into her wine glass it reinforced her desolation and loneliness. Nan had said, 'He's gone home'.

Away from her.

There was knock on the door.

'Rock Hudson here,' a voice cried out. 'The Mk 2 version, new and improved,' the voice added.

It made her jump, spilling her drink. She looked up and went to the window because she did not recognise the voice at first. A tug on the curtains to one side and there he was with a large bunch of flowers in one hand. She steadied herself. At first, she had trouble breathing and after a few seconds realised she was having a panic attack from the shock – then she also realised that she had suddenly wet herself.

'Oh God! Why now? Why is he here? He can't see me like this!'

In her moment of chaos and panic she cried out, 'Go away… go away,' while standing up, desperately looking for a way to hide the evidence of the embarrassing turn of events, her trouser suit bottoms with a nice dark patch.

And suddenly there he was standing in the doorway of the door she had completely forgotten to lock when she had returned, looking at her.

Not only was she mortified, she was also very angry. She picked up a small wicker basket from the table, throwing it at his face, furious at him for seeing her weakness while inwardly she shrank in a shame and humiliation she could not grasp.

How dare he see her like this!?

He ducked, placed the flowers on the table then and, in a couple of bounds, was right beside her trying to grasp her hands while she continued to try and hide her embarrassment, attempting to turn away from him or sit back down. But he would not let her.

'Stop!' he commanded masterfully, grabbing her shoulders and – once again – taking and holding her tight against *that* wall. He held her still. 'Stop,' he repeated but now more softly. She didn't move. He put his finger to his lips in a 'shush' movement then looked her in the eyes and asked, 'Did you not hear what I said earlier when you were in the hall? You did overhear, didn't you? I meant it to be so. Just move your head, no talking.'

She nodded.

'And yet you still came home… you left us. You left *me*. Why?'

'I was angry… I'm angry now!'

'Well I'm bloody glad it wasn't an ashtray you threw and *now* you must tell me – everything. I won't leave 'til you do, and I'll keep my hands to myself. Please tell me what happened to you.'

Olivia was in turmoil, worried that if she related what had happened he might politely offer some platitudes afterwards saying something like, 'I'm sorry to hear that and completely understand why you feel this way,' and then say goodbye, that she was 'damaged goods'.

She looked at the flowers. In the depths of her turmoil the flowers reminded her that what her nan had been saying all along about him may be true so she whispered, 'Alright – I will tell you.'

Chapter 65

Vi's tale

I was horrified with the tale she told.

When they were much, much younger Vi and her elder sister Laura were at a friend's gathering one evening many years ago. She had noticed her sister being led upstairs, rather reluctantly she thought, by one of the lads. Vi's sister was friendly with this man but Vi thought that that's all it was, just a friendship, so was a little concerned and it was getting late. She became increasingly worried. After twenty minutes, she ventured upstairs and immediately heard muffled cries from one of the bedrooms as if a struggle was in progress – and then a scream. Vi cried out for her and banged on the locked door.

Then another scream from within.

Suddenly the door was unlocked and her sister came staggering out, half naked, blood dribbling down her legs, gasping and struggling for breath, collapsing into Vi's arms. The man – he was more than just a lad, older – came running out, dashing down the stairs while trying to pull up his shorts and was out the front door.

Vi remembered his face.

Laura had been brutally raped – so badly in fact that she needed surgery. The police and hospital were involved of course; he was identified and jailed for two years. Two years!? It was Vi who picked him out and gave evidence.

A year after he left jail Vi was just getting into her car in one of those scrub-land car parks on the edge of town when from behind a hand came over her mouth, another hand forcing her into the car. She was told to drive – or else. A knife and broken bottle were shown to her.

It was him.

She thought the end of her life had come and started screaming while being forced into the back of her car, struggling and fighting as hard as she could. Memories of what he had done to her sister came flooding back. She knew what was in store for her... the same. All she remembered was being punched repeatedly and hit around the head with some metal object to silence her and a vague recollection that he might be reaching for his knife in his pocket. 'Please God, not the broken bottle,' she had thought. Then he was clawing at her clothing trying to rip her underwear off, forcing his fingers in making her bleed, but mercifully, a shadow fell over them, and voices, the voices of two middle-aged ladies who were now banging on the roof and the windows, knowing that someone was in trouble. This was sufficient to panic the attacker away from her, as he looked to escape.

One of the ladies had said her screeches sounded like a wounded animal being killed.

Her face was a mess of blood. The pain came later... excruciating pain. Her face took weeks to heal and get back to shape.

They knew who he was but he was never caught – believed to have left the country.

As she had been relating her story I noticed a softening in her voice and tears forming in her eyes so I moved closer to her.

'Oh Vi... what an absolute bastard! I can't imagine the terror you must have felt then... without those two ladies...? I hate to think. I understand now why... you've been hesitant...'

She nodded. I couldn't help it but I started to shed my own tears. I had to look away. 'My God – and look what I did... what I tried to do to you... I feel so stupid and you obviously had good reason for wanting rid of me.' After several seconds, I managed to compose myself. 'No wonder you feel...' I stopped, and then continued, 'Did he say anything to you during the attack?'

Again, she nodded, 'I don't know what he may have said later – he was shouting something – but right at the beginning I knew he wanted to repeat what he had done to Laura and rape me too... he said something like "This is for the jail, you deformed little witch! I'm going to make you ugly, make sure that nobody'll ever want sex with you ever!" – I can't ever forget those words. That's when he started to hit me. I thought he was going to strangle me or cut my throat.'

The doctors had suggested that he probably had a sharp ring on his finger to cause the injuries she sustained.

And *deformed little witch*? Ouch. Those words must have surely wounded Vi.

I was moved to tears once more.

I put my arm on her shoulder as a comforting gesture as she sniffled, wiping a tear from her eyes. 'Now I understand and I'm glad you told me.' Her emotions and tears made her scars on the side of her face more vivid, more prominent, but I reached up and touched them, sliding my hand across her brow. 'Vi, he failed,' I said as I planted a light kiss on her forehead.

It was now that I detected Vi's barriers were crumbling.

There was an awkward pause so I reached for my keys in my pocket.

'Don't you dare!' she said out loud, with some desperation in her voice. I was momentarily surprised at the outburst. What had made her say that? I was only going to lock my car.

'Don't what, leave?' I stepped back a little.

'Of course not you blinking idiot!' she answered, practically shouting at me. There was an awkward period of silence, then, 'I heard you say you were getting married…? I heard you say it… *who* are you marrying?' she asked, as more of her self-control slipped judging from this sudden, abrupt manner of her question.

I remembered some of Susan's words from earlier: "Young man — please don't play with her heart," she had said looking at me earnestly then.

We both stood there looking at each other for five seconds, neither moving but I could see that her expression was one of anguish, extreme agitation, and also of anticipation, watching my face for the slightest hint of forgiveness, resignation, or anger and for an answer from me.

Again, 'Who are you going to marry… who were you talking about?'

'You.'

'What...?' she said, stumbling over the word. 'Me…?'

'Yes you! Olivia, will you marry me?' I smiled while slowly raising inviting arms ready to embrace her.

She launched herself at me with a short cry of delight followed by sobs – it was almost like an upright wrestling match as we hugged and hugged and hugged. And kissed. She completely broke down in my arms. Eventually, 'Yes! Oh Robert… my heart broke when you walked away –

when you said goodbye. You looked so hurt. I thought I'd lost you forever before I even knew you.'

I pulled her face closer then I move my lips slowly onto hers with a soft brush of our lips just for a second or two, mingled with hot tears. Then her lips momentarily crushed mine. I felt her arms and body crush me to her, then relax measurably, her arms moving to my head, pulling lightly.

That touch, her smile, and her now husky voice. 'I don't want you to leave. Please don't go... I want you to stay,' she said as I was trying to understand why occasionally she still trembled, her hands shaking.

Then I realised something – just as she suddenly remembered – I could feel her trousers were wet. I pushed her away to look down. 'Spill something Vi? You are all wet... you'll have to change those,' I said as I swept her up in my arms. 'Do you want me to carry you upstairs...?'

'No, no Robert, I'll be alright.'

Did he know? And had he deliberately made it easy for her by saying 'spill'? But now she didn't care. 'I'll take the opportunity to freshen up, have a shower, if you don't mind.'

It had happened before if she wasn't careful with drink – a glass or two followed by a shock, a cough, or excitement... then wet panties! Should only happen to women who have just had children, she was told. Wrong!

She added, 'I was worried that now you know my story, you wouldn't want me... I'm always afraid Robert. I've always been afraid and get panicky but when I first see you. Well, somehow I knew you were different. Before, I didn't want you to leave thinking I was just a stupid, paranoid woman. Now you properly know the reasons,' she murmured quietly, looking down into her lap.

We sat together. I explained why I had come back – I wanted to set the record straight knowing what had occurred the last time we met... the misunderstanding.

'Yes, I know... I'm so sorry. I hope you're not angry with me... I feel awful about it. I just panicked. I hadn't realised that nan had said anything to you.'

'Oh, she did – but not everything. It's one of the reasons I'm here... it will only make sense to me when you tell me what happened to you... and now you have.'

351

'It's happened a lot to me in the past – I'm used to it, that's why I was not surprised when you said you wanted to leave earlier. It has complicated my life. It all started with people seeing my hands Robert…'

'Yes – Susan told me.'

'You don't think less of me, do you?'

'I know as much as I need to know already – that I love you.'

It became time to fresh up.

Reader, there's no way I could leave this woman.

Chapter 66

Nerves

She was transformed. After a shower, she looked warm and soft with a lovely fragrance that began to play havoc with my senses. Her eyes were shining bright.

I looked into them. 'Honestly, love, all I want to do is to hold you close forever, your warm body against my old leathery skin, your soft skin against my flesh, your perfume, your smell... nothing else. Besides, after *that* kick I'm not sure if...'

Two seconds of serious concern and astonishment on her face, her hand to her mouth before I laughed out loud. 'Joke!'

She hit me playfully. 'Don't say things like that... I was worried. I was very worried back then that they had hurt you more seriously with that kick.'

'What – some permanent damage, like not being able to 'perform'?'

I tell you what everybody, Vi is a good blusher.

Earlier she had been drawn and white; now her colour was returning.

'I saw the scars on your face when I sat close to you when we first met and... I have to say that you have the most beautiful hands in the world, oh yes, do you think I didn't know then? I can see past all that. It doesn't matter to me.'

'Do you mean that?' She beamed a smile.

'And stop crying Vi... you'll run out of tears at this rate.' That's when I took her hands into mine, so soft, so limp. Pulling her closer and looking into the depth of her eyes I said, 'You have a permanent blush on your face Vi. It's so endearing but there's absolutely no reason for you to be embarrassed – and I knew you were for me in the first five minutes I met you.'

Vi could not conceal her joy. A huge weight had been lifted from her constant worry but now, in the short space of just a few months, she had been both assaulted and proposed to by this man, something that could not have been further from any thoughts she may have had for her life! She had to phone Nan. And it had all started with a dropped cushion in a car park and a pair of forgotten glasses. Furthermore, she could not yet grasp how, in an even shorter time, from just an hour ago, they had changed from snarling adversaries to lovers, well, not quite lovers but it was her grandmother who, on the phone, brought her back to reality with her usual directness, after telling Olivia how happy she was at the news. She was all unversed in the ways of her sex, and by nature too guileless to attempt to disguise her feelings – one reason she found it difficult to even look into his eyes or even talk of intimacy without acute embarrassment and some trepidation.

'Young lady, you do know what is likely to happen tonight in your house? I assume that's where you'll both be staying tonight?'

'Oh Nan,' she said pausing, a worried tone that asked, 'what am I going to do?' Vi was suddenly dreading the thought. 'He'll want to... Nan, is it just me but every time he looks at me I get the impression he's undressing me.'

'He was doing that the first day you two met! And yes, he will young lady – you can bet on it! But Olivia, you'll be fine. For what it's worth, I'm sure he will do the right thing by you this time!'

The more she thought about it the more anxious Vi became – and of course he probably didn't know *everything*, not even Susan really knew everything, although she had hinted that she had thought Olivia may still be a virgin. This increased her anxieties. Would she disappoint him – what *was* he expecting?

'Nan wants to speak to you,' said Vi, holding out the phone to me, now grinning like a Cheshire cat.

'I'm so thrilled young man, congratulations – oh, and thank you from me. She can't hear us, can she?' asked Susan. 'I can't really believe it.'

'No.' Vi had moved into the kitchen.

'Mr Temple, please be careful, now she's really worried about what happens, what you'll be expecting of her; you know she's worried.'

'I understand completely Susan and to be honest, I'm *also* worried how she will feel and respond so I'm just as nervous. I will treat her as gently as I can – I won't do anything that frightens her. You never know, nothing may happen.'

354

'Ha! I can't see that happening,' she scoffed.

Vi returned and I closed the door, walked her to the very same spot against the wall of our last encounter and gently pushed her against it while embracing her so that she could 'feel' me.

'That's because of you.' She understood.

Then I stepped back and added, 'I *should* have done this the first time. It would have saved all this heartache.' I noticed that every time I touched or caressed her, her eyes would almost roll up into her head.

I continued: 'Vi, I know you're nervous, I am too, it's been a long time for me as well so I'm as nervous as you are. I won't to do anything you don't want me to do, but let's look at the issue of intimacy, something I know is worrying you... am I right?' She nodded. 'And no one has ever seen you naked... nobody, have they?'

She remained motionless, not looking into my eyes, then she slowly shook her head putting both arms on my shoulders.

'I'm going to say some things that may be on your mind. I may be too direct but here goes. Neither of us is exactly young – we're not young kids are we, so we can have adult talk. I already know about your scars and your fingers. Oh yes, I could see when we first met how you were trying to hide them but Vi, I didn't care – I *don't* care.'

She responded with a whisper, 'It became standard practice for me to do this, almost automatic to hide them; I was particularly scared after we started talking because you suddenly became the only person I was truly worried about knowing this – and about how you might react.'

I put my finger to her lips then went on.

'So what about other 'private' things? For instance, apart from your scars that I know of you may have a huge birthmark on your left thigh, or on your bum, but... I... wouldn't...care.'

'Like me, you will have wobbly bits, maybe all in the wrong places, but... I... don't... care.' She actually smiled with a little nod in acknowledgement.

'You may wear pink knickers – as I've already seen – or white knickers, black knickers, or even 'big' knickers, but... I... don't... care. Er – no thongs please, slutty. Actually, I... don't... care.'

She briefly looked away. As I spoke I began to move my hands softly over her 'little black number' she had put on, reaching down and touching her curvy bottom and then lightly caressing her breasts, my attentions not unwelcome.

'When you are in the nude, you may observe your boobs hang differently or point in a slightly different direction, but... I...don't... care. For myself Vi, when I look at my own body in the mirror, ogling at my own pitiful, personal endowments, my *thingy* hangs slightly to the left. But... I... don't... care... and nor will you!'

She put her hand to her mouth while looking at me.

'Shocked... shall I continue?' She nodded again.

'And who knows that during sex, you may be a shrieker, a hummer, a giggler (really?), a gasper, or maybe just quiet, but... I... don't... care as long as you don't say that the bedroom ceiling needs white-washing or something!'

Her mouth dropped. 'Oh, that's rude! I don't know what to say,' she said as her gaze turned away from mine. She's burning again. Then I took another shot.

'And you might pee yourself when you sneeze... or something like that. But... I... don't... care.' That one hit the nail right on the head. Sharp intake of breath.

'Goodness! You knew didn't you – I'm so embarrassed, so embarrassed.' If she was burning before, she was aflame now because she knew it to be true sometimes.

'Not at first – but then I realised. And some women don't like you seeing them naked, or squirming and gasping, so they want the lights off. But... I... don't... care whether it's lights off or lights on. I'm telling you all this in advance to put you at some ease later my darling. We all have our little defects or irregularities with our private pits and parts. But all this is just between us and no one else. So whatever transpires, you are definitely no freak to me.'

As I've mentioned before, Vi blushes well. She was probably born blushing. She was on top form right now, but her previous trembles had stopped.

That's my girl. Getting better.

Then I said, 'Vi – it's getting late and I'm knackered. It's been a long day... driving, the traffic; I was up quite early too and I've not been sleeping too well. Aren't you tired – all the emotion? Can I use your settee just for a little while to catch up? Now that I know *what* I know about you, I should probably stay at arm's length, perhaps even sleep in my car tonight and give you peace of mind. I don't want to go home today – I just want to be near you.'

She paused as the implications of my suggestion sank in as she looked at the couch, which was also one of these pull-out beds, knowing that it could be bigger but I just wanted to rest awhile. 'No Robert, don't be silly, you can't sleep in your car you'll – you must stay here in my house, besides... I want you to be near.' I detected uncertainty in her voice so I looked at her directly to meet her gaze, 'How near?'

Once again, her cheeks flushed. 'I don't know, I'm not sure. Oh Robert, I'm no good at this – I haven't done this before,' she said falteringly as she looked at me for help.

'Well, let me make up your mind for you,' I responded, 'I've already dragged you inside once before but I won't have to drag you upstairs, will I? Look, it's best you go upstairs and sleep in your own bed, Vi, for now? I can sleep down here. Is that okay – is that close enough? And we'll take stock tomorrow.'

An imperceptible nod of her head. 'Yes alright – at least you will be close.' I think it was then I realised that Susan may be right when she had used the word 'intact'; Vi was probably still a virgin and totally unversed in any of the sexual arts, but I still found this hard to believe if her kisses were anything to go by.

There again, a kiss is just a kiss... even kids do it. I did drop off for a short while and when I awoke it was almost pitch black. As I lay there I thought, 'To hell with this,' and climbed out of my makeshift bed and went upstairs to Vi. Her door was closed but not locked so I went in. I heard her stir as I approached and noticed she was pulling her bedclothes open for me. I climbed into the bed and lay down beside her, her arms reaching over my body. Then I pulled her in close to me for another kiss. She put her soft hands on my face as I did so. We just lay there awhile.

'I'm glad you came up – I was feeling lonely and cold and I was hoping you were feeling the same. I've been lying here unable to sleep a wink and if you hadn't come to me, I was going to come down to you.'

'Would have been crowded in that bed. Anyway just remember what I said – that I just want to lie with you, skin to skin, does that sound strange?' I placed my hand on her shoulder and said, 'It's all right Vi – I'm guessing that this is your first time, am I right?' An imperceptible nod was her answer then she turned into my shoulder. I continued, 'I just want to hold you and touch you. I'm in heaven right now.' I couldn't see the expression on her face, so I snuggled up beside her once again to keep her close. She then slowly moved her head on my chest, her left leg moving slowly up and down over mine. Absolute heaven, reader, tender, warm, bliss – her soft, smooth skin. Wonderful – I had forgotten what it was like.

'Olivia, to think – I didn't even know you a few months ago although I felt that I *did* almost from the first moment we bumped into each other in the car park.'

After a pause she said, 'Yes, I did too, that's why I was getting angry with Nan when she said rude things to you. She was going to spoil everything!'

Chapter 67

Passion at 1:58

It was no good – too much temptation, way too much. It could not last *just* canoodling. Her arm came over my head to help me get closer. She said nothing at first, only pulling herself close, her hands stroking my face and hair. We remained like this for a little while longer as I noticed that her breathing becoming heavier. Then a gentle action with her arm – was she giving me a signal? Then she said, 'Will you touch me? Please touch me Robert.'

That *was* a surprise coming from her... and those words.

I think because it was now completely dark she felt more comfortable. I slid down and pulled her underwear off and slowly moved my mouth up her legs, kissing all the way.

'What...?' she murmured but I think she had guessed already as I moved up her body and began kissing the inside of her thighs, then my tongue became busy for the next few minutes. Indeed, she was warm, sweet and wet. Her breathing turned into shallow pants, her hands and fingers now gently massaging my head while pulling me closer. My mouth moved away and up to her tummy, passing Pinky and Perky, then to her face. Another kiss and then I slid in slowly and as gently as I could.

She cried out with a low gasp.

I knew her past, knew what she'd been through.

'Tell me if I'm hurting and I'll stop.' She shook her head.

And we were on our way, and I moved real slow.

Reader, I shan't go into the details on what followed except to say the on the first occasion, because it had been such a long time for me, I simply exploded inside her.

Well, alright then, some details.

Vi

The moment had arrived, the moment she half-dreaded – anticipation with mixed feelings of fear, of excitement, of desire. She had no idea what to expect and could only recall from her previous time in the hospital following the sexual assault and subsequent medical examinations and treatment. Was it going to be like that – a rough and violent probing, another painful experience; probing that would make her cry? Each examination had resulted in yet more examination with peculiar looking instruments – and humiliatingly, by male doctors sometimes. She never, ever again wanted anything to do with strangers poking around in her nether regions. But here *he* was, doing just that but in a kinder way.

Now, as she felt him enter, she waited for the pain – the excruciating pain she had felt once before after the hospital's attentions after the pain-killers had worn off, waiting for him to undo it all: but it was a smooth movement, although for one moment she thought he was going to go right through her, forcing her to open her legs and bend her knees a little more. Each time he pushed she still expected pain but it never came even though at first it felt awkward and, she thought, a little sordid, his flesh inside hers.

Still no pain, but she was expecting it at any time because he was strong and hard, yet his body and arms were comforting. Her worry began to drift away while she became aware that now, each time he moved into her, she felt as if a tight string had been plucked. With a sting, with an itch, a sweet sting, a sweet itch and a small thrill. Then it would disappear only for it to return each time, just a little more intense, a little sweeter. Now she realised she was crying out involuntary, softly for each movement and that her arms were tugging at him.

From his breathing, she knew he would not be far off from releasing his pleasure. Then she sensed his sudden rush as it happened. How he now shuddered, now feeling hot and full of him in his climax. He was gasping and clutching but there was no violence, only the feeling of his strong arms around her back, his kisses on her neck and cheek and then onto her breasts.

And throughout, Vi was aware each time he pushed that she was ascending to a wonderful place but not quite getting there... not this time. Pleasant – but frustrating.

For me

Time passed as in a dream and there was no yelling, no shrieks and no cries, just quiet satisfaction, whispered moans and heavy breathing. I also felt some hot tears before she lapsed into a gentle slumber as I did too after a short while.

Truth be known, the first time was more fun for me that for her. She was unversed, uncertain, perhaps defensive – she had her hands against my shoulders as if she was ready to push me off at any time if it wasn't going well for her, but eventually her arms relaxed against me.

'Vi, you were wonderful,' is all I said and she hugged me tight. The second time, however, it was more equal in enjoyment, with her feeling less tense, more confident, and me in a wondrous place.

What awoke me at 1:58? Vi's arm had knocked the clock over probably, I don't know, but that was the time displayed on it as I put it back next to the bed: and she was half on top of me, totally out of it, soft and limp. It was pitch black but I was staring upwards lying on my back. As soon as I had moved, Vi woke up with a start and the first thing she did was pull me closer. I took it as my cue and soon realised we were both primed, truly, and latched together.

Only a few seconds had passed when I realised her finger-work was a great deal more vigorous on my back this time, becoming almost like a kitten's claws, digging in, clutching. This continued for a little while longer and then suddenly, she arched her back, grabbing my flesh in handfuls saying, 'Uhhhhh... Robert... Robert...' as she clamped me down and squeezed her legs tight. She wasn't screaming, but I nearly was – with her nails! And then she nipped my shoulder. She held this stiff position for about twenty seconds then slowly collapsed flat, gasping, breathing in short bursts before subsiding into a deep slumber. I must have followed seconds later.

Wow!

Vi

Vi felt that the second time was just completely enjoyable, with no fear, only pleasure... but still not reaching the top of the hill, just as before. But when they awoke in the dead of night, he brought her to heaven.

This time, she felt the sweet sting and thrill sensation start as before, then becoming fierce, much fiercer, and being combined with what seemed like a total body response that came together as one, until she burst with all her strength into ecstasy.

She had never felt that sensation before… ever… and was totally oblivious to his actions, knowing only of course that he was responsible. She was briefly aware that she was now completely out of breath, laying there panting until she drifted into blackness once more.

Me

I was totally and utterly exhausted, shattered.

Every time I stirred during the night it seemed like a signal for Vi to clamp me right close in with inevitable results; I was just praying my old ticker was going to hold out…!

Vi

'Oh God,' she thought to herself, 'I'm so sore.'

And each time she stirred during the night it seemed like a 'come on' signal to him and he would be right there, ready, and she felt like it was just one after another, all night long, with short snatches of sleep.

It turned out that when we spoke later, neither of us wanted to be the first to cry 'stop!'

The next thing I remember is Vi rubbing my shoulders and saying, 'Robert, Robert… your back, look at your back… and there's little spots of blood all over the sheets.'

I could hardly open my eyes but I was aware now that my back stung just a teeny-weeny bit. And Vi was looking over it with gentle probes, while observing the sheets with a mixture of surprise and astonishment, worried that it might have been her who had bled as well.

'I think you'll find that the DNA under your fingernails belongs to me young lady,' I responded with a satisfied smirk.

'Oh dear, oh my goodness,' she exclaimed as the realisation hit her – that it was her vigorous exertions that had resulted in numerous small scratches, some that had drawn blood.

'I was in agony Vi, but only for a short time, both ecstasy and pain all rolled into one, wonderful… you minx you!'

I said she was a blusher – now she was blushing for England. And the way she was reacting to it all, I think she was in rebellion against the obvious… that she was responsible. 'Oh, I'm so sorry Robert, I didn't realise – I didn't realise I was hurting you.'

'Don't you ever stop,' was my response. 'But don't think that *that* 'moment' always happens – it won't.' Then she realised that her top half was completely exposed to me as she was leaning over my back with them hanging down; she hurriedly snuck back under cover. As I pulled her closer I moved my hands down to her thighs. 'Why not?' I thought, but her hands came over mine to stop me.

'Robert, please don't… I'm sorry but I'm sore… and so tired.'

'That makes two of us then Vi!' I said chuckling.

And not just my back either – my poor 'John McGrobbin' was throbbin'. It had been a vigorous night.

Vi eventually put on her dressing gown and came back two minutes later with a small bowl of water and some cotton wool and began to clean up my back with lovely soft dabs.

We then continued to rest. We talked, touched. Eventually I said, 'You know what we have to do now Vi…? We will have to go and see your lovely nan.'

'Can't we stay here just for a little while longer? I feel so safe and content with you.' That made me sit up. Those two words, *safe* and *content.* I knew who had used them last. 'What's the matter Robert?'

'The words you used just then, what made you say them? Do you really feel that way?' It was the best I could think to say while my mind was racing, thinking hard.

Vi nodded, 'They just popped into my head.'

'I know Susan gave the game away when I first visited by revealing which year you were born, but *when* were your born exactly?'

'September the 3rd,' she answered. 'Why?'

Got that – stored it.

'Really? Susan said April 17th.'

'She gets mixed up – that's Laura's birthday. And you?'

'Can't remember – it was either Feb 29th or Christmas day, before they kept records…'

'Be serious!' When I told her, she said I looked good for someone in their sixties.

'Just 'good'? I feel disappointed.'

Chapter 68

Susan happy

Yet again I entered Susan's room, only this time with Vi holding onto my arm. My God, you should have seen Susan's face. As soon as she saw us her face lit up.

'Oh wonderful, wonderful,' she exclaimed. 'At last!' Vi was smiling – no tension but probably a tad nervous in front of her nan's stare. 'What have you two been doing?'

'Sleeping,' I answered, 'amongst other things…'

'So you've had sex!' she said almost joyfully. 'I can see it in her eyes.'

Here we go, nice one Susan, and probably bloodshot eyes if they were anything like mine.

I was surprised with Vi's reaction. She just looked at me then put her arm around my waist, spluttering out a giggle like a school kid.

'Yes Susan, at 1:58 to be exact, didn't we darling – and I have the scars to prove it!' This resulted in a jab in the ribs. 'Would you like to see them?' I asked laughingly, as I made to lift up my top.

'NO! Don't you dare!' she whispered hard at me, then realised I was joking.

'Vi, remember, your nan was once a young girl so she would not be shocked – and your granddaughter certainly hides her light under a bushel Susan,' I said turning to her.

Nan was nodding, so I walked over to her and whispered close to her ear, 'Earlier, you said to me "dry as an old crone", remember? Not so Susan, *definitely* not so – in fact the opposite.' Vi was throwing a puzzled look at me so I said, 'Tell you later love.'

Never.

Susan then said to me, but not quietly so that Vi could hear too, 'I don't know what you've done but I've never seen her looking so happy or excited, and no man has ever called her 'darling'. She is a woman transformed. She has never flaunted her wares that I can remember, but you've made an old lady happy. You seem to have the devil's touch with her.'

'Well, can you remember your first time, eh – and how you felt?' I asked.

'Some alley with some Yank if I recall,' she said matter-of-factly, quietly.

'I didn't need to know that Susan. As for Olivia, I'm thrilled myself,' I said, turning to Vi with a big smile. She was beaming like a school prize-winner.

The conversation and atmosphere that afternoon was certainly better than on my first visit – Vi visibly relaxed, Susan with no barbed remarks.

'Susan, we must take our leave. Your Olivia has just whispered in my ear that she wants to go home so that she can have her wicked way with me again.'

'Oh, behave yourself! That's not true nan! He's so cheeky,' she exclaimed – already knowing it was a leg-pull. But I had caught a bewitching glance in her eyes.

'By the way Mrs Kelly, or Nan, or Susan, there is no actual *date* on your mum's headstone. When exactly did she pass away?'

She pondered for a little while. 'If I recall, it was a bingo day – that I *can* remember, which was always on a Tuesday back then and I think it was December 6th because we normally played bingo in the afternoon.' Susan paused, recalling from her memories. 'We were getting ready to go when the hospital rang and asked us to go there. We were going to visit afterwards in any case. I shall never forget that phone call. She had taken an unexpected turn for the worse after being ill for a week or so. She passed away later that evening.'

I put my hand on her shoulder and said, 'Don't tell me too much Susan...' This was because I was having my own pangs of emotion.

Susan tugged at my arm and whispered to me, 'Thank you for coming young man – Mr Tits – and you *will* tell Olivia one day, won't you?'

I nodded, knowing exactly what she meant. At the same time, I was trying to do some math in my head.

I took some snaps before we left her room – one with Vi and her together, one of Susan alone, and one of Vi on her own.

'Your nan is something else isn't she – a shocker, a real feisty dame!'

'But I've never seen her so calm, relaxed – even happy,' said Vi.

'I think that's because she knows *you* are happy, that you've pulled a hunk, maybe an old hunk,' I said with a huge smile. Every time I joked with her she had the habit of slapping me playfully.

And I did say hunk, not husk.

I clipped Vi's picture to a message and sent it to Becky. The message was along the lines of, 'Back with Olivia (Vi)... everything ok. She reminds me of somebody... couldn't be happier.'

Becks: 'Yikes!' Good news. I know who you mean! Double Yikes! Where did you stay... hotel?

Me: No.

Becks: Naughty boy!

Me: All down to a pair of glasses. Tell you later.

...

We were back in her house. When we sat down and started petting, that same red mist came down. I was carried away again, but gently, as we were both suffering just a little. 'I saw the look in your eyes back at the care home... I was right, you little minx?' This resulted in a dig in my already maimed back. 'Ouch! Look Vi, each time I get you on my own all I want to do is do bad things to you... can't help it.'

As we lay there afterwards like two lovebirds, we talked. More background on me, more on her. I told her about my past – didn't dwell too much on my marriage although I did tell her she died as a result of a car crash on her way to school (a teacher). Told her what I did, about my music, about the gang and the dancing, about my very early years.

Vi spent all her life in and around Bury with work in a flower shop, library and her present job and she still did some part-time work in the flower place.

'Well like I said Vi, kiss you or salute you... the kissing won, hands down.'

She was excited about the music and dancing. She said she always had the tranny on in the back of the flower shop while she worked – and missed it when she worked in the library.

'With me and with the gang, you'll be surrounded by music – that's if you want to be.'

'Music? Do you know something Robert?'

'What?'

'Last night I dreamt of you and I dancing together in a dream.'

'So, last night Vi, what happened?' She knew what I was referring to because I was pointing at my back with a smile on my face.

There she goes again, beetroot red.

'Come on... tell me,' I said with an inviting look on my face. 'No one else is listening. Remember the intimacy chat we had...?'

'No. It's embarrassing. It's alright for you, you know about these things but I don't.'

'What – female things? You had a climax, right? I noticed almost from the start that something was different. Your hands, they were more... frantic?'

She nodded but would not elaborate.

'Well, for me it was fantastic! To be honest, that's the best shag I've ever had... ever! And I'm sorry for saying it like that.'

Apologies for the language, reader, I don't normally use profanities.

'Robert! So crude...!' but I could tell she was pleased.

'Now you know why sex is important in a relationship, it's another form of communication.'

...

Later, I had a question.

'Vi, as we walked towards your nan's room earlier, it was the first time I've actually seen you walk other than a couple of steps – I noticed how you walked, how you carried yourself; you are unhurried – you move with a wonderful poise and elegance. Along with your eyes and soft voice I think it is *that* which drew my attention when I first saw you. You carry yourself very well. Did you go to 'Dork School' or something?'

'Dork school?'

'Yeah, like a finishing school, where they send 'young ladies' to knock off the rough edges. You know, if you have a stooping gait, a plodding walk or amble along knock-kneed or pigeon-toed, eat with your mouth open, cackle when you laugh, chew gum, stand with your feet pointing inwards, how to get in and out of a low car without showing your 'whatsits': all that sort of thing. I'm not talking about silly, weird catwalks like models do. The army do the same when you learn to march – deportment and all that…'

'No, is that what they do in Finishing Schools?'

'So I'm told, apart from the marching – but you'd be a dead loss, you'd be teaching them! To me, you seem to do everything right, and do it effortlessly… the epitome.'

She beamed at me.

'No regrets Vi?' She shook her head. 'What about the ravish bit…well, nearly rape?'

'Yes. Part of me didn't want to stop you, but I would have felt horrible afterwards – and I think you would have too,' she added softly.

'You are so right, I would have, I already did. I realised just in time. Actually, I thought I'd blown it by groping you and trying to get your clothes off, that I had crossed the point of no return. Not one of my finer moments Vi, but it's when I saw you, watched you in the garden and cast my covetous eyes over your backside that was facing me, and then your startled look, your voice, I'm sorry, but a gust of passion swept through me. I wanted you – right there and then. Actually, I knew within ten minutes of meeting you. Same feeling, wanting your body *and* your soul – if that makes any sense.'

'I thought you were teaching me a lesson, punishing me for what happened to you.'

Eventually the time came to leave. As I gazed into her eyes she started to weep and I could see fear in here face as she looked into my eyes. 'This is hard for me…'

'Vi, what's the matter…?'

'That you are going Robert – that you have to go home. In my whole life, I've never felt so happy as these last two days. I worry that you won't come back and just a little part of me thinks… I'm sorry to think this Robert but that you've had your gratification, your fun, that I've had my use and it will be 'goodbye', and you'll never want to see me again. I'm sorry if I have a suspicious mind.'

A touch of insecurity here perhaps.

'That wasn't just fun – that was magic!' I shook my head as I embraced her. 'Vi I said I'm going to marry you okay? I'll ring you tomorrow. I have a gig in two days. Right after that I'll be straight back. And then if you can get a couple of days off, I'll take you back to my palace, but mark my words sweetheart, we *are* together and will remain so. You do realise that we now have a chain of events to follow – all the arrangements, so we'll have plenty to talk about shortly. You will also come to realise that there are some very good people about – like my gang for instance – and that not all men are slimy lounge-lizards. I know you told your nan about me mentally undressing you almost from day one each time I saw you – absolutely true I admit it. You were playing havoc with my senses. I think it was your air of vulnerability.'

She was stirred to smile, which helped disperse some of her sadness.

'You said many things about your music; what tune would you dedicate to me right now? Please tell me Robert.'

'Off the top of my head… snap choice,' I pondered a moment, '…if I could choose a record to dedicate to you right now it would be – well – it would probably be *Endlessly* or *Something.*'

'*Endlessly? Something? Nothing Compares 2U?*'

'By Brook Benton and George Harrison.' Most have heard *Something*, less so with *Endlessly,* but in my view both appropriate for Olivia.

This time, reader, my journey home was one of complete joy and happiness. No bleeding noses, stained shirts, bruised ribs, scuffed arms, flattened cojones or dead legs. I'd forgotten all that, and had forgiven. All pain was gone.

Now I was just dog-tired. I decided to tell my troupe next time we gathered again – a gathering I would arrange for tomorrow. But first, I had to do something important. I needed to get her a ring so I detoured through Newmarket, my spirits high. They were even higher as I walked out of the jewellers with the ring safely in my coat pocket – and one grand lighter in my other pocket.

My gang actually knew little of my exploits in Bury apart from the fact they usually ended in disaster and black eyes, so I had been rather reticent in revealing too much about Olivia. But tomorrow I could tell them more – much, much more. I was excited as hell.

And I knew the gang would be too, especially Becky.

Chapter 69

Cruel diversion

'Beep, beep, beep…' I heard in the distant corners of my mind, becoming louder, then voices, two or three of them. Then I was aware of movement right beside me with my arm being lifted and someone else forcing my eyes open, shining a light into them.

I wanted to speak but could only mumble. What's going on, I wondered?

'He's coming around. Quickly, go and get Dr Smeathers right away.' This was followed by footsteps and the sound of trolley wheels on hard, smooth floors.

I was in hospital again, reader.

My head hurt and I could see flashing lights without being able to focus my eyes on anything, but I knew somebody was sitting near me.

'Mr Temple – can you hear me?' I croaked an answer while nodding at the same time. 'You were in a serious road accident and you've just regained consciousness…' etc. etc.

Yes, on my return that day after leaving Olivia a truck had taken me out – some nutter driving in the middle of the road had hit two cars, one of them mine. I can't remember any details except waking up in this bed.

'When?' I had asked the doctor.

'Three weeks ago; you've been in a coma and heavily sedated for most of that time – you've only just properly come around… and actually you were lucky. The other car driver was killed.'

My injuries? Concussion, dislocated shoulder, something wrong with my foot. For several hours as I slowly emerged from my condition, my sight returning, I suddenly realised… three weeks? THREE WEEKS?

'Does she know – does Olivia know?' I asked the staff frantically.

'Who is Olivia?' was the response.

The gang turned up the next day. What a tearful gathering that was, mingled with some happiness – to see me recovering. And of course, they knew nothing – nothing at all about our latest news, something I was going to announce at our gathering.

I broke down in front of my troupe when I told them what had passed between us and of our plans, and what she must thinking now with no word from me.

Nothing.

My phone was eventually retrieved and when we had made a call to Olivia, a voice said it did not recognise the number and all calls to me had gone voicemail – the lot.

When Becky had eventually found out the care home's number, they had instruction to refuse the calls. I was beside myself. My life was seemingly wrecked, and God knows what she must be thinking. I just could not stop weeping in sheer frustration.

Where was Vi? What would she be doing right now? I was beginning to think the worst but surely she would realise – after what I had said before I left – that I would not do something as base as walking out. My pessimistic mood had me thinking she was cursing me as a bare-faced liar, a con man, despicable and much worse that the smarmy lounge-lizards I had talked of.

But I knew where Susan was so I endeavoured to start there.

...

My sheer determination accelerated my recovery – as soon as I was able, I was out. At present, although I *could* now walk and my head ached sometimes, my shoulder was recovering, walking was more comfortable with the aid of a stick and would remain so for another two weeks or so. But I could drive now, so off I would go back to Bury. However, before I left, when I phoned Ivy's Care Home I was given the dreadful news – my worst nightmare – that Susan would no longer talk to me and in any case, Olivia had indeed joined a convent 'discernment group' only one week ago.

And she did not know about me.

I implored the voice on the end of the line to please tell Amy to tell Mrs Kelly that I had just come out of hospital. ...'Just tell her that please,' I had asked.

But where was the convent? Well, I popped into the estate agents who had the signs in Vi's garden posing as an interested party – that I might be able to put in an offer, and by the way, who was the owner? etc. etc.

It's amazing how people will talk when they want to sell you something – and the fellow, in his thirties, let slip the word 'convent'.

'Convent? Really, I didn't think there were any this way. Oh well, fancy that,' I had said innocently.

'Oh yes, there's one at…' blah blah blah.

Job done.

'Well Tom – take me there,' I said out loud to my dashboard.

I patted my coat because inside was the ring. It had taken some time before I suddenly remembered I had actually bought one, such was my memory at the time – almost non-existent.

The 'Discernment Days' establishment was a pleasant looking, three-storey large building partly clad in a green mantle of creepers with a one-hundred-yard-long drive – a hard sand and pebble arrangement. Wooden benches adorned the sides of this wide track and it was evident that some nuns were toiling amongst the plants and surrounding gardens, reminding me of times past with Vi. I viewed all this from outside, by the rather unimpressive arch-gate entrance. There was too, an obligatory sign indicating 'Reception' so it wasn't exactly Fort Knox.

Chapter 70

Dudgeon

Vi

It was three days now and not a word from Robert. Her calls repeatedly went to voicemail. From the wild heights of excitement, anticipation, joyousness and happiness, the wonderful contentment she had briefly experienced, she had plummeted into dudgeon, complete and utter despair and depression, railing at the cruel world while almost driving herself into a catatonic frame of mind.

All those sweet words he had uttered, 'Not all men...' etc. 'There are some good people...' etc. 'I'm no lecherous monster...' He had had his fun, had taken her body and was gone. Where had he gone? To that other woman that he pretended not to have? And yet she had even said so to him that a part of her thought he would do this! What a complete and utter fool she had been. Now she had only hatred for him. But she did wait yet one more day – hope against hope. Nothing, so she contacted the Holy Sisters, her mind made up to re-initiate the process.

She knew from her past enquiries that an almost 'work-experience' system was available for women who were considering this vocation – a discernment period. This period would last one to two years working as a novice, generally in normal civilian casual dress, informal: they would work alongside sisters in activities such as teaching, helping the poor and in healthcare. The groundwork had already been set up previously – all that was required was a phone call.

She made that call with darkness in her soul.

...

I called up on the voice box by the gate with a request to see "Olivia", a newly joined nun, please. The voice answering asked me to come back later as she was attending an 'induction-awareness' meeting, or leave a message, and who I was, etc.

I replied that I had something belonging to her that I wanted to hand over personally.

'We will tell her you have called. It's Mr...?'

I didn't answer as just then a supermarket van appeared, the driver leaning out and speaking into the box. The gate swung open so I simply nipped in through the gate behind it and hobbled up the lane to the entrance.

A lady at a desk looked up with some surprise as I approached but before she could say anything I boldly announced that I had, 'A delivery for Ms Olivia Dawson,' as I handed over a gift bag containing both my ring and a letter that gave reasons for my 'disappearance'.

'Please ensure she gets these,' I asked in my sweetest and saddest tone, before hobbling outside with an exaggerated shuffle movement to the nearest bench I could find.

She followed me out, holding my bag, and asked in a rather officious tone, 'Who are you?'

As I made a pained attempt to stand up, before sitting back down again, with a grimace on my face, again exaggerated, I said, 'It's all in there... everything... and I shall stay here until I know she has accepted it. I do apologise but I'm not moving.' The poor lady was rather flustered but turned around and went back inside as I called after her, 'And thank you.'

For one hour, I waited before the lady and a nun came out together with the nun now holding my package: I could tell it was bad news.

I was told, kindly, that Olivia did not want my offering and asked that please, she would not like to be disturbed any further. My package had been returned to me unopened so she remained ignorant of events since the day I last left her. At first I was in shock; I looked up at all the windows wondering if she was looking down at me. I crumpled into quite sobs while the two looked on, the nun asking if I would like a glass of water. I shook my head but then asked if she could assist me back to the main gate. I shook my head once more and asked them to please leave me on my own.

I couldn't stop bloody crying. All this for nought – and she doesn't know! This was the worst part of it – me knowing that she *didn't* know the reasons for my absence.

Another half an hour passed; eventually I stood up feeling cold now and began walking back up the lane, putting my flat cap and sunglasses back on. The concussion headaches had not yet entirely gone and the sun was low in the sky and bright.

Olivia, on returning from a class, thought about the package and was quite certain she knew who it was from but no names had been given. She was absolutely sure that she was not going to be caught up again – if it was from him – in any of his scheming webs of entrapment, so she had resisted looking at the package. She knew it was not from her family as Nan would have informed her in advance.

As she came down the central stairs she gazed out of the large window that looked over the front gardens. She had been there for four days now and the view always pleased her senses; she could see the expanse of the garden and shrubs, the small allotments, just a few small trees. There was a digger excavating a new trench to update the drainage over there on the left, while the fraternity were now involved in clearing and tidying up.

One of her individual tasks, a new responsibility within the confines of the gardens, was a small vegetable patch which she was about to set upon and her mind would never forget that lesson in decorum regarding her short dress and the lecherous Mr Temple. She was embarrassed just thinking about it!

She also noticed the old man, probably one of the old-timer janitors, wearing a flat-cap, slowly – almost painfully – making his way up the path towards the main gate. She had yet to meet all the staff – it would take time to get to know all the faces.

'Oh, poor dear,' she muttered. On the way to her patch she would give him a helping hand. Ah – he's made it to the next bench, she observed; she would soon help him to the entrance.

Bouncing down the staircase she reached the entrance area where she noticed Sister Renee also looking up the lane at the old man.

'I have it under control,' Olivia happily announced to all who could hear, 'I'm going that way – I'll help him.'

'He must be in some pain – earlier he was sat just out there, almost crying,' said Sister Renee.

'Crying?'

'Yes – like he had lost a family member. It was upsetting.'

'Ah poor man,' said Olivia, hurriedly walking outside, excited at being able to show 'a good deed', missing the words that followed her out of the door.

'It was him who…'

She picked up a trowel from one of the tool baskets lying on the path edge in preparation for her task and walked towards the old man sitting down on the last bench, who it appeared was staring at his shoes. Then she noticed he was attempting to get up but had knocked his walking stick off the arm-rest. He looked a dejected, lost fellow and was unaware of her approach. She went straight to his walking stick and crouched down to retrieve it for him just as he did so at the very same time.

'It is alright – I will pick it up for you,' she said as she took it in her left hand.

It was the soft voice.

He looked up, startled, while taking off his glasses and was about to say 'thank you' to this angel. They turned to look at each other, recognition was almost instant.

'YOU!' she exclaimed out loud, recognising Mr Temple, now minus his shades.

It took Olivia just one second for her pent-up anger, her seething resentment and recent bitter heart-ache memories of the last few weeks to surface, resulting in her bringing a massive right-hand slap across his face while shouting, 'You pig!' before realising she might have still be holding the trowel, which then fell to the ground.

His cap and his glasses had gone flying and were now on the path, the glasses broken. He had been caught off-balance and fell over the side of the arm of the bench, lying on his back.

Olivia was horrified, frozen to the spot now realising at once the magnitude of what she had done in that explosive second – and then two sisters came running over asking, 'What has happened… what have you done to him?' 'Olivia, Olivia,' they cried for some explanation. A more authoritative voice arrived:

'Olivia, go inside at once to my office… off you go …now!'

'But…' she turned to look down at him. She thought she'd really hurt him. His eyes were blinking, his head shaking. 'I didn't…' she mumbled before dropping his walking stick.

'Get inside at once!' the voice repeated. Then turning to the other nuns, 'You must tend to him and ensure he is alright then get him inside as soon as you can. Oh, what a mess... Lord have mercy... and bring his bag too.'

Me

Although I was quite capable of walking my way out I was reluctant to leave this calm place, knowing that Olivia was in there somewhere ignorant of events, so I stopped at each bench wondering what my next course of actions could be. And I could not avoid choking on my emotions – I felt as if I was at a funeral but instead of internment. 'Dust to dust' and all that, my heart, my love, was still beating inside that building somewhere – a heart that had rejected me. Forever it seemed.

I decided I would leave my fortunes to fate and placed my small bag on the bench beside me. I would leave it there for a nun – or anybody – to find and just maybe – maybe – the truth would be revealed about events, and my true feelings for Vi. What else could I do? I didn't want the ring, it was for her and nobody else.

I heard someone approaching as I stood up, knocking my 'third leg' off the bench. I bent down to pick it up only to be stopped in my tracks by a voice offering help... none other than Vi's dulcet tones. Of course, I realise now that with my dark glasses on and wearing a flat cap she would not have recognised me until close up.

I heard her shout, 'YOU,' as recognition sunk in, complete surprise on her face. Joy filled my heart. I had so many things to say to her – and to give her my ring that I quickly looked at lying on the seat. I should not have taken my gaze from her otherwise I would have seen her face change, distorted into fury and anger as she let loose with her hand, taking me completely unawares. For a moment, I saw stars – not the pretty kind.

I lay on the pathway utterly bewildered and realising, once again, that I might be bleeding. Nuns came to me dabbing at my face talking and calling for help while helping me back on the bench. Vi was looking at me with both hands around her face, stricken it seemed to me, before she was led away. It was my nose and the side of my face that took the brunt of her blow.

Chapter 71

Pathos

'Please explain to me what happened in the garden – what was that all about Olivia? You must tell me. You realise of course we can't keep you here behaving like that.'

'Mother, sorry, I…'

'I take it you know this man from the past – is that correct? And did you not realise he was already lame? The clue – a walking stick?' Olivia nodded. The shame that would fall upon her, her new colleagues knowing, a nun hitting an old, lame man.

In pain, was he? Well serves him right thought Olivia – well 95% of her did, then she felt guilty at the irony of her new vocation. 'What about my pain, my heart-ache,' she asked herself?

The Mother continued. 'So why Olivia, why did you hit him? Had he done something to you in this 'past' of yours? Is this why you are here?'

She nodded. 'He was cruel to me.'

'Could you not forgive or turn the other cheek my child? How was he cruel?'

'He gained my confidence with false promises. He tricked me. He asked me to marry him.'

'And you agreed, and he then took advantage of you…?' Olivia nodded.

'He took my soul and my body – all on promises. Then he left me. I wanted to hurt him and I'm glad I have,' she responded with a flash of defiance.

'Oh, violence and temper? Now you've treated *him* cruelly, you were angry. So why is he here Olivia? He's a long way from where he lives apparently. He's come quite far – to see you. Are you sure you have not misread the situation?' She slowly shook her head. 'Have you looked at this? It was on the bench where he was sitting. Have you not opened the letter? It's addressed to you as you are the only Olivia we have. Perhaps you should do so and read it now.'

She shook her head while taking the little bag from the Mother. Strangely, she began to fear its contents, now realising that, as before, she may have acted impetuously. But how was she to know? Olivia opened the letter and began to read. Mother nun had noticed how this potential novice was slow and gentle in her movements as she watched her with the letter.

Olivia's eyes moved across the paper as she read. Slowly her pallor changed until she was deathly pale. Tears began to stream down her cheeks. The letter fell from her hand, fluttering to the floor. Olivia lowered her head into her hands and sobbed out loud.

'He was in hospital – *and I didn't know*! Oh – I must see him. I must see him. Oh mother, mother!' The Mother could now see real fear in her eyes.

Then Olivia realised what the small package must be. She removed the attractive wrapping and opened the little box. She was struck dumb – astounded. An Engagement ring. It was beautiful.

He had been true! She felt as if her heart had been pierced. She was devastated.

He had bought a ring on that very same day, the letter had told her. This made her feel dreadful, wretched, her senses lost in numbness.

'May I...?' ventured Mother, who had bent down retrieving the letter. Olivia nodded and watched her face intently looking for some guidance. 'Oh mercy,' she said eventually. For a moment, they sat there. She continued, 'You have come here for peace – wanting to profess faith in the Lord, and yet you could not extend any faith towards this Mr ... er... Temple, could you? And your outburst of violence... we can forgive you for that but what about him? Have you apologised to him?'

'No, I haven't seen him. I must see him,' she responded in a soft voice, almost a whisper, realising that she had wrought her own emotional destruction and could not bear the thought of facing him and then, inevitably, losing him. She would have to leave. He must now despise her.

She could not forget that look she saw in his face after his beating many weeks ago. And was he hurt now?

'We are responsible for his welfare while he is here in our establishment. The last thing he was expecting was to be assaulted by a novice nun. God knows what he must be thinking. It seems to me that he is a good man. He came by to do the right thing so you have a choice Olivia, I will not influence your decision. That is for you to determine. You *do* want him to remember you in a kindly light…? Otherwise he will always harbour poor memories of you and your lack of faith. You don't wish that to be the case do you?'

She shook her head.

'Please wait here Olivia,' she said as she motioned to a nun sitting quietly by the door, who then left the room. A minute later she returned with Mr Temple. The mother motioned him to a chair next to Olivia. She stole a glance at him and was relieved to see only a single plaster on his face – not swathed in bandages, considering her last sight of him after the blow. She looked away not wanting to see his eyes, deeply ashamed. He would no doubt not want anything to do with her after this.

Chapter 72

Made Up

Vi

The sister opened up the dialogue, asking how he felt now; had her girls tended to him well? etc.

'Yes,' he replied, 'apart from one.' Olivia flushed at this deliberate jibe. 'But I will survive, I've had worse. It was only my head – no vital organs.'

Olivia detected that 'Temple understatement', that self-deprecation, self-mocking, the light humour even while she was slowly dying inside. Oh, how she loved him, wanted him and his forgiveness, right then.

'Good. Mr Temple, I understand Olivia would like to say something to you,' she said turning towards her, raising her eyebrows in invitation.

'Mr Temple...' she croaked in a husky voice, struggling to maintain composure. Her voice was caught on emotion, preventing her normal clear tone.

'Olivia, you must look at him, come now.'

Olivia coughed. 'Mr Temple, I'm sorry. I'm sorry for what I did to you... I'm sorry, so sorry; oh Robert, I didn't know that you had had an accident... oh, dear, oh dear... if only I'd known.' Tears were flowing freely now as she went on. 'I'm a disaster where you are concerned – I bring you nothing but trouble. I can't seem to do this dance or play this game very well. I no longer trust myself to do the right things anymore. Please forgive me. Mother, please put me out of my misery and let me leave. I know I can't remain here... I just want to go home.'

'And Mr Temple... Robert, what say you?' asked the mother.

Olivia was looking at him, slowly shaking her head in quiet despair, then she looked down at her feet, not really knowing where to look, feeling both wrecked and wretched. Just a few weeks ago she had been lying in her bed in his warm, comforting embrace and full of happiness with a new life to look forward to... this man, whose lips and hands had touched every part of her naked body and had brought her to a quivering, trembling ecstasy, this man who had completely removed her veil. But now she realised that she had brought only ruin to herself and her nan would be horrified with what had transpired. She could hear it now. 'You silly headstrong girl' – oh yes, she would get the blame.

She became aware of his presence right beside her – he had moved his chair to close to touch hers. What was he going to say, that he never wanted to see her again?

She just felt sick.

Me

I don't like watching a creature suffer and when I saw the state Vi was in I had to say something. There was part of me that understood her sudden outburst and was all too aware how she must have perceived the situation of my absence.

'Sister, I don't think she would cope on her own so I'll take her to a place where they will look after her – where she'll be safe.'

'Mr Temple, I don't need your pity if you don't mind, thank you. I shall be fine by myself,' she replied in a broken voice.

Wow, more defiance, and back to 'Mr Temple' again. Some steel, some pride. It must have taken courage for her to have said that – her inner turmoil manifested itself by her attempt to control her breathing, her bosom rising and falling fast.

'No Vi – I will take that course of action I've already determined for you.'

Her lips moved as she shook her head. She wanted to say something but crumpled just a little. Then she stood up, shaking her head vigorously saying, 'No no no – I'm not going to be given over to any shrinks or special homes. I only slapped him Mother. I'll be alright. Let me go,' she said casting me a withering look.

'Sit down Vi,' I said, pulling her back into her chair. But before I could continue, Mother intervened.

'What have you in mind Robert – are you able to help Olivia? Are you too angry with her for what she did, have you forgiven? I am worried about you, young lady.' she said now looking at her.

'Actually, I think Olivia knows me quite well now and I believe that with a simple question that I'm about to ask her she will know what's going to happen and how I feel about her right hook,' I continued, saying all this with a serious countenance. I leaned in close – very close so I would not be overheard. Her lips were quivering as she instinctively shifted away from me, looking worried, but with a firm pull I kept her close. I could feel her resistance – a strong resistance that indicated she was ready to break free at the first opportunity. Then I whispered to her almost cheek-to-cheek:

'My God Vi, you are going to pay for that slap... *later*.' I paused while that sank in.

She gave me a searching look then began whispering to me while her hand gently moved to mine. 'Please don't leave me Robert, don't leave me, don't leave me,' as she started to weep, her breathing troubled.

Ignoring her pleas, I cut across her words and I whispered, 'What colour is your underwear today Olivia?'

Two seconds passed. Her jaw dropped as I looked over her face. 'Oh, I'm guessing pink – judging from your cheeks Vi. No, wait a minute, maybe red...?' I said looking directly into her eyes now, a smile edging onto my face. Then I saw her eyes slowly light up and felt her resistance collapse. A wonderful smile broke as she then pushed her face into my shoulder with a choking sob and she continued to sob for a minute or so.

'You sod,' she replied, also in a whisper. 'You bugger... I was in despair... I thought you had forsaken me.'

'Do you think I'd let you slip away from me like this? Did I not say I loved you Vi, that I want to marry you? Did I not say all these words? It is I who will take care of you. No 'shrink', just me. But if you want to stay here, well, I shall not stop you. It's up to you – but you would break my heart if you stayed.'

She grabbed my arm and looking into my eyes, 'Robert – I will always want to be with you. Does that answer you?'

Meanwhile the sister observed our close mumbles with a puzzled expression but she too smiled on seeing Oliva's happier countenance and our closeness.

'We are fine now sister – thank you. I'm happy and I think Vi's happy too,' I said looking into her eyes. Vi nodded.

'You have both restored my faith in people. It is wonderful to see such things,' the sister said. And looking at these two she could see that silent language lovers have.

From experience, she knew that life has its ups and downs and that character cannot be developed in ease and quiet. It was the experience of these trials of suffering that the soul was strengthened, whether the farmhand, the teacher or the engineer.

It took two days for Vi to relinquish herself from her 'discernment' obligations with me staying at her house overnight before bringing her home. I had done the best I could to make a welcoming house, with an abundance of flowers in each room; the fragrance was immediate as I unlocked and opened her door, and with great risk to my leg I just about managed to carry her over the 'threshold'. Then once we were through I asked,

'Upstairs Vi – straight to bed?'

She nodded.

'And do you want me to be naughty?'

She nodded again, giving me a sly look.

Vi had many loose ends to re-establish: take the house off the market; her memorial job – this was easy as the post remained unfilled – difficult to find people to do that kind of job, and she was always welcome to help out in the flower shop.

And Susan was rejuvenated. I had never seen her so happy since... 1944?

Still with me reader?

Chapter 73

No surprise

I organised a gathering of my dancing team for the next evening at our local. I went into more detail about my visit, leaving out the naughty bits of course, telling them more about Olivia and what a rascal Susan was. Keith cracked up laughing. 'Must meet her... again!' Of course, we had forgotten.

Keith then offered some words, 'You know, it's actually *her* that brought this all together. If she had not interfered you may well have gone your separate ways like ships that pass in the night. She was the catalyst and from what you've told us, Olivia's vulnerabilities played into your hands, you spawny bastard.'

I hadn't looked at it like that but he was right. And Becky was overjoyed, especially when she pulled out the picture I'd sent of Vi. Then she asked, 'Bob – you know who she looks like don't you? Uncanny.'

'Yes, of course I do.'

I explained the slight shading on the side of her face – the result of an accident. Later I told Keith and Becky the real story. Becky was upset to hear of it. 'I don't want anybody else to know,' I had added.

Matt and Ruby were grinning – first time they had seen a photo of Olivia. 'Bloody hell... similar features; to think that I danced with her great-grandmother. I suppose it's to be expected but even I can see how she must have caught your attention Bob.'

'You don't know the half of it,' I said. 'Wait 'till you find out when she was born. Tell you later...'

As they chatted and asked questions, I then told them about her hands.

I waited until two pints had gone down to liberate the imagination and then asked, 'You know the strange business about the dance in Bury...?' They all nodded.

'How can we forget?' said Keith.

'And me,' added Becky.

'Well, we thought it unexplainable, not possible, weird, creepy, that no one would believe us, would they, but I suppose these events can happen, maybe? Then in the first few minutes talking to Olivia when we were with Susan, Olivia asked me, "Do I know you from somewhere – have we met before?" I felt like saying we had, but we hadn't, or had we? It spooked me I have to say because it was manifestly evident with her appearance who her family was, and we seemed to hit it off straight away. I also asked about the headstone with no date on it, which is unusual, eventually finding out from Susan that Grace's passing was in December 1966, December the sixth in fact. I suppose I could ask Susan if she would like that added. If you are allowed to, that is. Olivia was born in 1967 on September the third, so she's closer to your age Becky.'

A few comments were made about the 'swinging sixties' and all that but on my journey back I'd had time to do some thinking about those two words 'safe and content'. The two words gave me a clue… a clue associated with the dates, a clue I'd toss into our discussion without saying anything immediately. It was Ruby who casually muttered how sad it was that Grace had passed away at a relatively young age. I pointed out that Grace had actually had her children later in her life so she wasn't *that* young when she died.

'It's a shame, she missed seeing her great-grandchild by, well, nearly a year,' she said with a sigh. There was a continued silence for several seconds, when I believe a penny had suddenly dropped because both Becks and Ruby said out loud, almost together…

'Hang on a minute, those dates – what were they again? That's about nine months!' An eerie silence followed.

'*To the day!* It *is* nine months' I said, '…and yes, I've been thinking about this all the bloody time I can tell you!'

'Oh my God, you don't think…?' exclaimed Ruby.

'What, a kind of re-incarnation, is that what you were going to say?' I asked. 'Grace dies and at the very same moment, right on the button, Olivia is conceived – or thereabouts.'

Out came the smart phones – the 'net' was interrogated.

'Oh my God,' cried Ruby. 'You're right – those dates are just about spot on!' She looked at each one of us in turn, her mouth wide open.

Even Keith was silent for a while, then, 'Do you think words or memories can move across? Can a reincarnation take up a previous personality? Is there a spectral gap that can be crossed?'

'Well, when I first saw Olivia I was struck by certain traits that mirrored Grace and I was certain that my eyes had looked into those eyes before. Remember, one of the first things she said to me after only a few minutes was, "Do I know you from somewhere?" It floored me because I'd had the same feeling about her. Then she uttered those very same two words, the exact words Grace had spoken when we danced. Anybody *not* believe in re-incarnation…?'

At this point, Becky looked at me. Earlier I'd had taken her – and only her – to one side briefly for a quiet word about other words spoken, about the more intimate words both Grace and Olivia had uttered, inviting me to *touch them*. It was then I told Becky that we had indeed shared intimate moments during that evening in Bury and this was when Grace had spoken those words, words repeated by Olivia in a similar intimate moment.

'Oh my God, I don't know what to say Bob. It is real spooky – almost like a ghost story,' she had answered.

There was silence for a while before Ruby asked, 'Do you think it could be a fluke, just a huge coincidence? Let's check again, let's work out the time again between the dates. What does nine months equate to in weeks? Look at your iThingy to confirm it. Mine says those dates are good.'

'Yeah, I reckon,' said Matt.

'And those two words…' said Becky.

'Do you know what buddy? I think you just may have a Grace Mark Two. We have to meet your lady, Bob – get her down here,' said Keith.

They all nodded.

'Will do.'

…

There was no need to wait too long. We married within two months, with my gang and just a few others in attendance, including Susan, who beamed all day long.

Becky practically fell in love with Olivia the moment she first set eyes on her. 'Absolutely adorable,' she whispered to me and Keith. 'And I can't get over the way she looks, her mannerisms. I *also* feel I know her just a little bit. But Christ Bob, you've landed on your feet with her.' Keith was nodding.

'Hey, it was a tough battle I can tell you. It wasn't all plain sailing as you saw.'

'I am stunned,' added Matt. 'I danced with Grace, didn't I? Olivia is just a touch taller but it's her presence and movement – difficult to separate them apart.'

Did the spirit and the soul of Grace, just as she passed away, move at the right moment across to Olivia? Some societies believe it, but for me? Well I already knew the answer to that, knew within five minutes. And did my visit to the grave trigger something, guiding me back to the care home?

One day I will have to tell Vi about the past.

Maybe.

THE END